No Place for a Child

Donna Richards grew up in coastal B.C. and spent most of her life in the Lower Mainland. When her four children moved on, she left her academic life to rest and write. Recently she and her husband moved to the South Cariboo, where she continues to write.

No Place for a Child

by
Donna Richards

Ottawa, Canada
2002

Copyright © by Donna J. Richards
and Borealis Press Ltd., 2002

*All rights reserved. No part of this book may
be used or reproduced in any manner whatsoever without
written permission except in the case of brief quotations
embodied in critical articles and reviews.*

Canada

*The Publishers acknowledge the financial assistance
of the Government of Canada through the Book Publishing
Industry Development Program (BPIDP)
for our publishing activities*

National Library of Canada Cataloguing in Publication Data

Richards, Donna Jean, 1949-
No Place for a Child / Donna Richards.

ISBN 0-88887-213-5

I. Title.

PS8585.I1735N6 2002 C813'.6 C2001-902348-3
PR9199.4.R43N6 2002

Cover design by Bull's Eye Design, Ottawa
Typesetting by Chisholm Communications, Ottawa

Printed and bound in Canada on acid-free paper

Table of Contents

Chapters

the One through Whom all things are possible

and to my mother, Alice R. Mowbray

1.

Old and New

Everything hurt. Her legs had passed the tingling stage of being asleep and were moving from shooting pains to an ache in each one. She struggled to swing them beneath the table as best she could, hoping to relieve the pain and restore circulation. But oh, she was tired! Her head throbbed and squeezed, and her throat continued to constrict around the lump that had seemed lodged there for hours, perhaps forever. Worst of all, her whole belly hurt. But still she sat, valiantly trying to finish the bit of dinner that remained before her. Usually, Misty ate the things she liked the least first, saving the best for last, but this night, her first in a new home, she had tackled the best first, hoping that she could get things she enjoyed past the lump that threatened to choke her as she sat at the foreign table with strangers. Now she was stuck with a pile of lima beans.

'God,' she thought, 'please help. I'm doing my best, but these things get stuck. Did You really make lima beans? I know You are supposed to be the Creator of all things, but I also know that every *good* thing comes from above. Lima beans just aren't good. Can that old devil make some things, like lima beans and mosquitoes after all? I've tried pretending these beans are something else, one of the wonderful foods You surely made, and I've tried pretending they are swimming in a delicious creamy sauce, but they are just beyond me tonight. And I'm getting so very tired. What do I do? The woman said I had to stay here until I'd cleaned my plate off, and I'm trying, God; I really am. But if I don't go to the bathroom soon, I'm going to have other trouble. Of course; she couldn't have meant anything ridiculous like I couldn't move at all, could she? Thanks, God. I'll just go to the bathroom and come back and try again.'

Gently, she pushed herself over the edge of the chair, wincing as her aching feet touched the floor. Avoiding the living room where the new people sat nattering away in the scratchy voices that almost made her shiver, she limped quietly through the kitchen to the bathroom. Whew, that took care of that pain. As she washed her hands at the basin, she tried shifting from foot to foot, twisting the free foot around. The pins and needles began to return rapidly, accompanied by sharp shooting pains, but she clenched her teeth and hung on, riding out the unpleasant sensations. It took a little while, longer than she thought, but she headed back through the kitchen, relieved to have only the headache, the lump in her throat and the dreaded lima beans to deal with.

But she was wrong; there was more. She jumped as a hand slammed down on the table when she slid back into her chair.

"I told you to remain where you were until you had cleaned off your plate! Who do you think you are to disobey me? Did I give you permission to go to the bathroom? Don't you know that thousands of children the world over would give anything for this good food, and here you are turning your nose up at it and disobeying me as well? You've a lot to learn, young lady, if you are going to stay here. I don't see why ..."

The throbbing in Misty's head increased and the lump in her throat all but choked her as the words continued stabbing her, rising and falling, poking and jabbing, hitting and stinging. Never had she been so harangued. Never had she been so hurt. Never had she been so tired. Almost against her will, she retreated inside to a safe place, her eyes widening, darkening slightly and glazing over as she travelled to her old world—a serene world, a warm world, a friendly world. She could almost smell the ocean air, hear the gentle wind whispering secrets in the trees, see the waves rolling and unrolling, gently stirring the clean, white sand along the shore. She felt her whole self lift upward as she imagined the shining gulls rising on the off-shore up-draft and soaring over the endless shimmering water. Always the birds seemed to carry a part of her with them as they rose high into the clear blue sky. Always she wondered if they felt anything when they flew into the fluffy clouds that floated lazily high above the water. Was it damp against their faces? Was it harder flying? Did their feathers ruffle differently? Did it hurt at all like running in thick tall grasses sometimes hurt her a little?

She jumped as the hand banged down on the tabletop again, snapping her back to the noisy and troublesome present. She focused her eyes carefully on the woman in front of her, trying to make sense of the tirade, trying to do the right thing. The Captain had told her that morning to do her best to please these new people so that she would be happy and thrive there, but it all seemed too much for her. The woman's words had come at her so fast that she could hardly sort them out or make sense of their meanings. She knew from the noise and anger that she had done many wrong things since arriving, but she wasn't sure what they all were, other than not getting permission to go to the bathroom. What could that mean? Why would she need permission to take care of natural bodily functions? And permission to leave the table? Well, she would have excused herself, but there wasn't anybody there to speak to when she had got down. The throbbing in her head increased, adding to the staccato sound of this woman's words jabbing at her.

"Answer me, child!"

But Misty was at a loss. No true question had been asked. She didn't really know what the trouble was. She just felt terrible, as if she were not only wrong but also despised somehow. She swallowed hard, though her mouth was dry and the lump in her throat so big she was sure it could be seen from the outside. Slowly, she picked up her fork and skewered a lima bean, hoping to put right the terrible wrong she had done. Silently she prayed for God's help once again. Unknowingly, she closed her eyes as she put the lima bean in her mouth. Down came the fist on the table again.

"Oh, that's enough! All this wincing and flinching over food. Just go to your bed. I hope you can be better behaved when I take you to get new clothes tomorrow. This is much worse than I ever thought it would be. Now get to bed! We'll try again tomorrow."

Silently, Misty thanked God for hearing her prayer and for the surprise answer. She had hoped only that He would enable her to swallow those beans, and instead He had rescued her from the impossible task altogether. Though her head and throat still hurt terribly, she felt much lighter as she paddled softly to her new room. From her little bag, she gathered her hairbrush, toothbrush and nightie and went into the bathroom to wash and get ready for bed. She could feel all kinds of aches and pains that she had never known before, but then never had she known such a long, long day. Maybe just this once, she'd skip brushing her hair out and rebraiding it to keep it from tangling and getting in her face when she slept. She was really too tired. Teeth brushed, face washed, she returned to her room and slid between the clean, white sheets of the narrow bed.

'Oh God,' she prayed silently, 'thank You for Your help. Thank You for staying with me even as the Captain said You would. Keep me safe while I sleep and show me how to live here. Please keep the Captain, all the animals and Miss Lily safe too. Say "Goodnight" to Gran and Gramps for me. And please, Father, help me.'

Only when her little arm automatically dropped to the side of the bed and did not find the familiar and comfortable soft fur of her faithful brown dog did Misty feel the tears begin to spill over and slide quietly down her cheeks.

* * *

It had been such a long day. The Captain had wakened Misty even before dawn, and together they had tended the animals and set out to walk the length of the island to the dock where Old Lundstrom was to pick her up in his fish boat. Along the way, Misty sometimes walked with Captain, holding his big warm hand in hers, happily describing some nearby flowers, ferns or light patterns, or perhaps the glittering of the sun on the water or the way the clouds formed shapes in the sky, bringing the pictures vividly before the Captain's windowless eyes, for he was blind, had been since what he called the Great War. Despite Misty's active imagination and uncanny ability to describe and understand, she simply could not imagine war, not war such as she read about over and over in the Bible, not war such as the Captain occasionally mentioned when he did have to account for his blindness or his scars. Nothing in Misty's world suggested the propensity for evil that is inherent in mankind, so she simply couldn't imagine men so set against each other as to maim and kill one another. No, Misty couldn't imagine war.

She didn't think of the Captain as blind; he was just the Captain, a wonderful man, full of life, full of love, full of laughter. She had been describing things for him ever since she could speak, simply because he had asked her questions that elicited descriptions. After a while she developed the habit of describing, of talking aloud when she was with him, seeing for him, reminding him of the beauty that is all around. In turn he answered many of her questions about how things became so beautiful, not insulting her with the dismissive "God made them that way" but launching into explanations of how God made flowers with full life cycles, reseeding themselves naturally every year, spreading from meadow to meadow with the help of winds, birds and animals. Misty thrilled to his explanations even as he thrilled to her lively descriptions.

Sometimes as they walked, Misty would scamper from his side, running ahead to gaze across the ocean from the hill where they walked, scurrying from side to side to get a closer look at toadstools growing beneath the ferns or at the light playing in the lacy leaves above or at nests and burrows of her many feathered and furry friends. She'd call out her discoveries as she found them, delighting the Captain as he walked surely along the well-worn path, his dog, Pilot, at his side. As always, Misty's faithful brown dog was with them. He and Pilot were fast friends, but Rusty followed Misty, returning to Pilot only when Misty returned to the Captain. And so the four made their way along the island as if this were an ordinary day, not the last morning they were to share.

Midway along they stopped to see Miss Lily, whose beautiful gardens and house nestled in the middle of her large property that bordered the Captain's to the west and Misty's grandparents' home to the east. Misty ran ahead, reminding Rusty to heel as they wound their way up the rose-lined path to the verandah where she could see Miss Lily watering her hanging baskets, squirrels scampering at her side. Miss Lily didn't keep what the Captain called domestic animals; she fed the wild ones who had become all but tame over the years. They'd even become used to Rusty and Pilot, but Misty was always careful to keep Rusty at her side so he wouldn't take a whim to chase one of Miss Lily's friends. Quickly Misty ran around to face Miss Lily, for Miss Lily's world was as silent as the Captain's was dark.

"Good morning," Misty said, looking up and speaking slowly so Miss Lily could read her lips.

Miss Lily bent down and held her arms out, receiving the hug Misty always had for her. "Come," she said in the low voice that had little tone; "I've set tea things in the back garden. Morning, Captain. Come along."

The garden was always a wonder and delight for Misty. In the centre was a birdbath and rose arbour, with birdhouses suspended in the safety of the trailing roses. To one side, carefully positioned to receive the gentle morning sun and be shaded from the more harsh afternoon rays, were table and chairs and the wonderful, magical swinging double seat whose gentle, rhythmic motion Misty so enjoyed, and all around were flowers, shrubs and trees. The Captain said Miss Lily had made a bit of England right in the middle of their island with her rambling gardens, her herb gardens and nut and fruit trees all carefully arranged to create something both practical and soothing. She didn't battle with the animals; instead, she planted enough for human and animal alike and even arranged a deer garden, a place the deer could munch so happily as to leave alone the parts Miss Lily wanted for herself and her other animal friends. There was a salt lick, some mangers where she placed sweet grasses for the deer, and all manner of plants deer favoured, grouped down by a small pond at the foot of the garden where they could graze and drink. The sights, scents, and sounds of Miss Lily's garden always filled Misty with a kind of awe. It wasn't as if Miss Lily's garden was more beautiful than the woods or the fields; it was just different. Here Misty knew a harmony of man and nature; in the woods she knew just nature. Both were beautiful. Both were wondrous.

As the Captain settled into his chair and Miss Lily carried the teapot to the table, Misty ran around behind the arbour where she knew the easel would be standing next to its table covered with paints, pallet knives, all manner of brushes, pencils, charcoals, and bits of cloth. Miss Lily's smock would be draped over the chair there, ready to put on whenever she sat to draw or paint. A gasp of surprise escaped Misty as she gazed at the canvas on the easel.

"Captain," she called, "Miss Lily has painted me in the garden! Oh, Rusty is there beside me. She has put me beside the pond with the floating lilies. The birdbath is behind me, a little to the left and the great walnut tree half shades Rusty but not me. The sun is shining on my braids, making the many different colours glisten and twist as they do, and my eyes are sparkling up, little yellow lights glinting out of the hazel colour. But I'm not looking out of the canvas. No, she has me looking up at a perfect little house finch who is clinging to the slender vine of the clematis that mingles with the roses. Oh, Captain, it is a beautiful picture, full of everything exactly as it is here in the garden! Oh, I didn't know Miss Lily could paint people too; I thought she just painted beauty, just flowers, trees, animals, the beach. But there I am, right in the garden. And oh, there is Nippy Tail sitting on the edge of the bird bath with his little paws in front holding a nut, looking just as if he's going to lift it to his mouth and start his little squirrel munching. What a happy picture!"

Misty ran back around the arbour and grasped the Captain's hand, squeezing it hard in her excitement. "When I look at that picture, I can almost smell the flowers it's so real. Aren't you happy to smell the flowers, Captain?"

"Yes, Misty, I am. And I am happy to have you paint pictures for me." With a chuckle, he added, "This time you have painted a picture of a picture, haven't you? Come now, eat the tea Miss Lily has made for us."

Before Misty could begin, she had to run around and throw herself into Miss Lily's lap. "It's a beautiful picture! Thank you for putting me in the garden with your beautiful things," she said as she kissed Miss Lily's soft cheek.

"There-there now, have your tea, Misty," said Miss Lily; "you can't stay all day today."

So Misty hopped down and took the seat between her two friends, pausing as Captain, his face lifted up, said simply, "Father, we thank Thee for this food, for wonderful friends, for peace, love, joy and strength."

She ate the biscuits spread with delicious currant jelly and drank the tea Miss Lily prepared from herbs grown in her garden. Around her the birds chirped, squirrels chattered, and leaves and blossoms rustled in the gentle morning breeze. Beside her, her friends quietly nibbled their biscuits and sipped their tea. Misty didn't notice that they ate little and silently brushed tears away from their cheeks as they tried to do justice to the delicious, light food. She was too taken with the garden and the new picture. Finished her food, she excused herself from the table, slipped down and ran down to the pond, hoping to see the deer.

"I'm glad you've caught our little jewel on canvas, Miss Lily," the Captain said. "Though I can't see it, it makes me feel better somehow, knowing you have the portrait with you. You won't mind if I come and sit next to it from time to time, will you? I'm sure if I sit next, I'll hear her voice and smell her hair and warmth, even as you can see the twinkle in her eye. Of course I'll have Rusty with me and he, too, will remind me. It's a hard day, Miss Lily, a hard day."

"Now, Captain," she said slowly and with an additional rasp in her low voice, "we've been blessed and we will be fine. There is no sense fighting against the inevitable, so we must just look on the bright side. They are right; it will be best for Misty to go to live in town and go to school. An island with an old blind man and an old deaf woman is no place for a child. She deserves more than that. We have to let her go. Besides, she'll be back someday, you'll see."

"Ach, Miss Lily; you're younger than I and have more chance of still being here when she does come back. It's a hard day. I'm trying for her sake, but it's a hard day. I know it's best to think positive, but tell me, what is this 'more' that you say she deserves? What more of God will she see in town? Oh, she'll see more of man, that's for sure, but more of God? Oh, it's a hard day."

"Now, Captain, God is in town too; you know that. She'll see facets of Him she hasn't seen here. Don't despair so. He'll tend to her even as He tends to us. But you are right: it is a hard day. I'll miss her terribly. We'll help each other. You stop on your way back and we'll take supper together before you go along home. I'll make soup, something light and easy for us to eat. Funny how the appetite goes when sadness comes. But here-here, we must take a lesson from the dear child. She doesn't look ahead and make herself all miserable with the troubles of tomorrow. Never was there a person so close to the Truth as Misty has remained. Try as I might, I still borrow trouble, as do you, and there is the child just living the moment God has given her. Call her now; we must carry on."

Misty came running the minute Captain called. Immediately, she began to gather the tea things, thinking she'd take them in and do the dishes with Miss Lily as she always did, but the Captain said gently, "Not today, Misty. We must continue or we'll miss Old Lundstrom."

It wasn't that Misty didn't know she was leaving the island. No one had ever hidden things from her or been in any way dishonest. When her grandfather had died two years before, she and Gran had carried on, learning to take on the tasks he had once completed. Gran, Captain, and Miss Lily all worked together, with Misty along side them as if she weren't a child at all, and they had managed well. But when Gran had died and Misty had ridden to the Captain's for help, things had changed. Captain was willing to keep her, as was Miss Lily, but orders had come for her to be sent to the mainland to the nearest town where she could have a proper life.

She had little curiosity about living in town, but Captain had tried to fill her in and prepare her for what was to come. Nothing he said seemed real to her, though: talk of cars and buses, schools and churches, stores and restaurants. These were all things Misty had read of, things that belonged in books, not things she need concern herself about. So though Captain had tried to prepare her, she had not ventured into the future, even in her mind. She was horribly sad to leave her friends behind, to leave her place behind, to leave her animals behind, and a lump such as she had never felt rose in her throat at such thoughts, but she just kept forgetting that she must go, so full and rich was life each day.

Even as she skipped along toward the dock, she was so taken with the world around her, with her world, that she forgot she was to board the boat and leave it all behind. So they moved along the path, one delightedly reporting all that she saw and felt, the other plodding along unusually quiet, each step that took him closer to losing her becoming harder to take. Despite his agonizing walk, the Captain thought the dock had never seemed so close to home.

Old Lundstrom was there, and the two men shook hands. As always, Misty laughed to hear Old Lundstrom say her name, for he said it in two words, "Miss T," not in the single word the Island folk always used. It sounded odd to her, but so did many of Old Lundstrom's words, for he had a thick Norwegian accent, giving his words a friendly but very distinctive sound. And Misty enjoyed sharing unusual names with such a fine fellow. Everyone thought of and referred to the gentle fisherman as Old Lundstrom as if that were a single word, yet all called him simply Lundstrom. He and Misty were fast friends.

She returned his friendly "hello" and darted off as she always did when he came to the dock. She was all over, skipping lightly to the bow of the boat, scurrying back to the stern, happy to be on the water once again. She loved the little skiff her grandfather had taught her to row as soon as she was able to hold the oars more than she cared for this big, noisy boat, but any boat was a delight, for the feeling of being cradled by the mighty sea thrilled her more than any. For a moment, though, as she ran to the Captain's side when she saw him hand Old Lundstrom her bag, her happiness vanished. She threw her arms around his neck and cried as she had when Gran had died. Tears ran down her cheeks and onto the Captain's shirt as he held her and rocked gently back and forth, his own tears dripping onto her thick, golden brown hair. Old Lundstrom moved away, leaving them alone for a time.

When Misty's tears had washed her hurt away, she kissed the Captain's rough, scarred and weathered cheek and said,

"Please, Captain, you will remember Rusty, the cats and old Nobbin, won't you? And you'll tend to Miss Lily, won't you? And you won't forget me, will you? I'll miss you so."

"Ah, Misty, you'll never know how much I'll miss you. Of course I'll look after the animals, and Miss Lily too. You'll be best if you do what they ask, Misty. Always try to obey. But don't let them corrupt you or poison you in any way. You're a special little girl. God will be with you." The old man bent again to give the child one more big hug before she stepped back onto the boat. Rusty leapt in beside her.

"No, Rusty," Misty said; "you have to stay with Captain and Pilot. Go back."

The brown dog sat at her feet and looked up at her, his head tilted to one side and his ears crinkled up as if to ask what this new command was. He didn't understand. Never had he been told to go back. As she looked at him, the tears sprang anew to Misty's eyes and she threw her arms around the dog's neck. His tail thumped against the deck of the boat, even as he carefully licked the tears from her face.

"Captain, why did you say Rusty must stay with you?" she asked.

"They said they wouldn't take a dog, Misty. Besides, town is no place for an island dog like Rusty. He's never seen cars before and would soon be hurt by one, maybe even killed, so Miss Lily and I must keep him here."

"Oh, that's right. Did you hear that, Rusty? You must stay here. Now go to Pilot and Captain."

But the little dog didn't move from her side, so she hopped back onto the dock and stood once again next to the Captain and Pilot, Rusty right beside her. Taking the Captain's hand, she kissed it, placed it on Rusty's neck then kissed the top of the dog's head.

"Bye, Captain. Bye, Pilot. Bye, Rusty," she said.

The Captain held Rusty firmly as she stepped back into the boat. Old Lundstrom hauled in the rope, called farewell and turned the boat away from the dock, while the small girl stood in the stern, waving to her friends ashore. A few more tears slid down her cheeks as she looked at the Captain, Pilot and Rusty, outlined as they were against the Island that had always been her world. But tears don't hurt. They cleanse. And as the chug-chug of the boat increased and the gentle roll of boat on sea increased with it, Misty soon became absorbed in the wonder of the ocean.

She had no sense of two hours passing while she moved about the boat, first watching the bubbles churned up by the propeller, then scampering ahead to watch the waves curl away from the bow as the boat cut through the water. Sometimes she'd stand with the warm wind flowing across her face, her braids blowing out behind her, enjoying the salt spray gently misting her all over. Then she'd run to Old Lundstrom to watch his gnarled hand on the wheel, his deep blue eyes scanning the water ahead, watching for driftwood and debris. He always seemed so much a part of his boat, his boat so much a part of the ocean, that Misty couldn't get enough of looking at him. The strength that comes from such unity seemed to spill over to her, making her feel secure and safe. From there she'd run out to the deck again, watching the gulls circling overhead, excited by their cries and squawks, wondering as she always did what they were saying to one another. She'd imagine herself flying aloft with them, looking down on the boat and the water churning out behind it and she'd hug herself with the excitement of such a feeling of freedom.

Misty was surprised to hear the throb of the engine slowing down. Looking ahead, she saw the harbour. It was as she remembered from her few visits there with her grandfather: rocks piled up to break the fury of the sea during storms, rows of docks tucked in behind the rocks and rows of fish boats tied to the docks. Above, the wharf was dotted with gulls, cars, and people. Old Lundstrom deftly manoeuvred the boat into its spot and secured it before retrieving her bag from the hold.

"Come," he said, "I have strict instructions to follow now. You must put your boots on before we get off the boat. In town, everyone wears shoes, even in summer, so you must have yours on. Yah, that is good. Now I must take you to find the woman you will live with. I know her a little bit from the bank in town, Miss T. She will seem strange to you at first, but you will get used to her. She wishes for you to call her Aunt Augusta, so that is what you must do. That is a good girl."

It was a good thing Old Lundstrom had taken her hand when they stepped off the boat, for, awkward in the boots, Misty tripped and stumbled a little. Suddenly she felt uncomfortable and uncertain. With the heavy boots between her and the dock, she was no longer sure of her footing, and the gentle rise and fall seemed unusually troublesome for her. Her feet, so long free from the encumbrance of shoes, felt pinched and constrained, and she found herself having to think about walking. Unused to thinking about herself at all, she was confused, disconcerted. It was as if all that was natural was being squeezed, forced away, replaced by something else. Concentrating on her heavy feet, she stumbled along beside Old Lundstrom up the ramp toward the wharf.

"Oh, there you are," she heard a shrill voice say as they crossed the wharf; "I thought you'd never get here. I've been waiting ever so long. Really, Lundstrom, you should take more care with time. Punctuality is important, you know. So here's the child. Hm. We'll have to do something about her looks. And she's tiny, isn't she? She must be ten years old by now; how can she be so small? Must be living in that horrid place; stunts a child's growth. And what hair! How ..."

But Old Lundstrom interrupted the stream of words, saying, "Now ma'am, we're here and we're safe, just as we were instructed. Small doesn't mean anything at all, you know. She's a good girl, you'll see. Be good to her. The old folk are going to miss her mighty bad. Me too. You take good care of her. Here's her things."

"Humph. Not much. Well, that's good. Won't have much to get rid of with such a small bag as that and if what's in it is a ghastly as what she is wearing, it will just have to be thrown out. Come, child; we must be off. It's late and we have a long drive."

Misty suddenly felt quite chilly and clung for a moment to Old Lundstrom's hand. He, unusually for him, bent his bearded, salt-weathered face and gave her a quick kiss on the cheek. The feel of his salty whiskers brought a moment of warmth to Misty, and she was able to let go of his hand.

"Bye, Old Lundstrom. Thank you for fetching me," she said, as she turned and followed the woman to the car she was walking toward.

Even through the cloud of having to think of her feet, her shoes, her legs, Misty was struck by the harshness of the woman's appearance. Her suit was a glaring, brittle red, the skirt shorter than anything Misty had seen before. Her hair was black and all one colour, no tones, no shimmering light, none of the subtle variation that brings softness with it. And it didn't move. Though the hair was short all over, somehow it didn't move, not even in the wind. And her feet! How could she clip across the wharf like that with such skinny, high heels on the bottoms of her red shoes? Misty guessed the shoes would be lighter than her own awkward boots, but she had to wonder how one walked on a slant like that, as if she were on her toes but with some kind of props for her heels. Suddenly her own feet felt a little less awkward, but she shivered slightly and turned to wave at Old Lundstrom before climbing into the car.

This was her first ride in a car and it wasn't suiting her very well. When she rode a horse or rode in a boat, she felt one with her carrier, was able to settle into the rhythm of the animal or of the sea; there was no sense of combat or even discordance. But the car seemed not to have a rhythm. It lurched and bumped along, sometimes from its own inherent roughness, sometimes from the roughness of the road. All of it seemed hard and unyielding, and Misty herself seemed to bump and jostle on the seat. Before long she felt quite battered. Her stomach also felt all out of sorts, something the healthy child had never experienced before. Then, too, the world moved so quickly by the windows that Misty couldn't feel one with that either. Absolutely everything suddenly seemed apart from Misty. For the first time she felt divorced from the world around her. For the first time she felt time drag.

Her uneasiness increased with every minute that ticked by, with every bump and jar, and with every lurch of her stomach. To make matters worse, the woman never stopped talking, adding her own noise to that of the car's engine. Never had Misty been so assaulted by noise, and it added to her discomfort and growing tiredness. Misty had long since stopped trying to hear the woman's words or understand anything she said, having concluded that she wasn't actually talking to Misty but was just talking. Vaguely she wondered if this were the "incessant chatter" she had read of in books, but most of her attention was taken with trying to endure the ride. As her tiredness and uneasiness grew, she slowly began to realize that she was beginning to feel as rough and battered inside as the ride itself was proving to be. Emotions that were new to her battled inside her as she clung to the cold car seat.

Misty had little experience with fear, but had known it once, when her grandmother had fallen down the stairs and lain in a heap at the bottom without moving. Fear for her grandmother had suddenly gripped Misty in that moment, and she had run as fast as she could for help. That kind of fear is instinctive not learned. Fear of other people, fear of the unknown, is learned rather than instinctive, and Misty had never learned such fear. Sneaking up on her now, though, was a stifling feeling that did resemble fear, for suddenly everything, including this woman, was not only utterly foreign to Misty but also abrasive. She tried to fasten her eyes on the trees that lined the sides of the road, hoping to regain a sense of belonging and safety, but they moved past in a blur, providing no familiarity or comfort. She took deep breaths, hoping to smell the familiar ocean scents, but smelled only the repugnant odours of vinyl, metal, road dust and exhaust. It was then that her head began to hurt and the lump began forming in her throat.

As the moments dragged by, Misty felt herself retreating into her own mind for rest. She was familiar with reaching out, wondering, imagining, pretending, and with talking to God silently, for these she had done all her life. But this was something new. This was moving inward in her thoughts; this was retreating, hiding and preserving rather than opening and growing. Bumping along the dusty road, Misty let the caustic grating of endless chatter and the harsh noise of cars fade as her mind carried her in to a safe place. Silently she asked for help, for rest, for quiet, for peace as her mind saw the faces of Captain and Miss Lily, the lithe forms of Rusty and Pilot romping through the meadow, the graceful movement of the tall trees bending in the wind behind the house and the soft colours of sand, field and flower blending into the safe blue of the sky above. Her mind returned to the picture she had seen just that morning, and she calmed a little, seeing herself back in the garden as Miss Lily had captured her. The senses of heavy time and passing miles faded as she slid back into her old world, and her eyes began to close.

Suddenly she was catapulted into the harsh, new world by the blaring of a horn. As the car screeched to a halt, Misty jerked, and her eyes flew open even before they had fully closed. The pitch of the woman's voice elevated and the sound escalated as she yelled something about lousy drivers before starting the car rolling once again. Misty found her heart pounding as if she had just slipped and fallen, and it took a while to settle because everything that now appeared before her eyes moved too quickly.

They had entered the town and there were many cars on the roads and many people hurrying about. The noise was almost unbearable as cars, buses, and people fought for the same small piece of roadway. Never had Misty seen such bustle, such pushing, shoving and scurrying about. The Captain had told her it was a small town, not like a big city, but as it was bigger than anything she had seen, it appeared impossibly crowded to her. She wondered why people couldn't walk together, why they seemed to tussle so as they moved along the sidewalks; she wondered why the cars couldn't move freely instead of all seeming to want to be first. She wondered where they were. Captain had said the town was on the ocean so wouldn't seem too foreign to her, but she couldn't see any ocean anywhere. In fact, the car was heading up a hill, which to her meant moving away from the ocean. She tried to filter out some of the noise and listen to what the woman was saying, but she didn't seem to know how, so she just sat stiffly on the seat, feeling the minutes drag again.

After reaching the top of the hill, the car moved along on the flat for a while before starting down a little. Not realizing how far inland they had travelled, Misty began to hope they would soon see the ocean, but they had barely left the crest of the hill when the car slowed and turned into the driveway of a large white house. Misty felt a little of the breath return to her when the woman turned off the motor, thus removing some of the noise that so bothered her. Even the woman's own words seemed to slow down enough for Misty to begin to hear and understand them again, so she obediently pulled the handle to open the door and step out when she was told to do so. She hoped to feel better with solid ground under her again, but as her feet touched the ground, she stumbled, tripped up again by the heavy boots that squeezed her feet. She concentrated on walking around the car without tripping. Her boots seemed to match the growing heaviness of her head and heart as she heard the woman say curtly,

"Well, hurry up then! We've wasted enough time today. Look at you—a perfect waif! But there's nothing I can do about it today. You'll have to hurry, for it's almost dinner time, and dinner must be ready when Hugh—you are to call him Uncle Hugh, mind—gets home from work. And that will be soon enough."

Misty's feet seemed even heavier as she walked up the steps to the house. She took her boots off by the door as she was told and followed Aunt Augusta through the house to a small bedroom that was to be hers. Even the house felt and smelled different from any she knew, but there was no time to think about that now, urged as she was to hurry. She stowed her bag on the shelf near the head of her little bed and went to the bathroom to wash the car and road grime off her hands and face before facing the woman in the kitchen.

"Well, I guess we can't expect you to get the salt and island dust and grime off you until we can wash your hair and give you a good bath, but at least your face is clean now. It will have to do. Now remember, be polite and well mannered at table. This is more of a shock for Hugh than it is for me, so you'd better make it as easy as possible for both of us. Go sit at the table until we come for dinner."

Misty's mind raced as she slid up into the chair to the side of the table. Wash off the salt and island grime? How could anyone think there was anything dirty about the ocean and the island? Here in this world full of dust and car fumes, someone called such natural things as the ocean grimy? And what was she doing sitting at a table when she should be cooking and helping in the kitchen as she had always done? Why was she to just sit and wait? Wasn't she to do anything here? And what did it mean 'make it easy for them' if she wasn't to help with cooking and setting tables? How could she make things easy for them if she wasn't able to work with them?

Again her head throbbed as she tried to sort through the strange new things, and again she could hear the voice nattering away from the kitchen and she began to feel tired all over. Again the lump rose in her throat. She wondered at it being suppertime, for though she hadn't eaten since her morning tea with her friends, she felt no hunger at all. In fact she wondered if she'd be able to eat anything. None of the smells coming from the kitchen were familiar, either; none of them gave her that little excited feeling that she was used to when she and Gran had cooked together and made such wonderful aromas.

A door slammed and a tap ran water somewhere, adding more noise to her confusion. Then, before she could even wonder, the woman came into the room, an odd looking man at her side.

"Thomasina, this is Uncle Hugh; Hugh, this is Thomasina," Misty heard the woman say as she gazed at the stranger, her confusion showing on her face. She felt perplexed to hear new names, for no one had ever called her Thomasina. She was also confused to hear such a stuffy kind of speech as if the woman were doing something rather than talking to anyone. And she was looking at a man so different from any she had known that she was momentarily stunned. No response occurred to Misty, so she remained silent.

Instead of addressing the child, Hugh turned to his wife and said, "Look at her, insolent thing, doesn't say anything to me as she should and looks at me as if I'm some kind of ogre. I knew it would be like this. Get me some wine and let's just get on with dinner. I'm tired."

Misty lowered her head, sensing she had done something wrong yet not knowing how she could have. She hadn't meant to seem insolent; she was just genuinely surprised at what she saw. Uncle Hugh wasn't very tall and had the most odd shape she'd seen, for his middle stuck out beyond anything else. He was dressed in a suit, the jacket unbuttoned but the vest straining across his middle, his shirt visible beneath it before bending around the mound of his belly and tucking into the suit pants that were fastened carefully below the huge bulge. Above his collar, a roll of fat shoved up against his very short, dark hair at the back of his neck and seemed about to choke him below his chins in front. His dark-rimmed glasses magnified his eyes in such a way as to make them appear to simultaneously stare and squint at her, and a tiny moustache made his upper lip both stand out and turn down as if in a pout. She'd never seen anything like this man.

Hers had been a world of tall workingmen, men whose muscular chests and arms seemed the biggest part of them. Hers had been a world of comfortable men, men dressed in trousers and shirts, men whose clothes weren't even noticeable, so suitable were they. Hers had been a world of old men, softened by white or grey hair and by exposure to wind, sun, and sea. Now she was looking at someone quite different, someone uncomfortable and hard. Now she was seeing someone grumpy and someone, she noticed even as she tried to keep her head down, with a glass in his hand, a glass he drained and quickly refilled before dinner had even begun.

The lump in her throat grew before Aunt Augusta appeared with the dinner plates. At home, they'd each dished their own dinner, but here Aunt Augusta appeared with the plates heaped up. Even on a happy day, Misty wouldn't have been likely to take so much food. She had no idea how she'd get through such a large meal, especially a large meal with a pile of lima beans.

* * *

So had begun her life in a new home. So had begun her battle with the lima beans. No wonder she had fallen asleep exhausted, the tears streaming down her cheeks.

2.

Changes

Sleep had always been a delightful thing to Misty, another of her friends. Sometimes she had happy dreams to bring her joy; other times she simply slept, but she always awakened refreshed and ready to begin a new day. As usual, she wakened early the following morning, just after sunrise. Immediately she began her first chat with God, thanking Him for a good sleep, for a new day, for all wonderful things He has made, but even as she thrilled at all the thoughts of the beautiful world and the joy of living, she slowly sensed something was different. Rusty had not licked her hand or her face. She couldn't hear him breathing beside her bed. Slowly she looked around her and remembered. She was in a new home in a new world. And she was quite alone.

'But,' she thought, 'life is good and wonderful and certainly not dependent on where I am, so I'm sure this will be okay. I'll just carry on as I always have.' Silently she asked God to look after Rusty, the Captain, Pilot, and Miss Lily; she asked Him to say "Good morning" to Gran and Gramps and to be with her and show her all the new things He must have for her in this new place. Then quietly, she got out of bed, turning to make it immediately. She straightened the covers, tucking things neatly in around the side of the bed and patting the bedspread until it was smooth. She noticed that her pillow was still wet, really quite wet on one side. She must have cried a long time last night, even in her sleep, but Gran had always assured her that crying doesn't hurt. Indeed, Misty felt so much better this morning, free of headache and that awful lump in her throat, that she thought Gran had shown herself right again, even after she had gone beyond where Misty could touch her. Practical as always, Misty decided that she must leave the pillow in the open air to dry, so instead of pulling the bedspread up over the pillow, she neatly folded the spread across the head of the bed and placed the pillow on top, wet side up, smoothing the pillowcase so all looked tidy. Satisfied, she took her little bag and went to the bathroom.

Her hair was difficult to brush out this morning, neglecting it as she had the night before, but she brushed and brushed as she had been taught. She felt a pang of loneliness, thinking of all the mornings she and Gran had sat side by side, Gran brushing her long, shiny, grey hair, Misty brushing her long, very curly, very thick, rich golden-brown hair, while they listened to the small music box that sat on the dressing table in Gran's room. They had often laughed about Misty's hair, for it really was thick and curly and could be very difficult to tame, like some wild animals and, Gran said, some wild people. If she didn't braid it, Misty was soon lost in a nest of frizz blown about by the wind, but the braids always worked well. So, they'd sit, side by side, Gran deftly braiding her hair and pinning the braids up around her head, Misty braiding hers and letting the braids hang down her back. Usually she tied them together to keep them from falling forward and getting in her way. If there was anything Misty didn't like, it was having things get in her way, distracting her from the ease, freedom and joy she found in living. So, this morning, she tied her braids together that they might stay put. That was her hair taken care of for the day. Idly she wondered if there were any music boxes in this house, anything that tinkled out such delight or sounded musical at all.

She became aware of how quiet the house seemed. There were no sounds of fire crackling in the stove or fireplace, no sounds of animals or life. She couldn't hear wind anywhere. She couldn't hear waves lapping against the shore. Neither could she hear any people, and that she liked! So she made a mental note that morning was a time she could enjoy quiet, even if it did seem somehow too quiet. Perhaps outside she would find things more familiar; perhaps she couldn't hear wind in the trees only because she was inside.

Replacing her little bag in her room, Misty quietly walked through the house. She ignored her boots by the back door and stepped out onto the dew-laden grass. Ah, that felt good.

Looking around, she saw that there were trees here, but only short ones. A row of fruit trees stretched along one side of the house and a thick lilac hedge closed in the other. She couldn't see any evergreens as far as she looked. But there were a few birds hopping about in the fruit trees, and Misty walked to that side of the house. Looking up, she saw a perfect place for sitting in the branches of an apple tree and quickly climbed up to nestle in the crook of the main branches. Even from here she couldn't see any evergreen trees, but it was a wonderful place to sit.

She saw that the house was much taller than she had thought, that it must have another storey above the one she had seen. She saw, too, that the house was on a hill, the land sloping away into the distance where two mountains seemed to come together forming a valley, the floor of which she couldn't see. She looked up, but saw nowhere that she could climb higher for a better look. Instead, she let her gaze move around the place she must learn to call theirs and saw a pond near the lilacs on the other side. It had lily pads floating in it and reeds growing up out of it and, as she stared hard through the leaves, she saw the glimmer of gold that told her there were goldfish in the pond. She breathed deeply the warm summer air, but did not feel the familiar salt tinge to it. Still, it was blossom-scented and quite nice. The sounds of the little birds helped her know she could belong here, know that this, too, could be a friendly place.

Happily, she let her mind travel home. She knew Captain would have fed the horse and the barn cats by now and have scattered feed for their few hens; he'd be moving about in his careful methodical way, with Pilot at his side. Pilot was just a dog, but he had all kinds of ways of helping Captain, of steering him clear of trouble that the old man could not see. When Captain went for his swim in the ocean, for example, Pilot did not swim with him but ran along the shoreline barking. By listening to Pilot's bark, Captain could swim parallel to the shore and needn't worry about being lost at sea. No one had taught Pilot to do that; he just did. Misty could imagine Captain this morning swimming with Pilot barking along the shoreline and Rusty paddling along behind him, for Rusty loved to swim. She couldn't imagine Rusty ever taking over Pilot's job, but she had always been happy to see Rusty swim behind Captain, not getting in his way, not bumping into him as the dog often did her when they swam together.

Gran had told her that animals had more sense than people did and were much more help. Gramps had corrected Gran and said, "Not sense so much as instinct. Animals are uncluttered by the sophistication that gets so much in man's way. They trust their instincts, and their instinct is to live with nature and with others, not to get ahead. They are not interested in success, just in living." Even in her thoughts and even after yesterday, Misty didn't see much difference between the dogs and the people she had known, for Gran, Gramps, Captain, and Miss Lily also just lived and worked together, but she trusted what Gramps had said. She smiled as she wrapped her arms around the apple tree, content and full of the best of life.

Her reverie was interrupted by a shriek coming from the house. Misty heard the abrasive voice of Aunt Augusta screaming.

"Thomasina? Thomasina. Thomasina! Oh, the child is gone! The ungrateful wretch is gone. What are we to do? Hugh! Do something; say something."

"Really, Augusta; she's your problem, not mine. But I can see life will never be the same here. You do something, and do it now! I want my breakfast and I must not be late for work. Leave the dratted child and tend to me now."

"But Hugh," the voice replied at a frenzied pitch, "she's gone. Her bed is all made and she's gone."

Only then did Misty realize that she was the cause of all this ruckus, so quickly she scrambled down from the tree and ran in the house to put things right.

"Good morning!" she said brightly, as she entered the kitchen where Aunt Augusta stood all dishevelled and distraught, while Uncle Hugh sat in a chair at the small kitchen table, glowering because his coffee wasn't ready. The sight of Hugh's scowl quickly choked the words that had risen automatically to Misty's mouth, so she didn't tell them she had just skipped outside to see the trees and birds and breathe the fresh morning air. Nor did she tell them how lovely it seemed outside. Instead, she just stopped and looked.

"There she is gawking at me again," growled Hugh. "Do something, Augusta, now!"

Poor Augusta didn't know what to do. Nothing seemed right. Her world was upside down all of a sudden. Quickly she tried to put it right.

"Thomasina, you must go to your room and stay there until Uncle Hugh has had his breakfast and is ready for work. I'll deal with you after he has left. Now go!"

Misty didn't move, but she looked around the room to see who else was there, who the woman was talking to. There were just the three of them. She frowned a little. Then she recalled the Captain reminding her that Miss T was short for Thomasina. They had been calling her! She'd have to try to remember.

"Move!"

The anger in the voice jolted Misty into motion, and quickly she hurried away and into her room. She sat down on the edge of the bed and, for the second time in her life, became aware of time moving slowly—very slowly. She heard sounds in the house now: chairs scraping, voices rising and falling, taps running, feet walking heavily across the floor. The minutes dragged by as she sat, an unusual dullness beginning to roll over her, threatening her usual morning thrill. The room was dark and seemed small. Wanting to resist the creeping dullness, she rose and went to the window to open the curtains and let the light in. They were pretty curtains, she thought, but they seemed all tangled up somehow as they criss-crossed and draped, covering the window entirely. She couldn't see how to pull them back and let them hang neatly to the sides of the window as all curtains at home had done. Then she noticed a solid looking heavy material behind the flimsy curtains, a small ring dangling from the bottom of it. Gently she pulled the ring. The blind lowered more. She pulled again and up shot the blind with a snap. She smiled to see the sunlight brighten the room, expanding it. Outside, she could see her apple tree and she reached behind the soft curtains and opened the window itself that she might hear the birds chirping. Leaning out a little, she breathed deeply and tipped her face up to the morning sun. It was warm, gentle and fresh. Though the thrill of morning did not fully return, the dullness that had been threatening faded.

She turned to look at the room itself and was pleased, for through the soft curtains, the sunlight cast patterns on the opposite wall, outlining the leaves of the apple tree and making her bed seem as if it were in the midst of the orchard itself. Misty decided to leave the blind up at night that she might not miss any of the morning sun. She noticed a small dresser in one corner of the room and a closet door to its side. There were a few shelves on either side of the bed, which stood centred on the wall adjacent to the window. In the bright light, she noticed that the soft curtains were flecked with tiny pink dots that matched the pink trim on the lampshade and the pink flowers on the bedspread. Though pink was Misty's least favourite colour, she decided the room was quite nice, despite being so different from the one at home. Idly she wondered why there was a small pink mat on the floor beside the bed when there were no dogs here to sleep on a mat; she reasoned that it was just a bit of warmth for feet hitting the floor in the morning. If that were the case, she must move the mat closer to the head of the bed, for when her feet swung over, they hit the cold floor.

As Misty rearranged the mat, she also thought the dresser drawers would be a better place for her few things, so she unpacked her bag. In one drawer, she put her underwear and nightie, carefully folded and tidy. In another she put her few shirts, her pants, and her shorts. In the bottom drawer, she carefully placed her favourite sweater, the only one she had brought. Opening the closet, she found a hanger for her jacket. She decided her hairbrush should sit on the doily on top of the dresser; she didn't need a mirror to look in when she brushed and braided her hair, so the tall dresser was a good place for her brush and the strands of cotton yarn she used to tie her braids. Maybe she would have a place in the bathroom for her toothbrush; in the meantime, she'd put it on the dresser too. She stowed her empty bag in the bottom of the closet and closed the door. There; she was done. It didn't look like home yet, but it was tidy and her things were put away, so she sat back down on the bed to think.

Misty knew only a life that simply unfolded naturally, so though her mind was always alive and active, she had spent little if any time thinking of what to do or how to behave. She was a spontaneous child rather than a pensive or hesitant one. She was also a naturally happy, delighted (and thus delightful) and peaceful child. Her world had been one of co-operation, of comfortable co-existence, of simple and true living. She had learned much, having been taught very little. Like a tree springing up near life-giving water and growing and filling out unassisted (and unhampered) by humans, Misty was a life, growing, unfolding, bursting forth in bloom. To others, she was refreshment and hope, like blossoms in springtime. All life seemed to well up inside her. Even now, sitting on the narrow bed trying to think, Misty found herself so full of the newness and freshness of the morning that her mind would not pursue thoughts of people, herself or her adjustment. Spontaneously, silently, she chatted to the Creator of all goodness, the giver of life, thinking and feeling her delight in the leafy shadows on the wall, the happy bird-talk outside her window, the warmth of the sun on her back. With it all, she asked that He might keep her safe and show her what to do next.

She was used to working along with her people, used to being active, so this was an unusual morning for her. She wondered why she couldn't have made coffee for the grumpy man, why she couldn't have fixed him some breakfast. She wondered why she had been up for so long and hadn't eaten anything, why she must be apart from the people and doing nothing. Her automatic, unthinking response had always been to help, to wade into the middle of what needed doing and simply work. Yet here she sat—alone, idle. Suddenly she wished she had thought to bring some knitting. At least she could have been making strips for rugs or squares for blankets. She thought of long winter evenings when she and Gran had sat comfortably together knitting or stitching quilt pieces, making things. Already she missed the quiet sense of creating something, of turning a single thread into something useful and warm.

Another new feeling began to rise in her, unsettling her. She slipped off the bed and walked about the room, a strange restlessness beginning to take over. She even felt her forehead wrinkle in a bit of a frown. She needed to do something, not just sit, not just wait. She wanted to live. Again, silently, she called out to God, this time for help and comfort. She went back to the window and leaned out, face turned to the sun's comforting warmth.

"What do you think you are doing now?"

The voice startled Misty, and she bumped her head on the window frame as she pulled back into the room.

"Really, child, you are a problem. Who gave you permission to open the blind and the window? Who gave you permission to just take over here? Who said you could move the mat? Where is your bag? Oh, I see you've just moved in, just taken charge, put your ugly things away. Didn't they teach you anything? A mere child, just pushing her way around. Nobody warned me that you were difficult. They just said you were left alone now. Ah, what is this? I see you don't like the way I make beds and have taken it upon yourself to do it differently. The pillow goes below the spread, you imbecile, not above. Looks like you can't get anything right either." As she scolded away, the woman grabbed the pillow. Finding it damp, almost wet, her tirade veered off in another direction: "Crying, I suppose. Blubbering in your pillow at night. Well, we'd better get one thing straight right off; there will be no crying, whining, or whimpering in this house. You'll just have to buck up. Children are enough trouble without a lot of crying. It will get on my nerves, it will, to have you crying. I won't have it; do you hear? None of it! Do you hear me? Answer me, child, when I speak to you."

But Misty stood rooted to the spot, eyes wide, body tense. The little pain of bumping her head should have faded by now, but she was aware of the throbbing of yesterday beginning to return. As the woman carried on, Misty also felt the lump rising in her throat. From the bits of the ranting that she had managed to comprehend, she knew an answer was expected, knew she should speak, but she could not find anything in the tirade to respond to, so she remained silent even as the woman picked up where she had left off.

"Say something! You've been nothing but disobedient since you came. Outside in the morning without asking. No shoes on your feet either. Up and prowling about the house when the rest of us were sleeping, snooping about, I suppose, looking for trouble. And look at you, those ridiculous braids all tied back as if you don't have hair at all, and where on earth did you get such clothes? Whoever put you, a girl, in pants? Really, I just don't know where to begin. How could I ever have gotten myself into such a mess? What … "

Misty could not decipher the words or sentences through the noise, could not follow what was being flung at her, just stood there feeling alone and attacked. As the voice went on and on, Misty began to retreat to a safe place. Her eyes took on the faintly glassy look as she silently asked God what it all meant and what she should do, and felt herself drifting off to the warm, quiet of the farm she had left behind. She could almost smell the hay in the loft of the barn, see kittens in little hay nests their mother had made for them, hear the nickering of the old horse below. Outside, the chickens would be scratching about in the dirt, their little clucks and chucks filling the yard with comfortable sounds, friendly sounds, natural sounds, sounds that didn't have to be understood or wrestled with. Through the beauty in her mind, Misty saw the answer: she must ignore the noise and listen only to the words. Silently she asked for help as her eyes refocused on the wall behind the noisy woman.

She heard clearly, "Come, then. We'll just have to begin at the beginning. I'll get us some breakfast and try to explain."

Misty realized that the woman's tone had changed. The anger seemed gone from the words and was replaced with something else, something she would come to see as resignation. It was easier for Misty to hear the words and their meanings when the anger was gone, so she walked with the woman to the kitchen and heard and understood her say, "We eat our breakfast and lunch here at the little table, taking only our dinner in the dining room. Sit down while I make you some porridge; you need something that will help you grow. I'll just have coffee and toast, so it won't take long."

Misty did sit down, for she wanted to do right as was her nature and as Captain had suggested, but it was difficult to simply sit and watch someone else work. As long as she could recall, she had been making porridge along side Gran, but watching Aunt Augusta, she soon realized she wouldn't know how to use such a stove as this. Instead of burning wood and heating the whole kitchen, this stove had little knobs on the front. When the knobs were turned, small flames grew under the rings that were slightly raised on the stovetop. She wondered what made the flames since there was no wood, but she didn't ask. She learned best by observing, so she watched quietly. She saw that moving the knobs clockwise made the flame grow bigger and moving them back counter clockwise made them grow small again. To get the coffee perking, then, she would turn the knob far around; just before it bubbled, she'd have to turn the knob back, and to keep it warm, she'd have to have it as close to the twelve o'clock position as it would go and still keep the flame flickering. So, if she were working at this stove, instead of moving the pot from the stove's hot spot directly over the firebox to its coolest spot at the back, she'd leave the pot still and turn the knob instead. That didn't seem difficult and wasn't in the least confusing. Left alone in the quiet, Misty was learning what she needed in her new life.

She wondered, too, about this woman moving around the kitchen in a robe and slippers, her hair all untidy. Gran had a robe, but Misty had seen her wear it only when she had to get up in the night and once when she had been sick for a few days after having fallen down the stairs. Back home, people dressed when they got up. But then back home, people had to go outside to get wood for the fire. Here, there was no wood, so no need to go outside. Perhaps a robe was okay here, then. But Misty didn't have a robe, so she needn't think further about this difference.

Before Misty knew it, Aunt Augusta put porridge in front of her and sat down with her own toast and coffee, immediately biting into her toast. Misty looked puzzled for a moment, as she was used to a pause of thanks before beginning to eat together, but she adjusted to what she saw and reached for the cream pitcher. The woman's hand reached out as if to stop Misty, but she seemed to think better of it and with a slight sigh, withdrew her hand. Misty poured milk onto her porridge, paused and began to eat slowly as was her custom. The porridge did not taste as good as what she was used to, and instead of the cream she had expected, there was milk, very thin milk, but she ate quite steadily, though without much appetite. A small glimmer of fear gripped her, as she studied the size of the bowl and realized it held more porridge than she could eat in a single sitting. Just one night in a new home and she had learned fear. The porridge began to resemble a pile of lima beans; however, it did taste better than lima beans, and she carried on, hoping that there would be no repeat of the previous evening.

Not surprisingly, the woman finished her toast before Misty had finished her porridge. She rose, poured another cup of coffee and sat down with a sigh. "Well," she said, "I'll assume you know nothing, for it seems you haven't been taught anything at all, and I'll begin. At least you seem to know that children are to be seen and not heard. I've barely heard you utter a word since you came. You go too far, though, in your adherence to that rule. You must reply when spoken to. Otherwise, it is true: children are to be seen and not heard."

As Aunt Augusta paused to take a sip of coffee, Misty processed the information given so far. She had always chatted easily with the folks on the island, which, she reasoned, was the same as replying when spoken to, so that shouldn't be a problem. What, however, might the rest of her words mean? Seen and not heard? Back home, there were no differences between children and adults; they were just one co-operative group of people. Here, it seemed, some differences were being spelled out. The new tingle of fear flickered through Misty as it dawned on her that this world was very different, that she was seen as different, that she was to be treated differently, but that she must learn. The fear grew as she also realized that if she was to be treated differently, then she couldn't depend on learning by observation, for there were only adults to observe here. She would have to listen carefully.

by observation, for there were only adults to observe here. She would have to listen carefully.

"Now today we will begin to put things right. I will take you shopping for clothes. Nothing you have is suitable for a little girl in our home. Your clothes all look homemade to me and only store-bought clothes will do for us. And pants will not do for a little girl. You're much too plain. Little girls are meant to be pretty. Perhaps if I can get you looking right it will be easier for you to behave right. We haven't got all day, late as we are this morning, so you'll have to speed it up a little. You finish your porridge while I get myself dressed and made-up so we can go. And for goodness sake, let's not have every meal a battle. Eat more quickly, child, and do finish everything I give you, without making faces."

How Misty wished for Rusty or the cats or even the chickens, any of whom would gladly have finished her porridge, but she was alone now that Aunt Augusta had gone off to dress. She wondered what "get made-up" meant as she wondered what much of that chatter had meant. She knew only that she was to hurry and that they were going out to fix her. Funny; she hadn't thought anything was wrong. Now she must hurry. The porridge was simply impossible, but she could hurry to clean up the kitchen so she'd be ready to go. Never had she left a messy kitchen, not even to move on to another chore like laundry, so she automatically got down from her chair and gathered dishes. She couldn't find a slop or compost pail anywhere; she guessed she'd have to ask. Meantime, she washed the remaining bit of porridge down the sink as she rinsed off the dishes ready for washing. It felt good to be cleaning and tidying, to be bringing order out of chaos, to be restoring cleanliness. She was struggling a little as the sink was really too high for her, so she pulled one of the chairs over by the sink and knelt on it as she washed and rinsed the dishes. She wiped the table and the counters off and was looking around for a tea towel to dry the dishes with, when Aunt Augusta returned, dressed in another short-skirted suit, this one a brittle orange every bit as garish as the red one she had worn the day before. Misty was about to ask where she could find a tea towel when even her thought was interrupted by yet another explosion.

"What are you doing? Who said you could get down from the table? Did you finish your porridge or have you done all this just to hide the error of your ways? Who said you could clean up? What on earth kind of child are you, just taking charge all the time? Adults take charge. Children do not. Have they taught you nothing? Will you ever learn anything? Oh, what am I to do? I thought I was taking such a sensible approach and here you have me all upset again. Is there no end to the trouble you stir up? I just can't think ..."

Misty stood rooted to the spot once again. Around her, the kitchen looked tidy, with only the clean dishes draining in the rack needing to be dried and put away. She had even rinsed the sink out when she was finished. All was as it should be if she'd only been able to find the towel. What, then, had she done to cause trouble, to make this woman so angry? Misty had very little experience with unhappiness and even less with anger so she had no way of understanding. She could only feel dreadful herself. She hated to think she was causing trouble, hated to find herself making others unhappy. She wished she could fix it, could do something or say something that would take away this anger. Instead, she felt the lump rising in her throat again and felt her head begin to tighten inside. She found herself clenching her fists, for she recalled one thing from the earlier tirade, and that was that she mustn't cry. It made no sense to her to hear that crying was wrong and bad; it contradicted everything Gran had said and everything she had learned from experience. But in an effort to please this woman and to undo what she had somehow done, she determined that, no matter what, she would not cry. So there she stood, unhappy and afraid, but hanging on. Silently she called out again for help.

Suddenly the woman flopped her hands down to her sides and said, "Oh, what's the use? At least you cleaned up the kitchen and saved me having to do it. Get your shoes on, child; we'll just forget this and try again. I am sure getting you looking better will make you behave better. Hurry. We'll go to the store."

3.

Shopping

Misty pulled on her shoes and walked to the car as quickly as she could. She tried to soak up a little of the warmth of the sun, hoping it would soften the block she was beginning to feel inside her, but there was no time. What a world this was. Sit and wait and then hurry and scurry. There was no rhythm here at all, at least nothing she could settle into, and she felt tired though it was still morning. Again the car felt foreign to her, the shiny hard seat as unwelcoming as the metal dashboard, and again the noise grated on her. As they rode along, the world closed in on Misty as the trees were replaced with buildings all lined up close together and the road filled up with cars. The noise was horrendous to the child who was used to gentle sounds of trees and ocean. She recalled her bit of wisdom from the morning and tried to ignore the noise, but soon realized that she'd have to experiment and practise, to find ways to ignore it, to block it out. She was tempted to retreat inside once again, but the woman's voice drew her attention. She struggled to listen, not wanting to cause more trouble.

"We'll soon be at the shop. Now I hope you can behave yourself and not embarrass me. These shopkeepers know me and are important to Uncle Hugh in his work at the bank, so you must be ever so good. As it is, I feel awkward taking you in looking as you do, so you just have to be on your best behaviour."

As Aunt Augusta manoeuvred the car into a parking spot, Misty wondered about this "best behaviour" business. She couldn't recall having heard or talked about behaviour before. Was behaviour a part of living? If so, what part of living might behaviour be? How was she to be on her best behaviour when she didn't know what behaviour meant? And what might embarrassment be? How was she to avoid embarrassing Aunt Augusta? And what was the matter with the way she looked?

She was clean, tidy and comfortable. Was there more? These thoughts were all new to her, and she felt uncomfortable thinking about herself. She couldn't recall doing that ever on the island; in fact on the island she had not thought or wondered about people at all. Instead, she had wondered how things work and how they live and how they grow; she had wondered about life and the wonderful world around her, the perfect world that was so beautiful and so intricately made. Never had she wondered about people, except as they were a part of that world. Again Misty felt tired with the weight of not only new experiences but also the need for new thought.

Misty was shocked when she got out of the car to feel Aunt Augusta grab her hand. Strangely, the touch made Misty feel at odds with everything. Though Aunt Augusta was touching her for the first time, there was no sense of unity or even of union between the two. It was as if instead of spontaneously and mutually linking up to move ahead together, one person had grabbed the other to drag her along, to take control. Misty felt herself cringe a little and hoped she hadn't pulled her hand away. Though she didn't like the feel at all, she was determined to avoid any more outbursts, determined to avoid offending this woman. In her innocence, Misty even hoped to somehow bring a smile to Aunt Augusta's face someday. She seemed so unhappy always. Concentrating as she was on her hand and Aunt Augusta's unhappy face, Misty found it difficult to keep up. Again she became aware that there was no rhythm. Aunt Augusta hurried along at a frantic pace, as did all the people on the sidewalk around them. Misty began to feel grateful for the hand, though it did pull her along so. She was almost overwhelmed, not just by all the people hurrying about, but by the disharmony of it all. Had she not been struggling so hard to keep up and to keep her hand from pulling away, she'd have noticed that tired feeling growing inside her.

When they entered the shop and the door closed behind them, she felt a bit of relief as the pace slowed down, Aunt Augusta let go her hand and as the street noise was shut out by the door and muted by the racks and racks of clothing she saw inside the shop. A slight frown wrinkled Misty's brow as she noticed a smile, the first she'd seen, appear on Aunt Augusta's face. Something looked wrong with the smile, something that caused Misty's frown, but she couldn't understand what it was. Immediately, she was distracted by Aunt Augusta's voice; the quality of it was different from any Misty had heard until then as Aunt Augusta began:

"Good morning, Milly. Yes, I do need your help today. I have a task that seems just beyond me and I'm so glad you are on today. I'd have just died if I'd had to depend on that young woman you have working here sometimes; she simply won't do. I'm sure you will sort things out, though. Now will you look at this? This is the child we've taken in. Look at her, such an embarrassment. I hardly know where to begin."

"May I suggest, Ma'am, that we begin at the beginning? What is it she needs?"

"Why everything, just everything. She didn't bring much with her, and I'm going to throw it all out anyway. She has atrocious things, all plain and homemade. She doesn't even look like a little girl. Fortunately, Hugh says I'm to spend whatever it takes to fix the child, so we have free rein today. I'm depending on you now and I'm really very tired so will just sit down a minute while you do some measuring and begin with her underthings and a robe. Perhaps after a little rest, I'll feel up to choosing some appropriate dresses and such. She doesn't even have a coat or any decent shoes. Look at those ugly boots they've kept her in. Oh, I'm so tired."

Misty felt relieved to see Aunt Augusta sink into a chair and grow quiet. The woman called Milly seemed calmer to her, and she thought she'd be better off with her. So she followed her to the back of the shop and into a little room separated from the rest of the shop by a curtain. There she took off her clothes as she had been told by Milly, leaving only her underwear on. Milly came in with her tape measure and little pad of paper. Silently, Misty held out her arms as directed while Milly measured around her chest, waist and hips before measuring her arms. Milly's eyebrows went up, but she didn't say anything, just measured again. She frowned and moved to the other arm, carefully stretching the tape from armpit to wrist.

She shook her head and muttered a soft "how could it be?" before writing the numbers on her little pad. She did the same when measuring Misty's legs, first raising her eyebrows, then frowning, then shaking her head before writing her numbers down. She asked Misty to stand on a measuring stick, and as Misty did so, Milly squeezed her foot and wrote more numbers. Finally she put the tape around Misty's head; before recording any numbers, she applied the tape once more, pulling it tighter. Again she frowned as she wrote a number down. Misty had never seen as many frowns and unhappy faces as she had in just that one morning; she began to wonder if everyone in the town was unhappy, but her thoughts were interrupted as Milly asked her how old she was and what grade she was going into.

Even before Misty could open her mouth to answer, Milly carried on with, "Must be about seven or eight, probably Grade Two or Three," making Misty wonder if she'd ever learn to live in this world. Finally she had heard a direct question, part of which she understood and knew the answer to, only to have the woman answer it herself as if she weren't even there. It bothered her that the woman's own answer was wrong, and Misty wanted to correct her but she wasn't given a chance to speak, as Milly kept on talking, listing all kinds of clothes that she'd need. Misty needn't have worried, however, for Aunt Augusta's tinny voice interrupted Milly's list of words.

"No, no, Milly, you see what I mean about impossible? The child is ten, just a runt, living deprived on that island with nothing but old people. She's positively scrawny, and look at how brown she is, allowed to run free all over like the animals I suppose. She looks grubby, all weather-beaten like that. I don't suppose she's had a hat on that woolly head of hers."

"Never mind, Ma'am. I'm sure we can at least make a start. Scrawny is easily hidden with clothes, you know, though we may run into some difficulty. I can gather the underthings she'll need, if you just tell me which kind you want her in, and I'll be fine fitting shoes and a hat, but you may have to make her clothes. Her arms and legs are very long for her body size; I'm quite sure nothing ready-made will ever fit her."

Misty had never felt as naked as she did standing there with two women criticizing her body; to make matters worse, it was chilly in the little room and she began to shiver a little. She wanted to curl up and hide somehow, but there she stood, clad only in her underthings while the two women stared at her.

Aunt Augusta was horrified at what Milly said; it was bad enough that she herself thought the child looked a waif, but to have someone actually see, record and state just how hopelessly disproportionate she was with a bitty body on spider legs and great gangly arms hanging at her sides made Augusta quite angry. Huffily she said, "Oh, don't be absurd. Of course you have clothes to fit. All children fit into store-bought clothes, no matter how awkward and gangly they are. Do you expect us to stoop to homemade or to waste the money on having clothes tailored for her? You'd best just get on with finding clothes that fit. Of course we'll take the underwear with the lace trim. Just look at her in that plain stuff. Ridiculous. And I'll have none of those clunky oxford shoes that all the mill-workers' children are wearing. We'll not have her looking like those riff-raff. It would never do for someone in Hugh's position to have a child in his home looking just like the others. No, fetch those patent leather party shoes; she'll wear those to school. I assume you do have those to fit, of course. Really, I may have to think of going elsewhere if you can't meet our needs."

Even through her discomfort, Misty couldn't miss the impatience and hint of disgust on Milly's face and she wondered if she had done something to upset her too. The kind of social comment that was going on right before her was utterly incomprehensible to her; she didn't even know what a mill-worker was, never mind why someone living in a banker's home shouldn't look like someone living in a mill-worker's home. Neither could she know that Milly's own brothers were mill-workers, so Aunt Augusta's huffiness was insulting Milly. But she could hope that she hadn't been the cause of Milly's discomfort, for she had stood still and done what she was told without comment—unless the very look of her waif-like body with gangly arms and spider legs had caused the offence. Once again, Misty wished to curl up somewhere but couldn't. Again, she shivered.

"Oh there she goes," exclaimed Aunt Augusta, "shivering and carrying on as if we are torturing her. Really!"

At that, Milly's professional aloofness began to give way and she stepped in. "Now, Ma'am, it is chilly in here, and perhaps we'd best start trying clothes on her. I've gathered the underthings and sent the boy for shoes to try on her; we'll just try some dresses while we wait. That will warm her up a bit."

"Well, fine. Pretty dresses. You must get pretty dresses. I want her in pink, with lace, frills and bows. See what you have."

"For school, Ma'am? You want those clothes for school? Surely nice cotton dresses and some skirts and blouses would be more appropriate and serviceable, much easier for you to look after. What grade did you say she was in? It will help me choose appropriate clothes."

"How on earth am I to know what grade the child will be in? She's never been to school. I'll not allow her to be placed in the First Grade, of course, at her age, but heaven only knows what they'll do with her. I'm sure I don't. Grade doesn't matter to clothes anyway. She need only look pretty. Get some pink party dresses."

Something in the woman's tone convinced Milly that she must just do as she was told. The same thing made Misty shiver again. She wished she could wrap herself in the curtain but she dare not risk doing so with Aunt Augusta standing there. Misty wished with all her might for the warmth and comfort of the sun or of the fireplace glowing as it did in the winter evenings or of the faithful little dog by her side. Somehow she knew that he didn't think her all gangly and awkward. If she looked so awkward, why had she never been awkward, she wondered. She didn't recall feeling at all disproportionate or gangly. The only time she'd been the least clumsy was when she first put on her heavy shoes in the winter, but the clumsiness left as soon as she adjusted to the shoes. Wearing them yesterday and today in the summer really made her have trouble, for she immediately became more aware of her feet than ever. Suddenly Misty knew that the key to smooth movement and comfort was complete unawareness of one's body and its parts. She had been clumsy yesterday because she was aware of her feet instead of being aware of her contact with the ground. She shivered again as she realized that she was now aware of much more than her feet; her arms felt so long that she was sure they brushed the floor, and her legs felt as long and thin as those of the daddy long-leg spiders she'd seen lumbering along; her body felt tiny, shrivelled compared to her limbs. Worst of all, Misty herself felt shrivelled under the harsh eyes of these critical women. It was still summer, but she had never felt so cold.

Even Milly's dropping the fluffy pink dress over her head didn't add any warmth to Misty. Instead, she began to feel fidgety. The dress was dreadfully uncomfortable. It hit her in all the wrong places, had much too much material everywhere and somehow it pulled at her arms. To her relief, Milly shook her head:

"You see, Ma'am. It's all wrong, and others will be like it. The child has no waist at all. Let me show you. Her bottom rib seems to rest directly on her hipbone so there is no space for a waistband, a belt or a bow. With her body this small, all sleeves are going to be too short for these arms and everything will pull. Her dresses will all tear if they fit this badly. The best thing would be to make clothes for her. We have patterns and fabric; made clothes fit better and are more comfortable. There really isn't any other way, Ma'am."

"I'll not have it! No child from my home goes about in homemade clothes. Do you understand? Just find the closest fit and have your seamstress do necessary alterations. Bring more to try."

Even Milly was cowed by the senseless stubbornness of the woman. As she brought dresses for Misty to try on, she began to feel sorry for the little girl before her. The child was unusually patient, having not uttered a word of complaint nor fidgeted about as most children do. She had not complained of the cold or of the tedium of putting things on and off, over and over. She hadn't even made faces, just shivered now and then. At times her eyes had taken on a kind of glassy look, but otherwise the child had simply stood still and co-operated. Milly decided the look was perhaps dreamy rather than glassy and she began to sense a kind of strength in the child. She was distressed to have to put her through this ordeal and wished she could make the woman see that the child deserved reasonable clothes and reasonable treatment. She made one more attempt, suggesting skirts and blouses might fit better and thus look better, but the woman was adamant. The child must look pretty, so must wear pink, frilly dresses.

Eventually, they found three dresses that could be altered. One could have the sleeves let down and the others could have the sleeves cut off and turned into short or cap-sleeves. Milly suggested a sweater to wear over the short sleeves, but Aunt Augusta didn't see anything pretty enough.

"Unless you can get one in her size with a beaded top, she'll just have to manage. You can't cover a pretty dress up with a plain old sweater. No, just bring some hair ribbons and barrettes that will match these dresses. The braids are going to go. She'll have to wear her hair in ringlets; at least it is curly enough for that. She'll also need socks with lace around the top. Just get the rest of those things and we'll leave. I'm simply too tired to do more now. You'll have the alterations done as soon as possible? I can't bear having her look like this any longer than necessary. We'll be in tomorrow afternoon to pick it all up. Oh, what a trial even this has turned out to be," she whined, as she walked out of the changing room, leaving Misty standing shivering in her underthings and Milly standing with armloads of fluffy dresses.

Sensing the child's fatigue and confusion, Milly whispered, "put your comfortable old things on and go with her. Somehow I'll get these done for tomorrow, and when you come to get them, I'll try once more to help you out." And Milly patted Misty's skinny, bare arm before leaving herself. Misty felt the lump in her throat about to explode and her head throb worse than ever but she hurried into her clothes, crying silently for help. She must not cry. She clenched her fists and hung on tight as she left the dressing room and followed Aunt Augusta out of the shop and to the car. She wondered if she'd ever get warm.

The vinyl of the car seats added to her chill, as did all the noise and confusion. At least Aunt Augusta was quiet. Misty wanted to pull her legs up shorter. Her feet didn't even come close to the floor, but in light of the shopping comments, they seemed to dangle far below her. She kept her gangly arms wrapped around her body, only partly to attempt to hold some warmth. Well, she'd learned about shopping, hadn't she? She concluded that she preferred sitting by Gran's side sewing. They had made all her clothes, some from material they had ordered from a catalogue, but most from clothes that Gran or Miss Lily no longer used. All of her clothes had been comfortable. All of her clothes had fit. There had been no trouble getting them, and she had not had to go among strangers and hear endless criticism of her body in order to have clothes. If shopping was one of the things people thought she'd missed by living on an island, she had to conclude that it was worth missing. She was exhausted, something she had felt only once before in her life, and that was yesterday.

As the car ground along, she retreated once again in search of quiet, rest, peace and strength. Her eyes took on the glassy look and her arms began to relax as she imagined the gentle movement of a rowboat beneath her, soothing her, calming her. She could almost hear the waves lapping against the sides of the boat as it bobbed along in the shallow water. She could almost see the movement of tiny fish as they darted about stirring up the sand on the ocean's bottom. She could feel the warmth of the sun as it streamed down from above and reflected off the water's surface. The brightness began to restore cheer to her troubled soul; the rest she sought seeped in. Her eyes began to close sleepily.

Suddenly they popped open again as the car jerked to a halt, but not before some strength had returned. She saw that it was sunny here too, as she stepped from the car and looked at the apple tree beside the house. The sun was high overhead now; it must be well past noon but she wasn't hungry and she headed for the apple tree. Aunt Augusta's shout turned her quickly toward the house, however. It seemed she was to follow her and do what she was told. Once again, she tried to listen carefully as Aunt Augusta spoke rapidly:

"I suppose it's not your fault, child, that you are so mis-shapen, but it really does make things difficult. Never has shopping been so tiring. I've always liked it. Well, never mind. At least you were quiet, and we did find some things. We'll have a bit to eat now and then we must walk through the house so I can spell out the rules for you. It occurred to me that I can't expect you to behave yourself when I haven't taught you the rules. We'll put that right this afternoon."

Misty was surprised to hear yet another tone of voice. This Aunt Augusta was a puzzle to her. She seemed to change wherever she went and with whoever she was around. But this was the softest Misty had heard. She thought maybe that a bit to eat would help make her warmer and ease the ache that continued in her head, so she set about to help, wondering what things they might make soup from. But Aunt Augusta jumped to find Misty at her side and quickly said, "No, you sit and wait. I'll just heat up some soup." So once again Misty was forced to sit idly.

But at least she could observe and learn. Against her will, her eyes bulged a little as she saw Aunt Augusta lift a tin from the cupboard. The red and white label clearly said "Soup," so Misty knew they didn't need to find things to make soup. This was new to her. She watched as the woman opened the can, poured it into a saucepan, added a tin of water, put the pan on the stove and, turning the flame up, gave the soup a stir. Misty wondered how the woman would prepare biscuits in time if the soup only needed to heat, but Aunt Augusta took crackers from a cupboard and put those on the table. There'd be no biscuits. Misty noted where Aunt Augusta got the bowls from and where the silverware was kept so she wouldn't have to root around looking for things when her turn came. She saw the cupboard for glasses and noted the water pitcher was kept in the fridge. Busy as she was observing and learning, the time passed quickly, and they were soon sitting down eating soup and crackers.

The soup tasted strange to Misty, a little tinny, but it was easy to eat, and the crackers were light and crunchy. Both Misty and Aunt Augusta were relieved that there was no struggle at this meal. When they finished, Misty took the dishes to the sink, an act which momentarily brought a dark cloud into the kitchen, for she had done something without being told.

However, even as Aunt Augusta began to exclaim, "What do you think you're doing?" she thought better of it and sat back in her chair, letting Thomasina clear up the mess. She was just too tired to try to tame this wild child. She did notice that Thomasina was quick, efficient, and very good at working around the kitchen but she still resented that a mere child was doing anything without specific instruction from her. There was so much to teach the child that she felt tired and had a sudden change of mind.

"Thomasina, I'm very tired and need a bit of rest before we begin this afternoon. I'm going to have some coffee before we start. You go outside until I call you. Mind you stay in the yard and don't do anything wrong."

Though Misty missed the first part of what Aunt Augusta said as she scrambled to remind herself that "Thomasina" somehow referred to her, she did hear the order to go outside as well as the explanation about coffee. Her impulse was to make coffee for Aunt Augusta, but she resisted, knowing that she must do what she had been told. She was learning.

Not sure what "the yard" meant, Misty decided to be safe and go to her apple tree. She was tired too and knew she could rest quietly up there. Settled comfortably in the crook of the tree, her back resting against one branch, her feet propped up on another, Misty took deep breaths of the fragrant orchard air and looked up through the branches and into the deep blue sky above. She felt her body relax and settle into the tree and she wriggled her back a little more firmly against the tree in expectation of the delight that always came with being at one with creation.

Instead, tears began to fill her eyes. Though she had grown up on an island with only four old people, Misty had never felt lonely. She had always been comfortably a member of that small group of people; further, they were each so much a part of the world that Misty found friendship not only in the many animals that shared the island with them but also in the very island itself. Even when she was alone, she felt only peaceful, comfortable and safe. Suddenly, here in a town filled with people, she experienced the first pangs of loneliness. Nothing here had made her welcome; nothing here made her belong. Her loneliness sprang from separation, not only from those she had known and loved but also from those in this new world. This world hurt her, and its people denied her the only way she knew of easing pain. This morning she had fought harder than she realized against crying from the pain of separation, of criticism, and of confusion. Though she couldn't have identified even the pain, what she felt was unsure, insecure and very tired, all things new to her.

Only as her body relaxed in the comfort of the tree, did the pain leak out in quiet tears. Safe in her tree, she naturally let the tears fall; they felt warm on her cheeks, warm and soothing. Feeling a great sense of thankfulness rise up within her, she wrapped one arm around a branch of the tree and drifted off to sleep.

She wakened refreshed and delighted to find herself in her tree. Looking around, she saw small finches flitting in the branches above her, not at all bothered by her presence or by the presence of the cat she noticed crouched on the ground below. She chuckled at the cat, knowing as she did that he thought he was nicely hidden behind a small clump of lavender, when he was clearly visible to her and the birds. Cats were funny to watch. This one was obviously not seriously hunting, probably only enjoying the afternoon warmth. Softly she called, "Puss, puss." He looked up at her but quickly turned away as if to snub her, cat-like. When she called again, he scampered away, vanishing out of sight. She wondered where he lived. She'd have to try to find out. Meanwhile, she felt warm to have seen him, to know he might come again.

Turning, she swung her legs down from the branch and stretched a little. She wiggled her toes and flexed her feet, enjoying the warmth and freedom. Tucking her hands under her thighs, she swung her legs gently back and forth, humming a little as she did so. What a wonderful place to have found! And hidden among the leaves were all kinds of apples that would come ripe in the early fall. What a treasure trove this was, for she loved apples fresh from the tree. Her humming turned into singing as feelings of familiarity and goodness rose within her. This tree was a little part of home and it was hers to enjoy. She felt strong again and wished she could live up in the branches of the tree.

4.

Rules, Rules, Rules

Instead she heard a voice calling, and a jumble of impressions and thoughts tumbled through her head bringing confusion with them. Dresses, arms, legs, cars, people all crowded into her mind, bringing with them a little chill, but through the jumble came the reminder from the early morning: "ignore the noise and listen to the words." She listened and strained a little. Then, remembering that she was to answer to "Thomasina" and come when she was called, she climbed down from the tree and ran across the lawn to the back porch. There stood Aunt Augusta, hands on her hips, a wrinkle in her brow.

"Please, child, try harder. How many times do I have to call? You must come immediately. And look! You've no shoes on again! Did I not tell you this morning that you weren't to run around like an animal? Did I not say I don't want you bringing all the dust, dirt, and grime from your bare feet into the house? Don't tell me you are going to be difficult to teach, too. Nobody said you were difficult. Well, I'll leave these outside rules for now and begin inside so you might be better when Uncle Hugh comes home from work tonight. He really can't abide disruption. Come now. I wish I could just write these things down for you, but that would be pointless. You can't read, of course, with no school. And at your age. Really! What were they thinking? How did ..."

Misty wanted to correct her, to tell her that she could read, had been reading for almost as long as she could remember, but Aunt Augusta kept on and on and on as Misty followed her into the house. She didn't seem to be giving any information, didn't even seem to be talking to Misty really, but just kept talking with that voice that could only suggest something wrong. Misty began to feel small again, small and gangly, as she realized that she had caused this by not coming soon enough when she was called and by her offending bare feet. She had come as soon as she realized she was being called and she simply hadn't thought to put shoes on. It was still summer, still warm, not a time to wear shoes. She made a mental note to wear shoes outside, always. She thought she'd also better practise saying "Thomasina" to herself; then maybe she'd learn to answer right away. That was two things Misty got from the many, many words that were pouring out of Aunt Augusta's mouth. Misty strained to listen to more of the words and found that the voice had changed again. The anger was gone and something almost flat had taken over; Aunt Augusta was beginning to give information about the house and the rules of the house.

Misty soon heard that there was no reason whatsoever for her to go to the basement unless she was with an adult. There was a bedroom down there and another room that they had once let out to a boarder; there was also the furnace, hot water tank, and the washing machine. Misty heard that as she had no use for any of those things, she should just stay away from the basement. She was also to stay out of the living room and the dining room unless she was with Aunt Augusta and Uncle Hugh and, when in those rooms, she was not to touch anything. Walking through the living room, Misty wondered why the fireplace had no ashes, but Aunt Augusta gave her no time to ask any questions, just continued on with her tour and her information. The door that was opposite the front entrance to the house was never, ever to be opened or touched—*never, ever*. Misty was also forbidden to enter what was called Uncle Hugh's study and she had no reason to enter the bedroom Aunt Augusta and Uncle Hugh shared either. Further, she had no reason to use the front entrance to the house. It really was a big house, but in the end, Misty realized that she was barred from most of it.

The list of things she was forbidden to touch was so long that Misty decided it best not to touch anything, for she'd never remember all that Aunt Augusta said. Not only was the list long, but it was the first such list Misty had encountered, so she found it a little puzzling and had to concentrate to stop herself from wondering why there were so many rules. Why did they have rooms they didn't use and doors they never opened? Why did they have things that weren't to be touched? Why was there a set of rules for her and none for them? None of this made sense to Misty; she couldn't see any reason for any of it. She forced herself to shut out the noise and her own questions and just take in the information.

She was never to run in the house. She was never to jump on her bed. She was never to jump on any furniture. She was never to put her feet on any furniture. She was never to go outside without being told. She was never to speak without being spoken to. She was never to yell, scream, or make any unnecessary noise. She was never to leave her things lying around. She was never to drop towels or clothes on the floor. She was never to interrupt. She was never to take anything. She was never to touch the stove. She was never to go into any cupboards or drawers. She was never to complain. She was never to demand anything. She was never to do anything without being told. She was never …

Misty began to wonder what she was ever going to do. As best as she could tell, she was being confined to her room, the bathroom and the kitchen, she wasn't allowed to touch anything, and wasn't allowed to do anything. She let many of the "nevers" go, for Aunt Augusta was saying things that were unnecessary, spelling out things Misty would never have thought to do anyway: yelling, screaming, running in the house, jumping on furniture, silly things. But what was left was making her feel small and crowded at the same time.

Aunt Augusta was right in a way; Misty had run free like the animals. But she was mistaken to think that made Misty wild. She was also mistaken to think that animals running free were chaotic or even disorderly. Had she observed the animals, she'd have seen that they move naturally and always with purpose, not wildly, randomly, chaotically. Misty had been free, but she, like the animals, was simply natural and unconsciously purposeful. Now, in the interest of what Aunt Augusta called order and obedience, Misty was being confined and being robbed of any purpose at all. How could she help people without touching anything? How could she even look after herself without being able to go from room to room, get things from cupboards, do things without being told?

As the list of "nevers" mingled in her head with this growing sense of loss of purpose and confusion about what she was to do, Misty struggled hard to refocus on Aunt Augusta's words. It was difficult to hear through a dull throbbing that had begun in her head, but she was determined. Ah, was there answer in the words? She must always do as she was told, and do it immediately. She must always show proper respect for Uncle Hugh and Aunt Augusta. She must always be polite and quiet. She must always wear shoes. She must always wear the clothes Aunt Augusta laid out for her. She must always make her bed. She must always wash her hands before meals. She must always eat the food that was placed before her—*all* of the food placed before her. She must always brush her teeth before bed. She must always sit up straight. She must always remember that children are to be seen and not heard. She must always …

Misty couldn't hear any more. There was no direction here, only longer lists. Her head hurt and her throat hurt. She felt small and cold. Without realizing it, she slumped down a little under the weight of it all and a frown furrowed her brow.

"There you are already disobeying. Didn't I just say you were to sit up straight? And you don't look the least polite right now. And here it is almost dinnertime, the time it is most important of all that you behave. You must try to understand just how difficult this is for Uncle Hugh and do all you can to make it easy for him. He's not used to having children around. Neither am I, for that matter, but Hugh is tired when he comes from work, so we have to make it easy for him, pleasant, you know. Do try your best, child. Now run and clean up for dinner. I wish we had new things that would make you more presentable, less offensive to look at, but that will be fixed tomorrow, won't it? Yes, things will get better tomorrow. Just do the best you can for today."

Though feeling somehow shrivelled and small, Misty also felt heavy as she went into the bathroom to wash her hands and face. Dread, another new feeling, filled her as she tried to make herself presentable for dinner. All she knew to do was wash herself. Her hair didn't even need tidying, as she had braided it well that morning. Presentable; she had never even thought of it before. Gran, Gramps, Miss Lily, and the Captain had all taken her as she was even as they had taken each other. As far as she knew, no one even thought about being presentable. What she saw in the bathroom mirror was a clean but strained face, a face she wouldn't want to sit across from, for it had no life, no happiness in it, nothing pleasant. She tried washing it again, tried putting warm water on it, hoping to wash away the strain. It didn't work. Silently she cried out for help, help to meet the coming dinner, help to carry this new weight, help to live with the pounding in her head and the lump in her throat and help with eating her dinner. She didn't think to ask for change outside herself, only for help with what she had to do. She heard Uncle Hugh come in, heard voices in the kitchen and the clink of decanter on glass. With one more plea for help, she pulled herself up as tall as she could and walked through the kitchen to the dining room.

Uncle Hugh was pouring another glass of wine and didn't look up as she sat down. Aunt Augusta was putting the plates down and chattering to Uncle Hugh, asking him about his day. Misty actually smiled and straightened up a little, thinking a surprised "thank You," as she saw that Aunt Augusta had not only dished her very little food but also not prepared lima beans or any other food that was hard for Misty to eat. Misty knew hope for the first time since leaving the apple tree; she knew she could choke this bit of food down. Noticing Aunt Augusta had begun eating, Misty began herself, taking care to sit up straight and to try to pay attention to the words being spoken so she might answer when spoken to. She needn't have worried, for they talked as if she didn't exist. Some of what she heard shocked her.

Uncle Hugh grumbled about the small portions of food on both Aunt Augusta's and Misty's plates. Misty frowned to hear Aunt Augusta reply, "Oh, we had a large lunch and ate it very late; we're really not hungry," for that was not the truth. Their lunch had been small, and though they had eaten late, it wasn't very late. She was puzzled to hear such exaggeration, something bordering on a lie. She had no way of knowing that Aunt Augusta was trying to hide a silly mistake she had made, a mistake for which Misty would have been grateful had she known. Aunt Augusta had prepared dinner for two as usual, forgetting that she must now cook for three. Because she always cooked at the last minute and didn't realize her mistake until the end of the meal preparation, her only recourse was to divide her own meal between herself and Misty and hope nobody noticed. As Hugh did notice and Augusta never admitted mistakes, she simply smoothed it over and tried to get the attention off her error by asking more questions about his day.

Uncle Hugh paused to pour another glass of wine before he continued his talk of loans, meetings, and people. Misty was shocked to hear anyone complain so much and criticize everybody he mentioned. She'd never heard so much talk about people, so much pointless talk, so much critical talk, and her instinct was to withdraw, to hide from the nastiness of it, but she forced herself to listen in case she was spoken to and must respond. She was doing well with her dinner, had most of it eaten, when she heard a slight shift in the intensity of Uncle Hugh's voice and realized the person he was now talking about was her.

"Am I going to have to sit at the table with this waif forever, Augusta? I told you to fix her today, to make her more presentable. She really is offensive. Look at her. Such a disgrace; not at all appropriate. Can't you get anything right, woman? Surely it was easy. I left the car for you, left you free rein with the money, and you couldn't even dress the child? I expected better and I won't take this. She makes the food stick in my throat. She even makes the wine turn sour in my mouth. Really! Something is wrong when a man can't come home to order and decency."

"Oh, Hugh, I am so sorry," Aunt Augusta gushed and almost whined; "I have tried. It was just dreadful! But it will be better tomorrow, for we've done the shopping but the clothes needed altering. Milly promised they'd be ready tomorrow afternoon. The child is much worse than you think. She's small and skinny with no waist, and her arms are inches longer than they should be for a body her size, and her legs are just as bad. Milly said that her head is also dreadfully big around but that she will be able to get a hat to fit and if nobody asks, nobody will have to know that her head is big enough to fit an adult's body and her body small enough to fit into a 6X dress. Imagine! Such a gangly, awkward child! I tell you, I was utterly exhausted by the whole ordeal and ..."

Misty felt herself trying to pull her legs up and scrunch her arms somehow. She put her free arm under her legs on the chair and tried to keep her other arm bent as she finished up her dinner. Unknowingly, she slid down a bit in her chair, hunched her shoulders over and stared down at her plate.

"That's enough!" interrupted Uncle Hugh. "I can see for myself the child is utterly hopeless. Unless you manage some kind of a miracle tomorrow, don't even bring her to the table. You'll just have to keep her out of my sight. And I certainly don't have to be tortured hearing all her exploits or what trouble you think she is. It was your idea to take her, not mine, and I won't pay such a high price as this. When I come home, I want peace and quiet. I want order. I want dinner. And I want someone to listen to me, not someone moaning on about a dratted child. And you'd better not let this kid interrupt your charity and social work. How will that look at the bank for me? Really, Augusta, I thought you could do better. I'm going to my study for the evening. Don't bother me. And keep the kid quiet!"

Though Misty was relieved to see Uncle Hugh leave the table, she had a new battle on her hands, for his last comment had reminded her that she wasn't to cry. Glancing at Aunt Augusta, she had seen such a look of pain crossing the woman's face that Misty felt her own tears rising up. She swallowed hard and took several deep breaths. She hated to see anyone look hurt, and her own confusion quickly left her as concern for Aunt Augusta took over. Quietly she got down from her chair and went to Aunt Augusta, putting her own small hand gently on the woman's shoulder. Aunt Augusta slumped down a little herself and started to reach her arm out to Misty. But as Misty looked up into her face, she saw the sadness replaced with something else and she jumped to hear the hand bang down on the table.

"How dare you!" Augusta exploded. "Look at the trouble you caused and then you dare to get down from the table before I told you to. Get to your bed and stay there you ungrateful, troublesome wretch! And no noise. And none of that senseless blubbering you indulged in last night, do you hear? Now go!"

Misty didn't have to be told twice. She felt as if she had been hit with something hard and utterly unyielding. As she walked through the kitchen to her room, a strange, cold numbness took hold of her. Mechanically she got out of her clothes, put on her nightie and crept between the sheets. She dared not go to the bathroom to brush her teeth; neither did she dare brush her hair. Even in her shock, she saw that she couldn't keep all the rules she had heard that day. "Always brush your teeth before bed" didn't go with "Always do as I say, immediately," when what had been said was "Get to your room and stay there," or with "Never do anything I haven't told you to do." It was all a hopeless mess and couldn't be reasoned out.

Like a wounded animal, Misty could do nothing but hide and try to lick her wounds. She burrowed further down in the covers, hoping for safety, hoping for warmth. She felt only pain and cold. She curled up in a ball as tight as she could. She pulled the covers over her head, her throbbing head. Still she felt only pain and cold. The lump in her throat threatened to choke her. Fighting as hard as she could, she wrapped her arms around her folded-up legs and body and held on tight, feeling herself shiver with the cold. Slowly she began to rock back and forth, ever so quietly, ever so slightly.

The gentle rocking motion stopped the shivering, and she felt her arms relax a little. 'Oh God,' she thought, 'help me. What is the matter with me? What am I to do? Aunt Augusta looked so sad, and I couldn't fix it—only made it worse. Please help her. And Uncle Hugh is miserable, but I didn't mean to make him that way. I don't mean to be so awful to look at as to make him unhappy. Can you help him? I can't. Maybe they can fix each other while I'm hidden away here. I didn't know I hurt people so much. Captain never looked hurt, but then he couldn't see me, could he? Miss Lily never looked hurt, though, and she could see me. Maybe if these new people saw me in Miss Lily's garden, I wouldn't look so bad. Is the town making me ugly?'

Even as Misty asked the question, she recalled the gentle voice of Captain saying, "Don't let them corrupt you or poison you in any way," and she stopped rocking and breathed deeply. Somehow she knew that a lifetime, even a short lifetime, of love and goodness could not be undone in just two days of confusion. The Captain had said she was special, not ugly, and she must not let poison in to change that, rules or no rules.

It was kind of stuffy under the covers, so she uncurled herself, rolled onto her back and folded the covers down below her chin. It was dusky in the room, but with the blind and window open, there were still faint shadows on her wall and the fluffy curtains fluttered a little in a breeze. Misty took deep breaths and felt some of the tightness leave her throat. She stretched and relaxed again, then turned toward the window. Propping her head on her hand and leaning on her elbow, she could see the branches of her apple tree beyond the window. She could hear birds singing their evening songs too and was comforted to think she was not alone in settling for the night, for soon the birds would grow quiet as they took to their hidden nests to sleep. The pounding in her head faded as she realized that as surely as the evening songs fade, the morning songs begin again, and she settled back on her pillow, safe in the knowledge that joy comes in the morning.

Oh yes, Misty had lost some innocence that day. She wasn't stupid; she knew that life here was different and would at times continue to be very difficult. She was more tired than she had ever been in her life and more wounded than even she imagined. She knew she couldn't begin to understand very much of what had happened that day. She knew she couldn't either undo what was done or put anything right, for it was all beyond her. She even knew a little dread, for though Aunt Augusta insisted that everything would be better tomorrow, Misty knew that meant going shopping again. What Aunt Augusta saw as a solution to a problem, Misty dreaded. But with the recollection of the good Captain's warning and the birdsong's reminder of joy, Misty's simple peace had returned, releasing her to live the moment. This moment, she was in a little bed, with fresh air blowing through the window and birdsongs refilling her heart with hope. This moment she could rest.

The tightness in her throat and the throbbing in her head disappeared altogether as she relaxed in the narrow bed. Recalling there was no little dog beside the bed, she kept her arms folded across her tummy and let the fading birdsongs become the background for a picture of Rusty romping in the field with Pilot, his little ears blowing slightly back as he ran. She closed her eyes, thankful for all she had, thankful for life itself, thankful that memories could carry her comfortably to sleep.

5.

A Presentable Look

Hugh and Augusta weren't really bad people, misguided, perhaps, but not really bad. Misty was just having the misfortune of encountering them at their worst. They were typical early middle-aged ambitious people, caught up in a career and position in the community. They had met at university, where Hugh studied Commerce and Augusta worked as a secretary in the Economics Department office. Hugh had visions of a successful legal practice and an eventual seat on the bench but he was just an average student, and his application for law school was turned down. He covered his disappointment and embarrassment by insisting that the real key to success was finance and he applied for positions in banking institutions throughout British Columbia. Augusta found him excitingly ambitious, and he found her supportive and attractive. If their aspirations made them less than curious and honest about the past, it bothered neither of them. He proposed to her when he had secured a position in a bank in the small coastal community where they now lived, and they had married before leaving the university and taking up their new position. For a few years, Augusta worked as a teller in the same bank Hugh worked in, and they saved money for a house. As soon as possible, they bought, and Augusta resigned her position and took up charity work, work they thought more helpful to their aspirations for a key position in the community. Hugh hoped to enter municipal politics.

It was difficult to settle into the community at first, for they were outsiders and, as is the case in small coastal communities, outsiders are frowned upon, suspect, not to be trusted. But with careful selection of people and persistent invitations which, once accepted, had to be returned, they eventually found their way into a small subcommunity within the town, and the private fears about the town that each kept hidden from the other disappeared as had other embarrassing things of their pasts. Fellow bankers, some teachers, doctors, shop owners, and lawyers formed the core of the subcommunity, all people who had come in from the outside.

Theirs became a life of bridge parties, golf, dinners and cocktail parties, a life which required that their home, their things, their clothes be fashionable. They had no time for children, had decided against burdening themselves with any. In fact, they knew very little about children and had even less experience with them. Augusta did occasionally visit children in the hospital in her volunteer work with the Hospital Auxiliary, but she kept her distance from them. Why she had taken it into her head that they must take this hopeless waif was a mystery to Hugh. Of course the money that was to come from social services for keeping the child would be welcome, and Hugh had easily calculated that they would get more than it would cost them to keep one child. Then, too, people would think him benevolent if he took an orphan into his home; that would help his career, he was sure, so it hadn't seemed a bad idea and he had agreed. Thus, a couple who knew little about children and who had selfishly indulged themselves for years, suddenly found themselves with a child. The vast difference between the mere idea of taking a child in and the reality of having a child in their well-ordered, settled lives had thrown both Hugh and Augusta into a nervous and impatient state. Change was bringing out the worst in each of them.

As Hugh sat alone in his study, he wondered what he had agreed to. Somehow the sight of the child irritated him. She seemed to threaten something, but he wasn't sure what. She took Augusta's time and attention and seemed to make her irritable, something he detested. The waif didn't look at all what he thought a child from his home should look, but he did believe Augusta's claim that she could fix that. But it was more than that. Those eyes looking at him were bothersome. He felt uncomfortable with her there, as if she saw something missing in him, and there was jolly well nothing missing. Of that he had made certain. He decided she'd just been spoiled and he knew Augusta would soon put that right if he told her to. With that in mind, he called Augusta to the study. He saw that she was tired and felt sorry for his earlier outburst, but of course he didn't apologize. He was, after all, the man of the house. Instead, he gestured to the chair next to his and put his feet up on the stool as she sat down.

"You're quite right, Augusta; tomorrow will be a better day. I'm sure the child is just spoiled, and I know you'll soon see that she learn better. School starts soon, doesn't it? She won't be around much then, and you'll be free to carry on as you always have. I've decided we'll also get her involved in all kinds of things that will help, so I'd like you to see about enrolling her in classes after school and Saturdays. We'll try ballet, tap dance, figure skating, piano, singing, art lessons, all the things you know little girls should do. We'll send her to Sunday School too; that ought to teach her to behave properly. We won't indulge her with money or with whatever things she wants, but we will see that she is properly dressed and has all the necessary lessons. That way we'll be doing our duty by her, she'll be busy and out of the way and, you'll be free to carry on. Life will soon run smoothly again, don't you think?"

"Oh Hugh; you are so right as always. I knew you'd find a solution. And I'm sure you are right. Life will soon run smoothly again. At least she's a quiet thing. There is one thing I must ask, Hugh. I'll tend to her clothes and all her lessons, but would you consider registering her at school? I'm sure they will listen to a man like you and place her properly. A man in your position can persuade the principal to do what is best for us, don't you think?"

Flattered by her confidence in him, Hugh agreed. Each felt more comfortable than they had since Augusta had picked the child up, for they had carefully made plans and a united front now. They were sure their idea of adoption would work after all. For a while before retiring for the night, they sat and chatted comfortably, almost excitedly, about all the advantages they just knew making an orphaned waif into a pretty, busy, successful little girl would bring them. They slept well that night, confident in the good they were doing.

Misty also slept well. She slept not the sleep of the confident but the sleep of the unself-conscious, and as she slept she enjoyed pleasant and peaceful dreams. She frolicked with Rusty in the meadow, visited Miss Lily for tea, rode old Nobbin through field and forest, walked with the Captain along the beach, sang with the birds in the woods. For a time she even dreamt of singing with the angels, of dancing on clouds with Gran and Gramps in soft, flowing robes, of floating breezily through the deepest of misty blue skies that stretched on forever. In sleep she was fully open to receive the best there is, and the best there is restores and refreshes fully.

She wakened smiling, the goodness of her dreams bubbling up within her and spilling into thanks. Outside, birds sang their happy, morning songs, leaves rustled gently in the breeze and the sun sent its beams of hope, warming all it touched. The rays stretched through the window to Misty's bed, blessing her, strengthening her, exciting her. Quietly she got out of bed and went to the window. Looking out, she saw the cat on the lawn beneath her apple tree and she grinned, thinking he must live nearby. She knew she mustn't run outside as she had done the morning before, so she just leaned out the window as far as she could and took great, deep breaths of the wonderful morning air and felt tingly all over. Happily she pulled back into the room, ready to tidy up and put things right for the day. After making the bed carefully the way she had seen Aunt Augusta liked it, she tiptoed to the bathroom to wash before returning and slipping into her clothes. She took her hairbrush to the window, undid her braids and brushed and brushed and brushed, letting the birdsong take the place of the tinkling music box that she missed so much. She could almost hear Gran's voice reminding her after Gramps had died that they must fasten onto the good things, must choose to live above the sadness, not deny the sadness but simply live above it by thinking of good, lovely, pure, true things, and she smiled realizing she had instinctively done what Gran had said. Oh, hers was a wise Gran, and the things she said were so easy to do, so right that they just came naturally. Very quietly she hummed the music box tune as she braided her hair. Pulling the loose hairs from her brush, she reached out and let them drift away on the wind as she and Gran had always done, let them float where birds could scoop them up for nest building and repair, and as she did so, she saw that even if she'd rather have run outside in the morning sunshine, there was still much she could do and enjoy from her window.

The sitting around waiting would be a little more of a challenge for her; it seemed so completely unnatural. But she knew that she must wait until Aunt Augusta called her from her room and she was determined to find the bright side to look on. Once again, she wished she had brought knitting and sewing things, but as she hadn't, she'd just have to find something else. Sitting on the bed made her feel useless and made her uncomfortably aware of time dragging, so she returned to the window, knelt before it and leaned her elbows on the sill. Watching the birds, the sky, the trees lifted her from the dullness of waiting and began to occupy and even direct her thoughts. She found herself in that kind of feeling things that Gran had said was a form of prayer. She didn't need words or even expressible thoughts; she simply felt goodness and safety for Miss Lily, for the Captain, for all the animals. Hearing the sounds of others beginning to move about the house, she thought of Aunt Augusta and Uncle Hugh and wished with all her being that they might be happy, might have a better day, might soften up somehow. She didn't think to pray for herself, didn't need to, for in praying for others and being thankful, she was herself strengthened, peaceful and ready for the new day.

Aunt Augusta opened the bedroom door when Uncle Hugh left for work. She sounded a little brighter this morning as she said, "Oh, you're tidy and ready. Come, we'll have some breakfast before we tackle your hair. We'll have to wash it and settle it into pretty ringlets. Good thing it is curly. How does it stay braided and neat so long? It must be days since it has been fixed. And who did it for you? Must have been that deaf woman. Too bad the braids look so plain; they seem to keep well. Ringlets will be much prettier on you."

Misty was momentarily taken aback by the chatter. Somehow she never had a chance to answer any questions that were asked; it was almost as if people didn't really speak to her at all, just prattled on. But when they answered their own questions, they were wrong. Of course her hair hadn't stayed neat for days on end! And why would Aunt Augusta think Miss Lily would braid Misty's hair? Miss Lily did her own hair, of course, but why would she do Misty's too? Misty was beginning to wonder just what and how these people thought. She also wondered how she should deal with this new way of talk. Aunt Augusta had said that she must answer when spoken to and yet she gave Misty no chance to speak, preferring to carry on and answer her own questions. Misty didn't feel spoken to at all, felt more as if she weren't really there, or were there but no more alive than the furniture in the house. Perhaps, like the furniture, she should remain silent. But it bothered Misty to hear wrong answers. Truth was important, so she must correct these false notions.

But just as she opened her mouth to speak, Aunt Augusta burst out in a much more rapid stream of words, prattling on about presentable hair and clothes and suitable lessons. Misty understood little of what she heard, but was happy to hear excitement in Aunt Augusta's voice, so it was easy to go quietly to her chair as indicated. This morning Aunt Augusta interrupted her own chatter to say, "I'll just put some milk on your porridge and then you can eat," not leaving Misty any time to naturally help herself and thus cause whatever offence she had unwittingly caused the previous day.

As Misty set herself to the task of eating her porridge, Aunt Augusta kept up her stream of chatter, leaving no time for Misty to so much as thank her for pouring the milk. As she ate and Aunt Augusta prattled on, it became clear that Aunt Augusta didn't expect any attention this morning so Misty felt free to travel in her mind. Her happy thoughts of the warm kitchen back home, the sunny breakfast nook, the nice tea that they always shared along with their porridge and the gentle laughter that often filled the room as they sang silly songs that they made up enabled her to finish off the whole bowl of porridge.

Finished, and seeing Aunt Augusta still sipping a cup of coffee, Misty was about to excuse herself from the table and start clearing up when she recalled that she was to be seen and not heard and to be quiet unless spoken to. She closed her mouth, forced herself to curb her instinct to help and strained to sit still and wait quietly. She didn't have to wait long, for Aunt Augusta had also remembered something. Recalling the child's work the previous day and thinking how nice it was not to have to tidy up, she made a quick decision and a new rule.

Putting her cup down, Augusta announced, "I think it is important that children have some chore to do. Yours will be to tidy up after breakfast. I saw yesterday that you can do dishes so I'll just have you do those. That way you can clean up while I get myself dressed and ready to go out. We'll see; I may have you do the dinner dishes as well, though I don't want you breaking my good things. These breakfast dishes don't matter so much. Do you understand? When you are done in the morning, then, you can clean up while I finish my coffee and get dressed. Oh, and don't drag the chair around the kitchen. There is a stool by the back door you can get and use, but be sure to put it back when you are done."

Misty was surprised at the excitement she felt to be told to do something she had always done; it was a little thrill of relief to be free from sitting and waiting combined with the ring of pleasure that comes with having purpose as well as being active. This was a much better day than the one before it!

Happily Misty gathered dishes, stacked them, filled the sink and carefully washed and rinsed them. From where she stood on the stool, she could see a little rack with towels on it that she had missed the day before, so she was even able to dry them and, having watched carefully at noon, was able to put them away as well. Oh, she did like to put things in order. It just felt so good. She wiped the counters and table, rinsed out the sink and neatly hung the towels and cloth before returning the stool to its place by the door. When Aunt Augusta returned, the kitchen was clean and tidy, and Misty was ready for anything.

Aunt Augusta looked better to Misty, too. Instead of the brittle looking suits of the previous two days, Aunt Augusta had on a dark skirt, a tan-coloured sweater and some flat shoes. She looked almost comfortable—almost but not quite, for the skirt was a little tight, as was the sweater. Seeing Misty take in her appearance and misunderstanding the look on her face, Aunt Augusta said, "These are just my house clothes; I'll change again before we go out, but as we're going to tackle your hair now, I put these old things on. Come, we'll go downstairs and wash your hair in the laundry tub down there. Bring the stool; you'll need it."

Misty grabbed the stool and followed Aunt Augusta down the stairs to the basement. It was a little dark down there and smelled different, not really damp like the cellar back home but stale and dusty. She didn't see laundry tubs anywhere, but there was a large white sink standing below the little window in the brightest corner of this part of the basement. Beside the sink stood a shiny white machine with a wringer at the top of it, which Misty recognized as a washing machine like the ones she had seen pictured in the catalogues at home. She wondered how all this was going to work. At home she washed her hair in the galvanized laundry tub, a tub that she first filled with water from the rain barrel. When her hair was all clean, she poured pitcher after pitcher of the clear water over her head until all the soap was rinsed out. Here she saw only the sink.

She needn't have worried because Aunt Augusta, assuming the child was too young to wash her own hair, was soon bossing her around. It was hard for Misty to stand still on the stool with her head bent over the sink while Aunt Augusta ran the tap water over her head and scrubbed and scrubbed the quickly tangling mass of curls. She was used to doing things herself. Besides, Aunt Augusta kept getting her fingers caught in the tangles and pulling Misty's hair. It didn't hurt so much as startle Misty and make it difficult to stand still as she had been told. The soap running all over burnt her eyes, and somehow Aunt Augusta managed to fill one ear with water, making the whole thing an ordeal for Misty, an ordeal that seemed to go on and on.

And that turned out to be the easy part. After the soap was all rinsed out, Aunt Augusta wrapped a towel around Misty's head and began to rub and scrub. Misty knew there would be trouble, for with her thick curly hair, rubbing was the worst thing to do. She herself would have patted and squeezed gently, avoiding tangling the hair further. Then came the worst part of all. Aunt Augusta tackled the tangled mass with a comb, a plain comb. She didn't run her fingers through first, didn't start at the bottom and work her way up to the scalp, didn't even start with a small section; she just plunked that comb at Misty's scalp and began to pull. Misty braced herself for what she knew would follow. Time and again Aunt Augusta pulled and yanked, muttering the whole time. Misty's head seemed to hurt all over, and she couldn't help but flinch sometimes but she hung on, seeing the anger beginning to rise. She wished she could just take over, could do it herself, but Aunt Augusta kept on, her seething muttering breaking into an angry tirade.

"This is impossible! What a mess, an utter disaster! Whatever am I to do? Hold still, child! All your squirming isn't going to help a bit and the more you squirm the longer this will take. Really! You are only hurting yourself and making this unnecessarily difficult for me. You know I told you to do all you can to help us. Don't move ..."

The noise of Aunt Augusta's angry voice added to Misty's suffering, and she silently cried out for help and strength. The day was quickly turning sour and it needn't, if only she could be left alone to tend to her own hair. As Aunt Augusta pulled hard on the comb that was lodged firmly in a tangle, Misty tried to concentrate on keeping her head still, pulling away from Aunt Augusta to do so. Snap! The comb broke in two, and both Aunt Augusta and Misty staggered backward.

"That's it!" cried Aunt Augusta, struggling to regain some composure. "I simply cannot manage this mess. You really are impossible, child!" she yelled and stomped away and up the stairs, much to Misty's surprise and relief.

Misty sat down on the stool and let her body go limp for just a moment before carefully reaching up and taking the broken comb from the tangle in her hair. A strange sense of puzzlement came over her as she gently but quickly and quite easily began to remove the tangles from her hair. Even using a broken comb, it didn't take long to work her way around the head of hair, taking one small section at a time and combing the bottom couple of inches, then the inch or two above and so on until the tangles were all gone. There was no pulling or tugging, no pain, no battle. She just combed out her wet hair.

Two things puzzled her: one was that somehow this had become for Aunt Augusta a battle, and the other was that though Misty had not broken any rules that she could think of, had done what she was told even though it seemed a silly way of doing things and had not spoken out of turn, somehow Aunt Augusta had decided once again that she was impossible. What had she done this time? She couldn't imagine. It didn't occur to her that it might not be her or even the hair that was impossible. Misty could not see her hair as impossible. It was just her hair. Besides, the island folk had all liked her hair. Gramps and Miss Lily liked the colours, for there was gold mixed in with the deep, rich brown and even some bronze tones, especially in the summer months. The many different tones made her braids appear almost striped at times, and they had all often chuckled at the effect such stripes could have. The Captain liked the feel of her hair, saying it was soft, silky and spongy and felt rich to him. Gran liked the curl, the thickness and the strength of her hair, saying it was perfect for the person Misty was. Misty had never questioned her hair; it was just her hair. She had, however, enjoyed the time shared with Gran caring for her hair. Now how could such hair have become impossible?

And how could something so far out of her control be causing trouble? Misty realized as she sat on the little stool that she was in another of the new pickles that seemed to make up much of this new life. She had combed her hair without being told and she was sitting in the basement without an adult. She couldn't think what to do, couldn't make her way through the rules to any kind of conclusion. She hadn't been called or spoken to, so she shouldn't either speak or go upstairs. Well, people in this world liked to say they should begin at the beginning, so she'd try that. Eliminate the wrong. She was where she wasn't supposed to be without an adult, so she'd best leave the basement. But, without being called, go upstairs where she knew Aunt Augusta had stomped? No, she'd best just go outside. It's what she'd have done at home, for she needed to dry her hair in the sun before she could braid it. If she braided it this wet, it would never dry properly and would smell sour. So, taking the broken bit of comb and the little stool, she opened the outside door, went up the few cement steps, found a sunny spot in which to put the stool, sat down and gently, rhythmically combed her hair as the sun poured down on her.

She'd always enjoyed this part of washing her hair. She and Gran would sit side by side on the rock wall at the back of the house and comb and comb, sometimes talking comfortably, sometimes singing little songs, sometimes just quietly enjoying the warm sun and clean hair. Today, however, she felt very funny inside. She could feel the warm sun, could feel the clean hair, could even feel the hair begin to lighten up as it started to dry, but none of these things gave her pleasure. Instead she felt kind of anxious as if she'd made a mistake or something, like the time she had forgotten to close the gate and the cow had gone into the garden. She'd felt so foolish then, but only for a moment; Gran soon forgave her and made her feel much better. But somehow this felt even worse than that. It was a puzzle to her. She couldn't recall sitting doing what needed to be done and feeling all wrong about it. She felt the hint of a lump rise up in her throat and began combing faster, hoping her hair would dry quickly.

But even as she tried to hurry the drying up, she realized that wouldn't solve any problem, for she didn't know what she should do next. The great lists of rules raced through her mind, faster and faster. None of them helped. In fact they all seemed to hit up against each other and jam like logs pounded, heaped and trapped against the wharf pilings in a storm, making things hopelessly confusing, making things impossible. She felt her head begin to throb and she combed faster. Should she braid her hair? Should she go inside? Should she return to the basement? Was she supposed to take the stool outside? Then she remembered hearing that she wasn't to go outside without being told. Talk about impossible! Misty suddenly knew that this new feeling was fear, learned fear. It seemed to go with rules, rules that she couldn't seem to get to work together. The feeling was wretched, even worse than the feeling of being wrong, a feeling that she would soon come to recognize as guilt. This was terrible.

Misty tipped her face up toward the sun and cried out for help, still rhythmically combing her long hair. The warm sun calmed her enough for her to feel her almost dry hair brush against her arm. It was time to braid. Quickly she sectioned the hair, divided it and braided, securing the ends by wrapping long, loose hairs around them. Finished, she picked up the little stool, walked quietly up the stairs, let herself in the back door and replaced the stool where it belonged. At least she wouldn't be where she had been told not to go.

As she entered the kitchen, she saw Aunt Augusta slumped in a chair at the table, holding a cup of coffee. Misty thought she should say something but couldn't think what, so she just walked over and stood beside her. Aunt Augusta jerked up, startled to see the child. Her face was a study and a puzzle to Misty as many conflicting emotions rose and flashed there at once. Anger, fear, outrage, self-doubt, surprise and relief battled for the upper hand in the woman. The surprise allowed the relief to win, if only for a moment.

"How ever did your hair get fixed, child? Surely you couldn't have done it yourself. You're much too young to be able to make braids at all, much less such tidy ones. How could it be?" she seemed to wonder briefly before her tone changed and voice began to rise as she rushed on anxiously; "You'd better not have left the basement, young lady, and found someone to do it for you. You'd better not be tricking me. But it couldn't be. I'd have heard you go. There *is* no one but us here; no one, do you hear? It must have been you. How on earth did you get those dreadful snarls out in order to braid it? Really, I just can't believe what I see. Why didn't you say something? Why did you sit so silently while I struggled so? You could have saved me a tremendous amount of work and no end of trouble. Now look what you've done! You allowed me to make a fool of myself, didn't you? You just sat and didn't say a word, and I worked and struggled, even broke one of my good combs. It's all your fault. Why must you make everything a battle? Why must you resist me so? And look, did I not say you were to have ringlets today, but you have braided that hair. Disobedient, always disobedient! Come with me and take those braids out. We'll have ringlets today, I tell you, ringlets!"

Poor Misty couldn't believe her ears. Again there were questions but no opportunity to answer and even as she stood there, the questions became accusations, and something that had seemed right was now being branded wrong. Truth be told, she wasn't sure what ringlets were. She knew curls; she knew waves, for her hair was curly and her Gran's was wavy, but she didn't know ringlets.

Silently and heavily she followed Aunt Augusta to the bathroom, unbraiding her hair as she went. She sat down on the edge of the tub as instructed and hung on tight as once again Aunt Augusta began dragging a comb through her hair. It wasn't as bad now, for Misty had taken the tangles out and the hair was dry, but still Aunt Augusta seemed rough. Misty sat very still as Aunt Augusta took small sections of hair, wet them and wound them round and round her finger, forming odd-feeling bouncy rings all over Misty's head. They were especially bothersome hanging in her face, but Misty was careful not to wince.

Aunt Augusta seemed to cheer up again as she worked, so though it was all taking a long time and Misty wasn't very comfortable, she began to feel better; the heaviness began to lift. Finally Aunt Augusta pulled the dangling rings away from Misty's face and stuck them back with a couple of funny clips, saying "These will do until we pick up your things at the store," and giving Misty's head a pat.

"That's much better," she exclaimed, smiling for the first time Misty could recall. "Have a look in the mirror, child."

Misty hoped it would look better than it felt; she seemed top heavy and tickly with all those rings sticking out and bouncing about. She felt oddly stiff as she stood up and stepped before the mirror, afraid to move freely and set the rings bouncing wildly around. What she saw in the mirror made her even more stiff. She didn't look like herself at all! She looked ridiculous, all hair, all hair that looked like a mass of coils or springs, sausages or something. Oh, it looked every bit as bad as it felt!

But Aunt Augusta was as happy as Misty had seen her, quite thrilled with the result of her work and eager to show it off.

"Yes," she said, "we're on the way now. You begin to look presentable, child! Let's skip lunch and go straight down and see if Milly has your things ready. I'll just change my clothes. You can go wait in the car."

6.

Suitable Girls' Clothes

Relieved to be free to leave the mirror and even the house, Misty started eagerly outside but soon found herself walking very stiffly down the steps, another new feeling taking hold of her. She felt silly, ridiculous, like some kind of clown or something, a puppet maybe. And she felt awkward again. Here she was trying hard to get used to shoes on her feet all the time, and now competing with her awareness of her feet was awareness of the bobbing mass of corkscrews. Her head felt absurdly big, dangerously big. She didn't know whether her feet or her head felt heavier. Standing beside the car she looked toward the apple tree, wishing she could crawl up there and braid the jumble of writhing snakes into comfortable order, wishing she could fix her hair so that she was no longer aware of her head at all. She was horribly uncomfortable with all this awareness of her hair and her feet and even her clothes. She felt herself hoping there were no birds in the trees to look at her; she was sure they would twitter laughter and fly away in fear, either that or try to nest in her hair! Unhappily she got in the car and closed the door. She couldn't lean back against the seat without squishing the mess of springs, so she sat stiff and very upright on the car seat and waited as directed.

Aunt Augusta came tripping down the stairs in yet another bright suit, this one the most brilliant (and hideous) pink Misty had ever seen. She was surprised to hear herself think the colour hideous; she couldn't recall being so critical before and she didn't really like the feeling. Silently she apologized for such a hard thought. The strange emptiness that seemed to accompany her stiffness was replaced with a bit of warmth when she noticed how happy Aunt Augusta seemed as she got in the car, started it and eased it out the driveway. As they drove along Aunt Augusta fairly bubbled over with how pretty the ringlets were, how much better Thomasina looked, how much fun the afternoon was sure to be, for with the new dresses, she'd be positively transformed. She even commented on how well her plan was already working, for look how much better Thomasina was holding herself now—sitting straight as she should. Oh, she was just so happy things were improving so much and so quickly; Hugh would surely be pleased this night. She chattered on in just such a manner all the way to town. Misty felt the bit of warmth crowded out by a sense of puzzlement, for she felt only uncomfortable and stiff, not at all pretty as Aunt Augusta insisted, though she realized that she wasn't sure what pretty meant. Beauty, she knew; prettiness, she didn't. In spite of her puzzlement, Misty sat straight and stiff but relieved to find Aunt Augusta so cheery.

She continued cheery and chattery even as Misty moved stiffly and uncomfortably at her side through the pushing, chaotic crowd on the street. Misty's new self-consciousness added to the noise and irritation of the chaos, increasing her discomfort tremendously. As they entered the shop and closed the door, she didn't feel the relief she had felt the day before; instead, she felt something new. Self-consciousness brought with it embarrassment; Misty was embarrassed—embarrassed by the very thing that made Aunt Augusta seem so happy, almost proud.

"Good afternoon, Milly," she trilled, "here we are and in much better condition today as you can see. I think the child has potential after all, don't you? Are the things ready? And are you ready to get us more things? I didn't order nearly enough yesterday, did I? Well, I'm much more able today. Turn around, child, and let Milly see how much better you look without those plain old braids."

Misty stood stiffly, but with her eyes lowered. She didn't think she could bear this kind of scrutiny. Somehow she felt as naked as she had yesterday in the dressing room and felt herself shrinking a little inside. She was grateful that Milly didn't comment on her hair, preferring instead to begin talk of clothes. She was also grateful for the feel of Milly's hand on her shoulder, gently leading her to the back of the shop; it made her feel a little less wooden. Had she known that Milly's reason for immediately beginning to speak of clothes and for putting her hand on her shoulder was that she thought the hair as absurd as Misty found it and felt sorry for her, she may have been something other than grateful, but with eyes downcast, Misty saw nothing that added to her discomfort.

Milly, however, had a plan. She had lain awake the previous night wondering what she could do for the poor child, for she had taken a liking to the silent, well-behaved girl. She did have the dresses ready, but she had thought of a way to convince Augusta to buy some sensible clothes as well and she began at once with her tactic.

"Yes, Ma'am, I have all the things ready. She'll need to try one dress on again, the one with the lengthened sleeves, just to make sure they are right and nothing will pull. She can get into that while I show you the other things I have taken out. Dr. Mac's little girl was in last week getting her clothes for school, and I thought you might like to try some things like she got on your little one, so I have some skirts, blouses, sweaters, and another dress out for you to try. The dress isn't cotton like the workers' children get; it is a new material, and Mrs. Dr. Mac thought it just the best thing. You know how she likes to be first to have everything that's new. We can't have her getting ahead of you, can we? So I found this dress in the child's size. You see it isn't pink, but it is a very pretty blue and has this bit of pink trim around the short sleeves and neck. I even found a pink cardigan that will set it off very nicely. No, there isn't beading on the sweater; they don't do beading for children, but there is just a bit of embroidery around the neck, so I thought you'd like that. It really is the latest thing, showing up in all our newest buyer's catalogues. And the skirts I have chosen are the very latest style and length. Judge Hawthorne's daughter is to have three of them, but you know we have to shorten them for her so they won't be ready until next week. Your girl won't need any lengthening or shortening of skirts, so you'll be able to have your girl's before the judge's daughter is out in hers. Then, too, I've slipped in two of those gym costumes that the girls need for school. Shall we get started, then?"

If Misty had known the agony of spirit it took Milly to play such a game, she'd have felt much less confused by what she heard. The woman had seemed so kind as she had led Misty to the change room, and Misty couldn't reconcile such nasty yet empty sounding chatter with the kindness she had felt. But Misty couldn't give it much thought, as she was not only braced for this dreaded session but also more uncomfortable than she had ever been. There she stood, corkscrews all over her head and layers and layers of pink fluffy stuff making her feel as if she herself stuck out all over. The dress felt scratchy and somehow binding despite its bulkiness, and Misty felt more gangly and awkward than ever, more gangly even than they had described her yesterday. She had that fidgety feeling creeping all over her, but she stood absolutely stiff and still, looking straight ahead, avoiding the mirror that she knew was behind her.

"Oh, marvellous!" exclaimed Aunt Augusta, clasping her hands together; "I just knew the child could be pretty. Why she doesn't look awkward and gangly at all! Isn't it a marvel what clothes can do for a person? This is just perfect. Are you sure those plain things will do as well, Milly? Surely she won't look as full and pretty as she does in these. Let's just try the matching hair ribbons before she tries the others on. Isn't this exciting? Why it's just like having a little doll. Hugh will be thrilled. I think she must wear this one at dinner tonight. Give me the ribbons, Milly, and turn to the mirror, Thomasina. Oh, even your name doesn't seem as bad in that dress."

Inwardly Misty groaned at what she saw in the mirror: a big, pink, airy ball of flimsy cloth, topped by a mass of wriggly corkscrews held back from what seemed a tiny face with two, pink, lacy ribbons. What she saw was almost as bad as how she felt. She looked away, but not before Milly had seen the growing sadness in her eyes. Aunt Augusta could see only the pretty vision before her and she continued her happy exclamations. "I just have to see the complete picture before we go on, Milly. Bring the shoes and socks. Sit down, child, and put these on."

Sit down? Misty wondered how on earth one sat down in such a mess of fluff and layers. She was sure the back of her was already on the chair she was supposed to sit on and didn't know where to begin. Seeing her confusion, Milly gently took her arm and backed her into the chair. The layers of fluff were forced out in front of her by the chair, making Misty at once both more uncomfortable but also sure she could sit down in the thing. The layers of fluff got in her way and masses of corkscrews fell forward blocking her view of her feet as she bent to put on her new socks and shoes. She tried shaking the ringlets back, but they wouldn't go. She tried pushing the fluffy fabric out of the way but she needed her hands free to get the socks on. Somehow she managed to lean on the dress with her arms while reaching with her hands to her feet. They could say what they liked about her gangly arms; she was glad of them in that moment. Now if she could just see through the hair to fasten the shoes up, she'd be okay. But she couldn't see and kind of groped about.

Aunt Augusta just continued to gush on about the pretty dress and the shiny shoes, but Milly noticed her struggle; without saying anything, Milly lifted back the ringlets while Misty fastened the tiny buckle on the shoe. The shoes, too, felt terrible. Though they were much lighter than her old shoes, they pinched somehow and didn't seem to cover enough of her foot. The single strap that went across the top cut into her a little and there was no room for her toes to move and yet the shoes felt as if they'd fall off. Besides that they looked silly, and she couldn't imagine how they'd be in the rainy weather. Standing down from the chair as Misty was told to do, she thought she'd never keep her balance. Her feet felt tiny and scrunched, her legs felt thin and long, body felt enormous, enshrouded as it was in yards and yards of pink fluff, and her head felt bigger than a beach ball and every bit as unstable. She was afraid to move lest she topple over. She wished the floor would open up and swallow her. But Aunt Augusta was thrilled, just thrilled. It seemed that Misty was exactly what she had hoped.

Misty suddenly felt utterly exhausted and wretched and couldn't listen to the excited exclamations of Aunt Augusta any more. The glassy look stole across her eyes as she escaped the only way she knew how, into the safety of her memories. She could almost feel Gran's soft cheek against her own as they sat together on the couch before the fire, looking through the bags of old clothes, choosing fabric for new clothes for Misty, paying attention only to the feel of the material and its suitability for clothes that would be warm for winter, cool for summer and allow free and easy movement. Gran had never worn slacks in her life but she very sensibly made pants for Misty, recognizing that pants were much better for riding the old horse, for climbing trees as Misty so loved to do and for many of the things Misty did with Gramps and with the Captain. Together they'd chosen the colours they liked best, colours that just blended in with Misty and with the world around, nothing that glared or clashed, nothing that attempted to compete with the beautiful colours of earth and sky, nothing that stood out much. Clothes were necessary and serviceable; they weren't even something to get excited about in themselves, but they were another means of drawing close to others. Misty could almost hear the thump-thump of the treadle as Gran quickly sewed up the seams while Misty, close beside her, hand-stitched button holes and hems. She could hear the funny songs they had sung as they sewed and could feel the warmth of companionable work. She smiled as she almost felt the softness and ease of comfortable, practical clothes as only Gran could make.

Milly was struck again by the strength that seemed to emanate from the child when she got that dreamy look on her face and she resolved to push ahead with her plan to help the child out. Ignoring the chattering woman, she reached out and began taking the frilly things off the child, discreetly attempting to flatten the mass of ringlets as she lifted the dress over the child's head. Misty's smile broadened as Milly's gentle touch mingled with the warmth of her memory. For a time Misty forgot her ridiculous hair as Milly's gentle manipulation freed her from the fluffy stuff, making her feel more like herself, more like the child Gran had so naturally clothed. The skirt and blouse Milly urged her to try on were such a relief after the gaudy dress that Misty was able to ignore the whine in Aunt Augusta's voice as she fussed about the plainness of such clothes.

"You're absolutely sure such plain things are in vogue, Milly? You're not just trying to embarrass me, are you? Why that skirt is plaid, just plaid! Is that really the thing? And heavens, it is long and dowdy, just straight with only that row of pleats around the bottom. Shouldn't it have gathers or ruffles or something? It really isn't pretty at all. Why, she looks like a schoolgirl. No, I'm not sure. Really, Milly, I have to trust you, but this is not nearly as enchanting as the pink."

Having seen the look of relief on Misty's face, Milly was encouraged to forge ahead. "Enchanting is all wrong for school, Ma'am. For school we must have the latest skirts and sweaters or blouses. Dresses are definitely passé. Why just think of putting this child in dresses when both the judge's and the doctor's daughters have come for skirts! You may as well have the child dressed like the riff-raff, as you call them. And Ma'am, I've chosen the very latest shoes to go with these school things, the very latest. Look at them! They call them saddle shoes. Aren't they just something? You can have white with navy or cream with brown. The other girls have the navy, so I've taken out the same for your little girl. Wouldn't want you not keeping up with the judge and the doctor, would we? Then too, Ma'am, there's the work. You'll soon find that the saddle shoes are easier to look after than patent and they'll wear much longer, especially when the rains come. The skirts and blouses will be much easier to care for than the frilly dresses and won't show the dirt nearly as much. You have no idea how grubby the children get from the desks and ink at school. You'll be much relieved when all is said and done, Ma'am. Come, let's try some more on."

Misty, more comfortable in the loose-fitting skirt and blouse that Milly had chosen, could finally begin to see what Milly was doing. Somehow she was choosing Misty's clothes for her. Relieved, excited and grateful, Misty took Milly's hand and gave it a squeeze. Further encouraged, Milly took one more step, a risky one, but one she felt was worth it. Handing Misty another skirt and blouse set, she turned to Augusta and said, "Let me show you the newest hair things while the child tries this set on. You know the principal's daughter has long hair. Well, she was in with her mother, and they have bought several of the new hair-fasteners, some for braids and some for ponytails."

"No, no, no. I won't have it, Milly. She's much too plain. She must have the ringlets. Braids make her much, much too plain. No."

"But Ma'am, what about these new fasteners? Look. They are elastic with these pretty bobbles on the ends, easy to use, practical, but with pretty bobbles, and the very latest thing. Here, let me show you how they work. You don't need braids for these; don't need to take the ringlets out at all. We can just tie the ringlets into a single ponytail or two bundles of ringlets, one on each side. Come, let's open the package of this pretty pink set and try tying the child's ringlets away from her face."

Aunt Augusta continued to look doubtful but she reluctantly agreed to try, saying, "You're sure she can still have the ringlets? They do make her more pretty, you must admit."

Milly wasn't admitting any such thing but she would push her advantage for the child, assuring Augusta that they had many pretty colours and shapes. One pair even had butterflies on them, and there were flowers and bows, all kinds of pretty things.

"Can you take those pink ties out of your hair so we can try these?" she said to Misty as she and Augusta returned to the room, the latest hair fasteners in their hands. Misty nodded as she removed the pinching and tickling pins with relief. Unconsciously, she tried to flatten her hair, make it more like her own, but before Aunt Augusta could exclaim, Milly continued;

"Here, just turn around so you can watch in the mirror while I show you how these work." She was very gentle as she gathered all of Misty's ringlets and pulled them to the back of her head. Holding the pink bobble at one end of the double elastic firmly in place with her thumb at the top of the mass of ringlets, Milly stretched the other end of the elastic as she wrapped it around the thick mass, separated the two elastics and popped the other pink bobble over the first one. With so much hair all wound into ringlets, it was a tight stretch, but the mass was secure. "There!" she said. "Simple and neat."

Misty was relieved to have the mass of hair out of her face, the silly ringlets at least contained and the whole mess pulled to the back of her head. She felt more secure than she had since

Aunt Augusta made her take the braids out, less like she'd topple over. These new shoes were also the most comfortable she'd had on, so she felt much better than she had earlier, not nearly so gangly. But Aunt Augusta wasn't so sure.

"Not pretty enough, Milly; not enough ringlets around her face. No, too plain. Let the hair go."

Seeing Misty's face drop a little, Milly pushed ahead, "Oh, but then she won't have these newest hair fasteners and won't be up with the principal's daughter. How about we try two clusters of ringlets, one on each side? (She didn't dare call them pigtails or Augusta would surely reject the idea without even trying it.) Come closer, child," she said, and deftly undid the ponytail and replaced it with two pigtails before Aunt Augusta could even reply. Milly was careful to have the pink bobbles showing to the front of the two tails, knowing that would help convince the vain woman. She herself preferred the child's braids, but since that was unthinkable to Augusta, Milly was determined to modify the ringlet mass as much as possible for the poor child. She could see that Misty was less happy with the two clusters than she had been with the ponytail, so she squeezed her shoulders as she turned her to face Aunt Augusta, saying, "See, Ma'am? The best of both worlds! Here you see the newest hair fasteners and all the ringlets as well. And the fasteners are so easy, the child can learn to do them herself."

Unaware of the morning battle with the hair, Milly had no idea she had just hit on the perfect argument, so she was a little startled to hear Aunt Augusta say, "Oh alright, Milly. If these are what the best girls are using, then these are what Thomasina must have. Be sure you choose the prettiest bobbles, though, and put out enough that she can have different ones each day. And you're sure those skirts are the thing now? Well, if you insist. We'll take the lot. I must say, for plain clothes, you've done quite a good job of selecting. I'll be sure to mention to my Hugh that you've served us well. And I'm sure when he sees the pretty pink and little shiny black shoes tonight, he'll be quite reconciled to the idea of having the child. It's difficult for men to adjust, you know. You'll throw her old things out, won't you? It will be best if the child wear the new dress home. Thomasina, get out of that outfit and into the pretty one."

Milly couldn't help but notice the sag to Misty's shoulders, so she quickly said, "Please, Ma'am, it may not be wise to throw her old things out; she should keep them for play clothes. And it really is too early for her to change into her pink things. Besides, I've already had the boy package it up and the patent shoes along with it. Don't you think you should leave her in what she has on for the afternoon? That way her pink thing will be sure not to get soiled before dinner. Having company are you? You have such a busy life. It must be difficult married to a man in your husband's position."

Misty relaxed a little as she heard Milly cleverly turn the attention off her and onto Aunt Augusta, for she sensed she could stay in the skirt and blouse. She really didn't like the ringletty pigtails; they felt heavy and springy, making her more conscious of her head than she liked to be, but they were much, much better than the mass of free ringlets had been. And the skirt and blouse, though not as comfortable as her old clothes, were manageable; she knew she could get used to them. She sensed that Milly had saved her from nothing short of disaster, and relief and gratitude rose up inside her, breaking out in a wide smile.

When Aunt Augusta had finished paying and was leading the boy carrying the bundles out of the store, Misty darted back to Milly, threw her arms around her and gave her a big hug. "Thank you. Oh, thank you," she said, before turning and running to catch up with Aunt Augusta. Fortunately Aunt Augusta had neither seen nor heard the exchange. As they left the store, Misty turned and waved, smiling the gratitude that still welled up inside her. Milly brushed a tear from her cheek, well rewarded for what had been one of the most difficult tasks she had faced in weeks.

The ride home was the easiest Misty had. Perhaps she was getting used to the town and the car, or perhaps she was just relieved. It had been a difficult day again, in ways, but the outcome of the various skirmishes had been better. Besides, she was more comfortable than she had been on the trip in. With her ringlets contained in the pigtails, she could lean her head back and relax a little. Aunt Augusta was quiet for once, quiet without seeming angry or distressed. So Misty was free to sit quietly in the car and take in a little of what she could see. She was beginning to adjust to the speed and to the number of things there was and was getting better able to pick out individual things from among the crowd. Occasionally she saw trees beside or behind the buildings and she noticed that the farther they got from the centre of town, the more trees and flowers there were between buildings. The land was quite hilly as if it may, like the island, rise up from the ocean on one side and sink back down to the ocean on the other. But that couldn't be, for she knew the mainland was much too large. She had seen maps, and her little island was a dot compared to the mass of land that was British Columbia, never mind the whole of Canada. Well, someday she would see why the land rose and fell so. Today it was just nice to feel that neither the land nor Aunt Augusta seemed quite so unwelcoming. Today, even in the rattly car, she could feel hope, not just remind herself there is always hope.

In fact Aunt Augusta too was relieved and she was doing some planning, some rethinking. The child seemed much better today. With the clusters of ringlets and the new clothes, even these plainish ones, she looked, well, if not pretty, at least more appropriate for a child from their home. Augusta thought perhaps she wouldn't have the child change for dinner that evening. Instead, she'd see how many of the lessons and things she could arrange before Hugh came home. That way she'd save the pretty dress for a day when Hugh really needed to be reconciled to the child and she could depend this day on the plain but suitable clothes and on the success of their plans for the child. Yes, that would be much better. If the child stayed out of her way, she could make all the phone calls she needed to make before dinner. So resolved, she glanced at Thomasina and said, "When we get home, I want you to play outside, without getting all dirty, of course, and without leaving the yard, while I phone and arrange for all your lessons and get dinner ready. I'll call you when it's time to come in."

Misty smiled to hear such unexpected good news. She'd be free to go to her apple tree and free from the dreaded pink dress. But Misty was about to experience the first effects of Aunt Augusta's efforts to tame her, to make her appropriate to a member of their household. As Aunt Augusta went into the house carrying the boxes and bags, having ordered Misty to leave her alone, Misty went to her apple tree, happy to see the bright sunshine still filling the tiny orchard. She stretched as she walked, turning all around, hoping to see the cat somewhere among the flowers and shrubs, happily settling for the birds she saw hopping about in the branches of the tree. At the bottom of the tree she stopped short, looking at her feet.

Suddenly, the shoes that had felt comfortable as shoes go seemed to look up at her, stopping her with their newness, their whiteness, their stiffness. Bewildered, Misty ran her hands down her skirt, feeling the new material, gently pulling the skirt out to its very limited fullness. The smell of the new material overpowered the gentler scents of the flowers and trees, making breathing suddenly difficult. Misty forced her eyes away from the new clothes and on to the tree with its branches as inviting as outstretched arms. She longed to feel the safety of the arms, the delight of the living tree, the life of clean air filtered through apple leaves. But she stood where she was, held hostage by the new clothes, the suitable girls' clothes that would not let her climb at all. The anticipated freedom and joy of the afternoon disappeared as Misty sat down at the base of the tree trunk, careful not to get the new clothes dirty. Deep inside the little girl something snapped, faintly, dully but surely, and the lump that rose to her throat was bigger and drier than any she had known before.

Inside, Aunt Augusta efficiently, methodically and very happily arranged the child's coming year. She successfully enrolled her in classes to be held after school and weekends: tap dance and gymnastics classes on Mondays, art lessons on Tuesdays, ballet classes on Wednesdays, piano and voice lessons on Thursdays and figure skating on Saturdays. It would be a nuisance having to drive her to the skating rink on Saturdays, a day they liked to sleep in, but she supposed she'd just have to make that sacrifice. To save Sunday mornings, she called the church office of the small white church within walking distance of their house and registered the child for Sunday School classes there. Of course she'd rather attend the bigger church in the centre of town herself, the church where the important people went, but it was just too much to ask to give up her Sunday mornings for any reason at all, so she decided on sending the child nearby. Besides, she wasn't sure the child wouldn't prove an embarrassment, so thought the small church safer. In just two weeks, school would begin, all the classes start, and the child would be well on her way to becoming the tribute to them she ought to be in her fine new girls' clothes. Hugh would be so pleased with all she had accomplished that day.

7.

School

The two weeks did pass by, not without some trials for Aunt Augusta, but with a great deal of encouragement as well. The child seemed much less impulsive as the days wore on, much less likely to do things without being told, much less likely to run outside or forget her shoes. She looked much better, prettier with the clusters of ringlets and the fashionable new clothes. Fortunately, she remained quiet; Augusta thought her becoming quite the demure little miss. Meals, however, were a trial; the child simply would not listen, would not do as she was told. Night after night, Augusta sent her to bed in a storm, for the child simply would not eat all her food. In fact, as the days wore on, she seemed to eat less, not more. Hugh had become so outraged that he had finally refused to let the child come to the dining room, so Misty ate alone in the kitchen. Still she didn't clean off her plate, and Augusta had to send her to bed, usually with a spanking for her silent refusal to obey.

It never occurred to Augusta that she was giving the child more than she could eat. Neither did it occur to her that rather than the improvement she was so sure she saw in all matters other than the meals, the child was, in fact, growing dull. The colour was fast fading from her cheeks. Dark circles were beginning to form under her eyes. The slightly glassy look that had occasionally spread across her eyes when she had first arrived was being replaced more and more by a dazed look. But Augusta saw none of it, looking as she did through her own selfish ambitions. She was so pleased with the child's improvement that she was sure the beginning of school would bring with it the solution to the disobedience at mealtime.

For her part, Misty lived between a cocoon of memories and a daze of bafflement. Robbed of the freedom to take refreshment from the orchard, robbed of the cleansing release of tears, she had withdrawn. Memories of home brought moments of pleasure and restored feelings of hope, but the continual barrage of angry words and senseless noise, the shock of being spanked for the first time and the enormous battle with swallowing food and the disappointment of her own regular failure to clean off her plate dazed her. Try as she might to sort through the rules and to deduce from Aunt Augusta's angry outbursts what she was doing wrong, Misty remained utterly baffled—baffled and exhausted. Then her head would ache with the swirling of rules and her attempts to sort them out and act appropriately, and she'd retreat again, more wounded than before. She spent most of her time in her room, alone, and very lonely. Only in her daydreams did she experience any comfort and relief from the loneliness that was quickly becoming a part of her life. From her memories and her habitual chats with God, she drew strength to face the next meal, only to fail again and be sent back to the little room, confused and wounded. She felt bad about the wasted food but was powerless to solve the problem; she simply could not eat as much as Aunt Augusta gave her. She seemed locked into a pattern of failure. Only her genuine desire to make people happy kept her going, kept her trying. Her wonderful storehouse of memories and the intensity of the life she had lived freely before coming here refreshed her and enabled her to carry on.

Finally the day dawned in September when the mood of the house seemed quite different, almost lively. Uncle Hugh had gone off to work, reminding Aunt Augusta that he had set everything up at the school and she need only take the child there to the principal's office. They were going to test her to see how close to the Fourth or Fifth Grade they could place her; the principal had agreed to sending the child to one of the assistants for a portion of each day to teach her to read and write. That way there would be no unnecessary embarrassment for Hugh and Augusta. Aunt Augusta was herself all dressed up and she had insisted that Misty wear the nicest of the school clothes; she had also insisted on arranging the clusters of ringlets herself so Misty might look as pretty as possible. Misty stood quietly, beginning to wonder if school might be some sort of solution to the worst of her problems. No one had yelled at her about porridge that morning, though she had been unable, as usual, to finish the heap placed in front of her. Aunt Augusta had instead muttered that it was probably the excitement keeping her from eating. Maybe Misty should feel excited. She had always liked books and, she reasoned, maybe school would give her things to do in the long empty hours she spent in her room. Maybe school would restore purpose to her life.

So it was with a bit of hope that Misty set out for school with Aunt Augusta. They were to walk so that Aunt Augusta could show her the route. Misty was relieved to see the way full of familiar things. As they walked up the hill, she enjoyed the trees and flowers that lined the road and she was excited to see several cats and dogs along the way. Aunt Augusta warned her to stay on the sidewalk and not cut across any of the lawns, especially not at the corner where they turned on to a slightly busier road. Misty was a little nervous to have to pass a shop where there were several people coming and going, but soon they were passing a row of tidy houses, many of them with children running out and scurrying along in the same direction they went. She cringed a little at the noise of children yelling and running, feet slapping on the concrete sidewalk, but as no one paid much attention to them, she relaxed a little as they carried on. At the end of the row of houses, the sky seemed to open up, to expand suddenly, as a field stretched out in all directions. Misty had pictured a small schoolhouse like those she had read of: Anne Shirley's school in Avonlea or Heidi's school in the village of Dörfli. Instead, in the centre of the field stood a large, yellow building, two storeys high, with a wide set of stairs rising up to the main doors and a covered walkway running from the bottom of the stairs to the doorway of a long single-storey wing stretching off to the right of the main building. Misty suddenly felt very small.

Children ran all around on the playground, some swinging on tires and canvas that were suspended on chains from pipe frames to one side of the building, others hanging by their arms and wriggling along pipe ladders that were suspended between tall metal frames that were planted firmly in the ground at either end of the ladders. More children ran around, shrieking and calling, some throwing balls, others chasing balls, and others hopping back and forth in squares that were painted on the ground near the building. Misty shivered a little, almost overwhelmed by the noise and a little frightened by the activity and the sheer numbers. She was actually glad to be with Aunt Augusta, who, undistracted by the noise or crowd, was leading Misty past it all and up the long staircase.

Inside, the building was more quiet, though very large and a little cold. There was a strange smell to the place, an odd combination of cleaning fluids, ink, paper, and chalk dust, and everything looked somehow tall to Misty. She saw many doors going into many rooms, each room filled with rows and rows of little desks. At least the desks were like those in books, as was the blackboard at the front of each classroom. A few adults moved quietly about the hallway and into various rooms, but Aunt Augusta led Misty through the door marked "Office." Inside there was a high counter behind which two women sat at large desks, sorting papers and looking over long lists. Behind them was another door marked "Principal." Through the glass window in the door, Misty could see a tall man sitting at a desk. Aunt Augusta cleared her throat, and one of the women stood up.

"We're here to see the principal. He is expecting us this morning. You'll show us in right away, of course." Aunt Augusta had adopted the same tone she had used in the shop with Milly, making Misty wonder yet again about this woman she thought she'd never understand. The tight tone had the same effect on this woman as it had on Milly, but the woman simply nodded, opened a small gate and led Aunt Augusta through the office to tap on the principal's door. He looked up from his desk and nodded his permission to enter. Though this man wore a suit as Uncle Hugh did, he looked slightly less uncomfortable in it and was taller and not as heavy as Uncle Hugh. He was neither welcoming nor intimidating, just seemed to be doing his job. He responded to Aunt Augusta's tinny greeting by saying,

"Yes, I did speak with your husband last week. We'll do our best for the child. I've decided to place her in a split Grades

Two and Three class at least until we can complete our testing and assess the situation."

"But that will never do!" interrupted Aunt Augusta. "The child is ten years old, and those lower grades are in this old part of the building, not the new part the older children are in. I won't have her stuck in here. I'm sure my husband clarified this with you. He told me you'd put her in Grade Four or Five. Really!"

The principal had dreaded just such an outburst. Augusta could be so abrasive and difficult; he had hoped to avoid such anger. However, he was in charge here and he'd just silence her and send her on her way. Speaking rapidly to avoid further interruption and difficulty, he carried on loudly and firmly:

"How much choice do you suppose I had? It's terrible the child not having been in school all these years. It was utterly negligent on their part. Had we known sooner, we'd have forced them to send her, of course, but we didn't know they had a child. It would be ridiculous for us to put an unschooled child in higher grades. As it is, we are taking a risk. However, it is a chance I will take for you; it really is good of you to take her in. It's good that she is small, won't seem so out of place in the lower grades, so I'm sure it will all work out. We have excellent staff here, and the child will have the best of instruction. If you'll just sign this paper I had filled in, you can go; your husband has answered all my questions and given me the information I need, such as he has. I'll get one of the older children to take Thomasina in hand this morning. I assume you'll come to get her today. We should dismiss early, around noon. Tomorrow will be our first regular day. Leave Thomasina with the secretary; she'll take care of everything from here. Good bye now."

Efficiently he dismissed them both and returned to his papers. As Aunt Augusta walked down the corridor, her heels clicking and echoing as she went, Misty felt very small once again and a little chilly. It was kind of hard to breathe in this place with its high ceilings and windowless walls. The light provided by the fluorescent tubes above was more harsh than friendly, and Misty found herself squinting a little. The secretary with whom she had been left had glanced at a large clock on the wall and decided there was no use sending the child outside, for school would begin in just moments. She'd wait until the classes had assembled, then take Thomasina in herself. The poor child looked quite frightened, and well she may be, having to move in with that uppity couple and come into a new school. Besides, much as she loved children, she knew that they'd make much fun of this new little girl, partly because she was new, partly because she was different, an orphan, and partly because of her name. What dreadful timing, that Gallico book coming out just last year and everyone being so taken with it. Children were often cruel in their carelessness, and the secretary was expecting the worst from them. Taken by the child's dreamy look, she immediately joined the ranks of Milly in feeling she must help her any way she could. Gently she took Thomasina's hand and began to explain;

"It is almost time to begin, so I'll take you to your class myself; there will be time enough at recess for you to get to know some of your classmates. I'm Mrs. Longacre and I'll be seeing quite a bit of you in the next few weeks as we get you settled. If you have any questions or any trouble, I'll try to help you out here. I know it isn't easy starting something new. You must miss your home, too. Is there anything you want to know now?" she asked, smiling.

Misty suddenly had so many questions she hardly knew where to begin but she did want to know what 'split Grades Two and Three' meant and where her classroom was and when the testing would begin, but as she opened her mouth, a loud bell rang, causing Misty to jump right off the floor. Mrs. Longacre chuckled a little in a friendly kind of way, before saying, "Oh, sorry. I guess I should have warned you the bell would be ringing. You'll get used to it. It will ring again in a few minutes. That was the warning bell, letting the children know they are to line up ready to come into the building. When the next bell rings, they'll file in and take their places. Then I'll take you to your class. Don't worry, Thomasina, you'll be fine. Just watch the other children and follow them. You'll soon fit right in."

Misty had to struggle to hear what Mrs. Longacre was saying through the clanging that kept echoing in her head. She'd never heard anything like it. Cowbells were gentle things, and the horns on the freight boats that had sounded when they docked at the island were mellow, almost mournful in their warnings, not harsh, clanging, and abrasive. Even as she thought about the comforting sound of a foghorn, the clatter of the school bell sounded out again, causing her to jump as much as before. It would take quite a bit of getting used to, she was sure. The harsh sound was soon followed by the tread of hundreds of feet as rows of children, all of them silent, all of them walking in order, in pairs, holding hands, entered the building. They filed in groups of about thirty into open classroom doors.

Misty was at once soothed by the order and confused by it; it seemed strained and unnatural. It struck her that the neat little pairs of children all marching stiffly along were as absurd as her carefully held clusters of ringlets. As much as she had found the noise outside overwhelming, she sensed that such clamour was more natural than this subdued but soothing regiment, much like the difference between her curls blowing and frizzing in the wind and the firmly held clusters of bouncing springs at each side of her head. She wondered if getting used to tidy rows of subdued children would be as difficult as getting used to clumps of ringlets.

Mrs. Longacre waited until the children had all disappeared into classrooms before leading Misty out of the office doorway and down the corridor where they paused at another doorway. Inside, the children were standing beside the desks while a woman stood at the front of the class, facing them. Mrs. Longacre knocked on the doorframe before the woman could begin.

"Miss Moore," she said when the woman looked up and nodded, "this is Thomasina, the new child you'll see added to your class list."

She glared at the class as she heard a few titters breaking out, then carried on.

"Thomasina has just moved here from an island and has not yet met any of the children. I'll send an older girl to show her around at recess. She'll be in your class, but I'll be taking her from time to time for the first few weeks as we determine what she'll need. Meanwhile, carry on as usual." Turning, she said, "Enjoy your new class, Thomasina," as she left the classroom.

A ripple of laughter that spread through the room was silenced as Miss Moore boomed out, "Class! Enough!" Misty was more startled by the shout than she was confused by the laughter and she stood, rooted to the spot until Miss Moore said, "Come in, child. Stand by the empty desk there in the back row for now. We sit alphabetically, so we'll have to rearrange several seats but we'll do that later. Right now we must get on with opening exercises. Class begin."

Misty was surprised at the silence that followed as the children suddenly became perfectly still, hands behind their backs, heads lowered, eyes closed. Then arose words with which she was familiar as, in unison, the children repeated the Lord's Prayer. Miss Moore noted that Thomasina joined the children, though she lifted her head up instead of bowing it. Still, she was pleased to see the child knew something.

When the prayer ended, the children took their seats and Miss Moore began what Misty soon learned was called "taking attendance." She read down the list of names, again arranged in alphabetical order, each child saying "present" when his or her name was called. One slightly scruffy looking boy, the biggest there, was reprimanded when he said, "here" in a very loud voice instead of the word "present" that was expected of him. Misty felt strangely excited by him and sorry when he was scolded and began to shuffle his feet. She got a little nervous, wondering when her name would be called and if she would do everything right, but it all looked simple enough. She kept repeating "present" to herself, over and over, practising, determined to get it right. Suddenly she noticed a few giggles followed by a hush.

Miss Moore called, "Thomasina," and the giggles turned to laughter, followed by the dreaded, "Class! Quiet!" Misty wondered what the laughter was about and why Miss Moore had stopped going down the list. She heard a few more titters as Miss Moore said clearly and carefully, "We do all know you are here, for we've been introduced. Thomasina, when you hear your name called, you must answer 'present' as the other children have. Do remember for tomorrow."

Misty's face flushed red as the children giggled and she realized her mistake. She had forgotten again. She was Thomasina. Miss Moore's repeated call to order saved her further embarrassment, but she sank a little down in her desk under the weight of all there was to learn. Frightened, she retreated, her eyes growing glassy as she almost heard the Captain call her Misty as she walked along beside him, enjoying the familiarity and friendliness of the sound. She recalled Gran telling her she was as winsome as the morning mist, so perfectly named. She wrapped herself in the warmth of the sounds of love, her people using her very own name, Misty. It was right.

A rustling of many papers and shuffling of books brought Misty back to the classroom. The children were getting things out of their desks as Miss Moore began to walk down the aisle toward her. Misty was amazed and excited to see the other children taking books, shiny new red pens, yellow pencils, and pink erasers and arranging them on their desks. In each row, pieces of paper were being handed back, each child taking one and passing the rest over her head to the person behind. Some were already bending over, beginning to write on the pages. Others were still opening the little bottles of ink that nestled in the inkwell at the corner of each desk. She could hardly wait to join them! But Miss Moore squatted beside her and said quietly,

"There is much to learn and decide here, so we'll have to go slowly with you at first. You see the little children, the Grade Twos, all use pencil. They have been taught to read in the basic books and to print. Those who are good with their pencils will be taught to use pen and ink during this year. Most of the Grade Threes use pen already. They have proceeded from printing and are beginning to write—in ink, not pencil. With thirty children, I can't take the time to start at the beginning with you, to teach you the alphabet, so we'll just have to fill in time until the assistant can get you started. I hope you learn quickly. It certainly won't look good on my record if you don't. It's bad enough I have Tommy to mar my record. Somehow, I have to keep you busy and quiet until you can be taught, so I suggest when I give an assignment as I have now, you quietly draw pictures. I don't expect much, but surely any child, even the unschooled, can draw pictures. You'll have to use the pencil; leave the pen alone. When we settle the desks, I'll just take the things you don't need away. You should find some crayons in your desk; you can use those for drawing if you want to. Remember, the children are writing about their summer holiday. You draw something from your summer holiday and hand it in with the others."

Misty wanted to tell Miss Moore she could read and write already but, as was usual in this world, she wasn't given a chance. Mrs. Longacre and Milly were the only two people who seemed to have actually spoken to her since she'd left Old Lundstrom at the Landing. Everyone here talked a great deal but always as if there were no listeners. She didn't like the feeling it always gave her or the position it put her in. Here Miss Moore thought she couldn't read or write and she could—in ink, too! She wasn't sure what she should do, but decided that doing what she was told would be the safest plan. All the other children were obviously doing what they had been told. Besides, drawing was as exciting as writing. So she took up her pencil, glanced out the window for a few minutes hoping for a drawing feeling to creep in and, when it did, she began.

She didn't know what was meant by "summer holiday" so just started in drawing her old home. Almost immediately she became completely absorbed in what she was doing, handily sketching the barn and the weathered fence that separated the small barnyard from the field that stretched out behind until all was obscured by the towering trees in the distance. She added a few chickens and a cat to the foreground before taking up the crayons to attempt to add colour to her scene. Misty had not been idle when she had stood for hours at the side of Miss Lily. She could work magic on paper.

She found herself having some trouble with the crayons, however, for they weren't at all like the pastels that Miss Lily had shared with her. Pastels flowed as easily onto the paper as pencil did, but these crayons felt heavy, thick and sticky. She concentrated harder and experimented, certain that there must be a way to add colour to her picture. If she could at least get the greens and blues, she'd be happy. She soon found that by tearing back the paper and using the crayon on its side, she could get quite faint colour to spread a little at a time. She felt the bubble of happiness rise up within her as she made the light green spread across the farmyard, mixing yellow in with it to give a truer sense of the grasses there. A little of the brown added made it almost right. Now if she could just get the darker greens in the distance and a good blue overhead, she'd feel that burst of satisfaction that she knew came with completing something well.

Instead, she heard a loud smack. Startled, she looked up to see Miss Moore raise a wooden ruler and smack it down on her large desk at the front of the class. All the children sat stiff, looking straight ahead. "Tommy! You must know by now that I mean stop when I say 'stop.' We must have order here. Thomasina; you'd best learn this too. Now be sure to put your name on the upper right hand corner of your work and pass your sheets forward. We have to assign monitors and reading groups before recess begins. Pass the papers forward."

Misty saw children handing their papers ahead of them and thought she should do the same, but her work wasn't finished. It felt dreadful letting it go when it wasn't done. Should she? Often Miss Lily had to leave a painting long before finishing and she'd go back when she could. Misty would do the same with this little drawing but how could she if she didn't have it? No, she decided she'd better tuck it inside the desk so she could finish it the next time Miss Moore told them to do something. She would put her name on it, though, but not in the top corner where the dark trees rose into the blue sky. There wasn't room there. Besides, Miss Lily always signed her pictures in the bottom. So, taking her pencil, Misty wrote her name in the bottom corner of her unfinished picture and tucked it into her desk before busying herself putting her crayons back in the package and gathering the bits of paper she had scattered all over her desk as she unwrapped and coloured. She tried to listen to Miss Moore, but none of the talk about chalkboard monitors and lunch monitors made sense to her and she didn't hear her name listed in any of the reading groups, so she sat quietly wondering when she would get to finish her picture.

The clanging bell interrupted her, causing her to jump once again, bumping her knee on the bottom of the desk and sending tingles along her leg. The other children stood beside their desks, so Misty rose as well. Row by row, the children filed out the door and down the corridor.

Misty followed along, but Miss Moore stopped her and took her aside when she reached the front of the class, saying, "Today you must wait here for the older student who is being sent to show you the playground and explain the rules. I'm sure she'll be here soon." Misty felt awkward standing in front with all the children filing past. She wished she could just go back to her picture. She really didn't like the sense of leaving something unfinished either; it unsettled her. She was most uncomfortable by the time a tall girl came to the door and knocked on the wooden frame.

"Ah, Judith, you must be here for Thomasina," said Miss Moore. "She has never been to any school, so you'll have to tell her everything. And don't forget to show her which line-up to get in after recess. Thomasina, pay attention to Judith; she'll take care of you. Off you go now."

As the two girls left the classroom, Judith immediately began talking in very hushed tones. "We're not supposed to talk in the corridors, but I have permission to whisper today so I can tell you the rules. So; one and two: no running and no talking in the corridors. Three: no going inside the building without permission during recess, lunch hour or before or after school, except for the big washrooms in the basement. I'll show you those first. Your class will use this stairway, so we'll go down here."

Downstairs, Misty was surprised to see a huge empty-looking room with one door off each side of it. Judith said it was where the girls from the lower classes lined up whenever the bell rang and where they sometimes played during recess on really rainy winter days. Through one door was a girls' washroom. Through the other was another such room and beyond that was a boys' washroom but, of course, girls weren't allowed through that door.

Judith carried on with her lists of rules as they walked out onto the playground. Misty struggled hard to listen, to hear anything through the noise of the children, all of whom seemed to be running and yelling both. Judith droned on with rules such as no going off the school grounds without a note, no fighting, no dropping garbage on the ground, no taking equipment without permission, no throwing rocks, no climbing trees, no playing around the teachers' cars, no pushing in lines for the swings … On and on the list of rules went. Misty felt her head beginning to swim with the list and the noise. Looking at the children made her feel dizzy; they ran round and round, here and there, but Misty couldn't see what they were running to see or to do. They just seemed to run and make noise. Before Misty could make sense of anything, the clanging bell rang through the din making Misty jump again and the other children stop their screaming and run to take positions in lines.

Judith said, "Go where the rest of your class is and get in line. Just follow them back to class." But Misty didn't move. All the lines looked the same to her and she didn't know which one to join. "Over there, silly," said Judith, giving Misty a little shove; "go there. I have to go to my own class or I'll be late, and that's against the rules."

Confused and frightened, Misty walked very slowly toward the rows of smaller children who were entering the large room she had come through to get outside. They formed four small groups before heading up the stairs; still Misty didn't recognize anyone from her own class. She hadn't paid much attention to individual children, and the groups all looked the same to her. Behind all four groups, she followed along, up the stairs and into the corridor. Only when the lines of boys filed from the other stairs, did Misty see where to go, for she recognized the big boy Miss Moore had called Tommy. Misty followed those boys through the classroom door. The whole class began giggling as she entered.

Miss Moore silenced them but stopped Misty in front of her desk. "I'll assume that Judith neglected to tell you to walk with the girls, not the boys, Thomasina. You will remember that, won't you? Take your seat please."

A sense of bewilderment and tiredness swept over Misty as she moved to her seat at the back. Though the walk down the aisle seemed long, she was glad to have to sit behind the children, for she felt uncomfortable with them staring at her. From the back she could try to listen to Miss Moore, but she must also study some of these girls so she'd know where to go next time. All she saw, though, were rows and rows of ponytails and pigtails, some blond, some brown, some very dark. A few girls had short hair but the other groups downstairs had also had several of those. One girl had on a sweater that was a different colour from everybody else's; maybe she could watch for that next time. Or maybe she'd just have to hope that she'd get better looks at the girls' faces sometime. Then she'd be able to tell some of them apart. Backs of heads didn't do much good, she decided, as she tried once again to hear what Miss Moore was saying but she found herself wishing she could go home to her little room. The thought surprised her, for when she was in her little room she longed to be back on the island. But now she felt so tired that even the little room appealed to her.

A small buzzer sound startled her, and she sat up very straight. Suddenly a voice filled the room, a man's voice, a disembodied man's voice. It was loud and very strange as it said, "Good morning. Welcome back to school."

Misty looked quickly around her. There was no man anywhere, and all the other children were sitting still, looking toward the front of the class.

The voice continued, "As you know, the first day of school we use mostly for organizing, for assigning classes and settling back in. You will be dismissed early today, but full classes begin tomorrow. I want to remind all of you that proper conduct is expected at all times, both on the school grounds and off. As long as you are here or on your way to or from school, you are a reflection of our whole school and must behave accordingly. Remember to walk on the sidewalks, to avoid running and pushing on the sidewalks and be sure to go directly home. There will be no stopping in the store, no walking on lawns, no …"

As the voice droned on with yet another list of rules, Misty thought it sounded like the principal she had heard that morning. The sound seemed to come from a little box high on the wall above Miss Moore's desk. Misty wondered if there were some kind of eye watching from up there as well, for it sounded as if everybody would somehow know everything that each child did. She found herself trying to sit up straighter, to seem the way Aunt Augusta kept saying she should be. Though there were far more rules than she could begin to take in, it did sound to Misty as if many of the rules were the same as Aunt Augusta kept repeating. But Misty had already seen that those rules not only hemmed her in as never before but also caused no end of trouble, for following one rule often meant breaking another. She began to feel chilly as well as tired.

Still the voice carried on, and Misty found herself fading away to a quieter place, seeing miles and miles of land without voices, hearing instead the happy sounds of birds and squirrels and the soothing sounds of wind. There was the gentle, whispering wind, rustling in the leafy trees, the stronger, whirling wind, creaking about the tree trunks as they bent in its path. Even the mournful, howling wind, swirling around cliffs, stirring up waves that crashed against the shore was comforting, almost exciting, for it blew life into things that were otherwise still. Misty hugged herself, feeling the thrill even the thought of fresh strong wind brought with it.

A loud click that ended the droning voice brought her attention back to the room. Standing behind her desk, Miss Moore took up where the voice had left off. "Now you all heard the principal, children, and I expect my class to be especially good. I am looking forward to beginning serious work tomorrow. We'll start with our opening exercises, followed by our health inspection. Remember to clean your fingernails before school so you get everything checked off our list. Remember, we want to get more stars than any other class in the primary division! Then it will be straight into reading and writing classes. We'll do arithmetic right after recess and spelling just before lunch. After lunch we have something different each day, sometimes science, sometimes social studies, sometimes art and sometimes music. And if we're all good, we'll have stories to finish up the day. There's lots to learn, lots to do, and I look forward to this class making me proud. I hope I won't have to send any of you to the principal's office all year, not even you, Tommy, so everyone must do better than ever before. And this year, let's have no failures, nobody repeating a grade."

Again Misty jumped as the bell rang out, stopping Miss Moore's urging. Misty almost welcomed the ringing in her head as it cut through some of the swirling thoughts. She didn't know what it all meant and she was confused by Miss Moore's voice; it was funny sounding, a little like Aunt Augusta's when she spoke to Milly in the shop, but even sillier, as if she didn't think the children could hear or think or something. Misty wondered why that would be a problem, since no one gave children a chance to answer or say anything anyway. She wondered also why they had spent so much time in the classroom after recess and she hadn't had a chance to get back to her picture. What had they done? Listened to rules, she guessed. But Miss Moore had said tomorrow would be different, so Misty guessed she would just have to try to find her way the next day.

She followed the class down the corridor and outside, watching the children scatter in every direction the instant they stepped outside, once again yelling and shouting as they ran. This time she saw them leaving the playground, so she knew it must be time to go home. She walked around to the front of the school and started toward the road before remembering the principal had said Aunt Augusta was to meet her that day. But nobody had said where to meet. She hesitated, confused again. At home, nothing had been so difficult. Everything had just happened. Never had she had to figure out where or when to walk. She didn't recall ever not knowing what to do or not knowing how to figure things out, yet here she was stuck in a mass of confusion.

'Oh God,' she thought, 'here I am again, just stuck. Is this the way You made the world? Is this the way you made people? How do I know where to find Aunt Augusta? I wish I could just float up above things, see everything like You do. Maybe then I'd know what to do. But I'm just stuck here. Will You help me now?'

As she looked around her at the last of the other children scurrying away from the school, she recalled Mrs. Longacre saying Misty could ask her anything. She turned and walked up the stairs and into the office. Even before she reached the counter, she heard Aunt Augusta's grating voice.

"Well, where is she? I've come all this way to pick her up, and you don't know where she is? What kind of teacher have you put her with that she just dismissed her with the rest of the class? That's fine for tomorrow but was just stupid for today. I told you she shouldn't be in that little class. No, I won't calm down! What if the child is lost somewhere? How will that look? And it won't just be me who looks bad; I'll be sure everybody knows that it was you who let her go."

Misty wished with all her might that somehow this would all end but she didn't know how to get anyone to notice her, didn't know how to let them know there was nothing to worry or argue about. Then she remembered people knocking on doorframes before entering classrooms, so she knocked quite loudly on the counter in front of her.

Mrs. Longacre leapt up from her desk and said loudly, "Oh, Thomasina. What a good child! You've done exactly right to come to the office. Well done. There's no need for any fuss, is there? How very clever of you."

As she exclaimed, Mrs. Longacre knocked on the principal's office door, and he and Aunt Augusta came out, Aunt Augusta accusing harshly, "Really, child! Whatever were you thinking, running off like that? You've given us all a fright and caused no end of embarrassment. You must be more like the other children and stop drawing all this attention to yourself. I trust this won't happen again. Well, I won't be telling Hugh this. Trouble, always trouble."

Misty's eyes opened wide as she tried to sort it all out. Mrs. Longacre had said she had done well, but Aunt Augusta said she was nothing but trouble. Misty looked from one to the other, puzzled. The principal rescued her by addressing the blustering woman.

"Now, Augusta, calm down. It was just a slight oversight, and no harm was done. You should be proud that the child had the sense to come here to meet you as we had arranged. I'm sure she won't be trouble. Why, I'll tell Hugh myself when we golf on Saturday how clever his little charge is! This is a fine beginning. Enjoy your afternoon. And Thomasina, we'll see you tomorrow," he said, as he ushered the two out of the office. Behind them, Mrs. Longacre shook her head sadly and vowed once again to find ways to help the quiet child.

Pacified by the principal's words, Aunt Augusta said she wanted to hear all about Thomasina's day as they started home. But Misty found herself assaulted with a steady barrage of words instead as Aunt Augusta prattled on about how exciting she was sure school had been and would continue to be and how easy it would be for Thomasina to fit in and make friends and how easy the walk to and from school would be for her and how fast time would fly as she was taught all the things little girls should know and how …

Misty grew tired with all the chatter and excitement, none of which seemed to have to do with her, and took solace in looking at the flowers that grew in people's tiny gardens along the way. There were some truly beautiful chrysanthemums growing along one little white fence, and there in the midst of them snuggled a small orange cat, almost the same colour as the rusty 'mums. It reminded her of her little dog whose brown coat had hints of rust in it, and she wondered what it would be like to walk back from school with Rusty at her side. She knew she'd like it, like to see him and smell him and feel his soft fur and his warm tongue as he rubbed against her and licked her fingers. But she was glad for him that he hadn't had to come here like she had. The Captain had been right; this was no place for an island dog.

Her eyes grew a little glassy as her thoughts turned to Rusty in his happy home, and she wondered what Miss Lily would think of the picture she'd begun that day. Miss Lily would be able to explain to her how the crayons worked. She was quite pleased with having found a way to make them blend on the page, but they were the most difficult things she had ever used to make colour. No wonder she hadn't seen any at Miss Lily's. She smiled to think of the last picture she had seen of Miss Lily's. Why she had caught the colour of Rusty's coat exactly! Misty was sure that was not possible with the crayons. But maybe she'd experiment when she got a chance. By the time they reached home, Misty was quite revived, soothed by her thoughts of home and excited to think about the crayons at school. She had something to look forward to.

But another meal awaited her—another large meal. Try as she might to finish off the big bowl of macaroni Aunt Augusta put in front of her, she couldn't do it. Was there no way she could please anyone? She braced herself as Aunt Augusta ranted on about starving children in China, about ungratefulness and finally about disobedience, blind disobedience. Misty felt tempted to simply stand up and turn around so Aunt Augusta could swat her backside and get it over with, but she sat still until she heard the inevitable, "Now get to your room and stay there!"

Wearily she went to her room wondering why she felt so heavy. The swat didn't really hurt, especially not through the thick skirt she had on, but every time she felt it, she was suddenly small, tired and heavy. It was like having failure rubbed into her, for she really did try hard to do as she was told. She couldn't recall ever having been told to eat until she had come here. At home they prepared the food together, helped themselves to it and sat down and ate together, ate because they were hungry, ate because it was another thing to enjoy together, ate as naturally as they slept and awoke. Here eating had become not only a huge undertaking but apparently something she simply could not do to anyone's satisfaction. Here meals were battles, battles which she always lost, though to hear Aunt Augusta carry on, you'd think Misty had won. Misty, with her inability to imagine war and fighting, could not see meals as battles between two people; the most Misty could see was her private battle to eat all the food. Time after time she lost and had the losing rubbed in by the hand that swatted her as she went to her room as ordered.

Once in her room, though, she could go to the window, look out and let the heaviness go. The apples were turning colour on her apple tree, some of them even falling on the ground below. She could almost taste them as she looked out and took great, deep breaths of the apple-scented air. It hurt her a little to see them lying there wasting. She and Gran would have gathered them and made wonderful pies and preserves. She had been disappointed, too, not to be able to help with the laundry. She had seen from her window the clothes blowing in the breeze one day, as they hung on two lines that stretched out from the house to a pole with a crossbar at the top. Laundry had always been a favourite of hers with the clean smells of soap and the freshness of air-dried clothes. She liked the sound of towels and sheets snapping as she and Gran shook the wrinkles out of them before hanging them on the lines. She also like the sounds of the clothes blowing in the wind, sometimes rustling, sometimes snapping as the wind rose and fell. Funny, though the clothes were firmly fastened to the line, they always looked so free to her, free to flutter, blow, dance about. She hadn't felt that freedom for a long time. But she drew strength from watching the clothes blow on the line and the leaves flutter on the trees. She even drew strength from the apples falling to the ground. This day, all thoughts of her failure to eat her lunch disappeared with the sound of a crow calling as he swooped down and began pecking at the ripening apples. Misty loved the crow sounds, so bold and friendly. She laughed to see the cat cower and slink away. She still didn't know where the cat lived but she had seen him often in the garden. She had even begun to think of him as a friend, though she hadn't had a chance to let him come to her, stuck inside as she was.

She really was becoming a puzzle to herself. In school she had longed for the quiet of her little room. In her little room she longed for the freedom of the island. Now she found herself looking forward to school again, or at least to getting back to her picture. Besides, Miss Moore had said they would have stories if they were good. She missed stories. She and Gran and Gramps had read many old books in the winter months. That's how she had learned to read, sitting on someone's lap and following along as they read aloud. Usually Gran read and Gramps sat in his old Morris chair beside the fireplace, the smoke curling up from his pipe. As soon as Gran became aware that Misty kept her eyes on the page, she had begun pointing at the words as she read them. Gran knew nothing about how to teach a child to read or when a child should learn to read; she just saw that Misty was interested and pointed things out to her. They hadn't any children's books, except *Heidi* and *Anne of Green Gables*, two of the first Misty could remember along with *Uncle Tom's Cabin*, so they read Gran's books, mostly, she said, the Victorians. Then, too, Gramps had read from the big family Bible every day and he soon started pointing with his finger too so Misty could follow along. At the same time Gran had given Misty pencil and paper and had her copy out the order lists for groceries and supplies that came from Woodwards and Buckerfields in Vancouver by boat. One of the first things Misty wrote out was a seed list. So, unaware of being taught anything, Misty had simply learned to read and write; it was all just a part of everyday life. Before she was old enough even to have been sent to school had there been one, she was reading to her grandparents as they quietly mended clothes and harnesses or quilted or tooled leather before the fire. Oh, how she missed the stories! But now Miss Moore had promised stories.

8.

The Office and the Alphabet

As Misty walked to school the following morning, she wondered what stories they would have that day, wondered if there would be the marvellous Old Testament stories of friends like David and Jonathan, strong men like Samson or wise men like Solomon. Or maybe she would hear once again of Tess or Jane Eyre or Catherine or, maybe the sisters Bennet. She skipped along, happily anticipating hearing of some fascinating character. Passing the house with the beautiful chrysanthemums, she remembered her drawing and skipped along a little faster, hoping to get back to experimenting with the crayons, completely unaware of the storm that was awaiting her.

As she approached the school ground, she slowed, mentally listing the rules she could remember. She heard the bell ring as she crossed to the bottom door as the girl, Judith, had shown her the day before. Inside, she looked everywhere for the unusual coloured sweater but couldn't find it. Of course; everyone was in different clothes! She felt shaky as she looked from group to group, trying to decide which one she belonged in; they all looked alike. Recalling Miss Moore's huffy tone when she had told her not to enter with the boys, Misty felt fear rise up. Children were staring at her now as the lines were all neatly formed and she was left alone. As Misty's eyes darted about from group to group, she suddenly noticed that many members in one group were giggling and tittering. That must be her class! She walked over and joined the group just as the second bell sounded and the groups started up the stairs. Misty felt relief flood over her, relief to think she had avoided being singled out as she had been yesterday. When the classes had entered their own rooms and the children stood quietly beside their desks, Misty knew she was right, for she saw Tommy beside his desk. She could hardly wait to sit down and get to her picture.

Once again Misty's head rose as she said the familiar words with the other children. Though she missed the music that had always gone with the Lord's prayer, for it was one of the things Gran often sang as she worked, Misty felt the words themselves draw her face upward, filling her with that quiet wonder she always felt was closer to God than to anything else. The shuffle of thirty children getting into their desks seemed almost rude after such an interlude, but Misty quickly turned her thinking to the desk and the picture. But nobody moved in their desks, so Misty remained still like the others. Miss Moore began.

"I have a few announcements to make before we begin this morning, Class. After reading your stories last night, I see I have to make a few changes. Some of you need to move to different reading groups than those I assigned yesterday. The following students come forward to get new books: Tommy, Brian, Jane, Greta, and Louise. Health Monitors, begin your inspections while I tend to these students."

Misty watched as Tommy and the other four children called went to Miss Moore's desk, and five other girls rose and, starting at the front of each row, looked at each child's face, hair, teeth, hands and fingernails, making little checkmarks on a sheet after they looked at each thing. Before the girl checking Misty's row got to the back, Miss Moore finished with Tommy and the others and called out, "Thomasina, come to the front."

Misty continued to look at her hands, wondering what the girl was going to check, wondering if she should do something before the girl got to her desk. But the girl paused and looked back toward Miss Moore as another ripple of giggles spread across the class.

"Thomasina, I said you were to come to the front and I meant now. The rest of you be quiet!" Only when the Health Monitor nearest Misty whispered, "Go!" did Misty recall that she was to answer to "Thomasina." Once again, she felt all the eyes on her as she made her way down the row to the front.

"I hate to have to send you to the principal on the first full day, Thomasina, but I'm afraid I have no choice. First, I assigned something and told you to hand it in, which you failed to do. Second, when I checked your desk to see how you had spent your time, I found crumpled up crayon wrappers and saw that you had torn the papers from most of your new crayons. That will never do. Then I found something in your desk that suggests that you are less than honest, so you will have to go to the office. Now I find that you are slow and disobedient, failing to come to the front when I call you. You'll have to take this note with you. It spells out your latest rebellion. Mr. Sullivan knows the other problems and is expecting you. Go now!"

Misty felt like running but could barely force herself to turn from Miss Moore and start the walk across the front of the classroom. Only seeing Tommy wink at her gave Misty the strength that it took to leave the room and head down the corridor toward the office. She walked slowly, a very slight smile accompanying the glassy look in her eye, as she thought of the winks Gramps used to send her way when they worked together in his workshop. Sometimes he'd make a great game of it, exaggerating each wink, crinkling up his whole face as he slowly shut one eye and squeezed it so tight even his eyelashes were scarcely visible. She'd wink back and he'd take another turn, this time winking the other eye. Back and forth they'd wink, alternating eyes and each one trying to make a bigger wink until they burst out laughing and began again with small winks. Sometimes they'd even play the game at the table while they were eating, and Gran would laugh and laugh to see the faces they ended up making as each one tried to make a wink bigger than the other. To their delight, they had noticed that one of the barn cats also winked quite often, though she seldom made big winks. Still, when one of them noticed her wink, they'd start the game again and play until they filled the barn with their laughter.

As Misty entered the main office door, she was buoyed up by the happy memories, no longer filled with fear or dread. Thinking once again of Tommy's wink and recalling that Miss Moore had said that he often had to go to the office, Misty felt the first little thrill of the hope of friendship in the making. The encouragement added to the refreshment of the memory enabling Misty to rap comfortably on the counter and look pleasantly and calmly at Mrs. Longacre when she looked up and said, "Ah yes, Thomasina. Mr. Sullivan is expecting you. Come through the gate there and I'll knock on his door and show you in."

Misty was grateful for Mrs. Longacre's hand resting gently on her shoulder and steering her into the office and up to the principal's desk. She enjoyed the slight squeeze she felt indicating that she was to stand still facing Mr. Sullivan, so she looked up at Mrs. Longacre and smiled her thanks as the woman went out and closed the door behind her. Surprised to see a box of crayons, a wad of crumpled wrappers and her own picture lying on the principal's desk, Misty was reminded of the note Miss Moore had given her. She thrust the note toward the principal even as he cleared his throat to begin to speak.

"I must say, I am surprised and a little disappointed to find you here so soon, young lady," he began, even as he unfolded the paper and read the note. "I don't often have my important administrative work interrupted by disciplinary matters in the first few days of school. Most children seem to manage to behave themselves in the early weeks, but then most children are excited to be back to their books after a long summer off school. I suppose you don't know enough to be excited by books, but what is this new show of resistance? I thought I had spelled the necessary rules out yesterday: all students are to respond when spoken to. Miss Moore finds you do not answer when called. This is much worse than I had thought. Do you not speak? What is going on in that unschooled mind of yours? I can't imagine what they were thinking, keeping you isolated on an island like that, without any people your own age, without school, without anything at all. It really is shocking even to think about, and here we are having to pay the price for it now, aren't we? Why never since being appointed principal have I had to deal with such neglect! I certainly hope you aren't going to be so headstrong as to mar my record as administrator here. That would be asking too much of any human. We can't all pay the price of other people's neglect. It is important that we uphold the standards of the school district, and I won't have a newcomer ruin the school's standing and my reputation in the district.

"So, let's begin at the beginning again. Here, we are orderly. Children speak when spoken to and do what they are told. Discipline and order are of utmost importance. You will line up with your fellow students. You will answer when your teacher calls on you. You will do what she says, when she says to do it. Look at this mess on my desk! What ever possessed you to ruin your crayons before school had barely begun? Have you not been taught to respect property, to appreciate your things, to make things last? We expect the supplies that we issue to last the entire term, not just one day. I must assume you didn't know that. Surely even you wanted your crayons to last, even if you don't know what they are for. You might have realized you would be given instruction and then would want the crayons. Surely, though unschooled, at ten years old, you could have figured that out. I am going to return the crayons to Miss Moore. You won't be given others, though these have no wrappers and are rubbed into odd shapes. You'll just have to manage with them, for I'll not reward disrespect for property by giving new crayons."

Misty clasped her hands together, trying hard to concentrate so she would not miss her chance to explain. Mr. Sullivan was clearly mistaken about her. Of course she knew those things and she hadn't ruined her crayons at all. If anything, they worked better now. She was relieved to hear she would get them back. But she couldn't see that she would be given a chance to speak at all. She wrung her hands together as she tried to keep track of the things she must explain even as she continued to listen to Mr. Sullivan carry on.

"As for dishonesty and slovenliness, we'll have neither here. Surely they at least taught you not to cheat, lie or deceive in any way. They are known as honest folk, though they are all quite strange, living on an island like that. They must have taught you to be honest. All Miss Moore could find in your desk was this drawing, a drawing far advanced for a child of your age. I agree with her that you couldn't possibly have done it yourself. Besides, there is a signature here on it, a signature that not only couldn't be your own as it is beautifully scripted but also contains neither your name nor your initials. Clearly, you have taken this from somewhere and hidden it in your desk. That will simply not do. As Miss Moore could find no evidence of work done during the prescribed time, she has no choice but to assume that you simply sat and wasted your time. We will not have time wasted here in my school. I assume that is clear to you now.

"Miss Moore does think, however, that you may have scribbled all over something and thrown it away; that would account for the mess your crayons are in. Now, you must learn once and for all that we do not throw anything into the waste-baskets without first receiving permission. Furthermore, nothing can be removed from the school grounds without permission. You will carry home with you only that which your teacher has ordered you to take home, nothing more and nothing less. Everything you do here is to be handed in. You failed to comply with that rule yesterday. I trust you will not break the same rule more than once.

"I am quite prepared to be lenient with you today, for I think it must be difficult to learn so much at once. However, I assure you I cannot be lenient forever. You'll simply have to try harder. Do what you are told and try not to cause more trouble. I will be keeping this picture, but you must take the crayons back to class with you. I am sure you will need them to fill your time with until we can get those tests done and you can begin to learn and then catch up with your classmates. Mrs. Longacre will give you a note to take back to Miss Moore. You'll get on better with Miss Moore if you answer quickly when spoken to. Now go, child, and please do your best."

The principal rose as he finished his harangue and gestured toward the door. Misty stood rooted to the spot, trying to think of where to begin speaking. Should she speak of her picture first, of reading, writing, crayons, dishonesty? She must explain. Surely it would be dishonest not to explain. But as she opened her mouth to speak, the principal repeated, "Go now!" before loudly calling Mrs. Longacre back into the room.

The lump rose in Misty's throat as she felt Mrs. Longacre's hand on her shoulder, leading her into the outer office. Gone was the smile; gone was the lightness of Misty's step. Instead, head down, feet heavy, she dragged herself along beside the secretary, wishing once again that she were somewhere else. Over and over Misty reminded herself that she wasn't to cry. She swallowed and swallowed, trying to win the battle against the lump and the tears that so badly wanted to fall freely. She was utterly confused, so confused that no single idea came to her. Instead, she just concentrated on not crying. Even when she sat down in the chair that Mrs. Longacre indicated she was to sit in, she continued to fight the battle, to refuse to cry, though her whole body seemed to want to slump down in a heap. Silently she cried out for help, though she couldn't imagine that help were possible. She was beginning to believe that the only help for her was to go back where she came from, back to the island where mornings were new, bright and fresh, where the only kind of tiredness was sleepiness from a long, fresh day, where people listened as often as they spoke, where life was simply lived.

Misty's eyes grew glassy as she almost heard Miss Lily's low, nearly monotonal voice followed by the Captain's deep, musical voice as they spoke to each other, exchanging so much more than information, doing so much more than simply uttering words. She began to relax as she almost heard herself describing the changing colour of the leaves to the Captain as they all three sat in Miss Lily's garden living together, fully, sharing so much more than even she could describe or Miss Lily could paint. She felt the lump recede as she almost tasted the fragrant tea Miss Lily served so beautifully, so quietly, so easily, and she felt strength begin to replace the confusion as she almost heard the little slurp the Captain always made as he drank. A slight smile even began to play at her lips as she relaxed into the chair, thinking of home.

Looking up to see the child sitting in the chair appearing so tiny and fragile yet somehow dreamy and safe, Mrs. Longacre once again felt an overwhelming desire to help somehow. No wonder the child hadn't answered when she'd called; she was probably exhausted what with being thrown into such a completely new situation all of a sudden. Once again the secretary felt a surge of impatience with teachers and principals, many of whom seemed to have forgotten the most basic needs of children, so filled were they with their sense of the importance of teaching. No one seemed to try to understand how difficult this move must be for a child. They seemed to think she would automatically know all kinds of things that no inexperienced person would know; they seemed to forget that there was nothing natural about many of the school rules. Even the brightest of children would not know which classroom to go to, which line-up to get in, which desk to sit in, which permission slip was needed for what. Come to think of it, it would be highly unnatural to assume one needed a permission slip to go back to the classroom to which you had been told to go.

Mrs. Longacre had a real soft spot for students who were sent to the office; usually they had made honest mistakes that were then interpreted by the staff as acts of insolence, disobedience or even rebellion. The whole experience was dreadful for the students, even the ones like Tommy who were sent often and pretended a brave indifference to the whole procedure. Unfooled by their brave fronts, Mrs. Longacre found little ways to encourage each one before sending him or her back to the classroom as required, always careful not to undermine authority, of course.

She very gently shook the little girl to get her attention and begin to explain the rest of the procedure, deciding as Thomasina looked up at her with clear, gentle eyes to accompany this new child back to the room rather than following the standard procedure of sending the child on its way. Again she placed her hand gently on Thomasina's shoulder and led her from the office, speaking very softly as they went, "You've had quite a morning, Thomasina, but you handled yourself very well. You were right to stand so politely and quietly and wait so patiently. Mr. Sullivan has a big job here. It was good of you not to waste any of his time. I'm to give your crayons back, and you must take this note to Miss Moore. It explains that all has been taken care of and the slate wiped clean. That means everyone just begins again at the beginning. So, you get a fresh start. You must knock on the classroom door. When Miss Moore says 'come in,' do so quietly, being sure to close the door softly behind you. Without disturbing the children, who will be working at their desks, take the note to Miss Moore and go quietly to your own desk. She will then tell you what to do as soon as she is free to do so without interrupting anyone else's work. I think they'll be doing writing exercises now, for it will soon be recess time already. I'm sure it won't be long before Miss Moore is able to tell you what she wants you to do."

Misty did as she was told, smiling once again at Mrs. Longacre before turning, knocking on the door and entering the classroom. The class was quiet, students bent over their desks, pens or pencils in their hands. Misty had just sat down and put her crayons back in her desk when she saw Miss Moore approaching with two small books in her hand. She bent down by Misty, putting the books in front of her. One was a half-sized scribbler with lined pages inside. The other was a thin alphabet book. Each page had on it one letter of the alphabet drawn very big on the page and two examples each of the capital and small version of the letter below. Miss Moore whispered, "I have got these Grade One books from which you can learn to print. Begin at the beginning and copy what you see. Fill each page in your little scribbler with the letter from one page in the printer. If you do them quickly and practice them over and over, you'll be able to print the whole alphabet in no time. You'll be able to work on them after recess, too, for we won't have you start arithmetic at this level, of course. Get your pencil out, then, and begin."

To say Misty was disappointed would be an understatement, but once again she was given neither time nor opportunity to object, explain or comment at all. As she got out her pencil and opened her cut-off scribbler, she wondered how she could be expected to learn anything by copying out and practising an alphabet she had known for years. But, wanting to avoid any further trouble, she set in, quickly and easily filling a page with big A's and little a's, big B's and little b's, head bent to her work, but mind elsewhere.

She imagined writing out orders for the Captain and wondered how he was doing without her to write the forms. He had a typewriter that he had used before she had taken over the task for him, so she guessed he would go back to typing out a list of things he needed instead of using the forms the stores sent with the supplies. They had always enjoyed doing the forms together, though. Sometimes she'd write out one list of things he needed while he typed out the other, clacking away at the old machine he used. Often he had said how grateful he was that he had learned to type when he had worked in an office for a while before he'd gone to war. Otherwise, typing would have been one more thing he'd have had to learn after being blinded.

Misty caught herself before she chuckled out loud to think what the Captain would make of her sitting at a little desk copying out the alphabet instead of making useful lists. She was beginning to understand what he'd meant when he had often laughed at some of the things he had been forced to do when he was in the army—"useless, mindless things," he'd said, "repeated over and over for no reason at all, except maybe to give us a good chuckle all these years later when we realized how silly much of it really was." Misty did smile as she carried on deftly filling her little book with the alphabet for no reason other than that she had been told to, but not a sound escaped her. At least she was free as she filled the pages to enjoy whatever thoughts came along keeping her from getting bored by it all.

The clanging bell sent her pencil across the page at an odd angle as Misty jumped once again. The other children immediately rustled their papers, putting their books into their desks and capping their inkbottles before Miss Moore dismissed them for recess. For the first time, Misty perceived the barely restrained excitement in the other children as they held themselves carefully in line, filing out in order, without speaking. She saw, though, that eyes flashed and looks went from one to another as messages flew back and forth, messages she saw but didn't understand. In those looks, all kinds of games were being agreed upon, as were meeting places and some tricks. Thus the minute the students reached the outside door, they burst forward, instantly forming small groups and beginning whatever game they had planned.

Misty was relieved they ran away from her, for she still found the noise and confusion frightening and preferred having time to look around and try to learn from what she saw.

Girls were running over to the swings and beginning to sway back and forth before swinging higher and higher. Misty was amazed at how high they could make the swings go; it looked as if they'd go right over the top. She thought she'd like to swing a little, imagining it would feel much like the big gentle bench swings in Miss Lily's garden and on the verandah at home, so she walked toward the playground swings.

She didn't get far before a small group of children began to circle about her, odd grins on their faces as they chanted, "Cat-girl, Cat-girl, dummy, dummy Cat-girl." Over and over they chanted as they skipped around and around Misty in a tight circle. "Cat-girl, Cat-girl, dummy, dummy Cat-girl. Cat-girl, Cat-girl, dummy, dummy Cat-girl." The chant grew louder and louder, and Misty's heart began to thump in her chest. She put her hands over her ears and tucked her head down, trying to fend off the chant that seemed to hit her, though the children never touched her as they continued skipping round and round. She crouched lower as they carried on, round and round, "Cat-girl, Cat-girl, dummy, dummy Cat-girl." Misty closed her eyes and wrapped her arms tighter around her head, trying desperately to block out the sounds, the attack, the words that just kept hitting her. She scrunched herself into a ball as tight as could be while still standing on two shaking legs.

Suddenly a loud and very angry shout interrupted the chant and sent most of the children scurrying quickly away. "Leave 'er alone or I'll bash yer stupid brains in. She's jist a new kid 'n' ya got no bizness kiddin' her anyway. Ya oughta be beaned, the lotta ya. Yer the worst kinda trash around, 'n' if I catch any 'a ya pickin' on 'er agen, I'll thrash ya. Now git!" Tommy gave one little boy that had not run quickly away a solid shove to emphasize his point before turning to Misty and asking, "You alright? Don't pay no 'tention to 'em. They don' know nuttin' anyhow. They din' mean nuttin'; jist a stupid buncha brats. Don' let 'em get to ya, 'kay?"

Before Misty could answer, one of the big girls that wore the "Playground Monitor" badge stepped up, gave Tommy a pink slip of paper and said, "Off to the office, Tommy; you can't knock little kids down and get away with it. You know that's breaking the rules. Go!"

"But they were pickin' on the new kid. Ya musta saw that. How come yer only sendin' me in? They were jist as bad. Aw c'mon. Whyn't ya jist ferget it? Gimme a break."

"Go now, Tommy, or you'll get another slip. No shoving, no fighting. You know the rules, and I saw you do it."

Tommy stomped off defiantly, leaving Misty standing alone and suddenly lonely. Nothing seemed right. She turned to the Monitor to explain that it was all her fault, but the Monitor was helping the little boy Tommy had shoved and paid no attention to her at all. There seemed once again to be nothing she could do, no one she could talk to, no way she could put things right. As always, she jumped as the bell rang out adding to her sense of helplessness. Slowly she followed the children to their lines and made her way down the corridor, into the classroom and to her desk in an orderly way. Tommy wasn't with the other boys or at his desk as Miss Moore gave instructions:

"Grade Threes, take out your arithmetic books and begin lesson one. You will use yellow notebooks for arithmetic. Don't forget to put your names on the front of your book. Grade Twos, take out your arithmetic books and we will begin lesson one in just a minute. Thomasina, carry on with what I gave you this morning. Tommy? Where's Tommy? I suppose he's been sent to the office again. What a year this is going to be! That's two of you on the first full day. Really! Well, I'll deal with him when he gets back. The rest of you begin your work as I directed."

Misty took her books out and picked up her task where she had left off, her hand automatically filling the lines with the alphabet while her mind listened to Miss Moore instructing the Grade Twos in their arithmetic lesson. They were reviewing the basics, according to what Miss Moore said, and were repeating in unison, in voices not unlike the chant she had heard at recess but with a very different cadence, addition tables: one plus one is two, two plus two is four … Misty might have chuckled to hear yet another of the Captain's examples of silly repetition had she not been preoccupied with wondering what might be happening to Tommy. He seemed to have been gone a long time.

She imagined Mr. Sullivan droning on as he had at her that morning and she felt bad that somehow she had been the reason Tommy had to stand before the principal. She didn't know Tommy, but from the little she'd seen, she guessed it wouldn't be easy for him to stand still and listen. Though it hadn't been hard for her to stand still, she didn't relish the thought of ever having to endure another trip to the office so she kept her hand moving quickly across the page, filling line after line with letters. She looked up when she heard a knock on the door and saw Tommy come in. His hand shook a little as he gave the slip of paper to Miss Moore, but he winked at Misty as he silently took his seat when Miss Moore told him to join the Grade Twos for arithmetic and try to get some answers right.

Misty returned to her own work. She couldn't concentrate on what she was doing, didn't need to, and she soon found the chanted addition tables just as silly and boring as her own repeated printing on the page. She knew, though, that she must not give in to the temptation to begin to embellish things, to turn the meaningless lines on the page into words, phrases, exciting sentences or to make the letters more interesting, drawing them into animals or people. No, she forced herself to keep printing, over and over the same things. She wondered if all the children had had to do this when they first started school. No wonder they were eager to run outside at recess, if they had sat for hours printing the same things over and over. Anything would be better than sitting like this.

If only she could print at the same time as she looked out the window, she'd feel less like she was wasting time. Surely something out there would occupy her mind while she kept this silly task up. There was clearly nothing inside the class to inspire anything but order. Since her book was almost full, she could at least risk a quick look outside. Pausing, she glanced at the treetops and the deep blue sky, all she could see from her desk. Even the colours were richer and warmer, more inspiring than anything inside the room. She wished she could switch to ink for a while; blue would be a nice break from the grey her pencil traced onto the pages. For the first time, she noted that the inkpot had been removed from her desk; she guessed the pen had been taken too. Well, that would be a temptation she wouldn't have to fight. On and on, she'd go with her pencil.

But the outside blues and greens had done their job, so Misty passed her time thinking of all the different colours of blue and green she'd seen at the island. There were so very many, for the colours of the sky and ocean both change with weather and time, never quite the same twice. Outside colours are so alive, more alive than any crayon can make on the page. Misty thought again of how Miss Lily so often captured colour that seemed alive on the canvas when she painted or sketched in pastels and wondered why the colours on the things around her inside were so dead—bright, some of them, but definitely not alive. At the front of the class, above the chalkboard, were posters, one letter for each poster. The first had the letter A and a bright red apple on it. The apple was all one colour, like paper or plastic, not like an apple at all. The ball on the B poster was all one colour blue, not like the sky or the sea, for they were never a single shiny colour blue but a mixture of moving blues, almost misty sometimes. The cat on the C poster was black, all black, not at all like the shimmery coat of even a black cat. Misty scanned all the posters, wondering why whoever made them couldn't have made them alive like Miss Lily made things. They were just dull, dull like printing letters over and over again.

Misty knew her letters were getting sloppy, not so much because she was tired and bored, but because her pencil was all dull. Gramps had sharpened pencils with a little pocket-knife, but Misty didn't have a pocket-knife, so she just carried on as best she could. She took to imagining that each of her letters was a different colour, the rich, misty blue of the early morning sky, the crisp, bright blue of the afternoon, the deep, deep blue of the very late night sky, the grey-blue of the sea just before a storm, the grey-black of the sea in the midst of a storm. On and on she made her letters, happy to be left alone to see beautiful things as she carried out her mindless task.

Miss Moore's voice calling for the class' attention saved Misty from really having to worry about what she would do when she ran out of pages, for her half book was almost full.

Arithmetic was over and they were to have a short lesson in spelling before lunch. Misty wondered what spelling might be apart from reading. She must listen carefully. Miss Moore soon explained that they would be doing three different things to accommodate the split class. There would be Grade Two spelling, Grade Three spelling and spelling bees. During spelling bees, the Grade Twos would be given Grade Two words and the Grade Threes would be given Grade Three words. The class would be divided into teams. As there weren't an even number of boys and girls, Miss Moore couldn't divide the class that way, so she'd made four smaller teams of seven each. Though there were thirty children in the class, Miss Moore was leaving Thomasina and Tommy off the teams for the first part of the year. They would work on their own during spelling, writing out the lists she gave them to learn. She read out the names that were on each team and showed the class where she would post the lists. Each team was named for a colour. The team that had the most stars at the end of each week would get a bigger star. At the end of the year, the team with the most big stars would get a prize. For today, however, the class would just practice a little spelling.

Miss Moore began the practice by calling Linda's name. Linda stood beside her desk, and Miss Moore said, "Baby." Linda said, "Baby. B-A-B-Y. Baby," and sat down. Miss Moore said, "That's right," checked something on her desk and called out another name. So it went, student after student spelling silly little words. When a student made a mistake, Miss Moore would call on her again, giving easier words until she got one right. Then she would give the child a list of the words she had got wrong and tell her she must practise them for tomorrow. The bigger kids were told they had to write the incorrectly spelled word out ten times and hand the paper in the next day. One little boy was told he'd have to stay in at lunchtime until he could get at least one word correct.

Misty had no way of knowing that the reason Miss Moore did not call her name or Tommy's that day was that she didn't have the courage to try either one of them. She'd rather not call on them at all than have the battle on her hands that she was sure she would have, for she knew Tommy would get most every word wrong and she assumed Thomasina would as well. She was not going to risk having to keep either of them in or, worse, having to send either of them to the office for the second time in a single day. Having two students sent in one morning was almost more than she could stand as it was. So even Miss Moore was relieved when the lunchtime bell rang.

9.

A Friend

Misty held back a little, unsure what to do about lunch. She had brought the lunch that Aunt Augusta had packed and had left it in the cloak room on the shelf above her coat hook just as she had seen the other children do, but she had no idea where or when to eat it, so she watched the other children. She followed along as they filed out as orderly as ever. Each child stepped out of the row just long enough to take the lunch from the shelf and get back in line as they passed by the coat hooks on the way out to the playground. There, as always, the children burst out in much noise and activity, seeming to run in every direction. Some children, mostly the boys, seemed to eat on the run. Most of the girls sat down in groups and ate their lunches. Misty decided she would eat her lunch on a swing, as there weren't many children there yet. She wasn't at all hungry and she stifled an inward groan at the size of the lunch Aunt Augusta had packed. There was a big sandwich, cookies and two pieces of fruit. Well, maybe here at school it didn't matter how much or how fast one ate. Nobody seemed to pay much attention to her, or to eating, for that matter. Slowly she settled on a swing, balanced her lunch on her lap and opened her sandwich wrapper as she swung ever so gently back and forth. She wondered if it was necessary to eat the lunch but she thought she'd better try.

Swinging slowly, she chewed away at her sandwich, noticing the level of noise on the playground increase as the eager students finished eating and paid closer attention to their rough games. She wondered how long she would be safe from the chanting of the children, not realizing that Tommy had scared them off at least for a while. He was busy playing tag with the older boys but he kept one eye on Misty the whole time, and the smaller students knew he'd be there in a minute if they hurt her, so they left her alone. Misty finished half her sandwich, wrapped the other half up, put it back in her lunch pail and took out one cookie. Oh, how she longed for a real cookie. These ones that came in a bag from the store were very, very sweet yet strangely tasteless. Without even taking a bite, Misty put the cookie back and bit into her apple instead. It was good to have an apple from the tree at last. So she sat, swinging gently and eating her apple. Children swarmed and ran all about, yelling and calling, some almost screaming as they chased each other in the strange game called "tag." Down on the field, she could see older children kicking a big ball around, moving from one end of the field to the other, back and forth, running, kicking, yelling. They seemed happy.

One of the playground monitors interrupted Misty's lunch and thoughts when she came up and said, "Time to give someone else a turn on the swing. Everyone has to share."

Misty looked around. There wasn't anyone waiting in lines or standing nearby at all, so she wondered who she was supposed to share with but thought it best to just get off the swing. The ever-watchful Tommy didn't agree. Up he ran, yelling, "Leave 'er alone, ya bully! Ya know we only hafta get off if someone is waitin'. Yer jist pickin' on her cuz she's new. Someone oughta monitor you guys!"

More than anything, Misty did not want any trouble, so she opened her mouth to say it was okay, but the monitor beat her to it. "Now look, Tommy. You'll get sent up again if you don't mind your own business. I'm just doing what I'm supposed to do. Nobody gets such long turns on the swing. There will be a line-up just as soon as the Grade Ones finish their lunches and come out, so I'm just clearing the way. You go back to playing tag before you're in trouble again yourself."

Misty saved Tommy then without knowing she was doing it. She had stepped off the swing and begun moving toward Tommy, turning his attention from the monitor to herself.

"Y' okay, kid?" he said. "Don't let 'em push ya 'round. Long as ya move around a bit, they'll leave ya 'lone. An' I won't let anyone bug ya like at recess, 'kay?"

Quietly Misty said, "Thanks, Tommy. I'm sorry you got into trouble this morning. You didn't have to. They didn't hit me or anything. But thanks anyway. Was it very bad at the principal's office?"

"Naw," answered Tommy, "I c'n take it. Bin there lots before. Got the strap, though. Sullivan wanted ta start me out right this year, he said, so he gave me three on each hand. Din' hurt too much, though. My hands are still tough from rope swingin' over the lake this summer. Gotta go, though; the guys'll be waitin.' See ya later!"

Misty took Tommy's advice and kept moving. She walked slowly around the playground, watching the children, looking at the school itself to get a better sense of its size and its layout, and enjoying the fresh air, especially over by the trees at the edge of the clearing. When the warning bell rang, she was startled but didn't jump as much as before. She was adapting a little, learning to shut out much of the clamour that was around her. Though she hurried across the playground to get in line, she found herself almost as reluctant as the other children to return to the classroom. She loved the late summer air almost as much as the clear fall and spring air and she had enjoyed her time outside. Besides, what might she have to look forward to inside? More printing letters? At least the afternoon wasn't as long as the morning, and she'd be able to enjoy her walk home in the fresh air.

Misty soon found she wouldn't have to do more letters that day. The whole class was to have a special group Social Studies lesson that afternoon. All would be expected to watch and listen to what Miss Moore had to say. Misty wondered what social things they would study but soon discovered that the lesson was in geography, for Miss Moore had a big globe on her desk and had pulled a huge map of the world down in front of the blackboard. It was really quite amazing to Misty to see such a large map that pulled down like a giant window blind. At home, they'd had much smaller maps, the ones that came in the National Geographic Magazine and some larger sea charts that Gramps had ordered from Victoria, but nothing as large as this. As Misty loved looking at maps, she felt quite excited. She immediately began imagining all the things that she, Gramps and Gran had read about far away countries, about deserts in

Africa and all the different animals that roam there, the tall giraffes and huge elephants, the zebras and lions. She looked forward to hearing more.

Alas, Miss Moore was droning on about globes and maps as if they were things in themselves instead of representations of and therefore windows to the whole world. Misty tried to listen as she heard about the globe spinning on its pin just as the earth spins on its axis and about the lines of latitude and longitude that divided both map and globe. She wondered if Miss Moore would ever get to a point about the world, about life. Instead, she heard that the globe was flattened into a map such as the one on the wall in the same way that an orange peel can be flattened if you cut it carefully into sections. Miss Moore even held up such a cut orange peel, one that remained joined at the top but dropped down in flat petals kind of like a flower instead of an orange. Misty wondered if that was a good illustration of mapping the world and thought not. Why didn't she just point to the map so the children could see where the countries were and compare them to the globe that was right in front of them? There were so many exciting things to see on a map; surely soon Miss Moore would get to them.

Misty waited eagerly, listening as hard as she could, fighting off her impatience, resisting giving in to her boredom. She heard Miss Moore explain about cartographers, men who make maps, and how important those men are. Then she heard about geographers and teachers, men who study and teach all about the earth, and how important those men are. Surely soon she'd have to get to talking about the world and all the exciting things about it, but instead Miss Moore went on to the importance of children having maps and globes, of atlases that important men had made for older children and how much the students had to look forward to when they moved into higher grades and could look at a whole atlas of maps of the world. The children should all be grateful for the wonderful globe and map the school board had provided for them and should respect them at all times, being sure never to touch them or get them dirty. She, herself, would always use a pointer when showing something on the map, not putting fingerprints all over. Misty wondered how else she might reach to point to, say, the arctic or even the northern parts of Canada and the USSR if she didn't use something other than her finger, but remained quiet. Realizing at last that nothing interesting about the world or life was going to come from a woman who simply wanted to assert the importance of the people who put things together for the school, Misty allowed herself to slip off to more fascinating things.

Her eyes grew glassy as she thought about the armchair journeys that she used to take with Gramps and the Captain. One winter night they had sat with a map and pictures of the Nile. Gramps had followed along on the map, and Misty had described the pictures to the Captain as they had all three ventured together along the mighty river. Once, when the maps and pictures had been of France, the Captain had added his own descriptions, had really brought to life the pictures that Misty described, for he had been in France during the war and had seen many of those things. They'd laughed so much at themselves for taking such journeys without leaving the warmth of the fire. But Gramps had also said that no matter how small your own world may be, you could always grow bigger by looking beyond it, by reading and studying and even by dreaming. So, together they had dreamed, learned and grown, all for pure pleasure and companionship. It was exciting to try to imagine flat land, desert land, frozen land when all Misty knew was such lush, mountainous land. It made a person feel small and big at the same time, small compared to a world so varied and large, but big to be part of something so huge. She smiled, recalling Gramps and the Captain both chuckling to hear her say it was good to feel big and small at once. There was more warmth in their laughter than in the fire itself.

The snap of the huge map rolled back up brought a shiver and a chill to Misty, as she was herself snapped back to the classroom. Miss Moore was wrapping up her lesson by saying, "So you see, children, without cartographers we would have no wonderful maps to study and we'd be unable to learn about the world. That makes cartographers very important people. Maybe some of you will want to become cartographers when you grow up, so we'll have to work very, very hard."

Misty forced herself to stop wondering if the cartographer that Miss Moore thought so important wanted people to look at his maps and feel the big and small in the world or to look at his maps and think about him and how important he was. Then she forced herself to stop wondering when they might be allowed to stop sitting around trying to listen and get on with some of the hard work she kept hearing about. Made uncomfortable by her own impatience and her critical thoughts, Misty silently asked forgiveness and followed a higher path, thinking instead of both the magnificent world represented on the map and the wonderful life that enables people to work. Miss Moore had shifted, too, and was speaking of the things to come as they worked along together, studying maps, pictures and books. She was looking forward to a great year with the children.

In preparation for dismissal, Miss Moore said she would collect the notebooks the children had worked in that day. She reminded them to be sure they had printed their names neatly in the top right hand corner of their books before passing them forward. Misty took her half-book out and neatly printed "Miss T" in the top corner as instructed and passed the book ahead as the other children were doing. She began to feel happy anticipation of walking out of the school and into the clear air. Odd, how stuffy it got inside a room with thirty people.

"Thomasina, what is this?" both sliced through and intensified the stuffiness, making Misty pull her arms close to her sides. "I distinctly told you to put your names on your books. What is this nonsense you've written here? I expected if you couldn't write your own name yet, you'd have me do it for you. Instead, you've put this silliness here. Your name is Thomasina; T-H-O-M-A-S-I-N-A; Thomasina. You will copy it one hundred times on a piece of paper tonight and hand it in to me in the morning. Is that clear? No excuses. Pick up the paper as you leave the classroom. Remember, one hundred times: T-H-O-M-A-S-I-N-A. It had better be on my desk first thing in the morning! Now, class dismissed."

Misty filed out with the other children, taking the piece of foolscap that was held out by Miss Moore when Misty passed her desk. Lunch box in one hand, paper in the other, Misty left the school alone and crestfallen, the anticipation she had felt gone. Instead of the promised story, a reprimand and command had ended the school day. She had failed again. Eyes down, she walked across the playground to the stairs that led up to the road, increasing her speed slightly as she heard a hissing behind her:

"Cat-girl, Cat-girl, dummy, dummy Cat-girl." The chant was just above a whisper, a few voices hissing in unison, "Cat-girl, Cat-girl, dummy, dummy Cat-girl; doesn't know her own name, dummy, dummy Cat-girl."

Misty sped up, but the hissing kept up just behind her, intensifying, increasing. Her ears began to ring and burn, and Misty broke into a run. Still she heard, "Cat-girl, Cat-girl, dummy, dummy Cat-girl; doesn't know her own name, dummy, dummy Cat-girl."

She ran faster, tears beginning to stream down her cheeks. Despite the voices hissing and ringing in her head, Misty sent off a silent but desperate "Help; please help!" as she fled along the sidewalk, looking for a place to hide.

"Stop! Now!" brought both Misty and the little band of taunters to a rapid halt. Misty watched in amazement as Tommy, fists doubled up, arms bent, walked steadily toward the little group yelling, "I warned ya. Leave 'er 'lone. One more word ever 'n' I'll beat yer brains AND rat on ya too. She does, too, know 'er own name and ya better stop callin' 'er Cat-girl if ya don' wanna bloody nose, d'ya hear? Ya think yer so big. What if yer moms see ya with yer prissy clothes all dirtied up? One more word 'n' ya'll go home so dirty ya won't think yer so big after that. Now git! All o' ya, and don' lemme see 'r hear ya near her agin. Git!"

Tommy poked the air a couple of times with one grubby fist, and the children ran more quickly than when they had been chasing Misty.

"Gee, I'm sorry," he said, walking over to Misty. "I wuz late 'er it wouldn'a happened. Ya better wait fer me after school fer a few days 'til they know I mean bizness. I live jist a mile er so past ya anyway, so we may 's well go t'gether. The guys won't kid me none. They know better by now. It's jist those prissy kids. Don' usually bother with 'em none, they're so stupid. But I'll get 'em ta leave ya' lone. C'mon. Y' okay?"

Misty was relieved to see Tommy, relieved to have the hissing chant ended, but she was suddenly so tired that she couldn't stop the tears running down her cheeks. She did hold back the sobs a little, but she was worn out and confused again. Tommy led her off the sidewalk onto a little worn path across the corner of some property. "Not s'posta cut this corner," he said, "but 'ts okay t'day cuz ol'man Mike ain't never home on Wenzday; goes fishin.' There's a place ta sit over here 'neath his apple tree. You c'n rest 'n' I'll git an apple. Sure git hungry a whole day at school."

Misty sat down beneath the tree and held her lunch box out to Tommy. "Here," she said between sniffs and sobs, "I didn't finish my lunch. You have it if you're hungry."

Tommy's eyes grew wide at the sight of sandwich, cookies and orange, and he said, "Are ya sure? Looks like ya di'n eat nuttin'"

"Help yourself, "she said, "just give me the napkin so I can blow my nose. You can have the food. They give me way too much to eat, and I never can finish it. Then they send me to my room. Maybe if you eat this lunch, I'll have enough room for dinner tonight. I'm not hungry at all, though. Gosh, it's turning out to be a struggle here. Too much food at home, the principal's office at school, have to write my name out and I don't even have a pencil. And then those kids! I'm sure glad for you, Tommy. I don't know what I'd have done. I could have outrun them I think, but I guess Aunt Augusta would be pretty mad if I ran wild like that, at least I think that's what she'd say. Thanks, Tommy. You won't get in trouble again, will you?"

"Naw, I don' think so. Pretty sure they won' tell this time. Usta gettin' in trouble anyway. Say, how come ya don' jist answer to yer name, though? How come ya put the wrong name on yer book?"

"Oh, Tommy, I just forgot again. I never was called 'Thomasina' in my life. My folks all called me Misty, and that's what I wrote on pictures and things. I can't seem to get used to Thomasina. But, Tommy, how come they chant "Cat-girl" at me and call me dummy?"

"Aw. They're jist stupid. There's a book about a cat called Thomasina, that's all, 'n' I guess they call ya dummy cuz ya never talk 'n' fergit yer name. I'll fix 'em though; don' you worry none. How come ya never talk, though?"

"When do children ever get a chance to talk here? Look at Miss Moore. She thinks I can't read or write or anything, and I can do all those things, but she yells at me and won't let me say anything. It's the same with Aunt Augusta and even the principal. Yesterday I drew a picture, and they took it and said I couldn't have done it, but they never gave me a chance to say I did or even to show them what I can do. They think because I've never been to school I don't know anything. How do I tell them, Tommy?"

"Gosh, I dunno that. I do know ya better not talk at the principal; he'll whip ya in no time fer that. Calls it 'talkin' back' and gives ya an extra strap. No, ya jist let 'em talk, take what they give ya 'n' leave. Ain't worth it to try to 'splain. Least I've learned that now. Only thing yer allowed ta say ta the principal is 'Yes, sir.' I reckon ya jist wait. They find out the truth sooner 'r later. Say, they usta call me Thomas, ya know, 'n' they said that was my real name 'n' I'd jist hafta git usta it, but they call me Tommy now. My pa fixt it up. They say he ain't no good, my pa, 'n' he ain't when he's drunk but he's real fine when he ain't drunk, ya know, 'n' mostly he ain't drunk. One time when he had ta go ta the school cuz me 'n' one o' my brothers got in a bad fight with some o' the rich kids, he jist told 'em 'no more Thomas.' Maybe yer uncle could fix it."

"Oh, he's not my uncle, Tommy; they just want me to call them aunt and uncle, but he wouldn't fix it anyway. They call me Thomasina, too. I guess I'll get used to it after tonight. Printing it one hundred times should remind me, don't you think? At least, if I can get a pencil and if I am allowed. There are as many rules in this house as there are at school. I haven't figured them all out yet. I never had rules before, so I guess I get mixed up. It seems I'm always making people unhappy or mad here and I've never seen that before. I wish I could be better."

"Aw shucks. It ain't you makin' 'em mad 'r unhappy; they're jist like that. Lookit how they harp at me. Don' matter what I do, they're never happy, jist holler about wantin' more. Funny thing, my pa ain't like that an' they say he's no good. I c'n do whatever my pa sez, no problem, but when they tell me ta do sumpin', I jist can't git it. My pa sez do the times tables 'n' I do 'em, but the teacher sez, 'Well, Tommy, do you suppose you might get one right answer today?' in that la-de-da voice, 'n' I git th' answer wrong. I don' wanna git it wrong, ya know; it jist comes out wrong. So, I jist stay in the same class. My pa tells 'em I c'n do it at home, but they don' believe him cuz they say he's no good, and when they test me at school, I fail. I figger it don't matter none any more. C'mon, now. It's gettin' late and we don' want more trouble fer ya. We can talk and walk."

Getting up and following along, Misty continued, "But Tommy, it's wrong, what they do. They shouldn't talk to you like that. And if you know the answers, there's no reason to sit in the same class over and over, is there?"

"I dunno. It's jist some kinda game. I learn better 'n' better to stay outa trouble. They don' notice, but I hardly ever go ta th' office like I usta; maybe only two-three times a week now. Usta go most every day. It's jist that I git so mad sometimes when they pick on new kids like you 'r when they git real stupid. My pa sez he's right proud when I git sent up for defendin' the little kids, but he gits mad when I'm sent up fer my own stupid temper. He figgers I'm doin' better, so I don' mind. B'sides it's fun at lunchtime and fun at home. Me 'n' my pa do neat things. We're buildin' a boat, ya know. But how 'bout you? You ain't got no nice home, do ya? Can't be good livin' with ol' Hughes."

"Well, I am having trouble, but I have a nice room and good memories for company. There's lots of birds outside, and I see a cat in the garden often. Maybe one day we'll get to be friends, but so far I'm stuck mostly in my room because I can't eat my dinner, so I haven't been near the cat. You know how long it takes to make friends with a cat anyway! I'm okay. I really miss my little dog and the Captain and Miss Lily. I wish I could write letters to them or something but I have no paper and don't know how to mail stuff from here. I'll be okay, though. Life is good even if sometimes things are hard. Besides, now I've met you, I have a friend."

"Gosh. Gotta cut now, Misty. I take the road down the hill here. You wait fer me here in the mornin'. Jist a minit." Tommy fished around in the bottoms of his pockets, seeming to search the very lining of his overall jeans. "Ah, thought I had one!" he said, drawing a stub of a pencil from deep within a pocket; "take this. It's jist one me 'n' my pa use fer figgerin' on the boat. Rub it on the side 'n' it'll sharpen up okay. Least that'll keep ya from the office tomorra. See ya in the mornin'!"

With a wink and wave, Tommy headed off down the hill. Misty took the few steps past the thick lilac hedge across to the driveway, feeling relieved and happier than she had since she'd left Old Lundstrom. Silently she breathed the deepest of thanks.

10.

Quiet Joy in the Evening

When Misty went into the kitchen and put her lunch box on the counter, Aunt Augusta was taking off her light sweater. "Oh, there you are," she said; "I've just come back from a meeting of the Hospital Auxiliary and I was a little anxious that you'd get home before me. If that ever happens, you must sit patiently on the back step and wait for me. I can't always get home just when I want to, you know. Sometimes meetings run late or there are important people for me to see afterwards. I expect, in fact, I'll often be late this year, for today they've asked me to chair the annual bazaar committee, and there's a tremendous amount of responsibility there. I'm thrilled, of course. I simply must put on the best bazaar ever. Oh, Hugh will be so pleased; it will be a boost for his campaign for city counsellor this year. Things are working out just as we'd hoped. It does pay to be in the right place and associate with the right people. And I'm sure you'll be able to help us with that, too. Why I know when you and Marilyn Murphy start chumming around, I'll even be able to get in with her mother. It's going to be so useful having a child after all. I see your lunch box is empty. That's a relief.

"I assume your day was just fine. Why I remember when I was in school, there was no end to the fun. I loved colouring pictures and doing the writing exercises; I could be so neat, you know, and chattering with the girls at lunchtime was such fun. Isn't it nice to fit in with all the right clothes and latest hair fashions? Why you know exactly where you belong just by looking at clothes, and that group at the top is just where you belong. I'm sure in a matter of days you'll know everyone who is anyone. It must be so exciting for you to finally be with children after all those ghastly years with crotchety and very strange old people. I don't know why we didn't think to rescue you sooner. Of course, it wouldn't have been nearly so convenient as now, nor did we need a child's contacts until Hugh actually enters the race for counsellor. I hear you are in Miss Moore's class. That turns out to be an added advantage, for they say she is seeing old judge Morris' son. That ought to be an in for us if she is properly impressed with you, so you be sure to be on your best behaviour at all times. Why there seems to be no end of possibilities after all. I'm just elated today. The chairman of the Auxiliary bazaar; I'm sure even you can appreciate that! We'll have to celebrate tonight! I'll cook some of Hugh's favourites. Why on earth are you just standing there, child? You know you are to put your other clothes on when you come home. Don't forget to wash your hands well. I do wish they didn't have all the children together; it's not right having you in with those grubby worker children. I wish we had a private school here. Now that would ..."

Misty wasted no time trying to pay attention to Aunt Augusta's prattle once she heard that she was to change. As she went to her room, she smiled to herself a little as she wondered what Tommy might call Aunt Augusta's voice if he called Miss Moore's "la-de-da." Misty wasn't sure what Tommy meant, but she was sure that there were more different voices and tones here than she ever imagined possible. Not all of them were easy to listen to; in fact, most of them unsettled her, confused her a little. She didn't feel comfortable with any of them, except the secretary and Milly at the shop, and even Milly had sometimes used an odd tone when she talked to Aunt Augusta. It was as if none of the tones or voices really fit the words or the people, and that lack of fit was distracting, confusing. Misty was uncomfortable, though, with feeling critical of the people, and she sensed that Tommy was being critical when he sort of mocked Miss Moore's voice. She was sure Miss Moore meant well, though she did sound funny, slightly tinny like Aunt Augusta. Still, it was difficult for Misty to get used to such a barrage of words and voices. Even as she washed her hands, she could hear Aunt Augusta continuing her talking in the background. She'd not stopped talking since Misty came in.

Misty thought she may as well slip into her room and start writing her name out. She quickly calculated that she could fit

"Thomasina" five times on each line; so only twenty lines and she'd be done. That meant she could use the bottom bit of the paper to rub the pencil up into a point. It wouldn't take long. She knelt at her windowsill and began. She was right; five fit just nicely on a line. She didn't waste any time day-dreaming at all, so she actually managed to finish her list, as she came to call it, even as Aunt Augusta continued her talking in the kitchen. When Misty had done the twenty lines, she carefully folded the bottom of the page above where she had made the smudges for sharpening the pencil. Licking her finger, she dampened the fold, pressed it hard again, then deftly tore off the bottom five lines. Before folding the paper and putting it with the clothes that Aunt Augusta had already laid out for the next day, Misty carefully printed her name in the top right-hand corner: Miss T. She tucked the pencil beside the paper so she could return it to Tommy and smiled, relieved to have been able to complete her task. So far, things were going well.

As she returned to the kitchen, Misty smiled, again thinking deepest thanks for Tommy, who had saved this situation as well as rescued her from those who had followed her after school. Tommy was the first comfortable person she'd met. Only the extent of her excitement at having talked with him gave her the slightest hint of how much she had missed comfortable people. Hearing Aunt Augusta talk almost frantically about bazaars and campaigns, Misty wondered if she'd ever learn to be as comfortable with her and in this new place as she had always been at home. She breathed more thanks for Tommy and tried to pay attention to Aunt Augusta as she set a place at the kitchen table for herself before going into the dining room with cutlery for Aunt Augusta and Uncle Hugh. Even this little task that Aunt Augusta had decided she was able to do helped Misty feel better than when she was left sitting watching. That, too, made her thankful.

Misty soon realized that Aunt Augusta was still talking about her own day and didn't expect any kind of response from Misty, so she felt free to slip into her own world as she worked. In her head, she began a little game, a game that she had played occasionally with Gran after Gramps had died, a game that was to become a lifeline for her before long. In the first while after Gramps had died, some of the days were really hard, and the loneliness they each felt at times would have been crushing had they not both felt free to weep. But as they struggled together to learn some of the tasks Gramps had so easily done, Gran had started the game meant to strengthen them and keep them going. She'd list something positive, something happy, some good part of what they were doing. Then Misty would take a turn, finding something good to look at. Sometimes they'd laugh and laugh when they had to list something almost silly in their desperation to see good in difficulty.

Misty wondered why she hadn't thought of the game before; it was a game she could play alone. So, she began to list all the things, even the tiniest things, for which she was thankful, and even as she began her list, she felt better than when she had allowed herself those critical thoughts of voices and such. She found herself thankful that Aunt Augusta liked to talk so much about herself, for it took all the attention off Misty. She was thankful that she had been banished to the kitchen to eat, for that, too, gave her time alone, away from critical eyes. She was thankful that she hadn't got into any trouble from Aunt Augusta after school. She was thankful that she was a tiny bit hungry and might be able to eat her dinner. She was thankful for hope.

And suddenly she was thankful for all those unsettling tones in voices, for they gave her clues. Even as Misty had occupied herself with her game, she had heard Aunt Augusta's tone change and she began to listen again, in time to hear something quite different.

"Dinner is almost ready now, and I must explain something quickly before Hugh gets home. I've spoken with several people today and decided that it will be fine for us to leave you alone for short periods when we must go out in the evenings. I wasn't sure, you know, just how old a child must be to stay alone. Hugh insists that it is unnecessary and wasteful to pay for a sitter when a child can remain alone legally at age ten. I'm a little uneasy because you haven't proven you can be trusted, but we simply must attend this meeting together this evening, so we are leaving you alone. The meeting begins at eight, so I don't see a problem. It is a school night so you should be in bed by then anyway, and there's no harm you can get into in bed. So, directly after dinner, you will prepare yourself for bed. I want you in bed before we leave. I'm sure we'll be back not long after ten o'clock, but you'll be sound asleep by then. I am going to trust that you will not get into any trouble. Is that clear? You will go to bed and stay there. And please eat all your dinner tonight so we don't have to be all upset when we leave for the meeting. You really can be a trying child. I'm not sure we have done the right thing after all ..."

Misty was free again as Aunt Augusta's voice shifted along with her subject. Misty wondered at Aunt Augusta's tendency to swing from one thing to another, to go from being pleased to have a child to worrying away about what a chore it was having a child, but she was almost getting used to it. She suspected that during dinner Aunt Augusta would be back exclaiming about how much use Thomasina would be to their election plans. None of it made much sense to Misty but neither did it really matter. She was beginning to recognize that Aunt Augusta talked a great deal but said little and meant even less. Talking seemed to be just something she did, like a nervous habit or something. Misty didn't need to try to understand either the words or the habit. Her only desire was peace, not just for herself but also for others. She longed to bring happiness to people, to see people smile, to share warmth and joy with others. She would, then, try once again to eat all of her dinner, not so much to obey Aunt Augusta or Uncle Hugh, but just out of a sincere desire to do what is right and to keep peace or even bring happiness. Misty knew, though, that she'd need help this night, for "Hugh's favourite foods" usually included lima beans. So even as she heard the car coming in the driveway, she sent up a prayer for help.

As Aunt Augusta and Uncle Hugh sat in the dining room eating and talking excitedly as expected, Misty sat at the kitchen table, picking up the game where she had left off as she ate. She was grateful for being able to eat alone so she could give the thanks that was due. She was grateful that the food was bland rather than spicy in some truly unpalatable way. She was grateful that there were mashed potatoes in which to try to hide her lima beans. She was grateful that lima beans weren't any bigger than they are. She was grateful that there was a slice of tomato that she could save for last so she could keep looking forward to something tasty. She was grateful that she hadn't counted the lima beans so wouldn't be discouraged at either how few she had eaten so far or how many there were left. Despite the lima beans, Misty was soon smiling to herself; her list was getting pretty desperate so kind of funny! They really did give her too much. She almost giggled realizing that she thought that even one lima bean was too much, but that wasn't what she meant. She would try to be fair. Surely no child her size could comfortably eat as much as Uncle Hugh ate, but that's how much they gave her. She had to keep trying. She was grateful that she had enough to eat. No, that really was desperate. She kept eating as she switched over to silently humming little tunes in her head, hoping to get her attention off food and just get the task done.

Hearing the sounds in the other room indicate that she was running out of time, Misty stopped her silent humming and sent up a plea for help, trying to chew faster. She was thankful for even the thin milk to help wash the lima beans down. Again she smiled, realizing that she had just given thanks for something that had seemed dreadful to her when she first came. She still missed the rich, whole milk from the cow at home, but she was, indeed, grateful for this store stuff after all. She kept on eating, ignoring the stuffed feeling that was all too familiar to her. Alas, she had run out of time and there was still food on the plate as Aunt Augusta came into the kitchen with their empty dishes. Misty swallowed quickly and braced herself, but the storm didn't come! Instead Aunt Augusta swept up her plate saying, "No time for any more tonight, young lady. At least you ate a fair bit. Now, I'll need you to clean up the kitchen while Uncle Hugh and I get ready. Work quickly so you can also get ready and be in bed before we go. Hurry up then."

Misty could hardly believe her good fortune but even as she got the stool and began cleaning up, she asked forgiveness and gave thanks. She had asked for help, after all; she shouldn't have been surprised to receive it. Still, this was more than she had expected. No more fight with lima beans this night and she could clean up the kitchen. Then she'd be left alone, truly alone, for the first time since she left the island. She felt rich beyond belief and hummed softly as she worked.

Just as she put the last dishes away and was folding the towel, Aunt Augusta entered dressed as Misty had never seen her before. She had on a deep purple dress with a short jacket of the same colour on top. Her earrings looked huge to Misty, as did the necklace and ring that matched them. By contrast, her hat seemed small and looked very precariously balanced on the unmoving hair. She was pulling on slinky, black gloves as she clipped across the kitchen in her high heels, fussing loudly, "Oh dear, I'm just not sure, and you're not ready for bed much less in it. Hurry now before Hugh is ready. You simply must be safe in bed, or I'll worry all night. Do I look fine? Is my dress straight? Does my slip show? Oh, this has to go well. Quickly, child, get to bed. Just leave the stool and hurry up! Oh really, life can be such a trial, so many little things to worry about ..."

Misty listened no more as she hurried off to get ready for bed. She was a little surprised that Aunt Augusta had not even given her a chance to answer those questions about her clothes, but she was grateful she hadn't, for she could not honestly have said that she looked fine. Misty thought she looked uncomfortable at best. She didn't waste any time getting her nightie on and getting into bed. It was nice to go to bed for some reason other than having been sent there for not eating her food. Aunt Augusta looked in the door and reminded her to stay exactly where she was and not get into any trouble at all before saying good bye, closing the bedroom door and hurrying out of the house. Misty heard the back door close, the car doors close and the car pull out of the driveway. She stretched and wriggled happily in her bed, breathing deeply, sighing contentedly as she let herself relax into the pillow. A great well of pleasure rose up in her as she turned her face toward the window, enjoying the evening light filtering through the thin curtain. The beauty of the quiet that filled the house stirred such joy in Misty that tears began to trickle down her cheeks, unnoticed. She sighed deeply again.

Misty was surprised to feel loneliness filter through the surge of joy. Had she thought to look back at all that she had been through since leaving the island, she'd have realized just how battered and exhausted she was. The new life in town with all its noise had worn on her just as much as the individual incidents in the life. The changes were phenomenal, almost as extreme as changes get. And yet Misty had not felt lonely out of need to talk to someone. It was not her instinct to seek people to help with her troubles. The island people had so unconsciously shared burdens that Misty had no concept of having ever had any. Her life had not included the kind of personal burden she now carried, and she had no desire or instinct to share those kinds of burdens with people, the burdens of pain, of confusion, of isolation, of being wronged. Instead she walked in her simple faith, leaning on the everlasting arms, instinctively calling out to the only one she knew could help. Her simple faith, her instinct to call out, saved her from accumulating burdens or from worrying about what was past. She was always simply relieved and thankful when a trial was over, when the help came. She seldom questioned the means of the help, so sure was she of its source. She was just grateful for all she was given.

But joy was different. Joy was for sharing; it increased when it was shared. It rose up and had to be shared. And joy rose up from many simple and beautiful things, from natural things. More than anything else, Misty missed solitude. Now that she had a little, she was overwhelmed with the joy of it. Simple solitude brought such joy that Misty, alone in the house, ached with the loneliness of having no one with whom to share. Even calling out her thanks to the source of both the solitude and the joy didn't seem to help. Instead, she became aware of the tears on her cheeks. Quickly, she wiped them away. But it was no use. She missed her little brown dog. She missed the Captain. She missed Miss Lily. Oh, what she would give to see them, to feel them, to be with them!

"Oh God," she cried out quietly, "please help me. I mustn't cry and get things wet. Aunt Augusta will be furious again, and I don't want to make her unhappy. Please look after the Captain and Miss Lily and all the animals. Somehow let them know I miss them. Can you give them this bit of joy somehow? They know the joy of the quiet. Bless them, God."

As Misty prayed, her tears dried and she felt a great warmth all around as she thought of the Captain and Miss Lily. It was almost like being with them to lie still and quiet in the great empty house and let herself recall the sounds, sights, smells and feel of her old friends. They were each so soft in their way, though the Captain often laughed about his rough face and work-worn hands. It's true that his face was scarred and pitted, and pieces of shrapnel still found their way out of his skin sometimes. He had shown Misty pieces that had come out, and later she'd been able to take a few out for him with the tweezers, for they did irritate him as they worked their way to the surface of his face. But despite the scars, shrapnel and pits, his was a soft face, gentle, kind and true. There is a softness that comes from deep within, not from the texture of the surface. Miss Lily also exuded that kind of softness. For the first time, Misty really appreciated the wholeness of the island people, the unity, the unselfconsciousness, the fit. They were easy people, rich people, full people. Oh, how she loved them! Somehow, she loved them even more now than she ever had.

"Oh, God," she carried on, "send them my love. Give them warmth like they have always given me. Thank You that even from far away, somehow I feel all their goodness and love. Give them mine, too. Take care of Rusty and Pilot and Nobbin and the chickens, Brownie, the squirrels ..."

Continuing in prayer, Misty experienced all the comfort and blessings of the sights and sounds of her old home. Her eyes grew heavier and heavier as she asked God to care even for the gardens, houses and barns themselves. Any lines between present and past blurred as she prayed, as did lines between asleep and awake. On and on she travelled in prayer. She was almost sure she could hear right in this house the steady, rhythmic, friendly and safe, squeaking roll of the rocking chair that Gramps had often sat in next to the stove when she was falling asleep. And somewhere in the distance, the safe, regular, deep ticking of the mantle clock assured her that all was well, reminding her that some things never change. Perfect peace enveloped her.

11.

Storms Break in the Morning

Misty wakened refreshed and strong in the morning. Aunt Augusta chattered on about the success of the meeting the evening before, excited that Uncle Hugh had secured the nomination for candidacy in the upcoming election. She assured Misty that they'd be even busier than ever and would need all of Misty's co-operation. Misty silently attempted to finish off her porridge as Aunt Augusta talked and talked. Again she was spared any conflict, for Aunt Augusta suddenly whipped the not empty bowl from before Misty, saying, "We're out of time; you'll be late if you don't hurry. Run and brush your teeth, and don't worry if I'm not home immediately when you get back from school. I have a tremendous amount to do today. Just wait patiently on the steps, remember. And for goodness sake, behave yourself at school! We simply can't have any fuss now that Hugh is officially in the running. You've not done a very good job of your ringlets this morning, young lady! Don't get sloppy now. Here, let me straighten that elastic before you run out. Take more care after this. That'll do. Here's your lunch. Away you go, and do walk like the little lady you ought to be. No running wild."

Misty slowed her pace to keep Aunt Augusta happy but she was eager to meet Tommy. She wanted to give him his pencil back and she may as well give him her sandwich and cookies so she wouldn't have to find him at lunchtime. She smiled to think of having only some fruit for her lunch. She loved fresh fruit.

Tommy was waiting just past the corner on the other side of the road. He waved as she crossed over. "Git yer lines done?" he asked, as they started walking up the hill.

"Lines?" she asked. "What do you mean?"

"Ya know, yer name printed out. It's called lines when ya hafta write sumpin' out over 'n' over."

"Oh," she said, "Yes, thanks. Here's your pencil. I couldn't have done it without you, but it worked out fine. See? It didn't take me long, either."

"Gee, that's real neat. Guess they'll be s'prised to see that, seein' they think ya can't write. Oh-oh! Look what ya did. Ya put yer real name up top. Better 'rase it 'fore ya hand it in."

Misty laughed in spite of the fear that suddenly gripped her. "Oh, Tommy," she chuckled, "here I thought writing out 'Thomasina' so many times would make me used to it, and look what I did! I put that on when I was finished!"

Tommy laughed too but stopped abruptly. "Better watch out. Maybe I sh'd call ya 'Thomasina' so ya'd get practised. We gotta get that off. Have ya got a 'raser, Thomasina?"

"Tommy, please don't call me that. You don't know how nice it was yesterday to hear my very own name for the first time in so long. I'll get it, I promise, if you'll only call me Misty."

"Okay, Misty, but what 'r' we gonna do 'bout that 'Miss T' up top? Must be sumpin'. I know, I'll borra 'raser from Bobby when we git ta school. I know he's got one 'cuz he was stuck doin' lines hisself last night 'n' there's one on th' end of his pencil. We'll hafta hurry, though, so we git there 'fore the bell. Sure hope it's a better day 'n yesterday. I'll watch out fer ya at recess and lunch, but I think they'll leave ya be. 'Member, keep movin'. One o' my little sisters'll probly find ya at recess. She ain't in our class but she'll be watchin' fer ya. She's got braids 'n' freckles. Name's Daisy. She's okay. C'mon, we'll hafta run a bit."

As they ran along, Misty said, "Take my lunch, Tommy. I just want my fruit. If you're always hungry, you may as well have my other stuff."

"Gee, thanks," he said. "There's so many of us, we don' always git much lunch, 'n' we never git cookies. That's swell. There's Bobby over there. I'll git yer sandwich while ya 'rase the real name."

Misty had just erased the offending name when the bell rang. "Thanks, Tommy and Bobby," she said as she headed toward the girls' entrance; "I guess you've saved me again."

"Good luck," yelled the boys as they ran to their own entrance; "See ya after school."

Happy to be able to identify her own group, Misty slipped easily into place and walked quietly up the stairs and into the classroom with the other girls, leaving the "lines" as Tommy had called them on Miss Moore's desk as she walked past. Standing beside her desk for opening exercises, Misty couldn't help but lift her face even higher as she repeated the Lord's Prayer; she had so much to be grateful for that morning that her face rose on its own accord. She was completely unaware of the frown deepening on Miss Moore's brow as the prayer progressed or even as the children took their seats.

"Attendance will have to be delayed this morning, Class," Miss Moore began in a loud, very tight voice; "I'm afraid we have some unpleasant business to attend to. Thomasina, please stand."

Misty, her promise to Tommy to answer quickly when called "Thomasina" fresh in her mind, rose and stood by her desk, steadying herself slightly with her right hand.

"Stand straight and keep your hands at your sides. I told you yesterday there was to be no deception, and the principal assured me that he had explained clearly to you that we tolerate no kind of deceit at all here. You have done your lines as directed, though you have clearly torn off the bottom of the page, which you were not told to do. Further, this sheet indicates that you know perfectly well how to print your name. No beginner could print that neatly or that small. So, either you have had someone else do it for you, in which case you are cheating, or you have deliberately misled us into thinking you are unable to write. Further, you have filled, I repeat, filled a notebook with the alphabet. One notebook in a single day! It is unthinkable. Have you no respect for property, for propriety? I distinctly told you to copy from the book. Instead, you have filled the notebook with the alphabet, not following the size, not using two full lines per letter as was done in the printer, but simply filling the book. Now, again, you have been deliberately, wilfully deceptive. I cannot imagine what compels you to be so difficult and so utterly wilful and disobedient, so headstrong, so …"

Misty was growing pale and beginning to shake under this sudden, unexpected barrage. The class itself, even those who had taunted Misty the day before, was visibly strained, almost impossibly still with tension. The air was stifling, the children barely breathing in their fear. Misty had to reach out to her desk to steady herself. Miss Moore's voice grew even louder as she interrupted her own list of adjectives with, "I said 'hands at your sides' and I meant it!"

Misty quickly pulled her hand back, willing herself to stop shaking as Miss Moore carried on, "Dishonesty is bad enough, but open disobedience will not be tolerated. Now stand up straight while I get to the bottom of this dishonesty. Is there no end to the trouble you can cause? Never have I had so much difficulty in the first week. Never have I encountered so many wrong attitudes in a single child. And such irreverence and defiance, standing during the Lord's Prayer with your head lifted high! Nothing shows your disobedience more than refusing to bow your head during prayer. And now you slump! How dare you stand there slumped down when I am trying to deal with you? Have you no concept of right and wrong? Straight means straight. Now stand up straight!"

Misty quickly complied, but Tommy had had all he could take. He sprang up from his seat and almost yelled, "Crikey, whyn't ya leave 'er alone? She ain't dishonest. Give 'er a chance ta' 'splain!"

Miss Moore wheeled around to face Tommy and shouted, "That is enough! That is enough from both of you. Come forward at once. I am taking both of you to the office immediately. Class, you will remain quietly in your desks until I return."

Seeing Tommy walk to the front of the room, Misty was able to force herself to follow him. Miss Moore grabbed Tommy by the ear and Misty by the pigtail and marched the two of them out of the classroom, down the corridor and into the office without saying a word.

The office grew silent as they entered. Her voice still very strained but much quieter, Miss Moore said, "Mr. Sullivan will have to deal with these two. My class is unattended, so I must return. I will send a *good* pupil down with the paper and book the principal needs to see regarding *this impossible and dishonest girl.*" She punctuated the last words with tugs on Misty's pigtail. Twisting Tommy's ear, she continued, "Tommy must be strapped for swearing, speaking out of turn, failure to respect authority, and for interfering, not to mention rudeness and disrupting the class. Good morning." Miss Moore turned abruptly and walked out of the office, leaving Misty and Tommy standing at the counter.

Seeing Thomasina's very pale face, Mrs. Longacre hurried around the counter and took her gently by the arm even while saying, "Now, children, you'll have to sit down and wait a little while. Mr. Sullivan is away at a meeting but he'll be back before too long. You surely haven't been fighting have you? Do I need to sit you separately or can you sit side by side in these chairs?"

"Course we haven't bin fightin'," said Tommy, as they sat down. "You know I never fight with girls. I'd never hit a girl. 'Sides, class had started. I oughta git the strap, she's right. I lost my ol' temper agin and bust out. I din' think 'crikey' was a swear, though, but I guess I'll know better now. I don' think I disrupted the class either. We weren't doin' nuttin'. Miss Moore was jist yellin' at Misty here, goin' on and on. I jist couldn' help myself but I shudda kep my temper, she's right 'bout that. Do ya hafta turn in Misty, though, Miz Longacre? She didn' do nuttin'. Honest. She did her lines 'n' everythin'. She even stood right up when Miss Moore called her, even though Miss Moore used th' name she ain't usta. How come no one lissens to kids? Miss Moore goes on and on 'bout Misty bein' dishonest, but she ain't. She ain't even had a chance ta be dishonest. Crik- I mean, crumbs, I don' think she'd ever tell a lie, nor hide stuff neither. Aw, shucks, Miz Longacre. Can't we help her? Jist give me some extra lickin's. I know better, but she didn' do nuttin,' honest, and she ain't had a chance ta learn all the rules anyhow. It ain't fair!"

Mrs. Longacre, with her huge soft spot for Tommy, interrupted before he got himself any more wound up; she could see he was on the edge of tears and knew he'd rather die than cry at his age and in the office at that.

"There-there, Tommy. I know. Sometimes life doesn't seem fair, and growing up is difficult, but it's never all bad, you know. You will have to try to find better ways to help your friends out, but just think, whatever happens today, your father will be proud of you for trying to defend someone you see as innocent." She glanced quickly around before ruffling Tommy's hair and giving him a quick pat. "That a boy, you calm yourself. We have to look after your friend here. Look at her. She's still pale as a ghost and she's shivering. This isn't a very good place for us to have to wait, is it? Tommy, you go get two cups of water and bring them to the nurse's room. I'm going to settle your friend on the cot in there and see what we can do about this trouble."

Tommy hopped down from his chair, eager to help any way he could, while Mrs. Longacre took Misty gently by the arm and led her to the nurse's room, telling the typist to take all her calls until she returned. As she'd be a while, she instructed the typist to get whatever papers Miss Moore sent to her as soon as they arrived. She was quite worried about the little girl, so pale and shivering, but Misty seemed not to want to lie down. Instead she sat silently on the side of the cot. Mrs. Longacre gently rubbed her back until Tommy came in with the water. "Here," she said, "try to drink a little. Tommy, you have the other cup."

Misty just held the cup in her hand and stared at it, but Tommy quickly drained his and sank into the chair across from the cot with a great sigh. "Aw, gee, Miz Longacre. I really blew it this time, din' I? Jist got the strap yes'day. Honest, I don' mean ta make trouble. My pa sez it's the red hair. D' ya think so? Maybe I sh'd shave it off if that's all thet makes me bad."

Mrs. Longacre chuckled a little, much like Tommy's pa did whenever he mentioned the red hair. "No, Tommy," she said, "shaving it off wouldn't make any difference—except get you in more trouble! It's just an old wives' tale anyway. Why look at your brothers and sisters. They all have red hair, too, and only you and Bobby lose your tempers very often. And we hardly ever see Bobby in here any more. You're getting better, too. Try not to be discouraged."

"But Bobby had ta do lines last night agin. Ya don' s'pose ol' ma—I mean Mr. Sullivan will give me lines t'day, do ya? I'd rather jist have the strap 'n' git it over. Writin' lines is jist awful, takes so long. C'n ya ask him fer the strap fer me? But nothin' fer Misty here, 'kay?"

"I expect you'll have to have the strap and some lines today, Tommy. You know speaking out, disrespect and swearing is a lot."

"Yeah, I guess yer right. Well, never mind; least I learn'd not ta say 'crikey.' Guess that's good. Must be runnin' outa swears I didn' know were swears by now. Is it okay ta say 'crumbs,' Miz Longacre?"

The secretary couldn't repress the smile that spread across her face but she managed to say seriously if not sternly, "Tommy, you ought to try to keep quiet, especially when you are angry. That way you won't make mistakes. Now, shall we wait for Mr. Sullivan or do you want to go back to class and come for your punishment when he calls you? I'd better tend to Thomasina, now."

"Shucks, Miz Longacre, couldn't ya call 'er Misty? She likes it better, 'n' lookit the poor kid. She don' look too good." Getting off his chair, he sat down beside his shivering friend and patted her shoulder, much like he did with his sisters when they got hurt. "Hey, Misty, it's okay, honest. Can't ya stop shiverin'? Ol' Moore din' mean nuttin'. 'n' Miz Longacre's here now 'n' she c'n fix things up. Ya don' never hafta be 'fraida Miz Longacre. An' she's a grown-up! Maybe they'll let her 'splain so Sullivan knows ya weren't lyin' 'r cheatin' 'r nuttin'. Soon's they know th' truth, everythin' 'll be fine."

But Misty had been so shocked, she'd gone kind of numb inside, numb but very cold. It was like her whole inside self was frozen. Her eyes, apparently staring into the glass of water, had moved past glassy and even beyond glazed; they were almost nothing more than mirrors. But deep, deep inside, encased in the ice that had spread so quickly across her, burned a tiny flame of righteous indignation, slowly, slowly melting the ice. Over and over, Misty silently cried, "Help Tommy, God. Please help Tommy."

She couldn't hear what was going on around her, didn't even hear the knock on the door, but she felt Mrs. Longacre pull her hand away and begin to stand. Misty reached out and grabbed her, spilling the cup of water as she did so. Surprised but not upset, Mrs. Longacre said quietly, "Tommy, you get the door. It will be the papers. Bring them here. We'll have to see if we can get to the bottom of this. Thanks. Now get some paper towels and wipe up the water. Misty doesn't seem to want me to leave her. I'll just rub her back a while longer. She's beginning to look a little better, don't you think?"

The colour was returning to Misty's face as she felt the warmth of the hand on her back and heard the gentle woman say her real name. Oh, there was hope. She struggled to focus on Mrs. Longacre, but kept looking at Tommy as he wiped up the floor. Dear Tommy, in trouble again because of her; that wasn't right. She felt a great fatigue replace the icy block and sighed before saying, "Thanks, Tommy. Thanks for helping me and for cleaning up, too. I'm sorry I got you in trouble again. Maybe you'd better not wait for me after school. I don't want to get you in any more trouble. You're a good friend, Tommy. I hope they understand it's all my fault, and you don't get punished. I'm so tired, Tommy, never been so tired, or I'd help you. So tired."

Misty's eyes began to get glassy, as she slid inside, seeking rest. She didn't resist as Mrs. Longacre eased her down onto the cot and covered her with a blanket. She snuggled into the pillow and let her eyes close as she drifted off into the deep misty blueness of sea and sky meeting together. 'So tired, God,' she prayed, 'so tired. Help Tommy. Help the Captain know I tried to do what I was told as he said. Look after the Captain, God; make sure Pilot barks faithfully while Captain swims and swims and swims.' Misty slid into sleep, comforted by the feel and image of the Captain swimming in the gentle, blue waves, rocked more gently than by any rocking chair.

"Is she gonna be a'right, Miz Longacre?" Tommy whispered. "D' ya think ol' Moore pulled 'er pigtail too hard? My littlist sister gits all pale and shaky and sleepy when she skins 'er knee 'r anythin'. D' ya think Misty's like that?"

"Come, Tommy, we'll leave her sleep. No, I don't think she's hurt that way; she's just worn out. It must be very hard to go from a quiet life with very few people to all this hustle and bustle and all these rules. She needs time to adjust. Sleep will be good for her. It solves one of our problems, too. I'll explain to Mr. Sullivan that she's not well today. That will give us all time to try to sort out what is the matter. I guess, since Thomasina's asleep, I'll have to ask you as much as you know. There have obviously been some big mistakes here. Look at this notebook. The child obviously prints beautifully and quickly; she's filled all but one page." Both she and Tommy allowed themselves a little chuckle over the full book as they closed the door behind them and went back to the office.

Glancing at the clock, Mrs. Longacre said, "Now, Tommy, the principal will be back very soon, and I want to call a meeting before anything is done about Thomasina or about you. You do understand that you'll have to have some punishment because you did lose that ol' temper again, as you call it. But I want some other things discussed first and I want you to be free to answer all the questions we need answered. I'll give you a slip and you can go work with Henry for the rest of the morning. Don't go out at recess either. He'll have plenty for you to do. I'll send a note to Miss Moore explaining that we are keeping both of you. I'll call you to the office when I need you. But before you go, at least tell me about the name. Why Misty?"

"Why it's short fer Miss Thomasina, ya know. It's th' only name anybody ever used 'til she got here. That's why she din' answer very fast sometimes. She jist wasn' usta Thomasina. I ast her why she din' git 'er uncle ta fix it with th' school like my pa did fer me 'n' Bobby, but she said 'er uncle calls 'er Thomasina too. Guess she's stuck with it. An' don' fergit, she c'n read 'n' write too. Thanks fer sendin' me ta Henry. See ya later." Tommy was off with a grin, for like all the children, he loved the janitor, and helping him was always fun, more fun than class.

Mrs. Longacre shook her head as she returned to her desk after looking in on the sleeping Thomasina. What a mess this had turned out to be! She didn't relish being in the middle of it, but that is exactly where she often found herself. She had earned the trust of the children simply by listening to them and loving them, but then, for the most part, she was free to love them. The teachers and principal had direct responsibility for educating them, whereas her responsibility was simply to the principal and the school board.

Of course she could never appear to take the children's part against the principal, but she could support them in almost silent ways. It wasn't that the principal or any of the teachers meant to disregard the children as whole people, but sometimes in their zeal for order, discipline and teaching, they overlooked the obvious. Miss Moore, for example, was quite a good teacher, but she was young and ambitious. Her own ambition sometimes drove her to slightly exaggerated expectations of her students' work and behaviour. She saw everything her students did not for what it revealed about the child but for how it reflected on her, so her view was sometimes a little askew. Somehow, both Miss Moore and Mr. Sullivan seemed to have overlooked the magnitude of the change young Thomasina had been thrown into. And now Mrs. Longacre realized that there had also been huge misunderstandings. Those she would attempt, carefully of course, to sort out.

Before going to the filing cabinet to retrieve Thomasina's file, Mrs. Longacre blocked a full hour off on Mr. Sullivan's morning schedule, writing "Conference" in the block. Glancing over the personal data of Thomasina and studying the picture the principal had placed in the file the previous day, Mrs. Longacre decided to call in the government agent who had placed Thomasina in the care of the Hughes. Looking in on the sleeping child again, she decided to have the school nurse in attendance as well. Unable to get an answer at the Hughes', she decided it best to have the principal schedule a separate interview with them later. She also decided against calling in a substitute teacher for Miss Moore, preferring to simply list the complaints Miss Moore had raised on a piece of paper; they could always call her if they needed clarification of anything. It would be best to attempt a discussion without a lot of emotions cluttering things up.

Glancing again at the picture, the book and the lines Thomasina had written, Mrs. Longacre saw that it was a simple mistake in a way. The child had been placed in the wrong grade. Wrong information had been given or wrong assumptions made. She wished they'd undertaken the placement tests before beginning school instead of delaying them. Unfortunately, the district supervisor who did the tests wouldn't be available to their school for quite some time. She'd have to see if she could arrange to have one of his assistants come. The sooner this was all done, the better it would be for the child. She made a note to call the district office as soon as Mr. Sullivan approved the plan. All that remained was for her to present the plan for the meeting to Mr. Sullivan as if it were something he had thought of himself rather than being a response to what he might see as a crisis.

The bell rang for recess just as Mr. Sullivan came in after his early meeting. "Good morning, Mrs. Longacre. Excellent meeting this morning. Is the rest of my day busy? I'm sure you've filled it up as always." He smiled as he hung his hat on the hook in the corner of the office.

"Yes; I'll be in to your office in just a minute to assist you in getting ready for your next meeting. I'll just get the files and see that the coffee is started." In fact, Mrs. Longacre went to check once again on Thomasina, who was still sleeping soundly, and to leave a note on the desk for the nurse, who would soon be in.

Taking the files, she went to the principal's office and began. "I discovered a discrepancy this morning that I knew you would want to take care of as soon as possible, so I've arranged a meeting next hour. It's about the new girl, Thomasina. I'm not sure whether some admission files never arrived from the school board or what has happened, but we haven't had accurate or adequate information. Knowing you would want to fill in the gaps and get the appropriate information, I have asked the government agent to come in. As the child is not feeling well today and I see we have no health records for her, I've also asked the nurse to come in. She'll check Thomasina before the meeting and will have a report. There wasn't any answer at the Hughes' but I thought you'd want to go ahead with the meeting and talk to them later. If we have questions no one else can answer, perhaps you might call Mr. Hughes at the bank. I've started putting together the things we have on file, including Miss Moore's observations, so that you can conduct the meeting from what we have. Before the meeting starts, I'll have a few notes added from what I've been able to learn myself. Would you like the meeting in your office or in the staff room?"

"The staff room would be best, I think. It will be free then, won't it?"

"Yes, that will be fine, then. And what seating arrangement do you want? Around the table or in the easy chairs?"

"I think with the government agent present, we'd best keep it formal: the table. Good work, Mrs. Longacre. It is best to sort messy things out quickly. What do I need to know about the child? You say she's not well?"

"Oh, I expect she is just exhausted from moving and beginning a new school. It is a radical change, you know. It appears that her general health is excellent, but there are no public health records for her."

"She isn't backward in any way, is she? She is small for her age."

"Far from it. I think she may even be advanced. I believe her size is fine. I knew her grandmother's family, small people all of them. You might want to recommend that people treat her extra gently for a while, though, just to give her a chance to adjust. This move for her is almost as drastic as for the little girl we had come from Yugoslavia last year. We ought to help Thomasina as we did her. Look how well she got on after the first month or so. But then once you have the tests done and the results compiled, many of your administrative problems with this admission will be solved. Perhaps we could arrange for a special examiner to come for Thomasina right away instead of leaving her in class. That might make your job easier. I'm sure the board would approve it, don't you think so?"

"Excellent idea. I'll convince the government agent. Would you introduce the meeting and give the information for me? That would save me having to go through what you've already prepared. Do you mind?"

"I'd be happy to. I'll call you when everything and everyone is in place. The rest of your schedule is there on your desk, as is the stack of papers for signing. I've checked them, and they are all in order. I'll see you in ten minutes or so, then."

So saying, Mrs. Longacre left the principal's office, relieved that everything had fallen in place so much to Thomasina's advantage. Poor child. She called Tommy on the public address system before going back to the nurse's room to check Thomasina. She was still sleeping, though the nurse was with her and had listened to her chest with a stethoscope and had taken her pulse. "I'm glad you're here," said Mrs. Longacre, "did you have a chance to read my note?"

"Yes. I'm sure the child's fine. Doesn't seem to have a temperature at all and her pulse is fine. She's certainly sleeping soundly, though. Must have been tired. Does she get enough sleep do you think? Are we dealing with any kind of neglect here?"

"No. None at all. Drastic, drastic change and possibly homesickness, though the child is astonishingly cheery and strong looking between her ordeals here. I've called Tommy to tell us the problem. I hope he can be quick, for the meeting starts in ten minutes. I'm going to need your help with this one. They're trying too much, too fast, especially since she's also having some trouble adjusting to living with the Hughes. Here comes Tommy. He'll fill us in."

"Good boy, Tommy. Now, we haven't long because we have to go to a meeting in less than ten minutes. As quickly as you can, tell us what you know Misty is having trouble with, what you think is unfair."

Tommy didn't waste any time, itemizing all that he knew Misty had found difficult and confusing. He was tempted not to tell about the food at home, thinking that would mean giving up his new-found extra food before it had hardly begun, but trying to help Misty was more important to him than being a little hungry sometimes, so he told them that, too. He even told them he already had part of Misty's lunch in his own bag. He remembered to tell about lending her the little stub of a pencil and explaining to her how to rub it to sharpen it, interrupting his quick narrative to ask Mrs. Longacre if she'd remind Misty to take her own pencil home when she had lines to do.

He hadn't thought to tell her. He ended by asking, "Ya c'n help 'er, can't ya? Gosh, she's still asleep. Ya gotta help 'er! Ya can, can't ya?"

"Yes, Tommy, thanks to you, we should have it all sorted out before you know it. She won't be punished either. You've done a good job and been a real help."

"What 'bout my whuppin'? C'n we git thet over with now? It's worse waitin' th'n jist gittin' it."

"Sorry, Tommy, we can't do that yet. I haven't spoken to Mr. Sullivan about it and won't be able to until after the meeting. Tell you what, though, you can go back to Henry for the rest of the morning. If I haven't called you by lunchtime, Henry will get your lunch from the cloak room and you can eat it with him."

"C'n I eat the stuff Misty gave me, too? Don' wanna do no more wrong today. She gave me cookies ya know!"

"Yes, eat that too, Tommy. And thanks again. We'll talk to you later. And, yes, we will take care of Misty."

"Thanks. Say, ya won' send 'er out on the playground 'lone will ya? 'N', don' let her walk home herself, eh? The prissy kids teased 'er awful yes'day. Is kids all rotten, Miz Longacre? Seems it sometimes, don' it? I tol' 'er I'd walk with 'er 'n' I will, so don' let 'er head out 'lone. 'kay?"

"Yes, Tommy; now away you go. We'll see you before too long."

As Tommy ran off, Mrs. Longacre turned to the nurse and said, "I can't help but love that kid. His only trouble is looking after other kids the only way he knows how. He's pretty perceptive. Didn't take him long to get to the bottom of Thomasina's trouble, did it?"

"You amaze me yourself, Jean," said the nurse; "this is only the second full day of school! Those kids will tell you anything, at least the troublemakers will. And then you manage to fight for them without the staff realizing what you are doing. You're quite the champion here."

"Kids need me, that's all. Now, we've work to do. Do you see from what Tommy has said what we need to do? I'm to introduce the meeting. You can pick up the direction from there. You're a champion yourself for these kids. See if you can get them to hold off on Thomasina's inoculation programme if they push for that. Let her settle in first. I'm sure she's not a danger to anyone. She probably hasn't had any of the basics. We'll ask her when she wakes up. Like Tommy says, all people had to do was ask her but nobody did. For now, I think we'd best concentrate on two things: buying her some time to adjust and getting to know what she can do and where she should be. I'm sure she's in the wrong class altogether. Let's go."

12.

Mrs. Longacre Steps In

While Misty slept soundly and Tommy chattered to old Henry, Mrs. Longacre deftly and calmly led the principal and the government agent to the only logical conclusions one could draw when presented with observations undistorted by selfish fear. She presented the picture Misty had drawn and coloured as well as the lines and the full notebook as examples of what Misty could do. While it is true that Mr. Sullivan had great difficulty accepting that an unschooled child could possibly know how to write and draw so well, he could not deny the evidence before him. The government agent admitted he had no knowledge of the child's capabilities at all. Like the others, he hadn't thought to ask or even observe what she could do; instead, he had just gathered the facts concerning her formal education and her health. But while both men admitted the evidence Mrs. Longacre presented, they insisted there were behaviour problems, the worst two of which seemed to be deception and disobedience. Only when Mrs. Longacre explained about the confusion arising because the child had heard only a pet name all her life and described some of the difficulty that any child would have adjusting to such a new life, especially when still grieving for her grandmother, did the men begin to realize there might have been misunderstanding rather than misbehaviour.

Both the principal and the agent agreed not only that Misty must be tested as soon as possible and placed in the appropriate class but also that no immediate or even early attempts should be made to begin any inoculation programmes or make any formal medical assessment mandatory unless the child became ill in any way. For the time being, the nurse would begin the child's health record by recording her age, weight, height, and birth date as well as her base-line vital signs: pulse, respiration, and temperature. All thought that information carefully entered on the appropriate card would persuade the health department that the school was fulfilling its responsibility by beginning the process of bringing the child up to the British Columbian standard of health care.

The government agent clarified that the child had not been adopted by the Hughes but was in their foster care, long-term foster care. The status was expected to remain unchanged indefinitely. He agreed, however, that though the Hughes now had full responsibility for the child, the island people could be contacted for any additional information that may be needed to explain any unusual behaviour. All decisions, however, must be made by the Hughes, including the decision about what the child was to be called. School policy was to use names as given on the register unless specifically and firmly instructed by the child's parents or guardians to use a different name or even a less formal one; it was thought that using formal given names helped establish discipline and control behaviour. All were quite certain the Hughes would respect school policy in the matter.

Mrs. Longacre agreed to talk to the child to glean whatever information she might need and to arrange for all tests. She recommended transferring her out of Miss Moore's class immediately, but the principal wasn't sure. He insisted that being able to print did not indicate anything about reading or comprehension ability and pointed out that they knew nothing of the child's arithmetical ability; while he had been forced to recognize that a child could learn some things despite being unschooled, he didn't think it possible that reading and arithmetic could also be mastered outside the school. Thus transferring the child right away would be premature. It was agreed instead that Misty would remain on Miss Moore's class list but would not attend class until all tests were completed.

The meeting was a success in the view of all concerned. Mr. Sullivan was sure he had impressed the government agent with the school's efficiency and concern. The government agent was sure he had illustrated that his agency had not been remiss with information; rather, the child simply had not been schooled or examined medically. There were no records.

The nurse and Mrs. Longacre had gained the time they needed to help Misty. Both wished they might have persuaded people to use Misty's familiar name, for they knew it would make the adjustment easier for the little girl, but neither was particularly concerned about it, for they knew only the teaching staff must use the formal name. Misty would soon be comforted to hear the familiar name from students and secretaries and, of course, old Henry. Mrs. Longacre had basically won almost free rein with the child, for she would not only arrange all tests but also have the child in her care until the placement was complete. She'd have Misty help out in the office and would learn by observation what the child was capable of. She would also give Henry some time with her. Nobody got to know kids like Henry did.

When the government agent left and the nurse returned to check on Misty, Mrs. Longacre turned once again to Mr. Sullivan and said, "There is one other matter. I didn't bring it up with the agent here, for it had nothing to do with him, and I knew you'd rather deal with it alone. You know Miss Moore sent Thomasina to the office this morning for deception. I'm afraid she also had to send Tommy for speaking out of turn and disrespect. He is working with Henry while waiting for his punishment. It seems Tommy suddenly felt so sorry for the little girl while Miss Moore was upbraiding her that he jumped up and told Miss Moore to leave Thomasina alone because she just didn't understand yet. He realizes that he must be punished because his temper did get the better of him again but he is sorry and was only defending the child. He has also been tremendously helpful to us with Misty. We'd have had much difficulty without him. And he took his punishment well yesterday, not trying to hide behind the wrong other children had done. Apparently children have been teasing Thomasina about her name quite relentlessly on the school grounds as well as on the way to and from school. Tommy might have tried to excuse his temper by telling on the other children but he didn't. That shows some strength of character, don't you think? Now Tommy's only concern is that you not punish Misty, for he is absolutely certain she did nothing wrong. Oddly, Misty's only concern is that you not punish Tommy, for she feels it is all her fault. The child was too shaken to talk much after the shock of being upbraided; all she did was apologize to Tommy and insist that it was all her fault. Perhaps if you strap Tommy for his outburst but do not assign lines, Misty will feel less that she is nothing but trouble for Tommy."

"Now, Mrs. Longacre, watch the names! You mustn't be so soft. Discipline and authority are of utmost importance. You know kids stick together like glue when there's trouble around. These children are just trying to avoid punishment. Miss Moore also indicates that Tommy swore. He'll have to write lines no matter what the new girl feels. It simply isn't her fault that he swears."

"Yes, Mr. Sullivan, I agree. However, this is a special case and Tommy didn't know that the word he used was a swear word. He does now, however. I do think this is not a case of children trying to cover for each other. It is much more that each assumes full responsibility. That indicates to me that each will learn from the mistake itself and doesn't need harsh punishment. Also, keep in mind the child is in a whole new world. Still, you must do your job. Shall I call Tommy right away so the task is over with?"

"Please do. Perhaps this time you are right. I won't assign lines for Tommy. I may have to give him the strap unless a good talking to will do. It may, since he's anticipated the strap all morning. Look, it's almost the lunch hour. Call him. We'd best at least be done so he can go to class this afternoon. Can't waste a whole day. Must say, I'm glad to have this muddle sorted out. You'll get the papers necessary for the testing ready for me to sign right away, won't you? I'll have to call the Hughes and explain about the testing. I'll do that after I've signed the papers."

Tommy soon arrived in the office looking solemn. Mr. Sullivan was surprised that his first question to Mrs. Longacre was about the girl not about his own fate. He seemed most concerned, especially when he heard the child was still asleep. Mrs. Longacre assured him he could see her after he had been to see the principal, so Tommy walked into the principal's office and stood before him, further surprising the principal by saying, "Mr. Sullivan, I'm sorry I lost my temper this mornin'. It was wrong 'n' I know it now. I'll try harder not ta do it agin. I didn't mean no disrespect, neither. I jist got mad. I'm sorry."

"Well Tommy, I see you have learned something this morning. Can I trust you not to interrupt Miss Moore again?"

"Yes, Sir."

"And you will not swear, even when provoked?"

"Yes, Sir."

"And you will speak only when spoken to?"

"Yes, Sir."

"If you promise me you will try your very hardest not to lose your temper, I'll let you go this time. "

"Oh, yes, Sir!"

"But Tommy, I do not want to see you in this office again. You really must behave yourself. Is that clear?"

"Yes, Sir!"

"Then away you go. *And no more nonsense!* Pick up your slip from Mrs. Longacre. Remember, I don't want to see you again. Concentrate on your lessons, Tommy. Work harder. Now off you go."

Tommy forced himself to walk, not run, to Mrs. Longacre's desk. Again the principal was surprised to hear, "C'n we go ta Misty now, Miz. Longacre? Is she gonna be alright? Man, how c'n she sleep so long? It's lunchtime. Why'nt she wake up? I already ate my lunch so how 'bout if I stay with 'er 'til school goes in? Poor kid. Whata mornin' fer 'er. Is it all fixt now? She wan't lyin', was she?"

"No, Tommy, she wasn't. Maybe you can help me find out just how much Misty can do. She won't be going back to your class. I'm going to have her help me and Henry so we can learn for ourselves where she belongs. You'd best stop by the office after school so you can walk home with her. Now let's go see how she's doing."

Misty had awakened just before the lunch hour bell had rung. It's clanging had served to remind her where she was, for on first opening her eyes, she was unsure. She had thoroughly rested while sleeping and wakened refreshed and restored. She had not so much dreamt of her old home as she had sensed the gentle and soothing rhythms of natural life by the sea. Her own deep and easy breathing had seemed a part, once again, of the ebb and flow of the whole of life, and she drew strength from the unity of if.

Though reminded by the bell that she was not only at school but had been sent to the office once again, Misty was not disturbed. This was a new moment, another beginning; she knew she was able to carry on. She did not, however, know what to do, so decided the best course of action was to do nothing. She would simply sit on the edge of the cot and wait. She didn't trouble herself with wondering what she should have done or what she could do or even with what she had done wrong. Nor did she wonder what was to come. Instead, she thought of how nice it was to feel warm again after feeling so cold when she'd gone to sleep. She silently thanked God for giving her rest; she had been very tired. She thanked Him also for Tommy; it was so nice to have a friend. She thanked Him for the Captain and Miss Lily and asked Him once again to look after them while she was away. Smiling, she imagined her old friends in Miss Lily's garden with flowers and animals all about and then thought of the beauty of the apple tree in her new home. She wondered if she'd see the cat there after school. She hoped so. She was smiling when Tommy and Mrs. Longacre entered the room.

"Yer awake!" exclaimed Tommy, running and dropping down beside her on the cot. "Boy, am I glad! I thought ya'd never git better! Ya sure scairt me! Ya look fine now, though. D' ya feel better?"

"I am fine, Tommy, just fine. I am sorry for the trouble I caused, though. I didn't mean to. Will you forgive me, Tommy?"

"Ain't nuttin' ta fergive, Misty. I'm jist glad yer better. Bad mornin' al'round, I guess, but it's lunch now. Gee, thanks fer the food. I ate it with Henry. Ya haven't met 'im yet, but he's grand. Ya'll like 'im. Shucks Misty, if ya hadn't had trouble I wouldna got ta see Henry. Then I wouldna thought ta 'pologize ta Mr. Sullivan. Henry's real smart 'n' he knows how ta help kids. Wonder why I din' thinka 'pologizin' before? My pa always makes me 'pologize. Jist din' thinka doin' it at school I guess. 'N' I'm sorry, too; I shouldna swore 'r bust out like that in class. Promised Mr. Sullivan I'd try harder. Anyway, it's all fixt up now. Miz Longacre did a meetin' 'n' everythin'. They know now ya weren't cheatin' 'r lyin'. Ain't that good? Din' I tell ya Miz Longacre could fix everythin'?"

"Now, Tommy," said Mrs. Longacre, "don't get carried away. I didn't fix anything. You showed us what trouble Misty had, so now we know what to do. I'm real proud of you, Tommy. You'd better go and run around on the playground before lunch hour is over and you have to get back to class. You need a little exercise, I think! Now remember, you come and get Misty when school is out."

"Right, Miz Longacre. Thanks. See ya after school, Misty."

Misty interrupted before Tommy could get to the door: "Tommy, I'll be okay walking home. Please don't worry about me and get in any more trouble because of me. You have to look after yourself, not worry about me. I'll be fine, honest."

"Nuttin' doin'. I'm comin' fer ya 'n' we'll walk home t'geth-er. Silly not ta when I go past yer house anyway. 'Sides, there won't be no trouble, will there, Miz Longacre? It'll be fine, ya'll see. I wanna walk with ya. See ya later!"

Tommy was off, bursting with energy, eager to get in a bit of tag or ball before he had to sit in class for the afternoon. Mrs. Longacre was left to assure Misty that she should accept Tommy's offer to walk from school with her. She wouldn't have objected to the arrangement even if she hadn't known as Tommy did that there would be no further trouble of the sort that caused Tommy to lose his temper. After the dressing down Misty had received in front of the class that morning, every student in there would be feeling sorry for the newcomer and ready to make friends with her. For a while, at least, that part of Misty's trouble had unwittingly been taken care of, another example of good coming out of bad.

Mrs. Longacre explained to Misty all that had happened that morning and what was to come of it. Gently she explained the tests that Misty would begin writing as soon as she could arrange for them before going on to ask for her help in the office and around the school while they waited. Misty was thrilled at the thought of doing something, of being a part of something, of being useful, and her eagerness showed all over her face. Before they could begin, however, Mrs. Longacre suggested they have some lunch. For today, they would eat together there in the nurse's office. Mrs. Longacre went herself to get Misty's lunch and things from Miss Moore's classroom before getting her own lunch and rejoining Misty.

"Are you sure this is enough food?" she asked Misty, as she opened the lunch box to reveal just two pieces of fruit.

"Oh yes, thanks, Mrs. Longacre. You can't imagine what a struggle I have trying to eat all the food here. It isn't that I'm ungrateful at all; it is just that there is too much for me. At home, we each dished our own meals, so I never had more than I could eat. Then, too, I was busy always at home and I was outside a lot. I think I was more hungry there than I am here. I don't mean to make people unhappy, Mrs. Longacre, so I try hard to eat all my food, but Aunt Augusta and Uncle Hugh are disappointed in me most every day that way. I'll keep trying. Somehow it will work out, I know. Things always do, don't they?"

"I suppose they do, Misty. That's certainly a good way of looking at things anyway. You just enjoy your fruit, then, if you know it's enough for you. I'm always more hungry at noon than I am in the evening. Funny isn't it?"

"Oh, maybe you're tired in the evening. You work hard here, don't you? I'd like to see if your typewriter is like the one the Captain has. It's a different colour and sounds different, but then you type faster than he does or than I do when I try to work it for him. I expect he'll be using it a lot now that I'm gone. Good thing he has it. The Captain's has Braille letters on most of the keys but it types plain. Does yours have bumps on the keys, Mrs. Longacre?"

"No, Misty, mine has letters on the keys. It probably just looks and sounds different because it is newer than the Captain's. I have some typing to do right after lunch. You can have a look at it then. We also have an extra typewriter in the office.

Perhaps I'll have you do some work on that if you are able. Did you do much for the Captain?"

"Oh, I wrote out more than I typed out for him. Writing is faster for me, and we had such fun doing his orders together. I sure miss the Captain. At first we'd do his lists and he'd have Gran or Miss Lily check them over to make sure I hadn't made any bad mistakes, but for a long time now, he hasn't bothered having them checked. Must be funny not having to write orders. Aunt Augusta just goes to the store, and she goes so often! We had to order at least two months at a time, so we couldn't leave things out. And doing the feed and seed ordering only twice a year was quite a big task. I miss it, Mrs. Longacre. I haven't done anything since I got here."

"You'll have more to do soon, I'm sure and you will get used to it, Misty. Tell me, do you print everything or can you write too?"

"Oh, mostly I write. Funny having to do the printing yesterday. At first it seemed so strange and slow because I hadn't done it for so long. Writing is much faster, don't you think? Gran told the Captain that I'd learned to write by accident because I was in such a hurry. Once she noticed I was joining my printed letters together in my hurry, she showed me what the written ones should be like. Mrs. Longacre, is there some way you could let others know that my people were good? I keep hearing people criticize them as if they weren't good to me, but we had a wonderful life. They were the best. I don't like to hear people say wrong things about them."

"Oh, they'll soon see better, Misty. As they see what you can do, they'll realize that no one neglected you and see clearly that your life was fine. Usually it is better to be patient and let people see things for themselves than it is to try to defend or even explain. Besides, if you think of it, not many people are critical, are they?"

"Hm. Guess I have only heard a few. And Gran also used to say most things were better seen than said. It's just that time seems funny here. Sometimes it rushes along and I am impatient and feel like I have to fix everything right away and other times it doesn't seem to move at all. At home, I never even thought of time. Things were so much more smooth and quiet there. Will I find the smooth path here if I'm patient, Mrs. Longacre?"

"I'm sure you'll find things a little easier each day, Misty, but it is definitely different here than it was on the island. Did you know I knew your grandparents? You must miss them very much. They were wonderful people, some of the best I knew. Now, we'd better clean up here and get to work. Just one other thing. You print, you write and you type some. Just lists? Or do you also write other things?"

" Oh, I can write anything. I did some letters for the Captain, too. I read, too, Mrs. Longacre."

"Yes, Tommy told us that. How did you learn?"

"I'm not sure. It seems like I've always read. I just followed along with Gran or Gramps when they were reading until I could start myself."

"Did you have Readers?"

"I don't know. What is a Reader?"

"A beginner book a little like the printer Miss Moore gave you yesterday, but instead of letters, it starts with simple words."

"Oh, no. I just followed along in the Bible and other books Gran and Gramps had. Miss Lily's books, too. Last few winters, I read to them instead of them reading to me. Want me to read to you?"

"Not now, Misty. Maybe later or another day I'll have you read to Mr. Sullivan, if you don't mind. I think he should hear you. Now, is there anything you'd like to do while I sort out some things to assign tasks for you?"

"Do you really mean anything? Anything at all?"

"Well, anything you can do within the office or the nurse's room."

"Oh, Mrs. Longacre, could I finish my picture? You can't imagine what trouble it has been to me to think it might never be finished. I came to school so excited yesterday to think I could finish it, and it was gone. Then I hoped Mr. Sullivan would give it back and I could finish it, but he kept it. It won't take me long, I don't think, but I'd feel much better if I could finish it. It looks so funny to me only half filled in. Besides, I'm just beginning to catch on to those crayons. Oh-oh. I'm not supposed to take the wrappers off, but they only work on their sides, Mrs. Longacre. How can I do that without taking the wrappers off?"

"Never mind the wrappers now, Misty. You've already taken them off anyway. Of course you can finish the picture. I'll get it from the file and get your crayons from among the things I brought with your lunch. Then you can sit over at this table and finish the picture."

"Thanks, Mrs. Longacre. I won't be long, I'm sure!"

Mrs. Longacre had recognized an opportunity to observe Misty and to put to rest all accusations about her artistic ability, but even more rewarding for her was seeing the life bubble out of the child as she took her picture and crayons to the table. "Not all of the crayons are peeled, Mrs. Longacre. May I peel the black? I'll need it to blend with the dark green of the trees. They're not quite right. It's a picture of our barn back home. Miss Moore said to draw my summer vacation, but I didn't know what that might be, so I just drew home. Was that okay?"

"You go ahead and peel all the rest of the crayons. They are yours. Summer vacation is what we call the time off school between the end of June and the beginning of September. Sometimes we call them holidays. Some people travel a little during that time. Others stay home. So, since you stayed home in July, you have drawn a picture of your vacation! Good work."

Mrs. Longacre found it a little difficult to concentrate on her own work, so taken was she with Misty. What a delightful and unusual person she was. And what talent! Misty was right; it didn't take her very long to finish the picture. When she had done the best she could, she took it to Mrs. Longacre and said, "There, it can go back in the file now that it's finished. It does look like home, but it's sure hard to get the colours right with crayons. I've never used them before. I wonder how you blend them better. They don't smudge at all, but I guess that's good in a way. At least it keeps them from smearing when you don't want them to and it keeps them from coming off on your clothes, too. That should keep Aunt Augusta happy. Why, if I'd used charcoals or pastels, I'd have dirty sleeves, wouldn't I? Is that why they use crayons at school, Mrs. Longacre?"

To be honest, Mrs. Longacre had never even wondered why they used crayons. It had always been that way, even when she had gone to school. She thought, though, that Misty had arrived at the most logical conclusion and marvelled again at the child's ability. How anyone could have thought her backward, slow, or deceptive was beyond her. Just for her own report to the principal, she thought it best to find out how Misty had learned to draw, so replied, "I'm not sure why the school supplies crayons, Misty, though your reason sounds good. Perhaps they are also a good price. What would you rather use or what have you used in the past?"

"Oh, Miss Lily has charcoals, different pencils, pastels, water colours, and oils. I like the pastels and water colours best, but Miss Lily says watercolours are the most difficult to paint well with. She also said that for some reason people seem to prefer oil paintings. She didn't understand that but she was happy to use either. You should see her paintings, Mrs. Longacre. She makes things seem alive even though they are just on paper or canvas. It's beautiful to see, and watching her paint is wonderful. It's like watching Gramps turn wood on the lathe or watching Gran quilt or the Captain weave. It makes huge bubbles come up inside me until I have to dance or run or sing to let them out. Guess that's why Gran and I sang so often when we worked around. Even Miss Lily kind of hums sometimes when she is painting. Do you know Miss Lily?"

"I did meet her once, Misty, but I don't know her. I have seen some of her paintings, though, and you are quite right. I didn't know the Captain did weaving. What about you?"

"Oh, I just did really small things with him. Mostly I sorted the colours for him so he could make the big blankets. They are beautiful, too, because the colours are so rich. He and Gran shared a lot of the yarns, you know. I really miss my knitting more than the weaving, maybe because I did more knitting than anything else—well, I guess more than anything else. I sewed a lot, and Gran and I really had fun quilting. I never made any quilts of my own, though. We always worked on the same one together. Gramps said it was amazing that no one could tell the difference between the stitches of an old woman and those of a young girl. I don't think it was amazing, though, do you Mrs. Longacre? How could it be when the old woman was the one who taught the young girl? You can't imagine how often I had to take my stitches out at first. I'd stitch away, and then Gran would remind me to check with my thumb like she'd shown me and sure enough I'd find I was doing only five or six stitches an inch instead of the eight Gran taught me to do. So, I'd pull it out and start over. It was fun, felt warm and good, you know. Still, it's knitting I miss most because you can always pick it up and do a bit and you can take it anywhere with you."

Even Mrs. Longacre began to get surprised as she listened to Misty talking so naturally and comfortably about doing such fine work. She knew beyond doubt that the child was not making anything up; she was just genuinely surprised at what the child could do, surprised at how the child had spent her time. Unable to resist, she asked, "What about toys and games, Misty? Which of those do you prefer?"

"Toys? Do you mean the wooden sailboat Gramps let me sail? It was real old, belonged to someone long since dead. Gramps said his uncle had made it. He found it one day when he was rummaging about looking for a special piece of wood, so he cleaned it up and painted it. Gran and I made sails for it. It took quite a while to get all the little strings hooked up for the rigging, but it was beautiful when it was done and sailed just like a large sailboat does. I liked that. But the little boats I made from the scraps of Gramps' wood were more fun, I think. And sailing shells was fun. Making things from sand was fun. Is that what you mean by toys?"

"Oh, I wondered about balls and pails, dolls and jacks, and the things you see the children play with at recess and noon."

"Oh, those toys. The funny cars the boys race and the dolls the girls giggle with. No. I didn't have those. Gran and I made lots of stuffed animals, though, and even some dolls. That was maybe the best fun of all. You know you sew or knit the pieces and it's quite fiddly work, but when you finally get to embroider a face on the doll or animal, it's like a new little life comes through. It's almost like seeing the kittens born in the barn, you know, only it's something you did all yourself. It was almost better than the painting!"

Mrs. Longacre could see the child hadn't needed toys as town children knew them. She'd been too busy. Still, for her report, she pressed on, "And games? I guess you didn't play tag or ball or those games that require other children to play with, but what about card games or board games?"

"Games? Hm. We played Scrabble once in a while. Gran really liked Scrabble. She said it gave her mind good exercise and settled her down when she might otherwise think worrisome things. So then we'd get out the board and play. She was right. Scrabble takes a lot of attention but it's just word puzzles and they're fun, don't you think? The Captain and I had a game of Chinese Checkers that Gramps had made. Instead of different coloured marbles, Gramps made different shapes so the Captain could feel them. That was fun. The Captain always won. He said it was because he planned ahead and I just liked hopping about, but what I really liked was watching him so happy. Otherwise, we just played our own games, winking games, singing games, word games, number games, laughing games. Miss Lily and I even played a painting game. We'd start with a blank page and using one colour at a time, taking turns, we'd see who could make the most variations of a colour or fit the most colours on a paper. Those were beautiful games! We'd even try to name all the colours and shades of colours. Sometimes we made story games. Yeah, I guess we had lots of games but only Scrabble and Chinese Checkers needed anything special for them. Mostly they were games we played while we were doing other things."

Mrs. Longacre began to see very clearly how Misty had learned so much that other children learned in school. Indeed Misty had learned far more than other children had learned either in or out of school. She also had to suppress a chuckle at the recognition that by government standards, the child would be considered deprived. No toys. No games. Indeed. It appeared that everyone was going to be in for a shock when the placement of Misty was finally done. Meanwhile, however, Mrs. Longacre needed to get on with her other work. She set Misty to the tasks of folding letters and putting them in envelopes and of tidying the office supply shelves and soon found herself smiling to hear Misty humming happily as she worked. Busy as people were, it seemed no time at all before the bell rang. Mrs. Longacre noticed Misty jump at the sound but didn't have time to comment before the grinning Tommy appeared, ready to go home.

"Before you go," said Mrs. Longacre, "you must take this letter. Mr. Sullivan was unable to reach the Hughes this afternoon, Misty, so he has written them a short letter instead. It explains that we have decided to begin your testing right away and that you will not be attending class until the testing is complete. Mr. Sullivan has decided it will be best to delay meeting with the Hughes until after everything is settled. This letter just lets them know what we are doing in the meantime. Be sure to give it to them as soon as you get home. Thank you for your help this afternoon. You work very well. See you in the morning!"

Both children thanked Mrs. Longacre and called goodbye as they left the office and school. The walk home was a very different one for Misty. As they crossed the school ground, children ran up and said "Hi." At first Misty thought they were talking to Tommy but soon heard them add "Thomasina" to their greeting. A few even called her "Misty," for Tommy had spread the word of the new girl's preference. All of them seemed a little shy, and Misty's own surprise at their greeting her at all didn't encourage any further conversation, but the ice was broken. She noticed some of those who had teased her the day before; they didn't greet her, but neither did they bother her at all. Instead, they simply stayed to themselves, sometimes glancing her way with looks that, if not friendly, were not hostile either. Tommy's sister, Daisy, joined them for their walk. Though like Tommy in appearance, she was much quieter than he was, almost shy, happy to walk or skip along just listening to the other two chatter.

Tommy was full of talk of the boat he and his father were building and was excited to hear Misty's tales of working beside her grandfather when he had built things, including the little skiff she had learned to row in. He could hardly wait to get their boat done so he could go out fishing. School may cut into his building time, but thoughts of school seldom cluttered the time he was free, so they chatted happily as they walked, discovering more and more things they shared. Misty soon discovered that Daisy was also a comfortable person to be with when the younger girl finally ventured into a slight pause in the conversation to admire Misty's curls.

"Oh," said Misty, "my hair just is curly. I can't think what will happen when the damp weather comes. Aunt Augusta insists on these silly ringlets, but my head will be a mass of frizz and tangles as soon as fall sets in if she doesn't let me braid it. Your braids are beautiful, Daisy, so shiny, coppery, and very tidy. I wish I could keep mine braided like I always did before coming here. Braids are so much more comfortable than this mess of curls, and much less work. Aunt Augusta said this morning I didn't do a good enough job of making these ringlets. She doesn't realize it is partly the change in weather. Did you see the dew on the spider webs this morning? Isn't it gorgeous? But my hair will soon look like spider nests or something, you'll see."

Daisy immediately saw the sense in what Misty was saying and stopped envying Misty her curls. Instead, the talk turned to the weather and the area, as Misty saw her chance to ask about the hills and where the ocean was. Tommy explained that when they got old enough for Junior High School they'd see the ocean every day, for that school was further up the hill and part way down the other side, overlooking the ocean. It wasn't all that far, really, only a few miles. It just seemed far because of the hills. The mountains with all their hills and crags did rise right up from the ocean all along the coast, making visibility limited almost as soon as you climbed away from the sea. Then, too, all the little rises and hills made natural divisions between small parts of their community, so the town seemed broken up in some ways. As they reached the corner where they should part, Misty thought to ask Tommy about the bottom of that valley.

"Didn' ya know? Why the lake's down there. We live 'most at the lake, least at the bay. It's a huge lake, jist huge, ya know. That's why me 'n' my pa 'r' makin' a boat, so's we c'n go fishin' in the lake. Bet ya c'n see the lake from upstairs in yer house. Whyn't ya have a look? There's a top window I jist know looks t' the lake."

Misty was amazed to think she was so close to a lake and was quite excited. Daisy suggested she come to their place on the weekend so they could walk the bit down to the log pond where the kids went swimming in the summer, and Misty promised she would ask Aunt Augusta, though she did wonder how she could go to Daisy's house when she knew skating lessons and Sunday school both started the coming weekend. Tommy assured her that would be no problem as she could come in the afternoon when Sunday school was over.

"Ask before t'morra so we c'n set a time ta walk up 'n' get ya if yer aunt sez it's okay," Tommy said. "T'morra's Friday already. Ain't thet great? I jist love the weekends. Me 'n' my pa'll show ya the boat. Maybe it's sorta like the one you had. This is great! Never knew no one who'd built a boat 'cept us. Wait'll I tell Pa t'night. Don't fergit t' ask. We gotta go now. It's late. 'Sides, there's yer aunt comin.' Ya better go. See ya in the mornin', Misty."

"Bye, Misty!" joined Daisy as the two coppery-haired kids began running down the hill, leaving Misty to walk slowly across the road and down the driveway, smiling to think of a huge lake so close and of going to see it so soon.

13.

Near Loss and Sure Gain: Tommy and Henry

Misty was surprised to see Aunt Augusta standing at the top of the stairs with her hands on her hips, her face looking as dark as the ocean before a storm. The smile vanished from her own face and she instinctively stopped at the bottom of the stairs and braced herself.

Sure enough, Aunt Augusta exploded: "What is this I see driving home? Did I not tell you this morning that it was of utmost importance that you cause no trouble today? How could you? How could you stand talking to those, those, those hooligans? Did I not warn you about riff-raff? And here you are, just the first week of school, talking to, standing with, goodness knows what with those hooligans. Why they are worse than riff-raff, the worst of the worst! Do you have any idea how many children there are in that family? There must be at least eight brats by now, at least eight! That is nothing short of irresponsible, plain ignorance, I'm sure. That alone should have told you to stay away from them. What ever will Hugh make of this? Here I am back from a hospital auxiliary meeting, and there you are cohorting about with the lowest of low. Whatever will people think? And wasn't that Thomas? Why, of all those hooligans, he is the worst of the lot, even worse than Robert was at that age! I simply won't have it; do you understand? Never again are you to associate with that family or any of their friends. Never! Is that clear? We will not have you associated with such people. Now, you will go immediately to your room and stay there! You'd better give some serious thought to your choice of friends, young lady. Now go!"

Poor Misty hardly knew what to do. Aunt Augusta towered above at the top of the stairs, glowering down at her, filling the doorway it seemed, making it impossible for Misty to obey her. She stood rooted to the spot, overcome by the woman's rage and her own position at the bottom of the stairs. Her mind swirled in confusion bordering on chaos, a throbbing beginning in her head as if the very thoughts themselves were hammering her, hammering, hammering through some kind of fog. The afternoon suddenly seemed dull, grey, as if night were already falling, snuffing out the light. Silently she cried out for help. Silently she battled the hammering, refusing to collapse, though she felt like it. Through the chaos, Misty discerned one thought: she must give the letter to Aunt Augusta. No matter this new rage all around her, she must do as she had been told.

Summoning all her strength, Misty put her foot on the bottom step and forced herself up. One step at a time, she pushed ahead, Aunt Augusta somehow seeming larger as Misty mounted each step. With just two steps remaining, Misty extended the letter toward Aunt Augusta, silently praying the woman would move, allowing her to go through the doorway and on to her room as commanded. Instead, Aunt Augusta drew herself even straighter and burst into yet another tirade as she tore open the envelope.

"Trouble at school, too, I suppose. I'll never be shocked again by just how wretched you are. Why, oh why didn't anybody warn me? Why couldn't I have guessed myself that you would be utterly hopeless and unmanageable? Riff-raff for friends, what could I have expected? No sooner do you associate with those hooligans and I've a letter from the school to deal with. How will I ever live this down at the next auxiliary meeting? How am I to put on the best bazaar ever when you thwart me at every turn? How is Hugh to win the election with you in trouble every minute? How do you expect to be any use to us when you cannot stay out of trouble? Really, I cannot deal with any more. I said 'to your room' and I meant it. There will be no dinner for you tonight, young lady. This is simply too much. Now, go!"

Aunt Augusta stepped aside, waving Misty into the house with an outflung arm, the unread letter clutched half-crumpled in her fist. Wide-eyed and very pale, Misty squeezed past Aunt Augusta, ducking beneath her arm and hurrying to her room. Closing the door behind her, she sank to her knees beside her bed, trembling and weak. The chaotic thoughts jammed, muting the hammering that persisted relentlessly and steadily, matching the pounding of her heart. Small as she was, Misty felt swollen with the enormity of her shock, a growing, throbbing ball engulfing her, frightening her with the threat of explosion. She wondered if the top of her head would just fly off, letting the pounding escape, leaving nothing but a chilled numbness. Frightened, she wrapped her arms around her head and held on, crying out at last. "Oh God, please help me." It was all she could say or even think.

Misty was not in the habit of kneeling to pray. Neither did she ever think about praying. She had dropped to her knees in sheer exhaustion, perhaps desperation, for through the chaos rose the knowledge that she was to lose her friends. Aunt Augusta was forbidding her to be friends with Tommy and Daisy, the only truly comfortable children she had found here. Grief rose up and silenced the chaotic thoughts, leaving raw pain throbbing through her being. It was the cold, her own shivering, that lifted her from the threat of defeat, forcing her to rise from her knees and tend to her physical needs, thus drawing her attention outward. Dully, mechanically, she changed from her school clothes into her warm flannel nightie. Funny to be so cold when the weather was yet warm. She put her bathrobe on as well, but continued chilly, so rummaged around until she found some warm socks and a sweater. She wished she had one of the old sweaters Gran had made; they were much warmer than these silly store-bought things that looked fancy but did no good. But Aunt Augusta had not left any of her comfortable clothes for her. She moved to the window, hoping to draw warmth from the light she saw filtered through the changing leaves.

Again she knelt, this time for comfort, the comfort of leaning on the windowsill and looking outside, the comfort of the kneeling position itself, the comfort of the thoughts she knew would come. She brushed the tears away as quickly as they fell, for fall they did when she saw the little cat below the apple tree. Oh, how she longed to scoop him up in her arms and bury her face in his soft warm fur, to hear the wonderful purr rise up in his chest and explode as she knew it would if only she could stroke him. No sound on earth is quite as comforting as the purr of a cat. Even as Misty's shivering began to slow just thinking about it, she noticed the cat trot away from the tree and she wondered once again where he went, where he lived, whose knee he might hop onto. Somewhere, she knew there must be a knee for the little cat, even as her knee had always been ready to accept the warmth of any of the cats who chose to hop up there back home. Misty's eyes grew glassy and the tears dried as she imagined herself back in the old barn, cats and kittens all around her in the loft.

The mother cat would never sit on Misty's knee when her kittens were up and playing; then she sat watching carefully as they wrestled and tussled, learning all the necessary cat moves in the course of their games. But once the kittens curled up for one of their many naps, the cat would stretch, lick herself a few times and then settle into Misty's lap and begin to purr deeply. Misty missed the steady companionship of her little dog, but for comfort, warmth and peace, she missed the cats. Leaning on the windowsill, Misty could almost feel the safety that emanated from the rhythm and unity of the barn. The scents of hay, grasses, horses and cats, so clean yet strong, fit perfectly with the even breathing or chewing of the horses and the purrs of the cats. Nothing jarred the peace. Nothing seemed out of place or intrusive. Even the clucking of chickens scratching about just outside the door blended into the scene. A small robin chirping in the apple tree outside Misty's window melded the two worlds for a moment, warming Misty with the harmony she missed so much before gently returning her to the present.

She was grateful for the cat, wherever he had gone. She was grateful for the robin. She was grateful that her predicament at least protected her from a battle over dinner. She was grateful for time alone. She was most grateful of all that she could see beauty and life in the trees, animals, sky and mountains, beauty that could not be marred by the constant clash of the people around her. She was grateful for so much that reminded her of her home, of peace, of living, and thus gave her strength to carry on, though the thought of doing so without Tommy and Daisy seemed daunting.

With the thought of the loss of her newfound friends, a hint of homesickness began to colour her thoughts of home. She didn't yet wonder why she had to come, was not yet tainted by the trials that persisted relentlessly in this new life. But deep inside, a vague sense of uneasiness, of loneliness, of homesickness took root, robbing her of some of the restorative power of her memories, tingeing the sensual nature of her memories with thought and a longing, not simply for what was gone but a longing to escape what was here.

Seeing the dusk beginning to fall, Misty rose from her spot by the windowsill and moved over to the bed, thinking that nestling down into the covers would remove the last of the chill that persisted. She tried pretending that she was a cat making a little nest in the hay of the loft, but nothing felt quite right. Instead, her mind was taken with wondering how she was to tell Tommy and Daisy that she couldn't go to their house and couldn't walk with them to school any more. She sensed they would understand that it wasn't her choice, but she also felt that it would hurt them nonetheless, especially since there seemed to be no reason not to be friends with them. None of it made sense to her, but the message had been absolutely clear and forceful, so somehow she would have to tell them. It never occurred to her to pretend anything or to try to avoid them. She must simply tell them Aunt Augusta had forbidden the friendship. She shivered despite the warm nightie and the covers. Funny, she'd never thought of coldness arising from other than the weather before, but this chill had nothing to do with the temperature, clothes or shelter. It was more distracting than being cold from not putting enough clothes on before running outside. Still, Misty wiggled down further in the bed, hoping to warm up.

Loneliness and chill interfering with her memories and imagination, Misty turned deliberately to her game, her grateful game. Reflecting on the day, she felt relieved as she thanked God for Mrs. Longacre, for the work Misty had been given to do in the office and for finally giving Misty a chance to speak. The time spent in the office had been good for Misty, and she was comforted to think she would return the next morning. It was a tremendous relief to have some of the misunderstanding cleared up. She had begun to feel deceptive, though she had not deliberately misled anyone. As Misty thought of all the things she had been free to say to Mrs. Longacre and the things she had shown her, she felt some heaviness lift from her, heaviness she had scarcely been aware of, and with the heaviness lifting, she began to think she could manage the next day even without Tommy's friendship. She sensed that she would be safe walking to school and on the playground and was thankful that somehow the children had stopped taunting her. It seemed that the school part of her life was going to work out. Misty thanked God for the hope that gave her that the other parts of her life would also work out, even as the Captain had assured her they would.

Easily, Misty turned then to thanking God for the Captain, for Miss Lily, for all the animals. The chill and loneliness left as she asked God to look after them, at times going into great detail of the things she knew the island people needed. They'd be getting ready for fall and winter now. She wondered how they would get the storm windows out and up without her help. This would be the first year that the Captain and Miss Lily must do it all alone. It would be hard work, and she didn't like the thought of the Captain up on a ladder having to feel his way around the window frame with one hand while setting the storm window in with the other, yet she knew they would not only get the job done but also enjoy doing it. She wondered if they would put the windows up on Gran's house and soon felt that they would, though there weren't people there to protect from storms. She knew they would protect the house itself. Misty felt her body begin to relax, the chill leaving at last, as she asked God to ensure no animals knocked the ladder over while the Captain was up it, asked Him to enable the Captain and Miss Lily to get messages straight, though the Captain's back would have to be to Miss Lily for part of the tasks. On and on she went with her requests, warmed both by looking to the needs of others and by the comforting thoughts of season changes and the security of having warm, safe places to live.

Misty loved each season for what it was and thoroughly enjoyed the changes between seasons as well. She smiled slightly, remembering a game she and her grandparents had had to give up. They had begun playing what they called "favourite things" one winter night when they had taken their hot chocolate close to the fire to draw extra warmth before going to bed. They began with food, each one trying to give the very favourite of all foods. Soon they were chuckling, for no one seemed able to decide on one. So it went, through favourite weather, favourite season, favourite clothes, even favourite colour. Gramps had ended the game with one of his resounding laughs as he said, "My favourite is the one right now; best meal is the one I'm eating, best season is the one I'm living, best time is the moment right now, best colour is the one I'm looking at, best clothes are the ones keeping me warm right now and best people are right here." He had stretched back in his Morris chair and sighed deeply and happily, concluding, "Only the truly rich enjoy their favourite things always, for their favourites are real and alive rather than ideal. We're too rich for this game." That was the only time they'd tried that game.

Before Misty could wonder if she was still too rich for that game, she received the answer to the question that had seemed unanswerable to her. Aunt Augusta poked her head in the door before retiring for the night and said, "I'll be driving you to school in the morning, young lady. That will take care of that riff-raff you've hooked up with. I must have a word with the principal. Hugh is as disgusted as I am. I'll give you and the principal a list of the people you must befriend. It's disgraceful that all the children are thrown into one big school. Silly small town, this. Perhaps Hugh will see to introducing a private school system when he is elected. Meanwhile, we will spell out which group you are to be a part of. You be ready on time in the morning and remember to take more care of how you look. Your hair was not pretty enough this morning. Leave yourself the time it takes to do a decent job. Now, good night." She closed the door firmly behind her, once again leaving Misty no opportunity to speak.

But no clear thoughts came to Misty's mind. She did feel relieved of the conflict of meeting Tommy and Daisy at the corner but not being allowed to speak to them or walk with them.

She'd been unable to sort out how she was to obey Aunt Augusta and let Tommy know she was just obeying her at the same time. Once she got to school, she knew she could send a message to Tommy through Mrs. Longacre or even could speak briefly to Tommy herself. She felt certain that it would be wrong not to speak to Tommy at all and was sure that when Aunt Augusta had calmed down, Misty could at least exchange a few words with Tommy from time to time. They just mustn't be friends. The only remaining problem was making sure Tommy didn't wait so long for her that he'd be late for school. She reasoned that he would see her leave in the car with Aunt Augusta and would carry on himself.

That settled in her mind, Misty listened briefly to the quiet creeping over the house for the night and let her mind drift to the pleasure of quiet, the quiet of houses tucked in for the night, fires banked, windows fastened shut, lamps blown out. She drew from the warmth of such quiet, such safety, such comfort, imagining as she did that all were at rest. At home, slow, even breathing of humans and animals alike had added security to the quiet. Even the occasional late night rocking of Gramps' squeaky chair had simply added its easy rhythm to the harmony, increasing both restfulness and warmth. Misty's eyelids grew heavy as she let the warmth of such night strength banish the chill of the day completely. Almost she could hear the steady creaking of Gramps' chair as if it were right there. Vaguely, sleepily, she wondered that the chair could sound so real, so close, so alive, so much a part of her new world. Its steady, soothing rhythm carried her safely to sleep.

Misty wakened refreshed and in plenty of time to take all the care needed with her ringlets. The crisp fall air that drifted in through the window brought with it the bubble of anticipation that she had felt each morning of her life. The damper of losing Tommy and of having to face an unhappy Aunt Augusta was eased by recalling that the burden of feeling so misunderstood at school had been lifted. She looked forward to seeing Mrs. Longacre and helping her. She was even a little hungry, having given most of her lunch away and missed dinner altogether, so she left her room unhindered by any fear or dread. It was another new day!

She ate her porridge, all of it, as Aunt Augusta prattled on about choice of friends, position in the community, importance of association and appearance, and putting things right at the school. She was much calmer this morning and had slipped into that talk that just fills up space without either demanding attention or battering the listener. It seemed to Misty that Aunt Augusta's relief to learn from the school that Misty would be tested and placed properly somehow over-rode her disgust at Misty's choice of friends. Though it made no sense to the child, she did comprehend that, to Aunt Augusta, Misty's having been placed in an inappropriately low grade was somehow a victory for the Hughes. Misty also deduced from there being no comment on her hair that she had satisfied Aunt Augusta in that small way. For herself, she was relieved to see Tommy wave to her as Aunt Augusta drove out of the driveway and passed him as they went up the hill. Tommy's lively grin somehow both smote and encouraged Misty as she heard Aunt Augusta say emphatically, "and I'll see that that is the last wave you get from such riff-raff as that." In that single grin, Misty recognized both the outward loss of a friend and the inward kinship that remains undisturbed by the events around us and the actions or commands of others.

At the school, Misty and Aunt Augusta went straight to the office, Aunt Augusta demanding to see the principal at once. Her voice grew louder and took on that tinny quality that grated on Misty's senses so badly as she began, "I'll have none of this continued association with such riff-raff as those bay children. Really, I just expected a school to have more sense than encourage such association, especially you knowing us as you do. We didn't rescue her from that dreadful island isolation to plunge her into the slums and we didn't take her so that her slum tendencies would drag us down. I demand to see Mr. Sullivan immediately and I expect you to keep her safe from those filthy people. Why they probably have all sorts of vermin about them. You do check the children for such things, don't you? Should I have deloused Thomasina? Oh, why didn't

I think of that? Who knows what dreadful things she has brought home, right into our home? Why on earth didn't you send a note to that effect instead of this notice of your placement blunder? Can't you people get anything right? Wait until I tell Hugh of this latest oversight. He'll have a thing or two to say, I'm sure. We've soon learned the trials of having children, haven't we? We've not had a peaceful moment since she came, and putting her in school, which we thought to alleviate the problems, has only made them worse. I demand immediate action here. Where is that Sullivan? Is he late? Why doesn't he come at once?"

Mrs. Longacre moved around the counter and gently put her hand on Misty's shoulder before addressing the irate woman. "Mrs. Hughes, calm down. In fact, Mr. Sullivan has stopped at the school board on his way in this morning to arrange for Misty's tests."

"Misty? Who on earth might that be? Why should such a child, any child with a name more utterly ridiculous even than Thomasina is, be given precedence over the child we've taken in? What sense of order is there here?"

"I'm sorry, Mrs. Hughes. I didn't know you were unaware of Thomasina's preferred name, the name she has known all her life. It is Thomasina's tests he is arranging. He'll be here shortly and will be free to explain it all to you. Let me just settle Misty with Henry; she's going to work with him for a while this morning until we have space ready for her here in the office."

"Just wait one minute. In the first place, the child's name is Thomasina, and Thomasina she'll be called. Her fool grandfather shouldn't have given her such a name if he didn't intend people to use it. As ridiculous as 'Thomasina' is, 'Misty' is just unacceptable altogether. We won't have it. In the second place, I will not have a child living under my roof assisting a janitor. Is Henry not the janitor? How could you even think to send the child to a janitor? Have you no sense of what is proper?"

Mrs. Longacre noted both Aunt Augusta's rising anger and Misty's slight cowering at the onslaught and decided instantly that Misty must take precedence over the difficult woman. Firmly and evenly she said, "Mr. Sullivan and the teachers will be more than happy that you agree with the school policy on names, Mrs. Hughes. You needn't worry about that. Forgive my mistake. As for working with Henry, you must understand that, though he is a janitor, the work he gives to the children is far from janitorial work. Henry is a vital part of this school's staff, invaluable to the children and to our assessment of the children. He will be reporting at the end of the day what he has learned about Thomasina's ability that will help us with properly placing her. You may take a seat and wait for Mr. Sullivan to come in or you may return home and I'll have him call you, whichever you prefer. Right now, I am taking Thomasina to Henry's room. Excuse me."

As Aunt Augusta sputtered on about schools, riff-raff, janitors and tardy principals, Mrs. Longacre firmly but gently led Misty past her and into the corridor, closing the office door behind them in an attempt to keep the irritating voice from travelling through the school building. Lightly, she said to Misty, "It's good to see you looking brighter this morning, Misty. I hope you don't mind going to Henry for a while. I didn't think you needed to stay in the office while Mrs. Hughes meets with Mr. Sullivan. I have good news for you. You have today free to spend with Henry and me, but we have received permission to administer the tests beginning on Monday. The school board is sending someone especially to complete the task so you won't be kept in the wrong place any longer. That's more than I had hoped for. It will be so good to have you settled. It can't have been easy for you, but you're certainly a brave and co-operative child and very strong. The folks would be proud of you, I'm sure."

"Thank you, Mrs. Longacre. I miss them so much. I really wish I could write them or something. Could you show me how to send letters? Funny, isn't it? I knew how to do it from the island but I have no idea how to do it here. I haven't any paper or money for stamps, though, so I guess I don't need to know how to mail things. That's okay, though. I'm sure they are all right. But I do need your help. Would you get a message to Tommy for me? I'm not sure what is right to do, exactly, but Aunt Augusta will not allow me to walk to school with them or to go to their house. Tommy and Daisy had asked that I go there on the weekend. Oh, Mrs. Longacre, I was going to see the lake! Is it at all like the ocean? I miss the ocean so much. Anyway, could you please just tell Tommy that I cannot go to their house and that I must walk to and from school by myself? Also, tell him I am sorry and that I'll miss him, but Aunt Augusta insists."

"Of course, I'll tell him. And I am sorry, too. Tommy and Daisy are good and lively children. I'm sorry Mrs. Hughes has decided to insist you form other friendships. But you will find other nice children, I'm sure, and you must do what the Hughes ask."

"Is it right, though, not to talk to Tommy at all? I don't understand why I shouldn't be friends with them, though I can just respect Aunt Augusta's wishes about that, but it seems wrong to me not to talk to them when I meet them. Surely Aunt Augusta didn't mean that I wasn't to talk to them at all, do you think?"

"I don't know what she said to you or has in mind, Misty, so can't really answer you. I do understand your feeling, though, for I think it wrong to ignore people or to treat different people in different ways."

"I get so confused, Mrs. Longacre, for all the rules people give me seem to snarl like frayed yarn and not weave together like good threads at all. If Aunt Augusta really means I am to have nothing to do with Tommy, how can I do that and 'be polite at all times?' Surely it is rude to ignore someone when he speaks to you, isn't it? I just don't know which thing to do. I guess that's why I seem to spend so much time here just standing and not answering at all. I can't sort it all out or work the rules together."

"You're doing just fine, Misty. Don't be hard on yourself. As for conflicting rules, I think we must try always to do what we know to be right. Sometimes that means looking beyond the rules. Just go slowly. A way will become clear before you. But why don't you ask Henry these things? He has been around longer than I have and has much more wisdom. This is his last year at the school, so you are very lucky you've come this year or you'd have missed him. After this year, he'll retire and spend his time in his orchards, I expect. Here, you knock on his door. This is it."

As Misty knocked softly, she said, "Oh, thank you, Mrs. Longacre. What am I to do here?"

Henry opened his door as Mrs. Longacre answered, "Anything that Henry asks you to do, any work he has."

But she wondered if Misty had even heard her answer, for on seeing Henry's wrinkled face and hands, Misty was almost transformed. Her face relaxed, her eyes widened and glistened and her mouth opened just slightly as she looked up into the kind face. She seemed completely taken by what she saw.

To Mrs. Longacre's further surprise, Misty became even more absorbed, almost as if she were transported to a different world, when Henry's face broke into its loving smile, and he said in his rich, deep voice, "Hello, little one. Are you to be my friend for the morning? I'm Henry. Just plain Henry. What about you?"

Henry bent down slightly and held out his large hand to Misty. She nodded as she reached her own small hand up to his. "Oh, hello. I'm Misty," she said in a soft voice that trembled slightly; "Just plain Misty."

As Henry's soft hand engulfed that of the little girl, her eyes grew even wider and she gave a delighted shiver as tears suddenly rolled down her cheeks. In one smooth, swift move, Henry knelt and gathered the little girl into his arms, drawing her close to his chest, rocking gently and stroking her hair firmly and slowly. Mrs. Longacre dabbed at her eyes with a hanky, but Henry let his tears fall onto the child's head. After a few quiet moments, he nodded at Mrs. Longacre, indicating she could leave. He had no questions for her, no need for anything. He knew nothing of Misty but what he needed to know, that she was a pure child who needed a little special attention.

Gently he rocked her as she wept into his great chest. As he sensed her quieting a little, he began talking softly in the most soothing voice Misty had heard on the Mainland.

"A good friend for me today, I see. It makes me real warm to meet someone who doesn't laugh when these old eyes spring a leak and wash away a little pain. Sometimes I hurt from the nasty things people do to each other and other times I just ache out of the fullness of love and the beauty around me. Either time, the old tears spill out, and most people make fun. I can see, though, that you're my own kind of person.

"Isn't it a grand morning, all crisp and clear, all bright and fresh? Why I thought my feet would dance of their own accord as I walked to the school this day. And then I got to thinking how fortunate I am to have this job, to have important, useful work to do, and to be free to work among all these lively children and I felt so glad all over I 'near bust' as Tommy'd say. Now to have a new friend all warm and gentle, it's no wonder I spilled over a little, is it? After a while, we'll go outside, you and I, to tend to the waste containers, and that will give us a chance to have another deep breath of that clear air, maybe take in some of the bird songs, too, if we're lucky. We'll have to watch we don't spill over again, won't we? But first we have a few things to do inside. Have you met my big mop, my very biggest mop? Come now, let me show you."

Misty lifted her head from the safe and now damp chest and stood back a little to look once again into the deep, open eyes. The joy she felt at seeing and feeling a soft, wrinkled person again and the comfort of being so thoroughly understood and accepted all glowed from her own eyes. It was almost like being at home again! As Henry stood and took her hand once again in his, and she felt the rough softness of old work-worn hands, Misty did burst out—singing a doxology. Henry brushed the new tears of joy from his cheek. This was a child unlike any other. He added his own bass voice to her child-soprano. The hush of the small room when they finished their praise was perfect.

Together the two turned, Misty easily walking with Henry to the cupboard. He removed the largest mop there, saying, "This is it, the one I use for the corridors, and it's your turn to ride!"

But Misty had seen other mops in the closet and quickly she reached in and took the smallest version of the shaggy dry mop that Henry held. Silently she adjusted the mop in her hand the same as he held his and took her place beside him. He smiled, understanding, and they set out together. In perfect silence they mopped the long corridor on the east wing of the main floor, but as they began the west wing, Henry smiled to hear the child humming softly but evidently happily. When that task was done, they cleaned the mops, replaced them and went outside, taking a large bin on wheels with them. Henry breathed deeply and looked all around at the trees, noting the birds flitting among the branches. "Nice, isn't it?" he said.

Misty was ready to talk, as he had known she would be. "Oh, Henry," she began, "it's wonderful, almost like home. I miss the ocean air, though, the salt tinge to it. The Captain said this town was on the ocean, but I haven't seen it and can't even smell it. I know the Captain never lies, so I must just not have found the ocean yet. He said I'd do fine here, too, but I haven't done. I seem to make people unhappy and make trouble everywhere I go. I can't find any rhythm here, except with you, Henry, and everything bumps and jars so. The Captain never was wrong, so I know it will be fine, but somehow it isn't yet."

Henry soon learned all Misty's trials and quickly saw her strength through it all. She never complained, just stated what she saw as the facts, as she genuinely searched for the way to have a smooth and comfortable life in the town. He recognized her discomfort with feeling as if she were deceiving people, though she had only been denied opportunity to explain, and once again wished that he could put the world right. It hurt the old man to see through Misty's recitation of her time here just how little respect she had been shown, but he remained quiet and continued to listen. Though it frustrated him to think he could not do anything about Misty's home life or the kind of people she seemed destined to live with, he showed no such emotion to the little girl. Instead, he calmly led her through the work outside so they would be sure to be off the playground by recess, knowing as he did that Misty would gain more by continuing in their quiet companionship than by being interrupted by the explosion of children onto the playground. As she continued recounting her life in town, he led her back to his little room where he put the kettle on to make them some tea. He always took a little tea and biscuits during the recess break in case Mrs. Longacre sent a child to him. He knew she would send no more this morning.

It was only when Misty poured out her tale of losing Tommy and Daisy as friends and not being able to see the lake that Henry turned her monologue into the conversation that she needed. He gave her a cup of the warm tea and said simply, "I am a bay person too, Misty. We've lived down that road for over forty years now, and it's beautiful down there. The lake stretches out for some twenty miles beyond the bay and there's a large island in the middle of it, rising right up out of the lake. We have a large orchard and our property runs down right to the edge of the water. The rest of the bay is taken with a saw-mill and log-ponds. It's a lively, grand place. You would like it, though it is not exactly the same as your island.

"But Misty, you have to learn that some people don't look at the beauty around them, and they look at work differently than you or I do. They see the kind of work I do and Tommy's pa does as dirty work and they think that only dirty or low people do such work. They have a notion that deskwork is somehow better. So they look down on us bay people. They are wrong, Misty, but we can't change them. All work that is honest is good and equal. Cleaning things at the school and harvesting fruit in the orchard is all honest. Working the saw-mill as Tommy's pa does is honest; it's hard work but it's honest. People here think that teachers are better than secretaries or janitors because teachers have more education than we do. But Misty, education is just education. We can't be judging people by how much education they have or don't have. Some teachers are honest. Some are not. Some janitors are honest. Some are not. It's who a person is, not what he does, that matters, Misty. But not everyone sees it that way. The important thing is for you to stay true and loving yourself, and the hard thing is to look for the good in people who have forgotten what is really important.

"You take Tommy, for example. Now you've been told you're not to be friends with Tommy, not to associate with him. Truth is, you are friends with Tommy whether you associate with him or not. People don't realize that friendship is a matter of the heart, not the mind or the skin. True friends have bonds that go beyond just associating, just chattering on the playground. Why, look how soon you and I knew we were true friends. Tommy is like that too. They can ask you not to play with him, but they can't take away what you have inside. So, Misty, you can honour Mrs. Hughes' request and still be true to your friendship with Tommy. The challenge for you is whether you can forgive Mrs. Hughes for forgetting what matters and judging Tommy so unfairly. I can. Can you?"

"That's it, Henry! Why hadn't I seen that? Of course I can forgive her. And I'll have to ask God to forgive me too. I haven't been very patient with Aunt Augusta and I have been critical inside myself. That must be what the Captain meant when he said I shouldn't let them corrupt me. I'll have to be more careful. But how do people forget so easily? Aunt Augusta is always so unhappy, Henry, and I can't seem to help her. I always make it worse."

"Well, little one, you deserve a fair answer here. She is unhappy and has been that way for a very long time. She is unhappy because she has forgotten what is important. You mustn't think you are responsible for her unhappiness or even that you make her more unhappy. As odd as it sounds, you mustn't try too hard to make her happy either. Instead, you must try to do what is right. That is the only way that you may be able to make her happy. We all have to tend to ourselves, Misty, to keep our own attitudes pure. That's all you can do. And you are doing a mighty good job of that, so try not to fuss.

"I am sorry you have learned loneliness here, but just think; you and I can be friends and Tommy and I are friends, so we're all three friends, aren't we? And I'm always around somewhere, Misty. You can find me if you need me or you can ask Mrs. Longacre. You'll see, soon you will find a place here in the school, even if your place at the Hughes remains strained for you. Those tests you say you'll have next week will sort things out in no time. Besides, with Mrs. Longacre looking out for you, you'll soon find your part of the rhythm here. There is one, you know; it just isn't one you have known before, and it is often interrupted by some kind of human calamity. Just think of mopping the corridor with me this morning. That's the rhythm I hang onto. Trouble is you are a child with a natural rhythm, the rhythm it has taken old folk a lifetime to settle into, and now you are trying to move in a world with the frenzy of middle-aged folk. Must make your head hurt sometimes."

"Henry, that is it exactly! I get such a pounding and swirling inside sometimes I can hardly move. Gosh, there's so much to learn here. I never was so aware of things before. Nothing ever took so much thought, so much figuring out. I just did things. I can't help but wonder if I'll ever get it. And I've only begun, really, haven't I? This weekend I begin more new things: figure skating and Sunday school. Is Sunday school like this school, Henry?"

"Not really. First, it's much smaller, especially if you're going to the little white church up the hill. It's short, too, only an hour or so. It will begin with some singing together before children form small classes by age, but all the classes stay in the one big room of the church, just gathered into groups by circles of chairs. You'll have a Bible story and lesson, a few questions, maybe something to draw or do. About half the people will stay after for church with their parents and the other half will go home. I expect you'll be going home, for the Hughes don't attend church much and never that one. It should be fun and easy for you, Misty. There's not all the noise of this school."

"Oh, that's a relief. I thought it might just be school on Sunday and, though I am beginning to prefer school to home, the noise of it all still makes me a little tired. I wonder about figure skating."

Henry chuckled. "I can't tell you about that one, child. I've never done that, though I did skate on the small lake when it froze over when I was a boy. I recall it feeling nice to glide across the ice and I liked the eerie hollow-sound of the skates on the ice. But you'll be figure skating. That's fancy stuff and it's in the arena. Say, you'll see the ocean! The arena is out past the High School, right on the ocean. You'll smell the sea there, Misty. You'll see the Captain was right! But now, we've more work to do. Let's get to it."

Old man and child worked happily throughout the day, interrupted only by Mrs. Longacre bringing Misty's lunch and reporting that all the tests were set for Monday morning, that Mrs. Hughes had gone home satisfied with the arrangements, and that Tommy understood Mrs. Hughes' directions and wouldn't wait for Misty after school. He wanted her to know that he would keep a watch out for any trouble, though, and wouldn't let anyone hurt her. Misty could have spent the afternoon working in the office, but Mrs. Longacre, Henry and Misty all knew instinctively that the day would be best spent with Henry.

Probably none of them realized just how much Misty gained by spending a day in the easy company of an old man, the only age Misty had been familiar with. She left the school yard that day strengthened, comfortable, calm, content to walk home alone, watching once again for glimpses of dogs and cats among the late flowers and gently turning leaves of shrubs and trees. She returned Tommy's wave when she saw him in the distance and smiled and nodded at children who called "hello" to her as they passed her or turned to go their own ways. Life was full of promise once again.

14.

Glimpses: The Sea and Skating

Misty waited quietly on the back steps for Aunt Augusta to return home. It really was a pretty place with the lush green grass surrounded by flowers and shrubs and the tiny orchard off to the side. The fish pond with its lily pads reminded her of Miss Lily's larger pond, and the distant mountains sloping down into the valley that she now knew held a lake filled Misty with that old sense of being big and small at the same time. She felt both full and empty. She was grateful once again for the solidity of the natural part of this world being so similar to that back home.

As she sat full of the beauty around her and the refreshment of her day with Henry, Misty saw the cat stealing around the corner and up the path. He crouched down a little near the other steps, the steps that led up to the stand for the clotheslines, and watched her, tail flicking slightly from side to side. Misty remained still and quiet, hoping he would come to her. The two sat still watching each other for a long time. Just as Misty felt she was about to be rewarded for her patience, Aunt Augusta's car pulled into the driveway, startling the cat and sending him running. To Misty's astonishment, he scurried up the clothesline stand, scrambled up the pole and onto the roof of the house. She had always thought he passed through the yard. Now she wondered why he'd flee to the roof. But then cats are funny things. She chuckled to think that her response to hearing a car might be the same. She still found their noise and their bumping unsettling.

Aunt Augusta came down the path chattering as always, but happily this afternoon. "Good girl. You did as I said. That's a relief. I've had such a good day, you can't imagine. I'm so happy to have that silly nonsense at the school sorted out. Mr. Sullivan is tending to everything. Of course, it was just misunderstanding. I knew a man such as he is couldn't have been negligent.

How would Hugh be content to play golf with anyone who didn't know better than to give you ridiculous names or put you with wrong people and in a wrong class? Hugh will be pleased that I've tended to it all and not had to bother him. And I've had a delightful afternoon of bridge with all the right people."

On and on she continued, full of talk that made no sense to Misty but delivered in a tone that Misty had learned meant she was free to do what was right and think whatever she wanted. After changing into her other clothes, Misty quietly moved about the kitchen, setting the tables and doing whatever she noted needed doing. Suddenly she realized that Aunt Augusta no longer exploded when Misty did something useful but without being asked. She bunched herself up in a little wiggle of happiness to realize that some things were getting a bit easier here. There seemed hope that she would identify and settle into what rhythm there might be.

Alas, she couldn't eat her dinner again, so the quiet was short-lived. Still, she was getting used to being sent to her room and she was happy to spend her evening thinking over the wonderful day she had spent with Henry and wondering if Tommy was happily working with his pa on their boat. She drifted easily to sleep that night, comfortable in the knowledge that friends are never really lost as long as we can think of them, remember them and care about them.

Morning brought new trials for Misty. Aunt Augusta was up early, fussing about getting Misty ready for figure skating lessons. She had to look just right, make her ringlets pretty and be ready to impress everybody. She also needed to eat a good breakfast, an even larger bowl of porridge than usual. Misty's confusion about what "impress everybody" might mean was soon forgotten in her battle with the porridge, a battle that was lost before it even began, so large was the bowl. As had been the case on the first day of school, however, Aunt Augusta did not lose her temper over the matter. Instead, when it was almost time to leave, she simply whipped the bowl away and ordered Misty to get ready and go to the car.

As they bumped along the road, Misty neither listened to Aunt Augusta prattling on about all the little girls and the importance of their parents to Uncle Hugh's election nor thought further about what figure skating might be or what she might have to do. Instead she looked eagerly around, watching for a glimpse of the ocean, waiting to hear its sounds, to feel its strength and peace. They drove through a forested area that was delightful to Misty despite her eagerness for the ocean, for these tall trees were as those at home: magnificent. Eagerly she watched for the squirrels she knew would be somewhere in the branches, for the deer that may be almost hidden among the trunks and undergrowth. So great was her pleasure in the forest that she almost forgot the discomfort she continued to feel in the rattling car. Unconsciously she took deeper and deeper breaths, trying to draw full life and strength from the beauty of this world.

Suddenly she strained to hear above the noisy car, wishing with all her might for the silent background of her old world. She sat up straight, leaning a little forward, turning an ear a little to one side, straining, straining. There! She heard it again: the cry of a gull! She tingled all over. A wide grin lit up her face and she leaned even farther forward. She hardly knew where to look and bumped her head on the windshield in her excitement. Instead of sliding back into her seat, she turned to the side, pressing her nose against the side window of the car, trying to hear the gull, trying to get closer to the ocean. Had she been free, she'd have run eagerly ahead, for she could sense now where the ocean was. She could feel it in the air, even through the noisy, metallic car. Misty could hardly keep her feet still, could barely contain her excitement.

Even the feel of Aunt Augusta's hand roughly grabbing her shoulder and shaking her a little didn't bring Misty fully back to the confinement of the car. Though she sat back a little in the seat where Aunt Augusta had pulled her, she couldn't hear the woman yelling about paying attention to her and being respectably dignified. She had ears only for the sounds of the gull and the ocean. And there as the road curved down the hill, Misty could see through a narrow scattering of trees the deep, moody blue of the sea. Her excitement suddenly flowed into the profound peace of fulfilment. As the car turned out of the trees into a large open parking area overlooking the ocean, Misty sighed deeply, full of the expanse of life before her. Her eyes wide but calm, she settled back against the seat of the car utterly content, at least content until the harsh hand shook her again and the grating voice pierced her reverie.

"Really, child, you are the most ridiculous thing I've ever met. What on earth are you gawking at now? I can't imagine what makes you so foolish. I begin to think you aren't quite right. It's just the ocean. There's nothing out there to gawk at or gape about. Surely you, of all people, know that. For goodness sake, pay attention to what's important. Now, we're going in to the rink to meet the other girls, get you into the right level and order your skates and skating clothes. Look smart and pay attention. Mind the people you meet. They matter."

As Aunt Augusta carried on about the idiocy of staring off into the ocean and watching gulls instead of going after the important people about you, Misty only vaguely felt herself jerked along by the hand toward the big, domed building called the arena or the rink. Try as she might, she could not keep her eyes off the ocean, the powerful blue-black of the depths in the distance yielding to the lively deep blue off-shore finally paling to the playful blue-green near the beach and rocks. It seemed to Misty to contain all of life. Somewhere in its expanse, every facet of being was stated, reflected, illuminated. She reluctantly turned her face away and looked in the direction Aunt Augusta tugged her only when they crossed the doorway and entered the building.

She found herself in a chilly, damp, cavernous room. In the centre was a huge sheet of ice, its length divided by blue and red lines, its centre marked with a large red circle. On all four sides of the rectangular ice surface, low wooden walls separated the ice from the stands that rose up as stairs high into the edges of the domed structure. The floors in the smallish area where they stood were wood, some spots of which were covered in a kind of coarse canvas. Aunt Augusta pulled Misty off to their right where people were clustered about the doorway of one of the equipment rooms. Misty recognized some of the girls from school who had taunted her on the way home and felt herself holding back and shrinking a little inside. The place seemed dark despite the many overhead lights. Aunt Augusta gave an extra tug on her arm, urging her along, even as she raised her voice slightly and began calling to the woman standing at the centre of the group.

"Oh, there you are," she began in the tinniest of her many tones; "we're here to register for figure skating and to order equipment. I see you have a large group. You'll recall I phoned late in the summer and you'll find the child's name on your list. This is Thomasina. She is ten, small for her age, but ten. I trust you will put her in the right group. I won't have her with the little children. I won't be embarrassed in any way. Do you see her name on the list? Please find it at once. We haven't all day to waste. Where are the parents of these other children? Why aren't there other parents here? What am I to do while you take care of the child? Who am I to talk to? Why didn't anyone tell me there wouldn't be parents here?"

"Ah, you must be Mrs. Hughes. You are a little early. We began registration of the returning students first. Thomasina is, I believe, a beginner. The other beginners will be along with their parents shortly, I'm sure. Perhaps you and Thomasina would like to take a seat over there on the bench while I finish up here. I won't be long. You'll be able to watch these older girls on the ice. They'll be doing some free practice this morning. Lessons begin next week."

"These are not older girls. They are Thomasina's age. What do you mean calling them older girls? I won't put up with this kind of distinction. People must learn to treat Thomasina as they do others her age. It's ridiculous, all this discrimination. I'm fed up with it and I didn't expect it here."

"Now, Mrs. Hughes, these other girls, whatever their age, have been figure skating for several years already. Some of them have begun competitive skating. As I understood you on the phone, Thomasina hasn't had any figure skating lessons at all. It would be impractical and dangerous to group the children by age rather than by level of training and skill. Thomasina must begin with the first class. There will be children her age in that group as well. Just you sit down while I finish this. Thomasina should watch the girls who are already on the ice so she can see the basics of what we do. Watch the girl in the deep blue skating tights. She'll give you a good idea of what we aim for here. Please, sit down."

Thomasina moved over to the bench to see the girls on the skates gliding smoothly and apparently effortlessly over the ice. Aunt Augusta stood for a moment, almost sputtering she was so flustered by the woman's having simply turned her back to her and continued with the task of registering and sorting girls. Unable to regain the attention of the woman, she joined Thomasina and huffed on about ridiculous rules and rude treatment. Thomasina, though, was fascinated by what she saw. First, the white skates with the glistening silver blades kept her attention. She wondered what they felt like and how one ever managed to stand in them, slide in them and, she suddenly thought, stop in them. Some of these girls could go backwards as well as forward and, to her utter astonishment, some twirled, spun and even jumped. Though the whole thing looked frightening to her, it also enthralled her, for the lithe movements and supple stretches of the girls gave her a shivery, rich feeling inside. She imagined it felt much like running free on the beach or stretching fully, arms above her head, to dive into the ocean. She longed for such free movement.

Only when one of the girls fell on landing a jump did Misty give a little shiver of fear, a shiver that was quickly banished by her attention suddenly being drawn to the skaters' heads. All of those who had long hair wore braids or had their hair neatly pulled back into ponytails. Unconsciously she put her hand up to her own clusters of ringlets, ringlets that were fast frizzing into mats in the dampness of the arena, and pulled them down, longing for the freedom of braids once again. Maybe skating would be a blessing no matter what falls she may have to take. Imagine being able to see the ocean every Saturday morning and to wear braids for at least part of that day! She felt herself shiver, this time with delight.

But her happiness was once again interrupted by Aunt Augusta's grating voice. "Really, child, stop pulling at your curls. You have them all messed up. Look at you. What will I do if any of the important people come in now? You're a disgrace to look at. Honestly. Didn't I tell you to take special care with your hair this morning? Nothing is ever right. And look at all these little children around. I'm not prepared to sit here much longer. We could at least be trying on skates or something. Everyone else seems already to have theirs. I don't see why someone can't tend to us."

So saying, she grabbed Misty's hand and hauled her over to the other equipment room, demanding someone measure the child's feet and fit her with skates.

"Do you have skates to trade in, Ma'am?" the attendant asked.

"Of course not! Even if the child weren't new to us, I wouldn't be dealing in used things. Do you really think I would put a child in skates that had been worn by someone else? Who knows what kind of filth there'd be in a skate? We want new. Brand new."

"Of course. Whatever you wish, Ma'am. I was just trying to help with costs. Most of the young skaters trade the first year or two. Only the more advanced skaters need new boots. Skating can be costly, Ma'am. We can help at the beginning, though we can't later on. Just trying to help."

"Well, I don't need your help! Now fit the child and bring new skates."

Poor Misty cringed as Aunt Augusta adopted a tone even worse than the one she had used with Milly in the shop or Mrs. Longacre at the school. She wanted to hide somewhere. The young man didn't seem bothered, however, as he turned to Misty and asked, "What size were your last skates?"

Before Misty could answer, Aunt Augusta exploded, "She's never had skates, for heaven sake! What would she do with skates on an island without ice? Really, young man! Pay attention to what I say and do your job. You are most inattentive. Did I not say she was new? Measure her foot!"

The young man rolled his eyes as he led Misty to a little stool and asked her to sit down while he got his measuring stick. He ignored Mrs. Hughes' continuing bluster and turned his attention to Misty, asking, "Do you skate at all?"

Quietly Misty said, "No," as she took off her shoe and put her foot on the measuring stick.

"Hm," he said, almost to himself. "I wonder if they know that. You wait here a minute while I go look at the list and see what I can find out. There are separate classes for learning to skate, classes that come before figure skating classes. I'd better check."

Aunt Augusta's voice rose as she saw the man leaving, but Misty refused to listen to her words. She was getting very tired by the conflict that she now realized arose wherever Aunt Augusta went. Nobody suited Aunt Augusta. Nobody did a proper job. Nobody pleased her. It seemed nothing was ever as she expected or wanted it to be. Misty's shoulders slumped a little as she waited on the stool.

When the young man returned, he had the registration woman with him. "It seems there's some mistake here," she said. "You do understand that figure skating lessons are for people who can skate, don't you, Mrs. Hughes? We have beginning skating lessons and beginning figure skating lessons. We don't start figures until the child can skate. It seems we've registered Thomasina in the wrong class. We'll have to change her to the learn-to-skate class. We'll still fit her with skates, but for learn-to-skate she'll not need skating tights. She can just come in a pair of pants and a sweater. The class is on Saturday afternoon. We block off part of the ice for the beginners to use while the lowest level of figures can use the other part for practice. Shall I move her, then? We do have room in the other class."

Misty cringed to see Aunt Augusta's face grow red and contort as the woman talked. She was not surprised to hear the outburst that followed, though she was surprised by its result;

"Well I've heard everything! You'll do no such thing. Why the child will skate in no time! She's not stupid, you know. I've never been so insulted in my life! Your suggestion is simply preposterous. Separating figure skating from other skating! Impossible. I know your little game. You'll put a nice child like this in with those ruffian boys who want only to play hockey. I won't have it; do you hear? You must have a beginners' figures class that she belongs in. It is completely unacceptable that you run things this way. Why when Hugh is elected, he'll see to your little sham school here. You'll find you'll run it right or lose your operating license, that's what. Just you watch. Come, Thomasina; there are more refined things to do than skate around on ice. We're leaving!"

Misty scrambled to get her foot in her shoe as Aunt Augusta grabbed her arm and all but dragged her from the building, half hopping, half stomping to get the shoe on. She had to stifle a chuckle as she realized what a sight they must make, Aunt Augusta clipping along, her minced steps matching the staccato of her angry voice, her face red and contorted in outrage, Misty dragged along by one arm, hopping and scrambling to keep up, her completely unruly mass of hair frizzing a full foot out from her head in every direction.

She couldn't help but be amused by the wild sight they must present and she wondered if the gulls were laughing at them or just calling their gull words to each other as they circled above the ocean. She smiled to hear them and felt herself refuse to struggle further. She simply stopped and squatted down to fix the offending shoe, breathing deeply of the ocean air. She ignored Aunt Augusta's shriek and subsequent tirade about disobedience and wilfulness as she adjusted her sock, fit the shoe properly on her foot and tied the lace carefully before standing up, looking over the wondrous expanse of the ocean and taking full, rich breaths.

Every sense was alive, at once reaching to the ocean and beyond and soaking up life itself. Misty could feel an ebb and flow of life inside her that matched the ebb and flow of the small waves, themselves but a miniature reflection of the steady ebb and flow of the tides. Misty thrilled at the solidity of the ancient and true natural rhythm and inhaled deeply, wanting to saturate herself in the fit of it all, as if in sucking in the ocean rhythm with its air she could force out all the conflict and abrasion of the town life. Only as the deep sense of belonging washed over her did Misty get a glimpse, a slightly frightening glimpse, of just how much this bumpy, cacophonous life had unsettled her, perhaps polluted her. Even as Aunt Augusta grabbed her hand again, jerking her toward the waiting car,

Misty feasted her eyes on the sea and drew great, deep breaths of the rich, regenerating air.

Inwardly, Misty struggled and fought as the car door slammed, the noisy engine started up and the car pulled away from the parking lot, leaving the expanse of sea behind. She yearned to stay, to hang on to every familiar breath, sound and sight, to feel once again the fullness of an unselfconscious life, to live in peace. Instead, the outraged nattering voice of the woman beside her threatened even what she had gained by her brief glimpse of the sea she knew so well. She felt energy drain from her as once again it dawned on her that she had been given a very brief promise of something only to have it snatched away. Just as she had gained and lost Tommy in a fleeting period, she had now lost in an instant the hope of seeing the ocean each Saturday. Aunt Augusta had decided: no skating. Misty strained to enjoy the ride home through the forest, but her disappointment separated her as the physical presence of the car couldn't. Try as she might, she could only see the magnificent trees; she could not sense the life in them. The hostile voice beside her, repeatedly, relentlessly spelling out a new kind of confinement stood between her and the enjoyment of the natural surroundings.

She had to escape. Her eyes grew glassy as she thought of the forest at home, the freedom of entering and leaving it as she chose, the fullness of being in it, of smelling the richness of forest growth, of hearing the happy life sounds of animals against the softness of the near silence of the huge trees, of feeling the life in the strong textures of spongy moss on pitted bark and rippled lichen on smooth limbs. Leaves would be falling now, covering the ground with springy carpet beneath which all kinds of nuts and seeds lay hidden. When she had walked through the woods gathering nuts, Gran always insisted that she leave plenty for the animals, and Misty always laughed, for there were more than enough for twice as many people and animals as were there. Misty could almost hear the squirrels chattering overhead as she rustled through the leaves, scattering them about and stooping to pick up acorns and put them in her basket. Oh, how she missed the richness of days filled with gathering, preparing, storing and creating, for there were many things to be made from the little caps of acorns. Glassy as her eyes were, the corners of her mouth turned up to think of the little acorn hats she and Gran made for the tiny knitted dolls and animals and of the acorn and shell pictures that she made with Miss Lily. Everything fit so well. Everything had a use. Misty sighed slightly as the sense of missing so much stole the refreshment of her memory from her. Just in time, she remembered the rule and fought against weeping, deliberately turning her attention to the road ahead.

She tried to sort out the angry sputtering of Aunt Augusta, wondering what was to become of Saturdays. She soon discovered that it wasn't just Saturdays she need wonder about. It seemed that Aunt Augusta had decided to cancel all the lessons scheduled for her. She heard grumbling about needless waste of money on a child that never behaved and looked wild no matter what they tried, about scheming teachers and about programmes that were stupidly planned and administered. She also heard, in quite a different tone, that it had become evident that they didn't need the child's time taken up with lessons anyway as they had discovered she was perfectly capable of staying on her own after school and even on Saturdays if need be. Misty learned that there was no need to get up ridiculously early on Saturdays and drive all about town and no need to spend money unnecessarily. It seemed clear to Aunt Augusta that there was also no benefit from having Thomasina in all these lessons that she had once claimed would make a proper little lady of her even while providing Aunt Augusta with contact with the important parents. Besides, the child looked so positively wild with her hair all sticking out that she'd have been embarrassed to have run into any of the important parents anyway. Her directions for Saturday were clear through the grumbling: this Saturday, Thomasina must tend to the offending hair before quietly doing whatever little girls do on Saturdays.

By the time they arrived home, Aunt Augusta had found a new way to look at the morning disaster and she presented her new decisions to Hugh cheerily, decisively and convincingly. Glimpsing the child, however, Hugh appeared to disagree on one point. "The child is a fright," he said. "You'd better tie that hair back in braids again. At least they were tidy. This is outrageous. If she can't do a better job of those curl-clusters, she must go back to braids."

"Hugh, how could you possibly disagree with me on this, and in front of the child! She looks positively plain, even homely in braids, and we simply cannot have that. This mess of hair must be her own fault. She hasn't looked like that before. I'll give her some of that new setting-gel I have, and she'll do a better job, you'll see. Thomasina, go at once and wash your hair. When you are done, come and I'll show you how to use the gel that will control those curls. Now!"

Misty felt relieved to be sent away from the escalating bickering of the two, for Uncle Hugh was insisting that it was all too much work and a senseless waste of time and money, while Aunt Augusta carried on about looking pretty. Even as she went down the stairs to the tub in the basement, Misty heard the voices elevating, heard Uncle Hugh ask why the child's hair should matter when she didn't see anyone anyway. They certainly weren't going to take her anywhere on Saturdays. She could barely be trusted at school, and look at the mess she'd made in just one visit to the skating rink. No, they may as well let her do what she would with her hair; she'd be seeing no one. "Besides, " he concluded, "she'll likely spend whole weekends in her room what with her stubborn refusal to eat properly. How she looks just doesn't matter then."

Gratefully Misty let the water run over her head, drowning out the further fighting. By the time she had her hair clean and combed out, there was a strained silence upstairs. Aunt Augusta said nothing as she left Uncle Hugh sitting at the table and led Misty to the bathroom, where she took out a jar of pink gel and held it out to Misty.

"Here," she said, "put a dab of this on each strand of hair before you wind it around your finger. When it dries, it will keep your hair in place. If that doesn't work, we'll have to wind it around rags to let it dry that way, so take care that you get it right this time. Hair can't be hurried, you know. And remember, beauty takes pains, so don't try any shortcuts. You will look pretty, do you hear? Don't listen to Hugh about hair. Men just don't understand these things. When you are done you can play in your room or outside, whichever you prefer. Just don't bother us today."

Misty hated the feel of the gel in her hair but she did as she was told, dabbing on gel and winding the wild hair carefully into little ringlets. She found herself wishing she had much less hair, as her arms began to ache with the task. Uncomfortable with such thoughts, she began her game, trying to think of one thing to be thankful for with each curl that she wound. She was grateful to have missed lunch. She was grateful for the cutting silence that had replaced the bickering in the house. She was grateful for free time ahead. She was grateful to be able to go outside. She was grateful for the hope of seeing the cat. She was grateful that the leaves were falling so she could enjoy them below the apple tree. She was even grateful not to have to have skating lessons or any of the others Aunt Augusta had threatened her with, for now that she could see beyond her disappointment of not seeing the ocean again, she recognized that the girls she had seen at skating were not ones she was comfortable with. Further, she assumed that skating, art, piano, all the lessons Aunt Augusta had arranged, would have been as trying for her as school had been. She was grateful that she wouldn't have the added struggles, for even she could see now that this new life was beginning to wear on her.

Even as she continued applying the gel and winding the offending curls, her eyes grew a little glassy as she wondered how long it had been since she had actually been hungry, had felt like eating, had been free to either enjoy eating as she had done at home or simply refuel her body without thinking, without struggling, without pain. She was suddenly more grateful than she had ever been for the wonderful food, the freedom to eat, the delight of meals shared in complete comfort, the ease of eating she had taken for granted all her life. Instantly she asked forgiveness for neglecting to be as grateful as she ought to have been. Immediately she continued silently, wordlessly, grateful for her old life. Mechanically winding those curls, she travelled wordlessly through the richness of the friendship of the Captain and Miss Lily, of Rusty, of Pilot, of the cats, of Nobbin, of the home, the beach, the trees, the boat, even the wind. As she felt thanks for all she had enjoyed, her task became easier and she was delighted to be able to give thanks for completing. She could not with any kind of sincerity give thanks for the ringlets that she discovered grew crunchy as they dried, but she could be grateful for being free to go outside.

Though Misty's head felt even heavier than usual with its carefully gelled, crisp curls, she was soon lifted beyond such physical concerns as she stepped outside and walked across to the apple tree. The air was clear and crisp, smelling distinctly of fall and healthily invigorating. Though she enjoyed the calming warmth of summer air, she was more stimulated by the fresher fall air and she turned around once, throwing her arms out at her sides as she did so, stretching to sense as much of the freedom as she could. Enjoying the feel of the cool air moving against her face, she turned around and around, feeling herself stretch inside as well as out while she turned. Finally, she tumbled to the ground below her favourite tree, stretching her legs out in front of her, imagining they stretched and stretched and stretched.

This town made her feel all crumpled up, shrunken somehow. She almost chuckled to think of Aunt Augusta's attempts to make her grow quickly by feeding her more. Though Misty knew she hadn't actually shrunk in height no matter how small she felt at times, even she could see that she was lighter than she had been when she came, for the loose-fitting skirts were now even looser. She wished she had a needle and thread so she could move the button over before she had to be afraid the skirts would not even stay up. But she didn't know where to look for such things in this house and was never given a chance to ask, so she just breathed thanks that the skirts were loose rather than too tight.

Misty leaned back against the tree and looked up, happy to see the blue of the sky through the thinning leaves. She rustled the leaves that were all around her, wondering how soon they would grow crisp or whether the rains would come before that and make them soggy. Though she loved the rain, she knew she'd best enjoy the last of the dry air before the weather changed. There wouldn't be much left. Happily she studied the sky and wondered for the thousandth time why the blue of even the deepest sky was so different from the blue of the ocean and why the changing weather was reflected so differently in the sky than in the sea. The sky never seemed as strong to Misty as the sea did, never seemed to show as much moodiness, and yet the sky stretched the world over, covering both land and sea. It was all wondrous to her and she felt the familiar thrill of being tiny yet huge at the same moment, of belonging but being distinct. 'Why,' she wondered, 'do I never feel this indoors?'

Even as the thought crossed her mind, Misty suddenly realized that being inside had changed for her, changed drastically since she had come here. Try as she might, she could not recall noticing such a tremendous difference in the freshness of the air between outside and inside back home. Oh, there was a difference, to be sure, especially in winter when the fires blazed inside, but that was just a matter of warmth. She was sure the air was as fresh, at least as breathable, inside as it was out. Here, though, the inside air was stifling—close, dead, and stifling. The air in the school was permeated with something stifling, something beyond the smells of ink, chalk, and new paper, even beyond the heavy muskiness of so many bodies in a single building; it was something close and almost palpable, something that made breathing as much an effort as a refreshment. The arena had also been heavy—chilly and damp, but heavy, as if the air were old and stale. And this house? Misty wondered how even she would describe such a thing to the Captain. Of course, you couldn't see the difference, for air is invisible, but the difference was so striking that it seemed as if you should be able to see it as well as sense it in other ways. Misty thought the difference best conveyed by the simple truth that for the first time in her life, she felt as much like running out of a place as she did like running into the outdoors. Misty was beginning to feel restless, to feel not just a longing to go home but also a desire to flee the place she had come to live in.

She shivered slightly, unhappy with such a thought. What was happening to her? She'd only been here a few short weeks and already she sensed that she was becoming spoiled, that she had somehow been unable to heed the Captain's warning. She had always been content on the island, never longed for anything else. Suddenly she found herself longing, not just to go back to the island, but to be anywhere but where she was. She wondered how Tommy and Daisy were doing and what the lake was like. She didn't like the feeling of disappointment that pursued her here. It was new to her, and not at all pleasant. Had she not known about the lake, she'd not have yearned to see it and had she not thought she would go to see it, she'd not have been disappointed to be denied such a privilege. She saw that one doesn't long for things not known. Still, she was sure she would rather have heard about the lake and be free to think about it and imagine it, though she couldn't see it. She was grateful, too, to know that just down the hill, just where everything looked like it formed a great valley, was a huge body of water. She was sure that somehow the freshness of the orchard air was enriched by the lake. Had she known that the lake narrowed into a very short river just beyond the bay at the bottom of the hill, a river that emptied directly into the ocean just three short miles away, she'd have been even more excited by knowing there was so much water nearby. As it was, she simply stretched again, breathing deeply, drawing strength from the lake-laden air.

Tommy had said he was sure she could see the lake from the house, from the top window. Misty let her eyes travel up, beyond the clothesline stand, beyond the pole and up the roof where the cat had scrambled. Sure enough, there was a gable in the roof with a window in the gable, and there, sitting on the windowsill was the cat. He looked small way up there, but Misty knew he was watching her, probably had been for some time.

"Silly thing," she said; "you should be looking at the view, not at me. Can you see the lake, Puss? Does it stretch way off in the distance? Is it the same colour as the ocean? Does it glisten in the sunlight and lap against the shore? Are the beaches the same or are there beaches?" On and on Misty questioned the cat who sat so far above her on the sill until her questions and thoughts faded into that blissful feeling of oneness with the world. Neither moved. Each was content, content to spend the afternoon comfortably resting in the richness of the outdoors, content to share respectfully the world that was theirs.

Only when Misty heard Aunt Augusta calling stridently did thoughts interrupt the calm; only then did she wonder what the cat was doing up there, how you got to the upstairs of the house to see out that window and what might be up there. But her thoughts were quickly snuffed out by the voice intensifying as Misty rose and hurried to the house. Dinner was ready. Misty took her place alone at the kitchen table, bowed her head in silent thanks and supplication and began the battle. She noticed some friendly-sounding chatter in the dining room and was grateful that both the earlier bickering and its subsequent cutting silence had ended. Misty had hoped that missing lunch would enable her to eat all her dinner, but despite the fresh air of the afternoon, she was simply not hungry. From a sense of duty and with an almost desperate effort to avoid conflict, she ate steadily and bravely, but the food often seemed to stick in her throat. She wasn't even half done when Aunt Augusta came to the kitchen, speaking very loudly.

"Well, I see you haven't got any better at eating. Keep at it. I just want to tell you Hugh and I have decided that you will attend Sunday School tomorrow, though I have cancelled all other activities for you. There's no need for either of us to take you or even to get up early in the morning. You will get up and dress yourself, not in your school clothes but in one of the dresses we bought. Wear the little black shoes and be sure to put your new coat on. And don't, for goodness sake, forget your hat. One doesn't go into a church without a hat. Be sure your curls are at least as tidy as they are now and be very careful you are clean. Walk up the hill as you do to go to school. Turn left at the street just before the school, then right at the first one after that. Go into the little white church that is near that corner. They are expecting you. Mrs. Norman will tend to you. And for goodness sake, child, keep in mind where you live, what family you are representing and thus how you must appear to others. Do not, I repeat, do not do anything that will in any way embarrass us. Now finish your food so you can go to bed early. You'll have to be up early to be sure you are neat and tidy for Sunday School. Hugh and I are going out for a while now. Be sure you eat all your dinner, tidy up your dishes and go straight to bed. No nonsense. We'll see you for lunch directly after Sunday School. Good night."

Long after Aunt Augusta and Uncle Hugh had left, Misty sat at the table, trying to force food down her unwilling throat. She didn't want to do anything wrong and didn't want to appear dishonest, yet she knew that she simply couldn't eat all the food. She also knew that she would be in trouble if she were still sitting at the table when they returned. Finally, as much because she was so very tired as anything else, she scraped the remaining food into the garbage, cleaned up her dishes and the kitchen and went to bed.

The thought of Sunday School in the morning didn't keep her awake. It didn't really even catch her attention. Instead, what prevented her from enjoying the quiet of the house and falling easily to sleep was the sense of having done something wrong. Though she couldn't see anything right that she could have done, any right way out of her dilemma, she felt somehow wrong.

Aloud but quietly she spoke; "Forgive me for failing again, for throwing away good food, for being unable to do what they want me to do. Please help me. What is wrong with me that I can't eat my food? Can You fix me or is there something I must do? Forgive me for wanting to go home. Forgive me for wanting other than what I have. Forgive me for wanting to run away, and please show me how to be content here. Thank You for providing a safe place, for a nice little bed, for fresh air at my window, for the little cat so high on the windowsill …"

As Misty carried on and on with her list of things for which she was genuinely grateful, she began to relax and to settle into a kind of even breathing, a sweet rhythm of old, the rhythm of her grandfather's rocker. She heard the steady creaking, back and forth, back and forth, back and forth, felt it close, real, comforting, solid as she drifted off to sleep.

15.

Sunday School

Misty noticed when she awoke that she didn't feel as fresh or as eager as she usually did in the morning. She wasn't tired either, however, and she was thankful for a morning alone, for not having to fight about breakfast and for being free to walk to and from Sunday School. She had no concerns about Sunday School itself, knowing only what Henry had told her and assuming that a school meant to be about God would reflect Him. Still, she had learned from even her short time here that one never knew what might be about to happen no matter what people told you to expect. She realized that her old habit of going moment by moment, though she had never even had to think about doing it, was turning out to be the best practice in this life. Here, though, like everything else, it seemed to take some effort. So she must, she decided, simply go one step at a time, beginning with getting ready to leave as Aunt Augusta had ordered.

She chose the least frilly of the dresses but still felt dreadfully uncomfortable and even fidgety in it. Her discomfort, though, was soon replaced by the trial of dealing with her gelled, but unruly hair. Oh how she wished Aunt Augusta would at least let her braid her hair at night. Alas, the woman insisted that hair ought to be free to flow across the pillow unhindered at night. As a result, Misty had wakened with the worst mess of hair she had yet encountered. In places, the hair was crisp, even crunchy. It felt unnatural. Though a few ringlets had held, most of her hair was simply tangled in a wiry-feeling mess that crunched as if breaking when she even tried to pat it flat. Attempting to comb it out, she soon found that little flakes of dried gel scattered about. Even worse, when she wet it, the brittle stuff turned immediately to slippery strands of hair. Misty shivered at the slimy feel of the ringlets as she made them but she was relieved to see they dried looking quite like they had the day before when Aunt Augusta had approved of her hair. Still, the whole process made her feel like she needed a bath, made her feel like dashing down to at least wash her hair. She resisted and continued winding the strands into the ringlets Aunt Augusta demanded.

Even with the ringlets contained in two pigtails, Misty had a struggle to find a place to secure her hat. She did manage to get it balanced between the two massive pigtails, despite its being a tight fit. Though the hat was almost bent between the pigtails, and the ribbons that hung down the back of the hat tickled her neck adding to her discomfort, Misty adopted her positive view, thankful that the tight fit would help keep the thing on. Still, try as she might to enjoy the walk to the little church, Misty was distracted by her head and feet. The little shoes pinched and seemed silly and fragile to her, making her almost afraid to walk in them, and the mass of crunchy curls with the little hat fit tightly between but tickling her neck made her afraid to move her head. Unnoticed by her, it also made her carry her head at an odd angle, chin down a little as if to hold things better in place. Before long her neck began to hurt with the unusual angle and effort to hold the head still. By the time she arrived at the little church, Misty was quite tired as well as uncomfortable.

To Misty's surprise, some children ran around outside the church, though they were dressed in clothes similar to hers. She wondered how they managed. She noticed, however, that most of the children stood in little groups just talking. The adults she could see as she walked up the short path were also dressed in stiff-looking clothes. Two men wore suits that looked as uncomfortable as Uncle Hugh's always did, and the women she saw wore nice dresses or knit suits and hats. None of them seemed too uncomfortable in the hats, though Misty thought they looked silly, for none of the hats would keep off the rain or keep much of a woman's head warm. They just sat there atop the head looking useless. Idly, Misty wondered why the men did not wear hats. Hadn't Aunt Augusta said that people must always wear hats in church? It seemed she must have meant only women and girls wore hats. There were certainly a lot of rules to learn in town, and none of them seemed to make sense. Why wear a hat that didn't keep the rain off? Why wear a hat inside at all? It suddenly occurred to Misty that when it did rain, these hats would be something else to attempt to keep dry, would simply be more work and worry. It was all beyond her.

Even as an efficient looking woman came down the church stairs and approached her, Misty realized that having clothes that match everyone else's did not make her fit in as Aunt Augusta insisted. In this group, neither did the clothes, as far as Misty could tell, identify which group a person might belong to. Instead, the whole group looked the same. Even the colours seemed somehow commonly agreed upon. There was a great deal of navy blue and deep greens and black, even among the young children. Nothing really distinguished anyone from the others, for all wore similar expressions. None looked interesting or alive, not even the children who ran about playing tag. There was something subdued about even them, as if their attempts to ignore the Sunday clothes weren't entirely successful. Misty once again felt restricted by what she was forced to wear here and felt even more uncomfortable as the woman said, "Good morning; you must be Thomasina. I'm Mrs. Norman. If you'd come inside with me, we can fill in a little paper before it is time to begin. We're very happy to have you join us."

As Misty walked up the stairs with the woman, she wondered about the brittle smile that did not extend from lips to eyes and about the hollow ring to the voice. Perhaps this was a friend of Aunt Augusta's. She did begin to chatter on, apparently unmindful of the child or her responses. While Misty filled in the little card with her name, age and address, she heard that the Sunday School had begun many years ago, was most important to the community, provided a fine service and was growing every year. She heard, too, that the children enjoyed the many activities and the opportunities that they provided to learn right living. The teachers were particularly concerned that they give young unchurched children such as herself every opportunity that their glorious Saviour would want them to have. She trusted that Thomasina would soon learn all about Jesus and would subsequently want to behave in right and proper ways. She noted that Thomasina was off to a good start, dressed so smartly and hair done so prettily this fine morning.

Taking the card from Misty, Mrs. Norman said, "You'll be in my class. I have the ten-year-old girls. After the open session, we meet behind that divider in the corner nearest the piano. I'm sure you'll enjoy our lesson today. We're learning about obedience. It's near time now; take a seat where you want, and I'll open the doors for the others to enter. I get such a thrill to think of the good we do here each Sunday morning. Seeing these lost ones come through the doors is such a joy to me."

Misty took a seat near the piano as the other children filed in. She noted that adults seemed quite evenly distributed among the children, all looking serious and stern. Only the woman at the piano smiled. Misty smiled back as she gently, expectantly, longingly took up the hymnbook that was on her chair. Though the cover of this was different from the old hymnbook that rested on the piano back home, Misty soon saw many of the familiar old songs that they had enjoyed so much. She felt excitement rise within her, excitement to hold a book in her hands again, any book, but even more, excitement at the wonder she knew this book contained.

The woman at the piano noticed a little glow showing on the new girl's face and carelessly brushed her hand on the keys in her surprise, sending forth some loud discordant notes and bringing stern frowns to the faces of the men now standing at the front of the little church. Somehow their frowns seemed out of place against the background of the altar with its crisp white linen cloth and its sturdy brass cross, which Misty knew to represent the Cross of hope.

One of the men cleared his throat and announced the opening song: "All Things Bright and Beautiful." The pianist struck the introductory chords with more enthusiasm than musicality, and all rose to their feet and began singing. Immediately Misty was absorbed in singing, lifted from even the discomfort of her clothes, moved beyond the distraction of the room. Had she been aware of those around her, she'd have been surprised and saddened to hear their dull, mumbled, dutiful rendering of the words and music, which were to them just that. Misty's clear, strong, joyous voice rang out across the room, singing praises, singing truth, singing hope and joy, singing life itself. These were no mere words and notes; this was an overflowing of the wellspring, an expression of Love. Misty felt joy well up within her as she sang the familiar verses.

As they went on to sing, "Jesus Bids us Shine," Misty's voice rang out clear and strong again, reaching even the ears of the exuberant pianist, who dropped the volume to hear better. This was something unusual. This was something worth listening to. But the stern leaders were dismayed at the pianist's lowered volume and one of them began almost frantically waving his arms, trying to get her leading, even drowning out the singing as she should be. The waving startled Misty and drew her attention into the room. Distracted, she lowered her voice, even paused, flustered.

Suddenly she heard the laboured sounds around her and became momentarily puzzled. There was no shining in this room. There was no joy. What was wrong? Was she wrong to sing? In her confusion, she found herself mumbling the words, singing stumblingly, uncertainly, unenthusiastically like the others, her eyes darting around almost frantically. She felt tears welling up, tears she didn't understand. She had to fight them, for Aunt Augusta insisted she not embarrass them, and crying in town was against the rules.

She ceased singing altogether, repeatedly swallowing hard and retreating. Her eyes grew glassy as she almost heard Gran and the Captain singing this song, singing with joy, singing of triumph, calling out, and she thanked God for the richness of such singing, for calling His people to shine, for the shining people Gran had been and the other island folk were. The tears abated and the lump subsided as Misty prayed joyously and silently amidst the dull, tortured singing of the people, until the love welled up within her again, her eyes closed and her voice rang out clear and true above the others in pure worship.

An odd quiet interrupted by shuffling of feet and scraping of chairs jolted Misty back to the room. Eyes open again, she saw people sitting down, settling into their chairs. One of the men at the front began to speak;

"That was good singing, children, just fine. We're lucky to have such grand hymns to join in, aren't we? Now, everybody bow your heads while Mr. Jenkins leads us in prayer."

Misty grew quiet inside and leaned a little ahead in her hunger. She hadn't heard prayer since arriving in town and she suddenly realized she missed it. But instead of Gramps' rich voice, or the Captain's spontaneous bursts of praise or Gran's expectant thanks for prayer soon to be answered, she heard a dull, sombre voice, carefully controlled and modulated, droning out formulaic things. Misty recognized some of the words from the Bible, some from the Book of Common Prayer, but she heard none of the promise in the words; she heard no life, no expectation, no praise. She did hear, as the voice droned on until rising for emphasis or in desperation, a strong admonition that the Good Lord enable the children to behave according to the traditions of the elders, that He strike fear in their hearts that they might grow in knowledge, and that He bring to their knees all that needed chastening. She was surprised to hear him ask all these things for the glory of God, for she could feel, sense, imagine no glory. In fact, she felt robbed, as if there had been no prayer at all. Quickly, silently, she asked forgiveness for such an uncomfortable reaction to prayer. She asked that He forgive her for losing sight of Him in this place.

Just as she asked God to shine some joy into these miserable people, to lift whatever saddened them so, take whatever was troubling them and put a song in their hearts, another voice interrupted her silent prayer, saying, "Thank you, Mr. Jenkins. Now children, how many of you remember the lesson from last week? What were we reading?"

Several hands went up. Misty noted most of the older girls who had taunted her so badly sitting together, each with her hand raised. When indicated, one of them answered, "We're studying the story of Moses leading the people out of Egypt. The lesson was about the importance of obedience."

"That's good. Mrs. Norman, put a blue star on the girls' chart; they've got the right answer to our first question again this week. Now, how many of you have memorized the scripture that went with the story?"

This time, more hands went up. Misty didn't like the looks on the faces of the children whose hands were up. Their heads all tilted a little to one side, their chins raised cockily, almost defiantly and their eyes flashed some kind of smug challenge or even accusation. They reminded her of Aunt Augusta when she was ordering people around, expecting they would meet her demands immediately, as if all other people were beneath her and owed her something. Misty wondered how learning scripture could bring such a look to these people. For her, learning scripture had always been sheer delight. It didn't take effort, wasn't an accomplishment; it simply happened and once it happened, sharing the scripture happened as well, quickly becoming another of the many games they had enjoyed so much on the island, spontaneous, co-operative, delightful. Taking turns saying scriptures that they knew had been just another part of living, another expression of Life itself. But already Misty could see that here this business of memorizing scripture was something else entirely.

Soon she learned. It was a competition. The stern man went on to say, "Your teachers will hear your recitation of last week's scripture, and we will report the winners next Sunday morning. Last Sunday, the eleven- and twelve-year-old girls' class had the most correct scripture recitation. Mrs. Norman, put another blue star on the girls' chart. Well done, girls. Boys, you'd better try a little harder. Look at those charts. We can't have the girls winning all the stars, can we? If you don't pick up soon, we'll have to begin contacting parents again. Here we are doing lessons on obedience and you have not obeyed, have not memorized your scripture. I'm sure you'll try harder next week. It's what good children do, you know. This morning, before we go to our separate classes and instead of our usual story, we have a special treat for you. Mrs. Norman has prepared a game for us, a Scripture spelling bee. We'll play girls against the boys and will alternate between teams, but anyone on the team can offer the answer. The team with the most correct spellings will win the star for today. Are you ready? Mrs. Norman, you can begin."

In the ten-minute eternity that the game took, Misty struggled painfully through confusion and even torment to suddenly realize that she was more disappointed than ever before. She hadn't realized she had come with expectations. But if she hadn't come with hope in her heart, she had felt hope and excitement while singing. The elation of worship had created an expectation of celebrating Truth here, of sharing Life. Instead, they competed, spelling scripture words, not surprisingly getting more wrong than right, for Mrs. Norman seemed intent on forcing them to learn not only all those tough Biblical names but also how to spell them correctly. Misty soon realized that her list of words all had to do with churches. The only connection Misty could make to the simple truth of Jesus was indirect and forced; she recalled that at Antioch (which the boy attempting the answer misspelled) they were first called "Christians." Back and forth, Misty was torn as the game went on. She couldn't understand the reason for the game and worse, she was disconcerted by what she saw the game bring out in the other children. They were cruel to one another. Instead of the joy that Misty had hoped for, had tasted, had expected, she felt pain, pain and disappointment. So shaken was she that she didn't even notice who won the game. She was, however, grateful that, being new, she was ignored, not expected to participate yet.

As the group broke up into the individual classes, Misty's spirits rose a little momentarily, for the pianist played "Onward Christian Soldiers" enthusiastically above the dragging of chairs and moving of room dividers. Misty could almost see Gramps' foot tapping in time to such a rhythmic call to life. She returned the pianist's smile as she moved to the group Mrs. Norman had indicated for her. Following the other girls, she pulled a chair into the circle they were forming around Mrs. Norman, whose chair sat before the board that formed the room divider. Misty saw on the board a list of girl's names, some with many stars beside them, others with fewer. Her own name had been added to the list and stood out, the only unstarred name. There were also some pictures up and a small chalkboard she assumed was for Mrs. Norman to write on. As the girls settled into their chairs, Mrs. Norman began.

"We have a new girl today, Class, so we'll take time for introductions and a few questions. This is Thomasina. She has just recently moved here. Perhaps each of you can introduce yourself and ask Thomasina a question about herself so we get to know her quickly. You begin, Maureen."

"I'm Maureen. I live up on the hill and my father's a manager. Where'd you get your strange name?"

Though taken aback by the question and its tone, Misty answered evenly, "I was named after my grandfather, Thomas. My people all called me Misty, though, and I prefer that."

The girls giggled and Mrs. Norman said, "We don't use nicknames here in Sunday School, Thomasina. Here, we must do all to the glory of God, so we dress well to honour Him, speak well, do all as if unto the Lord. Nicknames are much too casual. Next."

"Hi. I'm Diana and beside me is my twin sister Debra. We're the only twins in the Sunday School." The girl's boastful tone changed to contempt as she added, "Our Mom says the Hughes rescued you from your home. Why couldn't you stay home?"

"I'm not sure about being rescued," answered Misty, ignoring the girl's tone. "There wasn't anything wrong with my life, but my grandparents both died, and the Hughes thought it would be best for me if I came to town to go to school. There is no school on the island."

"I'm Mary-Ellen and my father is a doctor here and my mother is the head of the women's auxiliary. No school? No Sunday School either, I suppose. My mother says you must be backward, coming from the bush like that. Are you a perfect heathen?"

Misty looked at Mrs. Norman, hoping she would somehow rescue her from this interrogation. She struggled to get her increasing discomfort under control, frowning slightly as she fought to answer such a question. Was it a question? Must she answer? She wondered how people were supposed to get to know each other if all they commented on were their families. She also wondered at all these comments the girls reported coming from their mothers. What did these town people talk about all the time? Why did these girls feel free to ask anything at all and to report what their mothers had said? Was this the gossip she had read about and was warned against in the Bible?

She had always wondered what gossip was. She suspected she was beginning to see and she didn't like the feel of it. She felt much more attacked and scorned than she did welcomed or even just neutrally questioned. These were the girls Tommy had frightened away from her after school, but they had seemed to agree to leave her alone after the morning Miss Moore had yelled at her, yet here they were hurling questions at her in tones that cut deeply. She looked again at Mrs. Norman, hopefully. Hadn't Mrs. Norman just said that all must be done as if unto the Lord? Is this how people thought the Lord could be glorified? Misty struggled for calmness and clarity, not realizing how long she was taking.

"Thomasina?" prompted Mrs. Norman, "can you not answer that question? It is an important one, especially for Sunday School."

"No, I am not a heathen. I'm not sure what you mean by "perfect heathen," but since I am not a heathen, I couldn't be a perfect one."

Again the girls giggled before the next one introduced herself. "I'm Marjorie-Ann, daughter of the owner of the store you pass on your way to school. So, are you an orphan? Why did you live with your grandparents in the first place?"

Misty felt as if she'd been smacked. She was suddenly utterly exhausted and she slumped back in her chair fighting the pounding in her chest and resounding in her head. Thoughts hurried so quickly inside her skull, they seemed to jumble up, even to jam. Her head hurt, and things in front of her blurred. The room felt hot, stifling hot like the classroom at school. Breathing was difficult, and Misty was losing track of what she was supposed to be doing. Her eyes glazed over as she silently cried out for help.

Mrs. Norman, alarmed at how pale the girl was becoming, stepped in. "I think, girls, we'll have to leave the rest of our introductions until next week. Otherwise we won't have time for our memory verses or our lessons. Perhaps the rest of you can also make a point of meeting Thomasina at school during the week. You know it is important that we be hospitable, for the Bible instructs us so. Now, Maureen, your memory verse."

Misty continued her silent cry for help as she tried to breathe deeply and refocus while the girls took turns repeating the same verse from Exodus: "And Israel saw the great work which the Lord did upon the Egyptians: and the people feared the Lord, and believed the Lord, and his servant Moses." The dull, mechanical sound of the verse repeated over and over added to Misty's battle, for she was not only shocked to hear scripture sounding so empty but was also reminded of the relentless chanting she had endured on the playground. The thumping in her chest and head competed with the class for her attention, and she felt herself sinking way inside, found herself wishing her Red Sea would part so she could flee or even that it would simply wash over her.

"Please, please, God, help me. I can't take this. I can't hear. I can't see. Calm me with Your strength. Light my way with a pillar of fire; cover me with a cloud. Carry me." Her eyes grew glassy as she imagined herself sitting securely on her grandfather's knee where she had first heard these verses. He had painted such a wonderful picture of both Moses and the Lord. She felt herself lifted by both thought and pictures and she wished the class could have heard Gramps; then they couldn't sound so dull with their repetition.

Seeing the colour beginning to return to Thomasina's face, Mrs. Norman looked at her and said, "Of course there will be no star for you this week as you are new and didn't have a verse to learn. Make note of the verse for next week. Do you have questions about our memory work?"

Misty surprised herself by speaking through her fatigue as if the only important thing were Gramps' voice: "No questions, thank you, Mrs. Norman, but I know the verse and would like to repeat it please." Without waiting for a response, Misty immediately spoke the words, not mechanically, not dully, not scornfully, but as Gramps had read them, emphasizing as he had "the great work" and people "believed the Lord, and his servant Moses."

There was a hush when she finished, for everyone was affected by the life in Misty's rendition of the verse. Further, everyone was shocked that she knew the verse at all. Mrs. Norman seemed momentarily flustered, recovering herself and reaching to paste a star by Thomasina's name only when Maureen spoke excitedly, "Gee Mrs. Norman, that will give us the star for next week for sure. The whole class got the verse right today, even the new kid." Misty was too tired to hear the scorn that slipped into the last phrase. Silently she thanked God, her eyes growing slightly glassy again.

To her relief, the focus of the class shifted as Mrs. Norman read another short passage from Exodus, assigning it as next week's memory verse, before going on to insist that the important message in the verse they had just repeated was that God punished the Egyptians and would, she was sure, punish each child who failed to obey Him. She did not speak of promises, of the Lord, or even of Moses, just carried on about the horrible punishment delivered on the Egyptians. Misty could not continue to listen, though she did hear Mrs. Norman exhort them to be sure to be as the Israelites, not those Egyptians, lest they incur the wrath of God.

Silently Misty asked God to lift this unhealthy fear that held these people captive and reveal His love. She asked Him to take the frowns and make them smiles, to take the bitterness and make it sweet, to take jealousy and make it love. She asked Him to be as important to these kids as they seemed to think their fathers' jobs were. And she asked Him to give her strength.

For a moment, she felt relief to hear Mrs. Norman repeat her point once more in conclusion and begin handing out papers. "I've brought these pictures for you girls to colour. That's what we'll do in the remaining time. Do your best work as is fitting a godly young girl. Remember, the person with the most best pictures gets a prize at the end of each year. So far, Mary-Ellen leads that competition."

Misty was momentarily confused to see the piece of paper in her hand, for she had never coloured a picture she hadn't drawn herself. Further, she wasn't sure what the picture was meant to be. She saw the other girls take crayons and begin right away, however, so she studied the picture carefully as she reached for a crayon, keeping in mind that she wasn't to rip any wrappers off. Even as she wondered how she was to make a decent job of adding colour to the picture without tearing wrappers, she suddenly realized that the picture must be Moses before the Red Sea. It wasn't at all as Misty would have drawn him, and she really didn't know how she might colour the thing, for much of it would need to be very light earth tones, none of which were among the crayons. Glancing at the other girls at work, Misty saw that they simply coloured with whichever crayon they liked. She noticed further that they just filled in the outlined spaces, and she did mean "fill in." The papers took on the look of heavy wax as bright colours began to fill the papers. None of the pictures looked at all like people who had just fled a country after a long, difficult sojourn there, but Misty had no idea that, to the other girls, these were just pictures to colour, just lines on a page. They meant nothing.

Mrs. Norman interrupted her confusion saying, "Thomasina, aren't you going to join the girls? Our lesson again today is of the importance of obedience. God Himself calls for obedience. Did you not listen to the passage or the lesson? Choose your crayon and hurry your work or the class' good record will be spoiled."

Misty's pulse raced at the reprimand, for she really couldn't think how to begin. She was incapable of doing a picture just to get done. Though this kind of colouring only scarcely resembled anything Misty had learned was art, the end result was still to be a picture, something that should be as close to living as possible. How could Misty bring these lines on a page to life? Why did she have to feel so very tired just now, too tired to think clearly enough to choose a crayon that might bring life to a dead page?

Once again, Misty could do nothing but fold up inside, seeking the help she so badly needed. Her eyes grew glassy as she asked silently, "How would You make Moses look, God? How did You make Moses look? What crayon might I use to make his face more real, lined as it would be from his age and his trials as well as from his own early reluctance and self doubt but alive with the promise? And what about his robes and the robes of the people behind him? How do I make them show the dust and grime of the journey? And what colour was the Red Sea just before You parted it? Was it stirred up, angry like? I forget. Was there any storm?" Misty's face began to light up as her questions brought the story, if not the picture, to life.

Looking at the clock, Mrs. Norman decided to avoid conflict and possible disaster, though she did note to herself that Augusta was quite right; the child seemed unmanageable. Pasting a smile on her face, she looked down at Misty and said, in a voice so like that of Aunt Augusta that Misty almost shivered, "Perhaps for this week, you'd like to take the picture home and colour it there. We needn't hold up the class for a new girl. Now, everybody tidy up. It is time for closing prayer."

After a pause in which the girls quickly put away crayons and piled their completed pictures on Mrs. Norman's little table, Mrs. Norman, in a tone she thought most dignified and reverent, closed with the shortened benediction, "Now, may the Lord bless thee and keep thee and cause his face to shine upon thee." All the girls but Misty mumbled, "Amen."

The girls' giggling brought Misty's eyes open. They were laughing at her as she had sat quietly, expectantly waiting for the rest of the benediction, waiting for Mrs. Norman to ask Him to "be gracious unto thee, to lift up his countenance upon thee and give thee peace." Oh, how Misty longed for His peace that moment! But, flustered, she rose with the other girls and left the little building, alone again as the other girls clustered together talking quietly and giggling, not hiding their contempt for her. Outside, Misty noticed adults milling all about and recalled that Henry had told her some would stay for church. As she left the churchyard, she noted just two things: everyone there wore the same uncomfortable looking clothes and appeared to ignore her, and, sadly, she noted that she was tremendously relieved to be out of Sunday School.

Walking slowly home, Misty tried to sort out her troubled thoughts. She soon understood her sadness, for she had gone in innocence and was returning disillusioned. She had thought that Sunday School, as an extension of church and church as the body of Christ, the Son of God, would have been a place of worship, praise and joy, a place full of people like her beloved island folk, full of the goodness of God, full of desire for Him and joy for Him, so full that it was simply a part of them. Instead, she had seen no joy, heard no praise, sensed no worship. She had seen discomfort, fear, unhappiness and she had learned more rules but she had seen none of the love of God that she had expected. Silently she lifted her sadness to God, asking Him to forgive her and all of them for failing to honour Him. The heaviness continued about her. She wasn't sure why.

Then she remembered, recalled the "introductions," the accusations, the pounding heart. What had stopped them? What had suddenly taken hold of her so strongly, making her feel as she had felt when Miss Moore yelled at her? "What happened, God?" she wondered aloud. Her mind rolled back over the class, each girl, each question, and suddenly she knew. Misty had never felt there was anything wrong with her life. She hadn't even thought of its being unusual in any way. It just was as it was. She had never wondered why she lived with grandparents. Why would she wonder when her life was so good, so full? But the girl had clearly hurled accusation along with the question. Misty felt as hurt by her sudden introduction to gossip and the smallness of people, of church people, as she was threatened by the question, for whatever the girl's intent might have been, she had not in any way weakened Misty's confidence in or comfort with her family as she had always known it. No; doubt had not been cast. Misty's old security had not been threatened. But she was wretchedly hurt to see such cruelty and such shallowness and to hear harsh judgement of her people. She was at a loss for ways to befriend these girls, for they were the very girls Aunt Augusta expected her to befriend. She could not understand them.

"Oh God," she thought, as she continued her slow walk, "You love them. Please show me how to love them, too. Thank you for Gran and Gramps and for Captain and Miss Lily, for all my folks. Tend to them. Look after them. Help me here, Father, for I struggle. I'm so very tired. I was happy to leave that stuffy room, but now I feel myself dragging, unhappy to reach Aunt Augusta's. Forgive me, Father. Help me be grateful for what I have and not long so much for what I don't have. Thank

You that I have a safe place to live. Thank You that I can soon change out of these uncomfortable clothes. Thank You that my hat stayed on. Thank You that I have clothes. Thank You for the pussycat I see outside the house. Thank You …" As Misty carried on, she grew lighter and happier, even chuckling a little as she and Gran had done sometimes when their blessings game had bordered on the ridiculous. Dear Gran.

By the time Misty reached home, she was quite strengthened by her thoughts of the wonderful woman who had given her such a solid, joyous life. Aunt Augusta and Uncle Hugh, both in bathrobes, both drinking coffee and reading papers, looked up as Misty entered, only Aunt Augusta speaking. "Well, you look like you've had a good morning. I'm sure you must have, meeting all those nice girls your own age. Mrs. Norman assured me you are in with all the right children. You see, Hugh, I told you it would pay off buying this place so close to the hill. At least at Sunday School she is with only the right children. I suppose, Thomasina, that you have behaved well or I'd have heard by now. Mrs. Norman is on the hospital auxiliary with me, you know, so you won't get away with any nonsense there. Besides, it's church, isn't it? You have to behave. At least you looked respectable. I see the setting gel works well for your hair. That's good. We have had a lovely sleep-in and plan a very leisurely day. Can it be lunchtime already? You get yourself something, and we'll take our coffee into Hugh's study to get out of your way. Change and hang your clothes up nicely before you eat. You'd better enjoy your afternoon; rest up a little. You begin your tests tomorrow, and I expect you to do well. Do be quiet this afternoon, won't you? We're very tired ourselves, what with all our work and Hugh's extra work, and we also have a busy week coming up. That reminds me, I'll be late most every day this coming week. As the weather is changing, I'll leave the back door unlocked so you can come in and sit in your room until I get home. It will be damp and cold outside, I'm sure. Here, Hugh, let's take the rest of this coffee and move into your study. Did you see this notice of that Stinson man entering the election? Surely he doesn't have much backing. Why he's a mill-worker, isn't he? Whatever is he thinking?"

Misty was grateful that the closing study door muffled the voice, for she really was tired and not at all sure she could ignore the nattering that she knew would go on all afternoon. She breathed deeply as she hurried to change out of her uncomfortable clothes, happy to be free to take a small lunch and not have to endure another battle. She'd just take some fruit outside, she decided, smiling gratefully to think of an afternoon of rest.

Outside, she stretched and smiled to think that the one new thing that remained to undertake here was just some tests. Since Mrs. Longacre had arranged them and kept saying they would solve her school problems, Misty was sure that the tests could not possibly pose the kinds of trials that other new things had thrust upon her. Perhaps life was sorting itself out here. Perhaps the worst was over for her. Perhaps she could now find her place here.

Not stifling a yawn, she leaned back against the tree and allowed herself to think of home, of Rusty, of the Captain, of Miss Lily. Her eyes closed as she saw the Captain's warm face and Miss Lily's smile and heard the ringing sounds of their laughter. She could almost feel the furry little dog as he curled up beside her whenever she sat on the ground for long, and her hand reached out of its own accord. But the tears that threatened to rise as her hand fell on the emptiness of the leaf strewn lawn evaporated as sleep claimed her.

16.

Tests or Trial

Misty was so tired that she slept the afternoon away. Wakened by Aunt Augusta's call, she struggled to know where she was. As if through a fog, she rose and stumbled toward the house, rubbing her eyes, trying to hear what demand was being made this time. But she was relieved to see Aunt Augusta dressed up and to hear her say, "We've had an impromptu invitation to go out with the Wills for dinner. I'm sure you don't mind, as you never eat properly anyway. I've heated some soup for you and put out some crackers. Clean up when you are done, and remember, don't touch the stove. Go to bed immediately following your dinner. You look like you need sleep. We shouldn't be too late."

Misty sat down and gave the most sincere thanks for dinner that she had felt in days. Happily and easily, she sipped the soup, freely swinging her legs beneath the table. She was sure life was improving. After she had finished her meal, she cleaned up, fetched her hair brush and went onto the little back porch where she brushed and brushed and brushed her hair, trying to get as much of the flaky dried gel out as she could. Though she dared not wash it out, she accomplished much with her hairbrush and her patience. High above her the little cat watched, head tipped to one side. She noticed him only when she was finished and turned to go inside. "That's better, isn't it, puss?" she called. "You'd understand. Well, good night." She could hardly resist taming the hair into two neat braids but she controlled herself, taking consolation in her hair feeling better than it had since Aunt Augusta had produced the gel.

Comfortably in bed, Misty was surprised after a whole afternoon of sleep, to feel her eyes quickly grow heavy as she settled into the familiar, soothing rhythm of the old rocking chair. She smiled as she said, "Thanks for Gramps' old rocker and the nights he was up late. Tell him it was all for something after all. He thought the painful arthritis just kept him awake but he was making music for me to hear over and over when I came away. It's so nice, so even, so gentle. Why I can almost hear the deep mantle clock ticking along with it, can almost see the pendulum. Thank You. So quiet, so steady, so safe ..." As young as the night was, Misty was sound asleep and at rest.

Morning seemed to tumble upon her before she had had quite enough of the rest she needed, but the chilly morning air revived her quickly. With a little thrill of delight, she heard rain falling outside, swishing lightly in the remaining leaves, bringing some down with it. Misty loved the first rain after a long dry spell. She smiled widely as she took a few extra minutes watching out the window, listening to the different sounds, the pinging against the windowpane, the dripping in puddles and slight gurgle in the eaves. Taking a last deep breath of the clean-washed air, she turned to get ready for the day.

To her relief, her hair was a little less slimy when she wet the strands for their ringlets, but she knew this would be the day of reckoning. Even if her hair didn't actually get wet in the rain, the dampness of the air would make it wild. To her surprise, Misty felt excited at the thought. Always in the past she had not liked the feel of her hair springing and frizzing all about, preferring the tidiness of the braids, but having endured first springy and then crunchy corkscrews all about her head for weeks now, she looked forward to the freedom of natural curls gone to frizz in the rain. She also thought the wild frizz looked much less ridiculous than these silly ringlets she had been forced to make each morning. She was tempted not to bother, for they'd have sprung free by the time she reached school anyway, but she knew Aunt Augusta would never approve of just naturally curly pigtails, so she completed the tedious task, smiling almost impishly to herself.

As Aunt Augusta first raved about the importance of doing the best on the tests so those hopelessly bureaucratic buffoons at the school would finally give her the position the Hughes deserved then ranted about Thomasina's obstinacy in refusing to eat decent portions of food so she would quickly grow to a size more typical of a girl her age and thus more impressive and indicative of the good the Hughes had undertaken and were accomplishing, at great sacrifice to themselves, of course, Misty ate as much as she could before having the bowl whipped out from under her and being ordered off to school. Misty was glad to hear the door close behind her, shutting out the incessant criticism, which she now recognized as being directed not just at her but at everything and everyone other than the Hughes themselves.

The hood on Misty's Burberry covered only part of her hair and didn't stay on very well because of the mass of hair, so Misty soon stopped struggling and let the hood hang down her back. She enjoyed the feel of the rain and walked with her face lifted slightly to feel the freshness on her cheeks. Tommy and Daisy waved at her from across the street as they made their way up the hill. Misty smiled and waved back, happy just to see them. Tommy couldn't walk anywhere, so Misty soon watched their backs as they ran on ahead, Daisy's short legs hurrying to keep up with Tommy as he sprang along. Misty chuckled a little to notice that Daisy needn't have worried, for Tommy didn't run a straight line, instead darting here and there along the way, much like an eager little puppy does when walking with its master. Wistfully, Misty recalled feeling like Tommy looked and she frowned slightly to think that she no longer felt like that. Her feet felt quite heavy despite the wonder of the fresh morning rain. She shook her head a little to throw off the unpleasantness of the realization and turned her attention instead to the day ahead.

She wondered if she'd have time to see Henry that day, for she had so much to ask him about her disappointment of Sunday School. She'd also like to share her excitement over the ocean with him, knowing he would somehow understand. But it would probably be someone else's turn to spend time with Henry this day. Misty had other things to do. She looked forward to seeing Mrs. Longacre and even felt a little excited about the tests. Finally she would get to do something. Finally she would be able to show them that she was not backward. It wasn't important to Misty what people thought about her, but she was determined to show them that there was nothing wrong with her people. Hearing the children's comments yesterday and listening to Aunt Augusta's outbursts had revealed that people had very wrong ideas about the island folk, and she hoped that by doing well on the tests, she'd give them a better view or at least destroy their insistence that island people were backward. She began to hurry a little in her eagerness to get on with the task.

She was so wet when she arrived at the school that she went into the girls' washroom before going upstairs to the office. She didn't want to drip all over the floors Henry worked so hard to keep clean. Her hair was the mess she had expected it to be, but she took paper towels and squeezed it as dry as she could, at least dry enough to stop the still slightly slimy drips from running down her back. She soaked many paper towels before her hair stopped dripping but she stepped back from the little mirror, happy to see just plain natural curls. It felt good to shake her head and feel the hair move freely. With a little gleam of pleasure reflected in her eyes, Misty hurried upstairs to the office.

"Good morning, Misty!" called Mrs. Longacre. "Have you had a nice weekend? You look quite happy this morning."

"Morning, Mrs. Longacre. I feel happy right now," Misty replied, pleased not to have to answer the question directly, for she didn't know what she could say about the weekend. "Will the tests begin soon, Mrs. Longacre? I feel happy to do them, though I don't really know what tests are. I hope I can write something or make pictures or something."

"The woman who is to give you the tests is called Mrs. Wright. She will be here in about half an hour and will administer the tests in the nurse's room so you aren't interrupted. In the meantime, I need a little more help here in the office. I'm not sure that you will get to write much on these tests, Misty. I think they are mostly multiple-choice questions. Mrs. Wright will explain those to you when she comes. But I'm sure you will be free to do some writing after the tests are done. There will be some time between when you finish the tests and when you will get to go to your new class. Mrs. Wright must grade the tests and make her recommendations at another meeting with Mr. Sullivan. During that time I can give you some room to write here in the office. What would you like to write?"

"Oh, I'd like to write a letter to my people at home and I'd like to write a bit of a story, I think. I'd like to read too. I miss reading. But I had some strange things happen yesterday, Mrs. Longacre. In Sunday School Mrs. Norman gave us a picture—'to colour', she said. I couldn't seem to do it, maybe because it wasn't my own picture or maybe because the crayons seemed the wrong colours to me or maybe because I can't work the crayons with their wrappers on or maybe because I was tired. I don't know. But it wasn't nice, Mrs. Longacre. I felt all wrong. Will I have to colour on the tests? Could you tell me how to do it?"

Mrs. Longacre didn't know whether to smile or frown. She wanted to smile at the thought of a child capable of producing beautiful pictures with the barest of equipment being told to "colour a picture" but she was afraid Misty would misunderstand such a smile. Poor Misty was so serious, so earnestly wanted to do what she was told and took full responsibility for anything she seemed unable to do. It never occurred to Misty that maybe the task was silly rather than that something was wrong with her. Mrs. Longacre had to be careful how she answered, though, for she mustn't be too critical of the systems as they stood. She felt herself grow a little anxious about Misty's tests, however, for if colouring was a problem for Misty, many of the tasks on the tests would be as well, not because Misty was dull but because she was so bright, so far beyond some of the banal things children were expected to do and get excited about. She kept her anxiety to herself, making a mental note to record this conversation in her own file when the child had begun her tests. For now her task was to encourage the little girl.

"Well, Misty, there may be some colouring to do; I'm not sure. But if there is, you'll have your peeled crayons to work with, won't you? That will be a help. I think, however, you won't have to colour pictures of the sort you had in Sunday School. In town, children are given small books full of pictures like the one you saw yesterday. They are called colouring books. Children just colour the pictures with crayons. That is how most children are introduced to crayons. It is thought that they will learn good eye-hand co-ordination and tidiness by colouring within the lines and will learn good colour identification and co-ordination. For most children, that is their introduction to art. Colouring is supposed to be fun, Misty. Your trouble yesterday was that you have already done so much more interesting and satisfying drawing and painting that just colouring between lines held no interest for you. Don't forget, though, that the other children have had none of what you have had. They have no Miss Lily to watch and work with. Crayons and colouring books are all they know."

"Oh, of course. I really couldn't understand the colouring or the children. I guess I just thought everyone must have someone like Miss Lily. And I never thanked her, Mrs. Longacre; that's terrible. You see I must write a letter. But Mrs. Longacre, what should I do? Do I colour like they did when I'm asked? Should I just learn it? It doesn't look in the least like art to me, though I suppose anyone could fill the spaces with wax. That's what the other girls did. Why would I make something so ugly, though? But Mrs. Norman didn't leave enough time for us to do a good job. It would take quite a while to make a picture like that come alive, especially with crayons. Do I try, Mrs. Longacre? Or do I just do what the others did?"

"Well Misty, that's a good question. I don't think you can do what the others did; otherwise I'm sure you would have. I think you must do it your own way. Didn't you say the Captain told you to be yourself and not let them corrupt you? That's your answer, Misty. But other than Sunday School, I'm sure you don't have to worry much about colouring, for after your tests, you'll be in a grade that is higher than the ones where children still do colouring. You may even get pencil crayons to work with instead of the wax crayons the primary children use. I'm sure you'll find those better; they are coloured pencils and though not quite like pencils you are used to sketching with, they are more like those than they are like crayons. Perhaps for Sunday School, pencil crayons would help solve your time problem. How about if we do a little experimenting with them after your tests?"

"Oh, I'd like that, Mrs. Longacre. But I am getting a little bit nervous. Oh Mrs. Longacre, I never had so many strange feelings back at home. I still can't find real quiet here or any rhythm and suddenly I am looking in all the wrong directions, both ahead and behind instead of right here. At home, I never had to think at all or make myself think or be so aware of things or myself or anything. Here, I just struggle. Nervous now. I never felt fear until I came here, but I've learned that. Now I feel nervous. Isn't it kind of funny that I'd read about all these things but never felt them myself and only now as I feel all strange do I begin to see that this must be the feeling I read about? It's a good thing we read a lot at home or I wouldn't know anything that was the matter with me here, for all these new emotions feel as if there's something the matter, not something right. I guess I am learning a lot here after all."

Misty's little grin struck a note of sadness in Mrs. Longacre and reminded her of something Misty had said earlier that prompted a question that must be asked. "Why would you think that you couldn't do the colouring in Sunday School because you were tired, Misty? Are you tired today?"

"Oh, a little. That's another thing I've learned since I got here, though. At home I was sometimes sleepy at the end of a wonderful long day but I don't remember ever feeling tired. Here, I get tired often. But I'm not so tired this morning as I was in Sunday School. Before the colouring I had been all confused by everything, by singing that didn't sound like singing, by people who looked all uncomfortable and sad when they were speaking of some of the happiest things there are to think about, and I guess by the girls. They kind of hurt me, Mrs. Longacre, but I'm sure now they didn't know any better. Thanks so much for reminding me they haven't had any Miss Lily. I guess no Captain either, huh? I'm sure that will help me understand better. I do wish Sunday School were a happy place, though. It should be, shouldn't it?"

Mrs. Longacre didn't want to comment, for she knew and had many differences with Mrs. Norman, but she would not criticize another nor another's church. Instead she rested her hand comfortingly on Misty's shoulder and said, "Ah yes, Misty. And you of all people want to make everyone happy, don't you? I love to see the happiness bubble up in you. Try not to let it go, Misty, no matter how tired you get. Still, I'll have the nurse check you in a week or two. We must watch that you don't get too tired. Do you sleep well?"

"Oh yes. I have a nice room and I love sleep. Sometimes I have beautiful dreams and I wake up all happy inside. Sometimes I just feel so safe while I'm asleep. When I lie in my bed I can almost hear the sound of Gramps' rocker and I fall asleep sensing everything the even rhythm always meant to me. Last night I was sure I could also hear the deep even ticking of the old mantle clock as well. I sleep just fine. I used to wake up so fresh, though, always fresh. The last few mornings seem to have come a little before I'm ready. I wish I'd known to thank my people for the wonderful things they gave me but I didn't know until now how wonderful they were. I hope people soon stop saying wrong things about them, Mrs. Longacre. Do you think my tests will help?"

"I hope so. Mrs. Wright will soon be here. You'll have a break near recess and at lunch, Misty. Where would you like to have your lunch today? Shall we eat together or did you meet anyone at Sunday School you'd like to eat with?"

"Oh, I'd like to eat with you, Mrs. Longacre. Does Henry have anyone with him today? I could run down there at recess, couldn't I? I saw the ocean on Saturday just like he promised and I want to tell him about it. I don't want to neglect thanking people like I did when I was on the island, Mrs. Longacre."

"Yes, you can run down to Henry. I'll call you when it is time. But Misty, don't worry about not thanking your people. There are ways we thank people other than with just words, and I know you showed your appreciation all the time. I'm sure you gave as much as you received."

"Oh, thank you, Mrs. Longacre. I hadn't thought of that and it has worried me. I am sure surprised at how much I didn't know, though. I just keep learning and learning. I guess Aunt Augusta was right to insist I come to town. I'd never have understood home as well as I do now."

Mrs. Longacre smiled at the indomitable spirit of the child. She really was unlike any child she had known, and she had known many. She reached out and touched Misty's hair, saying, "Beautiful hair, Misty; it looks very nice today."

"I'm glad you think so, Mrs. Longacre. It feels much better this way, but I'm still hoping I can braid it again soon. I'm sure even Aunt Augusta won't try fighting the inevitable forever. Just think, with braids, I'll be able to forget about my head again. That will be exciting!"

Mrs. Longacre chuckled softly both amused by the child and not convinced that "even Aunt Augusta" wouldn't fight forever. The woman had a well-earned reputation for being immovable.

As Mrs. Longacre ruffled a pigtail slightly before once again giving Misty's shoulder a squeeze, Mrs. Wright arrived with a bundle of papers so large Misty's eyes grew wide. Mrs. Longacre dropped her arm across both shoulders, holding her firmly, hoping to calm the child's sudden fear. "Don't worry, Misty," she said; "just do what you're asked. Good morning, Mrs. Wright. This is Misty. Misty, Mrs. Wright."

Misty said, "Good morning" just as Mrs. Wright began, "Misty? I've come for Thomasina. Where is she?"

"I am Thomasina," replied Misty, "but I've always been called Misty and prefer it."

"Oh," said Mrs. Wright, slightly bewildered, not so much by the explanation as by the child's voice. It was very musical but even and calm, very adult sounding, she thought. "Well, I'm afraid I must call you Thomasina as directed; I like the name very much, myself, though Misty also sounds lovely for you. Well, we have very much work to do today, so we'd best begin."

The woman's tone went through several changes in even such a short exchange. Her initial outrage was quickly modified by the powerful impression the child had upon her, but the efficiency for which she was known became most evident in her final statement. Misty felt suddenly chilled a little, for she had begun to sense that efficiency sometimes carried with it inflexibility, and inflexibility caused her no end of trouble. However, recalling that these tests were an opportunity to clear her people of unfair judgement of them, she willingly followed Mrs. Wright into the nurse's room to begin.

When Mrs. Longacre interrupted them for a recess break, she was a little concerned, for Misty looked quite pale. Instead of sending the child to Henry, she decided she'd best walk with her. So, saying she'd join Mrs. Wright in the staff room for a cup of coffee presently, she took Misty's hand and went into the corridor. "Are you okay, Misty?"

"I think so. I'm tired, Mrs. Longacre. It's as bad as the colouring was. Every new task she gives me I feel almost blank at the beginning. Something always seems wrong or impossible to me, and I kind of freeze. I guess I'm not doing too well, either. She's getting pretty frowny and very quiet. I wish I could have a little sleep. I wonder how many more papers she'll give me. The pile that I've done is still smaller than the other pile. What a peculiar business, Mrs. Longacre. I can't figure out what it has to do with anything. I can't seem to understand. She has me circling things and filling in little dots. It's very odd. Those ones that you called multiple-choice seem not to have a right answer or seem to have all right answers. I wonder why I have to fill in only one circle when all the answers could be right. It might be easier to keep going if I could figure out what any of it has to do with living."

"Try thinking of it as just a silly task, like the colouring. At least that will free your mind to answer the questions. When it is all done, we'll have a look and see how it connects to living, shall we?"

"Oh, yes, that will help. Thanks."

"How about a little fresh air? Do you think that would help, too?"

"Fresh air? Oh yes. I mean no. Not with the other kids today. I'm too tired."

Mrs. Longacre felt her own shoulders slump for the child but she forced some cheerfulness into her voice and said, "Oh, but the girls will all be in the big activity room, and Henry can take you for a short walk off the grounds. How about that? I'll spin out the time a little for you so you get at least twenty minutes. I'm sure that will help."

"Oh, thank you, Mrs. Longacre," Misty said as she knocked on Henry's door.

"Look who's here!" said Henry, his voice full of warm surprise. "God's good to me today, He is. Hello. Hello."

Misty threw herself into the great arms that folded immediately and easily around her even as Henry looked questioningly over the child's head at Mrs. Longacre.

Speaking very quickly Mrs. Longacre said, "Middle of the tests, Henry, and Misty is very tired. Take her for a walk off the grounds; she needs some fresh air, but keep her away from the children. Have her back in twenty minutes. I'm off to buy the child some time and see what else I can do."

Henry rocked slightly back and forth as Mrs. Longacre hurried off. "Let's see what I have here for you to put on, my friend. It's raining cats 'n' dogs outside, and you've no coat. Isn't it a grand saying—'raining cats and dogs'? Why this early fall rain is just as wonderful as a whole sky of cats and dogs would be. When I walked up that hill this morning, I just had to take my rain hat off and feel the life on my head. People laugh at me, you know Misty, an old man walking in the rain carrying his rain hat, but I just couldn't help myself. Let them laugh, poor things. Laughter is good, and if I'm all they can find to laugh at, then I've done them a favour, haven't I? Shall I take my hat and carry it so we can give some other folk a laugh or shall we just leave it here and enjoy the rain? How about you wear the hat? I've this big old sweater I keep here too, but you choose."

Soothed by both the sound of Henry's voice and his wonderful words, Misty stood back and looked at him. "Oh, Henry," she said, "I'd love to wear your hat and your sweater too. Did you really make them laugh this morning? I walked to school with my hood off this morning too. You are right; it's wonderful rain. Come on. Let's go before we have to be back."

Henry draped the big sweater around the child and handed her the hat before putting on his own raincoat. He chuckled deeply as Misty, almost completely engulfed in the big sweater which hung to her ankles, grinned up at him from under the hat that seemed so huge on her. Taking her hand, he led her out the side door of the school's basement, breaking into a shuffling run as they crossed the bit of school ground to the alley that ran to the south of the school. Running along beside him in the baggy hat and clothes, Misty burst out laughing, her tiredness vanished for the moment.

"Feel like a big kid skippin' school," Henry chuckled as they slowed to a walk in the alley. "It's great fun, but don't you tell Mr. Sullivan I said so. Smell the rain, child. Is there a smell like it on earth, do you think?"

Misty took big breaths and just smiled deeply, squeezing Henry's large hand as she did. Pulling him a little to the side of the alley that bordered the forest, Misty held the big hat with her free hand as she tipped her head up to feel the large drops that dripped from the tree branches onto her face.

"No, Henry. There's no smell like it. But there are different rain smells. You know that. Why spring rain doesn't smell much like summer rain at all, and this fall rain has its own smell. And the rain in the forest smells different from the rain in the field. And it feels different, too. Oh, Henry. I asked to see you to tell you I saw the ocean on Saturday. You understand. It was wonderful, just like you said it would be. Rain air doesn't smell like ocean air and rain at the ocean smells different from rain anywhere else." Misty gave a little skip in her delight at walking along with someone who knew.

Not wanting to trouble her by drawing attention to having to go back to the school, Henry led her a different route back, saying, "Here's a treat for us. We'll get a good dose of the forest rain if we take this little path. I wonder if the old skunk cabbage pond is filling up yet. Let's have a look."

Misty laughed again to see Henry have to duck under some of the low branches in the little path, for he'd twist around and turn his face upward to catch some of the branches' drips, grinning as he did so. Playfully, she shook some water from a low bush, sending droplets all over them. Henry's deep laugh seemed to fill the path and run over into the woods themselves. She joined him, her young voice adding crystal sounds to his resounding bass. "Look," she suddenly interrupted, "is that it?"

"Yup, just starting to fill up. In a week or so, it will be a perfectly round little pond. There's an old frog lives nearby. You'll hear him from the grounds sometimes if you listen for him. Come spring, there'll be skunk cabbage all around the pond and tadpoles swimming in it. Tommy showed it to me one day. Trust him to know it was here; little imp isn't supposed to be off the grounds but he sneaks down here sometimes after he's had a trip to the office. It doesn't hurt anything. Gives him a chance to sort things out, you know. Sniff now, little one. Rain here smells even different."

The two stood side by side, tall, strong, old man with his hair plastered wet with rain, short, tiny young child, dry beneath the big floppy hat, faces lifted high, one weathered, lined and darkly tanned, the other soft, smooth and pale, both lit up for the moment, as hand in hand the two took deep, fresh breaths. A tear of relief joined the raindrops on Henry's cheek as he felt the tension drain from the child beside him. Together they turned and followed the path. Very softly the child asked, "What is it called, Henry?"

"I call it Tommy's pond, Misty. It's a secret place. He won't mind, though. I'll tell him I brought you."

"Thank you, Henry. Thank you."

Both were quiet as they walked, quickly again, back to the school. As they crossed the grounds, Henry was relieved again to hear Misty chuckle. "What a sight we must make now, Henry. And you are right. Let them laugh, poor things." Her chuckles turned to laughter as she added, "Maybe next Sunday, I'll borrow your sweater and hat for Sunday School. They surely need a laugh there."

Henry joined in her laughter, for they certainly were a sight to behold and it was delightful to laugh with others. But he also gave her hand a reassuring squeeze, for he shared her underlying sadness for the people who needed to laugh at others because they failed to see the things around them to laugh about.

As Misty took off Henry's hat and sweater in his little room, she smiled up at him and said, "I'll think about your hat and the rain and I'll be okay. Wish you had made up the tests, Henry. You'd know how many answers there can be. But I'm stronger now. Thanks. Guess I'd better hurry."

"Never mind how many answers there might be, Misty. Just give one of them. That's all they want, poor folk. And just remember, no matter what, you are fine—just fine. And I'll have a little chat with the Big Boss for you on and off through the day. Don't forget, He loves you. That's all that matters. Now off you go. Thank Mrs. Longacre for me. It was a great walk!"

Misty never knew that Henry closed the door to his little room, sank into his chair and wept when she left. As she resumed her task up in the nurse's room, the old man neglected his work, driven to pray without ceasing for the delightful, brave soul who was being so sorely tried. He thought his heart would break as he cried out, seeking the only help possible. It was quite some time before he could break through to thanks, so heavy was his old heart, but he did find himself praising God for the child and for the help he knew God could give. He ignored an almost tentative knock at his door but soon looked up, startled to hear the door open quietly.

"You are here," said a shaking voice, "please may I come in?"

Henry turned to see Mrs. Longacre peeking through the slightly opened door a little like a naughty child. He smiled at the sight and answered, "Of course. Come in. Come in. You look a little like Tommy when he's done something wrong. I'll put my kettle on here. You also look like you need some of my good tea. You in trouble like Tommy or just tired like Misty?"

Mrs. Longacre managed a feeble laugh at his description of her but she sank into Henry's extra chair with a tired sigh. "Just tired? Do you think Misty is just tired? Henry, I can't stand what they're doing. I don't ever recall being so distraught over a child before. Whatever is the matter with them? Can't they see? Don't they look? What do they think they have eyes for?"

Henry interrupted with a deep chuckle this time. "Now Jean, you do sound like Tommy. Watch out. You're winding up just like he does—and you don't have red hair! In a minute you'll be sputtering and stammering and you'll 'jist bust out' if you're not careful. Calm yourself a bit."

She joined his laughter, more fully this time, but again grew serious. "Henry, you are right; I need to be careful. I'm not sure what's got into me but I don't think I can take this. Mrs. Wright said that on the basis of what she's seen so far, the child is impossible. She's failing all the tests—failing them, Henry. What will we do? You know how inflexible Wright and Sullivan are. Always by the book, the book, the book. Do they even look at children? I had to come down, Henry. I was afraid I was going to lose my temper."

"Here, have some tea. Misty likes it. Even Tommy has a cup some days. So, Tommy's temper has finally rubbed off on you. I'll have to watch myself. I spend more time with him than you do."

Mrs. Longacre laughed at the comical face the old man made as he poked fun at himself and she felt herself relax a little as she sipped the soothing tea and listened to the kind and wise old fellow.

"I've had my cry and my prayer, Jean. That's the only reason I'm in better shape right now than you are. My heart breaks for the little Miss. She's just as brave as they come. We had a wonderful walk. Imagine that! She came in here tired and near broken and just a few minutes outside and she was back in one piece and fun—lots of fun. Those island folk sure have something right, or she'd not be like she is. She may feel that she's becoming polluted by this old town, but inside she isn't. She is getting tired and worn down, though. I'm worried about that. She's mighty thin."

"I've noticed. Her skirts are looser than when she first came. She says she just isn't hungry. I wonder if there's a way we could get Augusta to stop forcing food on her. I'm sure she'd eat more if she could just choose her own."

"Afraid I'll have to leave you to deal with Augusta. She won't even talk to me. Beneath her, you know. Bay man, you know. Poor Augusta. You'd think having Misty around would have softened her some. I'd hoped so, but it doesn't look like it. Imagine living with that child all the time and not getting happy? I can't understand it. Sometimes the strength of evil baffles me almost as much as the power of God awes me, you know. Both seem too big for me to imagine at times. I guess our poor little Miss had a rough go at Sunday School, too. Lordy, nothing seems to go right for her here. Do you ever wonder if she isn't an angel sent to shake us all up?"

"Feels like it sometimes, Henry. She's almost pure enough to be an angel. But you forget, we knew her folks and her life. Days like this make me ready to go off to an island. Well, never mind. I'd better get back before I am in trouble like Tommy! But Henry, if you think of anything I might do, please let me know. I've never felt so unable to help a child, nor so desperate to help one. Thanks for the tea and the talk. I think I can carry on without 'jist bustin' out.' Next time you have Tommy here, you'll be telling him I was the bad kid of the day, 'sent ta ol' Henry fer fixin'!'"

The two enjoyed a companionable and healthy laugh before Henry said, "Bring the child down for lunch if it'll do any good, Jean. Bad day, I think. Bad day."

"Thanks, Henry," called Mrs. Longacre as she left to return to the office. Henry turned back to his prayer. He felt suddenly old.

At noon Mrs. Longacre wasn't sure she shouldn't call the nurse. Misty was pale and appeared shaky even sitting at the table with the piles of papers in front of her. She seemed distant, her eyes looking almost vacant. It wasn't the glassy look Mrs. Longacre had seen before. It was more like the dazed look she'd had after Miss Moore had dressed her down. Mrs. Longacre forced cheerfulness into her voice as she stepped fully into the room and said,

"Good work, Misty. Only a tiny pile left. Look how many you've completed. But it's lunchtime first. Mrs. Wright, are you having lunch here or going elsewhere?"

"I'll be leaving and I'll have to be gone about an hour and a half, but that will leave plenty of time to finish these. We're almost done now. Is the child well? She seems weak to me, as if she has flu or something. Do you suppose she caught cold in the rain? She keeps shivering."

Mrs. Longacre wanted to scream at the woman, to ask why she, like everyone else, refused to talk to Misty, refused to treat her with the respect every human deserves instead of treating her as if she were mindless or even dead. But she controlled herself and said simply, "I'll tend to her, Mrs. Wright. You have a nice lunch, and we'll see you later, won't we, Misty? Come on, I've a nice treat for you."

Seeing Misty didn't move and her eyes were wide and glazed, Mrs. Longacre took her gently by the shoulder and led her from the room, straight along the corridor and down the stairs, talking evenly and gently as they went, "I've talked to Henry this morning, Misty, and he invited us to have our lunch in his little room. We're going to have a picnic there, just the three of us. Now the nice thing about having a picnic rained out is that there are no ants at indoor picnics, so we won't be bothered any. Only trouble is, it takes a little rearranging, so you and Henry will have to wait just a while until I gather our things and move them into Henry's room. I have a nice, light and very good lunch planned, one I'm sure you'll like. You won't mind waiting a few minutes with Henry, will you? And we have an extra half hour! Won't that be grand? You won't try to start without me, will you?"

Mrs. Longacre was tremendously relieved to see Misty shake her head and even look up at her and try a faint smile. Henry was right. The child was incredibly tough. She fought back tears as she knocked on Henry's door for the third time that day. "We're here for our picnic, Henry," she called loudly. "You will wait for me while I go and gather our food, won't you?" she continued as he opened the door; "I don't want to be left out."

Wordlessly, Henry gathered the little girl into his great arms once again, drawing her into the room as he did so. Mrs. Longacre said, "I'll be about fifteen or twenty minutes; remember, don't start without me." She closed the door behind her as she turned and hurried away to get food, leaving Henry to work his magic.

17.

Dust from their Feet

Gently Henry rocked the silent little girl, momentarily stunned by the difference in her. He had known it would be bad but hadn't imagined it this bad. He did the only thing he could. Still holding Misty tightly, he began softly, but firmly and fully; "Great God, the Father of all, thank You for this bright child, this shining light in our lives. Thank You that You care for each of us, Your children. Thank You that You never leave us. Forgive us our sinful ways, our small minds, our blindness. Forgive those that are hurting this wee one and help us to forgive them. Grant us Your peace, oh Lord. Heal our pain. Thank You that You have given all for us, that it is complete. Thank You that You suffered that we might be made whole. Thank You …"

As the old man cried out with tears streaming down his joy-lit face, the child in his arms shook with sobs—sobs of pain, sobs of fatigue, sobs of the great pleasure-pain that she was learning came with first receiving something she had missed so very much. Inside, the joy rose up pushing out the cold, forcing out the pain, replacing the dullness that had threatened all morning to suffocate her. The joy lifted her tear-streaked face up and illuminated it with peace. The sobs subsided, though the tears continued long. Her thin but clear voice soon joined that of the old man, thanking God for joy, for strength, for Henry, for prayer, for Mrs. Longacre, for this safe little room, for life itself and adding a loud, full "amen" as Henry concluded with the benediction she'd heard from Gramps' lips so often, the full benediction, spoken with life, with hope, with faith, as she had always heard it. She sighed deeply as the two continued silently, unaware of the hard cement floor on which they knelt together, no longer rocking, simply still and safe.

As one they rose, still silent, and moved to Henry's great chair, the child standing at his side, leaning against him, his arm wrapped comfortably around her tiny frame. Henry smiled to see peace and quiet strength showing again in her damp and very pale face. Seeing his gentle smile break through the concern she saw in his caring eyes, Misty reached up and patted his cheek, wiping the dampness with her small hand. "Sprung a leak, huh, Henry?" she said, an impish grin flashing across her face. Both laughed gently.

"Ah, little girl, you know the secrets of life, don't you? Have you ever been angry?"

"Yes, once. Not "bustin' out" angry, quite, but angry. Why do you ask?"

"First, you tell me when you were angry."

"It was when Tommy was telling me about failing his tests all the time. I was angry, real angry. It isn't fair, Henry. Tommy knows his arithmetic but he fails his tests. They make him repeat grades that he doesn't need to repeat. When he told me, I was angry. That's it; the only time I remember."

"Don't you get angry when you have to wear your hair curled or have to eat food you don't want or wear clothes you don't like?"

"No, I don't get angry at those things. I just don't like them but I'm trying to like them, Henry."

The old man shook his head, amazed at the wonderful simplicity of the child. "I asked about anger because one of the secrets of life is not turning pain to anger and not harbouring anger. I wondered if you even knew anger, you're so bright and you refresh so quickly. You're a wonder, you are."

"Why do you suppose I was angry about Tommy's tests? When people make bad comments about my folks, I feel hurt, not angry, but when Tommy told me about his tests, I felt only angry. It felt strange at first, but it didn't really feel wrong."

"No, anger isn't wrong. You remember the Book says 'Be ye angry and sin not,' so we have to expect some anger. Yours was the right kind, too, anger at wrong done to another. You were right not to sin in that anger, though. That's where Tommy runs into trouble with his 'bustin' out.' Say, let me tell you something funny. This morning, Mrs. Longacre came in here. Do you know, she looked and sounded almost like Tommy. She was just 'bustin' out'. Why I had to talk to her like I do Tommy, and her a grown woman! It was something to see."

Henry's great laugh filled the little room. Feeling the kindness and friendliness in Henry's telling as well as his laughter, Misty said, "You're exaggerating now, for sure. Mrs. Longacre? Bustin' out? Henry, I think you've had too much rain on the brain today." Her laughter added a richness to his.

And that is how Mrs. Longacre found them, to her intense relief and her surprise. She entered carrying a tray covered with a cloth that Henry immediately recognized. Putting the tray on the little table and stopping to take off her coat and hang it on one of Henry's pegs, she said, "So what on earth is so funny? Do I look windblown or something?"

Henry laughed louder as Misty said, "Why we were laughing about you, Mrs. Longacre. Henry said you were 'bustin' out' like Tommy this morning. I think he must have got too much rain on his brain, don't you?"

"He must have," she replied in mock horror. 'Why, I could never 'bust out' like Tommy!" Her laughter added to the others.

"Looks like you've been to my Christina's. You weren't speeding now, were you? You're awful quick back."

Seeing the twinkle in his eye, Mrs. Longacre ignored his comment about speeding and answered, "Of course I've been to your Christina's. Where else would I get a decent picnic lunch? She sent a message with the lunch too; said to tell you she'll be spending the afternoon in the grape arbour. Seemed a funny message to me. Do you always tell each other which part of the property you'll be in, even when you are at work?"

Henry chuckled. "Of course not. The grape arbour is my 'Stina's praying place. The message was that she's praying."

"Who is Christina?" asked Misty.

"She's my wife, Misty, and as fine a woman as you'll ever meet. Afternoon in the grape arbour, eh? She'll be as happy as can be that it's raining. Like you, Misty, she loves the rain. She'll have her wrinkled face tipped up to that wet old sky and she'll just be lit up."

"Oh, does she have a wrinkled face? I wish I could meet her and rub my cheek against hers. I miss softness, Henry. And a grape arbour! We had grapes at home, nice juicy, tart ones."

"Well, you'll like our picnic then, Misty, for we've grapes. Look." Taking the beautiful cloth from the tray, Mrs. Longacre revealed grapes, apples, cheese, light biscuits, and cookies.

Misty spontaneously clapped her hands together and leaned forward to smell the goodies on the tray. "Oh, Henry," she said, "smell the grapes. Smell the cheese. This is real cheese! Like home cheese. And the apples!"

Henry and Mrs. Longacre both chuckled in great delight to see the child's joy. Henry bowed his head and said in his rich, full voice, "Father, we thank Thee for this Thy bounty and ask that You bless it and minister strength to those who prepared it and those who eat it. In the name of the Father, Son and Holy Spirit, we pray, Amen." He frowned slightly to see tears coursing down Misty's cheeks but relaxed to see by her shining eyes that they were tears of joy.

"I'm just full up," she proclaimed; "that's two real prayers I've heard in a single day. Full up!" And with that she reached out and helped herself to some grapes and cheese, excited to have real food and to eat with friendly people. Her face as she tasted the food was pure delight for her two companions, and the evidence of her appetite relieved them of some of their worry. Mrs. Longacre saw in Henry's face that he would be bringing fruit and fresh cheese for Misty, and biscuits too, she realized, as she heard Misty exclaim, "Oh, Henry. You will thank your wife, won't you? These biscuits are just like home! I can eat them without even feeling it! And real cheese. Do you keep a cow, Henry?"

"Not any more, little one. But we get milk from Old Mac's cow, and my 'Stina makes cheese. I tell her it's the best, but she just shakes her head like I'm an old fool. Today, though, I'll tell her about your face when you ate her cheese. Then she'll know!"

But if the two thought Misty had forgotten her morning ordeal in her delight, they were soon to learn otherwise, as Misty, pausing for a moment but taking more grapes as she spoke said, "I really hate to have let the folks down. I don't mind that I can't do the tests; it's just as Tommy says, sort of.

But I really wanted to show people that my folks aren't backward. I can't do that. It's no use."

Seeing some of the joy go from the little girl's face, Henry said, "Why don't you sit up here on my knee and I'll tell you something important while you and Mrs. Longacre eat?"

Misty's face lit up again, as she perched herself on Henry's lap, leaned against his great chest and munched her grapes and cheese as he began;

"I'm not sure how much you know or remember, Misty, but I do know it's time someone told you the truth that wipes out these silly things you've heard people say about your folks. Then you'll know you don't have to show people any such thing. And I'm the one to tell you, for I knew your grandfather and I know the Captain. I know they'd both want me to tell the truth. Your grandfather owned the whole island you lived on, Misty. He bought it when he was just a young man. He was troubled for a time then by two things.

"The first was that he chafed under working in the city for another man. He was a good carpenter and a fine cabinetmaker, was a lover of wood who saw beauty in everything. He felt that his work should always be right, bring out beauty and glorify the Maker of the wood. But in Vancouver where he lived, people wanted things done in a hurry and done to fit in with what everyone else was doing. All the houses looked the same, and your grandfather thought them ugly and carelessly made. He was dissatisfied in his work there, and that began to bring with it dissatisfaction within himself.

"The second was that he was deeply hurt by the church. I know he wouldn't have told you this, Misty, for he seldom said anything about it, never wanted to bias anyone or to be a stumbling block. But you have had a taste and you need to know this. Your Granny was the most wonderful woman he'd ever met, and he loved her more than he imagined possible in life. She was just a bit of a thing, he said, and had the most beautiful gold-flecked eyes and hair, much like yours, Misty. He said the gold in her eyes were tiny bits of the gold-paved road in heaven, so pure and true was your Granny. But she was Catholic, and he was Protestant. Neither of their churches would marry them. They were strong, though, and knew God had brought them together, so they went to City Hall and were married there. Her church excommunicated her completely, wouldn't let her through the doors again. His let them enter but scorned them so thoroughly they weren't welcome there either. It hurt both of them, more for each other than for themselves, but most of all for God, for they knew that it was only the people, not God, who scorned them, and they hurt for the sadness, the smallness, the bitterness it all showed. So they came away.

"They stayed in town here a few months while your grandfather cleared a little of the land on his island. He built a kind of large box and covered it with a tent, and they moved in there while he built the house and his workshop. They were more than a year in that tent-box but they were as happy as could be, free at last from cruel tongues and from small minds. But best of all, they were free on the island to see God again as God is, not as people have come to represent Him; they were free to be the people God wanted them to be. Your grandfather was a great thinker, Misty, very creative. On the island, he was free to build as he wanted, to take the time he wanted, to try new things, to continually improve his skills. He made some of the most durable and handsome furniture I've ever seen. When they needed some extra money, he'd come to town and build someone a house, but never without an agreement that he could work at his own pace and have a say in the house design. He built our house, Misty, and most of our furniture. That's how I met him.

"Their life was a good one and your grandparents were the best people I've met, as selfless as people can be, I think. They were content but never complacent. They were full of life. And isolated as they were, they gave of themselves always and readily. Your grandmother would row for hours to take something to a family or an old fisherman she heard needed something. Back then, there were isolated people scattered all over the coast here but somehow they'd learn about the others in need. Most of the scattered folk were single men, some of them crabbed and hardened. Your grandmother somehow managed to tend to many of their clothes and to their souls. She'd climb out of her rowboat with her little basket of newly knit socks and mended shirts and a little fresh-baked loaf, and those rough old fellows would just melt. Bit of a thing that she was, she was never afraid, nor had she need to be, for even the roughest of them respected her more than even she knew. Your grandfather soon stopped worrying and fussing about her. He couldn't stop her anyway, wouldn't have, for he knew that she was doing right. If she wasn't daunted by the hardship of wind and weather, he wouldn't get in her way. She was like you, Misty, tiny but strong.

"Though they were alone, they were never lonely on their island. They simply didn't know loneliness, for they were full. But one day they added a different kind of fullness to their lives. Your grandfather was here in town working a job. He went to the tobacconist one noon for something for his pipe. It was a little shop, just a booth really, next to the old hotel. It was quite busy, for people bought their newspapers there as well as candy, tobacco and even some fresh fruit when it was in season, as people sold their extra harvest there. While your grandfather waited, he saw things that hurt and upset him, so when it came his turn to pay, he said, 'Captain, I'm finishing this job in about a week, and you are coming home with me. Do what is necessary to move out of your room and this place and be ready to go. I'll come by and help you clean out in the evenings.' I heard that he didn't argue, didn't even wait for a reply. He told me later it was because he was afraid he'd say something bad. That was one of the few times in his life your grandfather was 'bustin' out mad,' Misty. So he walked away.

"But he went back in the evenings and helped the Captain sell off most of his things and close up the little hovel he called a room. Your grandfather had seen people cheating the Captain day after day. He could tell coins apart, for each one is a different size, but the bills all felt the same to him, and time after time people gave him a one-dollar bill and said it was a five. The Captain trusted everyone, and they just walked all over him. Your grandfather had also seen the tired look that crossed the Captain's face when he heard people jeering at his scars and children making fun of him. They'd make faces right in front of him, thinking he couldn't tell what was happening because he couldn't see, but he knew. Even the room he lived in showed the disgrace of man, for it was unfit for anyone. The fellow who rented it to him over-charged him and never looked after the place. Nothing the Captain had seen in the war that took his sight and scarred his face hurt him as much as the people did when he came back home blind. They treated him like a freak.

"So your grandfather took him home, and your little Granny made a new man of him. He lived with them the first year while, together, they cleared the land at the far end of the island and built the Captain's house and furniture. Your Granny was always wise past her years, so the very minute the Captain came in the door behind your grandfather, she just brightened up and said, 'Oh, Thomas, you've brought me some help at last. I've been so tired this past while I wondered how I'd carry on. Hello, Captain. You can't imagine what a welcome relief you are.' Now Misty, your Granny never told a lie. She was often tired, for their life was hard work and she had to do many physically difficult tasks herself, though she'd have kept on forever, as you know. But she saw a way to restore life to the blind man, to give him purpose again, and she started right in. Hearing that he was a relief to someone and not a bother gave the Captain the first bit of hope he'd had since returning from the war. She set right in to make him independent. The tales the Captain tells now of how she did it are something! I'll tell only a few.

"Right off, she asked him to leave the white stick outside. You probably haven't even seen his white cane, Misty, for he soon gave it up altogether. He'd need it if he were in town, but there on the island, he doesn't need one. Your Granny recognized that he'd feel stronger without it, so, on the pretence of protecting your grandfather's fine work, she showed him how to move about safely inside the house without it. She was a wizard. But most wondrous of all was that very first day she set about teaching him how to cook. Now the Captain had never cooked much before he was blinded, so he had a lot to learn, but your Granny just set him to it. She declared her first rest would be from the work of cooking. She'd do the bossing, she said, but he'd do the work. She even had him packing the basket lunch that he and your grandfather took out when they worked on his new house. She figured out all kinds of ways for him to get the right things in the recipes she taught him. But you know those, Misty; you've seen the Captain's kitchen and watched him work. Just you remember, though, that it was your Granny who devised all those tricks.

"And your Grandfather, too. He soon began arranging tools in special ways so the Captain could find what he needed without hurting himself. Your grandfather claimed that he learned more about his own trade by working with the Captain than he'd ever known, for he had to learn more about feel himself in order to help the Captain. And so it went. That first winter they lived together, your Granny taught the Captain mending and basic sewing, she started him weaving—and he taught her basket making. Oh, he makes the finest baskets, Misty, as you know. The Captain learned to tend the animals without getting hurt and do everything he needed to live on his own. He was like a new man, the man you know and love.

"As his house neared completion and was about ready for him to move into, they got a dog for him, not the one he has now, of course, but company and help for him. He has paid his way all these years, Misty, earning money from his baskets and his weaving, but also working with your grandfather, who claimed that nobody could ever finish furniture as beautifully as the Captain does. Working by feel instead of sight, his sanding is perfect, his polish like none other. Yes, your grandfather together with your grandmother gave that man land and they gave him life.

"Miss Lily came later but much in the same way. She'd had a hard life, not because she looked different from other people, but because she is different, an artist through and through. Artists seem to see differently from others, see more than others, and they often think differently. Instead of just leaving them be as different as they are, other folk get uncomfortable around them and begin to criticize them, belittle them, try to make them like themselves. Miss Lily never married, either, and people don't leave much room for spinsters in their communities. They look at them as if there is something wrong with them that no man would have them. It wasn't that no man would have Miss Lily at all. She was just fully taken up with two things: her art and nursing. Did you know Miss Lily was a nurse? Well, she was. For years she travelled all around nursing sick folk and painting. People said it didn't make sense for one person to do those two things, but Miss Lily always said that nursing and art were perfect companions, for they are two parts of the same thing.

"You see the artist sees beauty everywhere, seeks beauty. The beauty moves her to create, not just to try to recapture what she has seen but to create more beauty that others might be lifted up. And she who so loves beauty cannot abide the pain of suffering. Even as Miss Lily needs to paint, she needed to do all she could to alleviate suffering. And so she did. She took all the worst jobs, nursed where others wouldn't go, never spared herself any hardship if she could help even one suffering person. From place to place she went, and always when her work was done, she'd leave behind some of her beauty, not just in the people she'd helped, but in paintings. Some of the poorest people in the world, people who have almost nothing else, have one of Miss Lily's paintings. People here scorned her, saying she should give them food, not useless pictures, but Miss Lily knows the importance of beauty to hope and to health. She ignored the criticism and did her own miracles.

"But after the accident that took her hearing, she didn't nurse. There was an explosion in a small camp where she had gone to nurse some children. Miss Lily's hearing never returned to her. She was herself a long time healing, for she was troubled with terrible pain in her head for almost two years after the accident. She was also lame in one leg, for she was near the centre of the explosion and was hit with a piece of metal. The leg was slow to heal, so she came home to rest and recover. I've never known whether she couldn't nurse without her hearing or if people just didn't want her help anymore, for we soon learned that if people thought her strange before the accident, they shunned her even more when they heard her early attempts to talk. That's when your grandfather met her and took her home.

"It happened much like with the Captain. Your grandfather was in town on a job and was doing a little shopping when he saw Miss Lily in the store, trying to get some things. He saw the pained look on her face when people ignored her, mocked her, pretended not to know what she wanted or what she was trying to say. Children were imitating her limp and her sounds, chanting at her, and, even worse, their parents didn't stop them. People can be dense, Misty. They thought because Miss Lily was deaf she wouldn't perceive their cruel treatment and they seemed to think that because she was different, she couldn't be hurt. Or maybe they just didn't think. But your grandfather saw it, walked right up to her and made her understand almost the same thing he had said to the Captain. It must have been a shock for a woman to have a man make her understand that she was coming home with him, but Miss Lily was tired and hurt, and your grandfather didn't give her any time to fuss. He went with her right that day and started packing her things. He went to the Land Office, too, just as he had done with the Captain, and he signed a piece of his land over to Miss Lily, just gave it to her.

"When he walked in the house with Miss Lily behind him, your Granny's face lit up and she ran over and hugged Miss Lily right off, saying, 'A woman! You've brought me a woman! And a beautiful one at that.' Nobody could say or do the perfect thing quite like your Granny, Misty. So Miss Lily moved in, and your grandfather and the Captain, together with Miss Lily herself, designed and built her home and started the gardens. Your grandmother set to helping Miss Lily speak again and enabling her to read lips. There are other ways for the deaf to communicate using sign language now, but Miss Lily just wanted to be left alone to live and to paint. With the Captain and your grandparents, their love and patience, she was soon able to communicate without difficulty. You know that too, don't you?

"None of those folk ever complained, Misty, or ever criticize that I know of. And none of them regrets or resents or is bitter in any way. Any of them could have been angry, 'bustin' out angry' all the time, but they saw a better way and followed it. Miss Lily is so grateful to have her sight so she can continue her art, that she never fusses about the hearing she doesn't have. The Captain is so grateful for the fullness of his life on the island that he never fusses about not seeing. The people that meet them soon forget that each of them has a missing sense, for they live more fully than many people who have not suffered at all.

"Some folk here criticize all of them for running away and even make up stories about why they must have had to run. But your island folk didn't run away, Misty. They just went to something better. They couldn't help the people around them and were continually hurt by them so they moved to where they could do good. I think it's a little like when Jesus told the disciples to let their peace come upon the worthy houses but to let it return to themselves if the place were not worthy. Then He said, "when ye go out of that city, shake off the dust from your feet." I think the island folk just shook the dust from their feet and took their peace where people were worthy of it. Your grandparents did more for a few than I have seen others do for many, Misty. You don't ever have to defend them—not ever. And you must never forget that you are one of them and every bit as good.

"As we've sat here and I've told you this story, I see more clearly than ever just how like them you are, right down to your gold-flecked eyes. It's like having your grandparents back here with us, Misty, and I thank you for that. You remember, too, that sometimes your Granny got tired. The city folk hurt her just like these town folk are hurting you, but she hung on to the right way until she could brush that dust from her feet. She never let those gold flecks in her eyes tarnish in the least. We don't know what path there is ahead for you, Misty, but we do know that, like your Granny before you, you are strong and you are gold-flecked. And we love you just like your Granny."

The room was quiet for a moment as all three let the impact of the story settle a little. Misty looked more steady than she had for days, strengthened by the truth as Henry had known she would be. Finally she said simply, "Thank you, Henry" and turned so she could hug him and softly kiss his cheek.

After a few more moments of quiet, the little twinkle lit up her eye and she said, "But Henry, I know you've got rain on the brain now. My Gramps 'bustin' out angry' indeed! First you accuse Mrs. Longacre and now my Gramps. You'd better wear your rain hat from now on."

The three laughed merrily together before Misty hopped down from Henry's knee and said without any hint of devastating emotion or fatigue, "We'd better get on with it, then. I'll go finish those tests just because Mr. Sullivan said I must. It won't take me long now. There aren't many left. I know what I can do no matter what these old tests say so I'll just go make those little crosses and fill in those circles. Kind of funny, in a way, spending a whole day filling in little boxes and circles. Wonder what Gran would think of that? I know; she'd think if it made people happy, it was worth doing. So if it's time, I'll just go make Mr. Sullivan happy. And I'll do it Gran's way. I think I'll have to make up a little song about circles and crosses, dots and boxes. Thanks again, Henry. And don't forget to thank your wife. I haven't had such good food since I came here. Give her wrinkled cheek a pat for me, won't you?"

All three were strong as Misty and Mrs. Longacre left the little room and walked back to the office. With a simple thanks, Henry turned to his work. Misty thanked Mrs. Longacre for the best picnic ever and walked calmly into the nurse's room to complete her task. Mrs. Longacre turned to a task of her own.

18.

Bustin' Out Meeting

Misty completed her tests quickly and left the pile for Mrs. Wright's assessment when she returned to the office as directed. Mrs. Longacre had another surprise for her: a gift. She presented Misty with a box containing paper, envelopes, a pen and pot of ink, a pencil, an eraser, and a note promising to mail any letters that Misty might write. Misty was so excited she couldn't speak, just threw her arms around Mrs. Longacre's neck and hugged her. She could hardly stand still as she clutched the box, looking at it with eyes alive and dancing. She was even so excited she almost missed Mrs. Longacre's announcement that she was done for the day.

"We will not have the meeting until tomorrow morning, Misty," she said. "We've already made you do too much today. Mr. Sullivan agrees that you can skip off home now and we'll see you back here in the office in the morning. Any particular work you'd like me to have ready for you? Or would you like to read here in the office while we have the meeting?"

"Oh, could I read, Mrs. Longacre? That would be wonderful! Thank you so much. I'll see you in the morning."

"Thank you for the picnic, Misty. I haven't had such a fine lunch hour for years. Good night."

Misty hurried home with her precious box, eager to set pen to paper. Aunt Augusta was not home, but the door was unlocked as promised, so Misty was free to go in, hurriedly fix up her wild hair to avoid any conflict with Aunt Augusta and then write. She filled several pages, not with complaints but with questions. At the end of her long list of questions, she stated simply that she missed them both very much but that meeting Henry had helped.

When Miss Lily got the letter and read it to the Captain, both wept, for they saw more in the child's simple statement than she ever imagined she put there. They knew life in the town.

Misty slept well that night and hurried off to school in the morning, unaware that the day would go down in the school's history as unprecedented and unforgettable. For a while she helped Mrs. Longacre around the office, working easily and cheerily with the women in there, often humming to herself. Mid-morning, Mrs. Longacre cleared off the little table that sat beneath the window in the main office and put down a book, saying, "I thought you'd like to read this book, Misty. It was new last summer. I borrowed it from the library in town, so you can keep it for two weeks. Will that be long enough?"

"Oh yes, Mrs. Longacre; I'm sure it will. *Thomasina!* The book about the cat! Tommy told me. Thank you."

"You can sit at the table there, Misty. We're about to begin our meeting in Mr. Sullivan's office. Ah, here come the Hughes now, and Mrs. Wright, too."

Sure enough, Misty could hear Aunt Augusta's voice coming down the corridor, probably disturbing every class she passed. As they entered the office, Misty could see Uncle Hugh trying to quiet the blustering woman, and Misty smiled slightly. She had seen so little of Uncle Hugh, she'd never thought much about how Aunt Augusta might make him feel sometimes. Though they seemed to think alike, Misty suddenly realized that Uncle Hugh was generally much quieter than Aunt Augusta. Despite Uncle Hugh's shushing and nudging, Aunt Augusta kept right on talking even after they took the seats that had been placed for them on the left side of Mr. Sullivan's office. Misty noticed that Mr. Sullivan stood at his desk, Mrs. Wright, with her bundle of papers on the side of the desk, sat to his right. Mrs. Longacre took a seat almost directly across from Mr. Sullivan, very near the office door. There were only two empty chairs in the room. After Mrs. Longacre had closed the door, Mr. Sullivan sat down. Misty turned her attention to the book, soon absorbed by the adventures of Thomasina and Mary MacDhui, barely aware of the low din in the principal's office.

Inside a struggle began. Mr. Sullivan started, efficient and proper as always. He introduced Mrs. Wright, and she took over for a time, efficiently stating the test results and her assessment of them. Thomasina had indeed done appallingly, failing almost everything, even the simplest of tasks. Though unemotional, Mrs. Wright did state clearly that she had never seen such poor results. Aunt Augusta was outraged and kept interrupting and muttering until Mr. Sullivan had to reprimand her much as he did the children, once raising his voice and seeming quite angry.

Finally he rose and said, "Hugh, if Augusta cannot behave as is fitting a meeting, she'll have to leave. We cannot accomplish anything with her continual outbursts. Shall she stay or will you be the only representative of the child?"

Hugh, shooting a fierce look at Augusta that silenced her, said, "We'll both stay, thank you."

Mr. Sullivan resumed his seat and the meeting proceeded. Both Mrs. Wright and Mr. Sullivan spoke of the test results, meticulously repeating the scores to clarify the only possible recommendation: that Thomasina be left in Miss Moore's class and have tutoring to get her caught up to the other children.

At that, Uncle Hugh had to lay a heavy restraining arm on Aunt Augusta, and Mr. Sullivan reminded her that she would be given a turn to speak, a proper turn as befitted business meetings. Now, it was Mrs. Longacre's turn to report. Apparently Mr. Sullivan had a different set of rules for himself as chairman of the meeting and for Mrs. Wright as examiner than he did for Aunt Augusta because both Mr. Sullivan and Mrs. Wright interrupted Mrs. Longacre frequently. As she evenly presented her report, a report that contained no test results but plenty of observations and information, the other two objected over and over, refusing to look beyond the black and white results, as they called them, in front of them. They even began to accuse Mrs. Longacre of fabrication and exaggeration, accusations which soon interrupted Misty's reading, for Mrs. Longacre opened the door and asked her to fetch Henry.

Misty was alarmed at the look on Mrs. Longacre's face, so alarmed that she ran down the corridor and slid down the banister in her haste to get Henry. She arrived at his little room quite out of breath herself but calling, "Henry, come quick! Mrs. Longacre looks terrible and sent me for you."

The old man turned from his cupboard and said softly, "Ah, little Miss. So it doesn't go well. Come then, we'll go up together. No need to run. I've to meet with the Boss as we walk." Misty walked slowly and silently by the old man's side, understanding and respecting his need. Just before they reached the office, he looked down at her and said, with his deepest smile, "It's good to see you, Misty. You look fine this morning." She smiled back and squeezed his hand.

As Henry closed Mr. Sullivan's office door behind him and took one of the empty chairs, Misty returned to her book, eager once again to enter Mary MacDhui's world, having found a friend in blind Thomas. Inside, Henry began his own report of Misty, slowly, calmly, evenly. Even the staid Mrs. Wright was surprised to hear that Henry actually added things he had learned of Misty, thus suggesting that Mrs. Longacre wasn't exaggerating. Or, perhaps they were both lying. After all, how could an old janitor know that the child could play the piano, could sing, had perfect pitch and could even tune a piano? The child was only 10. Besides, how often was a single child gifted in both music and art? No, there must be some mistake, so she objected again, insisting that the test results must stand. After all, the tests showed that the child doesn't even know her colours!

The only thing on the desk besides the tests was Misty's picture. Henry reached out and took it in his hand, saying, "Why don't you people see what is in this picture? Why can you look only at your numbers? Anyone who can do this kind of work with nothing but a box of school crayons knows more than her colours. You show me that test."

Both Mr. Sullivan and Mrs. Wright objected, thinking it ludicrous to show a test to a janitor, but Henry persisted. "Well, just ask me the questions on it, then. There must be an explanation for this."

Finally Mrs. Wright produced the test. On it were examples of the primary colours and below each example was a multiple-choice selection. The child was to put an X in the circle beside the right answer. There were no X's on Misty's paper. But neatly printed beside each colour was her own identification. Instead of putting an X in the circle next to blue, Misty had written "cobalt" beneath the blue dot, and so on.

"You see," Henry said, "the child has grown up with far more than the primary colours. She couldn't find the answers she thought fit best, so she printed them in. This shows that she knows more than the primary colours not less. Can't you see that?"

"Well that may or may not be so," conceded Mr. Sullivan, "but if it is so, it shows disobedience, a failure to follow instructions. Besides, on other tests there are blanks everywhere and nothing printed in."

Henry replaced the picture and shook his head as he sat back in his chair, saying, "Think of the child, not the tests. She doesn't belong in the Second Grade at all. Did you test geography? The child can read maps and tell you things about the world that aren't even in your schoolbooks. Did you ask her any questions or just have her fill in the dots?"

Mr. Sullivan's voice had begun to rise a little as Mrs. Longacre and Henry persisted and it raised even more as he said, "You people don't seem to understand. We have a system here, a method, and we must go by the book. There are rules, you know, rules for those of us who run the school just as there are rules for the students. We administer, but we must go by the rules. Now the rules state that when a child is admitted without records, we are to administer the tests and place the child where the test scores indicate, which in this case would not even have the child in school. The law states, however, that every child over the age of six years has a right to public education, so we have to take her. You see, we are already bending the rules in placing the child in even the Second Grade. According to these scores, she should be sent to a remedial class or even school. Can't you appreciate that we have already made all the exceptions for Thomasina that we think we are able to make?"

Had anyone looked through the glass door into the outer office, they'd have seen that Misty no longer read quietly at the little table. Instead, she looked toward the office, unable to ignore the rising voices. She had a look on her face quite unlike any that had appeared there before. But as the argument grew more heated, those inside saw nothing beyond the people in the room.

All were surprised to see Mrs. Longacre stand up abruptly and state loudly, shakily, her voice rising with every word, "I cannot believe what I hear and see here. Always I have told myself that, underneath, you do care more for children than you do for your methods and your rules, for your school and your position. Now I find myself embarrassed and ashamed to be associated with any institution that is so blind and heartless. You'll destroy this child for the sake of your silly rules and methods. I cannot stand by and watch. Further, my conscience will not allow me to continue in such a place. I will have to tender my ..."

She didn't hear the door open but she was stopped by a small, gentle hand on her arm. She looked down to see Misty beside her, an awesome calm about her. No one moved or spoke. The child looked up at Mrs. Longacre and allowed the impishness to flicker briefly in her wide, clear eyes as she squeezed the woman's arm and said, "Uh-uh, Mrs. Longacre. Be ye angry, but don't 'bust out.'"

Mrs. Longacre and Henry both smiled, but the room remained silent as Mrs. Longacre returned to her chair and Misty stepped toward Mr. Sullivan's desk and began: "I am sorry to have caused so very much trouble ever since I came here. Please don't be angry at each other any more. I am especially sorry I couldn't do the tests and I have somehow been unable to clear up any misunderstanding. It's time, now, for me to put it right. Please listen."

The group was shocked into silence and co-operation. Uncle Hugh could safely take his hand from Aunt Augusta, for she was rendered mute by this child's strength and resolve—or something. She couldn't have explained it if she had understood. Mr. Sullivan and Mrs. Wright had never had their authority so thoroughly challenged by a child and yet they felt not at all challenged, so completely taken were they with something in the little girl. Only Henry and Mrs. Longacre seemed comfortable rather than simply stunned.

Misty stepped over to the principal's bookshelf, removed a Bible, somewhat dusty, and returned to her place in front of his desk. She began where the Book happened to open and read clearly, unstumblingly and more meaningfully than some of those in the room had heard for years. She read on, stopping not when she might have proven that she could read, but only at a place in the text that seemed complete enough to her to interrupt without confusion or pain, for all books were alive to Misty and this one most alive of all. Henry brushed a tear from his cheek. The others remained silent for several moments while Misty replaced the book.

Finally Mr. Sullivan forced himself out of his shock and said, "But that is King James English and that is only the Bible."

Mrs. Wright added, "And reading doesn't indicate understanding."

Mrs. Longacre and Henry both shook their heads, but Misty quietly returned to the shelf and took down another book, a Grade Six history book, though she didn't know that. Opening it, she read as clearly and with as much interest as she had the other. When she stopped, she asked simply, "Which text would you like me to explain, or shall I do both?" Not pausing for an answer, she carried on, "This seems to be part of the description of what they called the prehistoric ages of man. This short piece is about the Stone Age, for it explains the development of tools made from pieces of rock."

Forgetting her task for a moment, Misty interrupted herself, some eagerness creeping into her voice as she said; "Gramps and I found some stone tools once when we were digging a new well. He showed me how he thought they might have made them, and Gran explained how they had had to fashion some cutting tools out of rock themselves once before their things came to the island. That's how I learned about the Stone Age, for after we went home, we ordered books from the library in Victoria and we read all about it. But that's beside the point.

"Let me see, in the Bible I read from the Gospel as recorded by John, part of the story of Nicodemus. You see Nicodemus was a Pharisee but he wanted to know about Jesus, so he sought Him at night to question Him. Jesus explained the importance of belief, showing Nicodemus God's love for man. Jesus commented on how hard it is for people to believe spiritual things when they do not even believe the things before their very eyes."

At that point, Mr. Sullivan decided he'd best interrupt again, for he suddenly felt uncomfortable and didn't like the thought of taking a Bible lesson from a child. Henry could barely contain a chuckle. Mrs. Longacre did not miss the twinkle in his eyes, but she, too, controlled her laughter. Both knew the principal was probably not aware of the personal timeliness of his interruption, for his face was almost impassive as he said, "Yes, yes, I see you can read and do understand. But is it the reading you understand or have you just remembered what you were told? Your reading comprehension tests were full of blanks, even those testing the very first Reader's level."

"Oh, that. Yes, I am sorry about that. I was getting tired when I did those and I got so confused I couldn't really see the questions clearly. Who is Jane, anyway? All I could think of was Jane Eyre and I couldn't figure out what she could possibly have to do with Dick Whittington, who was the only Dick I could think of at the time, so none of the questions made sense to me. And what would Jane Eyre be doing with a ball? I must have had the wrong Jane. I am sorry."

At this, Henry couldn't contain a chuckle. In fact, he could barely resist laughing loud and full. To his disgust, however, Mr. Sullivan pushed on.

"But your arithmetic was even worse, and reading to us from books shows us nothing of arithmetic."

"Yes, I know. I am sorry. Let me see; what trouble did I have there? I couldn't make much sense of what they wanted me to do. I can do arithmetic, if what you mean is figuring, but I don't know quite how to show you this. How about this? A bolt of fabric contains 25 yards of material, that's 75 feet or 900 inches. If the fabric is 45 inches wide and it takes one and a half yards to make a dress, you can make 16.6 dresses from a bolt, but since you don't want .6 of a dress, you'd make 16 dresses and something else, perhaps some aprons. Or you could make some of several different things. But I'm getting off track again.

A barrel contains three bushels and there are four pecks in a bushel, eight quarts in a peck, two pints in a quart and two cups in a pint. That makes about 384 cups in a barrel. It takes about twelve cups of flour to make four loaves of bread, so if you use four loaves of bread every six days, a barrel of flour contains enough flour to last just over six months, if you only bake bread. It takes only two cups of flour to make pastry or a cake and you don't make or eat those every day, so three barrels of flour would be plenty for a year."

Misty paused only slightly to do her calculations, surprising them all again. Though she spoke very calmly and was doing only arithmetic computations, she did these with almost as much life and enthusiasm as she had read. She couldn't help but enjoy doing the familiar things, and her pleasure shone through. Unlike Henry and Mrs. Longacre, who couldn't help but take great delight in the shock and even discomfort of the others, Misty carried on, oblivious to the impression she was making or the challenges her knowledge and ability posed for the principal and school board examiner. "Now," she said, "there are 144 cubic inches (1' x1' x1") in a board foot of lumber, and ..."

This time it was Mrs. Wright who interrupted; "Okay, child; enough. We see you know your quantities and measurements, and your tests do show that you can do word problems, which is strange, given you failed absolutely every other section of the arithmetic tests. Other children do fine on the rest of the tests and fail the word problems."

"Oh," interrupted Misty. "What you call word problems were the only part of the test that made sense to me, except for that one question, of course. Perhaps I was just too tired. Those tests came last in the day. I couldn't imagine that you wanted me to bother filling in all those little circles showing that two plus five is seven and eight times three is twenty-four. I thought you knew that I knew that. I'm sorry that you didn't. And I should have filled it in. It was the same trouble with the one word problem. Mrs. Wright, why would someone try to fill a bathtub with the plug out? Of course I could have calculated the rate the water was running out of the tub and the rate the water was running into the tub and subtracted the difference and divided it by the time, but I just thought anybody would plug the drain."

Again, Henry couldn't restrain himself, and this time Mrs. Longacre joined his laughter. Hugh and Augusta remained silent and almost expressionless, but the other two persisted. Mr. Sullivan sounded firm and a little frustrated as he said, "That was disobedient and unco-operative of you, child. It borders on arrogance. You seem to begin to display an attitude problem and you haven't shown us you know your sums or tables."

"Forgive me," said Misty. "Would you give me two four digit numbers please?"

Taken aback, Mr. Sullivan didn't respond immediately, so Henry said, "1587 4298"

"Thank you," said Misty. "Added, the two make five thousand, eight hundred, eighty-five. Subtracting the smaller from the larger, we get two thousand seven hundred eleven, and taking the larger from the smaller we get minus two seven one one. Multiplied they make ..." Here Misty's pause for calculation was slightly longer than the others had been, but surprisingly short. "Six million, eight hundred twenty thousand, nine hundred twenty six. Divided, the larger by the smaller, they make ..."

"Stop!" interrupted Mr. Sullivan. "You're just making fun of us now."

But Uncle Hugh had been calculating rapidly as she went. He spoke up as he scribbled on a small pad he had taken from his jacket pocket. "The addition and subtraction are correct," he said, even as he completed the other calculation, "and so is the multiplication." He couldn't resist emphasizing what he said with a little flourish of underlining on his paper, punctuated by a final dot.

Silence filled the room.

Finally Misty said brightly, "Isn't it fun? You see, one night Gramps and I were at the Captain's helping him mend fishnets. It isn't difficult work but it gets quite tedious, you know, and the Captain was telling us ways he had of amusing himself as he tied the little knots. Sometimes he attempted to calculate how many knots it took to make a standard gill net measuring ..."

Mr. Sullivan interrupted again, "Never mind the numeric details, child, just finish your explanation."

"Without the numbers? Well, it doesn't make much sense without the numbers but I'll try. He'd count the knots in an inch and multiply the inches in a square foot and just sit doing calculations in his head. Then he showed us how to multiply two digit numbers in our heads, then three, then four. We had great fun doing the mending then, calling out numbers and seeing who could get the right answer first. It took me quite a while to learn it, partly because I'd be having so much fun I'd forget to listen carefully to the numbers given. Then I'd be multiplying wrong things in the first place. Gran and I used to play sometimes, too, when we were quilting, for you must make eight stitches to the inch, you know, and if a standard quilt measures…"

"Enough! You'll make us all crazy with your number chatter. Now why didn't you do the arithmetic test if you can do multiplication? Must we test you again?"

"I am sorry, but I'm not sure about testing me again. You see, I do have trouble understanding the tests. I'm never sure what they actually want me to do, and it is very hard for me to do calculations without a reason. If you want me to pretend I'm playing the game with the Captain or Gran, I could, I suppose. But that reminds me. It occurred to me last night that the things you called geometry on the test are just quilting and building problems. I do know how to do angles, diameters, radius, area and all; I just didn't recognize it on the test. Sorry. You see, when you piece a quilt, the perimeter of the circular template needs to equal …"

"Alright! We don't need a lesson in quilting!" Mr. Sullivan almost exploded. "I think we may have heard enough from you, though we know nothing about writing or spelling—and those are the basics."

Here Mrs. Longacre stated simply, "There are no problems in either of those areas, Sir. I've seen writing and had Misty do work for me that is letter perfect."

"The name, Mrs. Longacre, the name! Let's have some sense of order here. And I'm afraid order it must be. It's all very well that you read so nicely and quilt and cook, young lady, but we are stuck with the bare facts, just the bare facts. Your tests scores are the lowest I've ever seen. You have left us no choice—none at all."

Uncle Hugh's hand returned firmly to the sputtering Aunt Augusta's arm. But Henry was the one to rise. He did so suddenly, though slowly, deliberately and forebodingly. He really was a tall, big man and he seemed to tower over everyone in the room as he spoke, "I'm an old man, ready to retire, doing my last year here and I've nothing to lose. But even if I had everything in the world to lose, I'd have to speak now."

Even patient old Henry's voice rose as he spoke, deepening and rolling almost like thunder as he continued; "You people have forgotten what school is. You have forgotten who children are. I daresay, you've forgotten your Maker. School is not here to provide you with careers or to serve itself. It is here for the children. It ought to be a place where they can learn and grow, where the kind of excitement this young lady has for numbers and thoughts is a common thing, not something so unusual you don't know what to do when you see it. If you must 'place' children, as you put it, then you can do that only by seeing what the child can do and where she would benefit the most, be best able to learn more and to gain more delight in what she learns. Instead of that, you have these old tests that show, not what a child knows, but if a child can give the answers you want in the way you want them. What you have just done and said is as great a disgrace as I have seen in all my years."

Pausing just slightly, Henry reached over and gathered all the tests off the desk in his great hand before continuing, "I'll just be taking these with me to the furnace room where they belong, and it isn't the child's work I'm having to burn, it's yours. Now I'm going to walk from this room because this meeting is over, do you hear? If the child has the courage to stay in this poor excuse for civilization, then you will place her in the Sixth Grade where she belongs and further you will show her the respect she deserves. You will have her assist those children who have trouble with your old word problems, for unlike your pokey teachers, she can give them the fun of the task; she can do more for those struggling kids than any of you, and she'll gain by doing it. You owe her that much after this unforgivable, puny, self-serving torture you've put her through. And if ever again I see or hear any wrong treatment or wrong comment, any wrong assessment or small-minded ..."

A small hand placed firmly in the old man's own stopped him. Misty looked up into the now red face, that little twinkle dancing in her own eye, and said, "Uh-uh, Henry. Be ye angry, but don't 'bust out.'" As the two walked from the office, Henry added his chuckle to the laughter of Mrs. Longacre, for Misty's part in the meeting had ended as it had begun.

Mrs. Longacre also gathered her things and left the room saying, "I'll add Misty's name to Mr. Broadmore's class list and arrange times for her to work with the younger children on their word problems. I'll also send the placement report to the school board."

Behind her she could hear Augusta begin to sputter on in a whole new way, suddenly as proud of the child as she had been critical. The secretary almost felt sorry for the dressing down Mr. Sullivan and Mrs. Wright were getting but she didn't step in to relieve Mr. Sullivan as she usually did. But the Hughes didn't stay long. They left the office, Augusta fluttering on about being late for her meeting and having so much to tell the ladies about the prodigy they had rescued from oblivion, and Hugh walking quietly just behind her, obviously happy to get back to the bank where things ran smoothly and always according to numbers.

Left behind, Mr. Sullivan and Mrs. Wright just looked at each other, neither knowing quite what to do or even what had just happened. Neither could afford to think that a child, a janitor and a secretary had somehow completely usurped their authority. It was unthinkable. A little awkwardly, they congratulated each other that the matter had been settled at last. Mr. Sullivan thanked Mrs. Wright for her work. Mrs. Wright assured Mr. Sullivan that the properly signed form that Mrs. Longacre was preparing would fulfil the requirements of the school board office. The placement would stand as the meeting had determined. Thus they deemed the meeting a success as Mrs. Wright left the office.

As the old man and young girl walked together to the furnace room where Henry did with the exams precisely what he had said he would, they chuckled and chuckled, first one, then the other, then together, chuckled and chuckled and chuckled. Finally Misty stopped and said, "Oh, Henry. I just 'bust out' didn't I? And I broke every rule. I went to the office without being asked. I spoke without being spoken to. I said more than, 'Yes, Sir' to Mr. Sullivan. I did every wrong thing, so I shouldn't be laughing. When I heard all that nastiness in the voices, all the sadness about me, I suddenly knew the time had come for me to put it right. It was like something taking over me, though I wasn't sure what to do, for I hadn't been asked to the meeting. But when I heard them in there calling Mrs. Longacre a liar and you a liar and I heard Mrs. Longacre about to 'bust out,' I guess I 'bust out' instead. We're all catching Tommy's disease! Even you, Henry."

"Yes, little Miss, thank you for stopping me. And forgive me. I shouldn't have gone so far. It's not God's way, is it? I was mad, though, wasn't I? You saved me more wrong, and I am grateful. Must remember to tell Tommy not to get discouraged. Why when an old fool like me still 'busts out' sometimes, Tommy can maybe take heart with the progress he is making. I'll set him to try to get the times down to just once in a wee while. Meanwhile, little Miss, we'd best have a brief prayer so this thing is over.

"Dearest Lord, forgive us our 'bustin' out' and wash us clean of sin. Turn us around, too, so we can start over fresh. Wipe from our minds and hearts any ill feeling or unforgiveness we have coming out of this meeting and give us the attitudes You would have in us. Thank You for fixing the problem and giving Misty a proper place here at last and give her all the strength and love she needs as she begins in her new class tomorrow. Thank You for Your great love and sacrifice and for the safety and hope You give. Bless us and keep us safe, we pray in the name of Jesus. Amen."

"Thank you, Henry," Misty said, wiping tears from her cheeks and slipping into one of the chairs in his room with a big sigh.

"Now, you're not going to slump are you? Why we've won this battle, little Miss!"

"I know, Henry, but I feel tired and not quite right. Did I do wrong? Would Gramps be proud? Would the Captain understand?"

"Think about it, little girl. You did almost what your grandfather did. You didn't sail in there to hurt anyone or do harm. You just stepped in to put things right. That's exactly all he ever did. And that is not wrong."

"But Henry, I might have hurt them or something. They didn't seem very happy at all."

"Sometimes the truth, and the truth of yourself is all you presented, makes people a little uncomfortable because it shows up the false. Those people had forgotten that learning happens even if there aren't any schools. They did have an exaggerated sense of their importance. I was the one who wasn't very kind about that, Misty, not you. You were pure and true, just showed them what you can do. But I laughed at them instead of with them once; I enjoyed their discomfort for a few minutes. I was wrong, Misty, and I'm grateful the Lord has forgiven me. I'll go ask their forgiveness as well, but not until I can do so without any further harm to them. But you? You have no such forgiveness to ask. I think you just feel sad that they are sad, and that is just a part of who you are, Misty. You don't like sadness any more than Miss Lily likes suffering. But this is sadness that couldn't be avoided, that they brought on themselves and that could lead to better attitudes. It's the kind of sadness that people sometimes have to endure to become better people. It's wrong to try to protect people from that kind of thing. You must be tired, though. It has been quite the two days for you."

"Will my new class be better, Henry? Can I look forward to it?"

"Well, it will be better for you to be there than in the Second Grade, more interesting for you, but it is still school, Misty, and still in town. It isn't back home. But yes, you can look forward to it. They have all kinds of books in Grade Six, and you love books, don't you? You'll also get some work to do at home, and I expect you'll like that too. And look, before you go back to the office, I have a little treat for you from my 'Stina. Here's a bit of cheese, a biscuit and some grapes. You take this little bag she sent and enjoy it, won't you? She'll have something to say to me tonight when I tell her I 'bust out' at the principal. She'll be grateful you stopped me. Thanks again."

Henry ruffled Misty's pigtail before sending her on her way. Though everyone was pleased with the outcome of the meeting, only Aunt Augusta walked away without regrets. The others each had some reason to wish it had never happened and that somehow it could be forgotten. But Aunt Augusta and her incessant prattle weren't the only reason it never was. It remains the only time a janitor settled an academic placement.

19.

Henry Packs a Bag

The results of the meeting brought some changes in Misty's life at school, though not all of them were good. She settled easily and quickly into her new class but soon discovered that she had to fight against boredom and its resultant persistent daydreaming, which frequently landed her in trouble. She lost track of how many times she had to write out, "I will not day-dream in class" or "I will pay attention in class." She was sure that at least as often as Tommy had been sent to the office in his early years at school, she wrote those lines 100, 200, even 500 times at night. She struggled while writing the lines to keep herself from making them more interesting, for she learned by not controlling herself once that she must simply write the words out. Getting the strap hurt more than she had thought it would, but physical pain recedes very quickly compared to the emotional pain that she suffered much more regularly than she did anything physical. Still, getting the strap carried emotional pain for Misty too, so she tried hard to avoid making them think she was insolent.

She soon realized that it wasn't the rules in school or the little rows of desks or the small stiff desks themselves that made her life difficult or made her feel hopelessly stifled and sometimes confused; it was that teachers demanded and insisted that everyone think alike. Everyone must not only arrive at the same conclusion but also get there by the same path. Misty's grades were never good, for she frequently forgot to stay on the singular intellectual path the school board had sanctioned. At times, she couldn't even see that path. Other times she was simply confused. Always, she felt outside, different, odd, and usually she felt sad, not so much that she seemed so different, but sad that all the people around her plodded dully, even unhappily along such a lifeless and, she thought, pointless path.

It hurt her tremendously that there was no excitement and no spontaneity in any of the learning that she did see. It confused her that things were separated into packages, things that she thought belonged together. In her confusion over why the geography of a country would be studied separately from the history of that country, she failed to give as correct, memorized responses, the details that for her had been rendered meaningless by their isolation. She continued unable to do arithmetic or spelling as ends in themselves, failing geometry despite being able to understand and calculate all kinds of angles for carpentry. And it completely perplexed her to be given as the only reason for learning a thing or "getting it right" grades. She was unable to learn something simply in order to get an A or a B or even a C on a test, for neither tests nor the letters assigned to them meant anything to her. To have information robbed of all its inherent delight, robbed of simply being a piece of the puzzle that allows us to understand our world and our God better than we did before, dismayed the formerly lively child.

In her pain, confusion, dismay, perplexity, she withdrew, eyes glassy, to a more lively world, a world of excitement, sense and peace, a world where curiosity itself led her to learning one thing after another, a world where liveliness and calmness together made ease and rest. Inside the classroom, the glassy eyes brought her some kind of scolding or punishment again and again. Out on the playground, those glassy eyes brought teasing and taunting, chanting and mocking, more of all the things that drove her to the safe place hidden by those glassy eyes in the first place. But Misty's survival depended on the odd cycle of moving through her two worlds.

Driven in part by their own jealousy that a new kid in Grade Two was suddenly put into Grade Six ahead of where a child her age should be, the children teased Misty mercilessly, at least as mercilessly as Bobby or Tommy would allow. One or the other of them always stepped in when they thought Misty looked tired or worn down or hurt by the children. Misty learned to hope it would be Bobby who stepped in, for he managed to have the others leave her alone without doing anything wrong himself. Occasionally, Tommy still 'jist bust out' and was sent once again to the office, not for defending her, but for losing his temper or whatever wrong thing 'bustin' out' had resulted in. On those days, Misty hurt to know that she still caused others pain.

Misty continued alone much of the time. Forbidden from playing with "the bay riff-raff" and told to befriend the girls from the hill, she ended up left alone. From time to time, she attempted to get to know and understand and enjoy the girls who had been deemed appropriate for her, but even when they didn't shun her, she soon gave up. She simply couldn't either do or understand what they did. They talked a great deal, but always about people, seldom saying anything kind and often giggling. Even the games of the younger ones were nothing but senseless gossip, or so it seemed to Misty. She preferred to walk around the playground alone, often eating a nice piece of fruit or cheese that she found in a little bag next to her lunch box most days.

Misty was grateful for the little bags of food that Henry's 'Stina sent for her. They continued to be the only food she enjoyed at all, for at home the battles over the meals continued. In fact, things at home were not at all improved by the outcome of the meeting. To Misty's relief, Aunt Augusta's initial flurry of bragging about the prodigy soon abated and her old impatience with what she saw as the child's disobedience and stubbornness returned. Misty found impatience and criticism much easier to bear than the boasting. When it was convenient, the woman boasted about what wonderful things they were doing for the clever young girl and when it was more to their advantage, she complained bitterly about the trials the child presented, thus emphasizing the sacrifice they were making. In fact, they made little sacrifice at all, for they continued either ignoring Misty or scolding her. There remained only the two main battles: meals and ringlets, both of them fought and lost silently on Misty's part, loudly on Aunt Augusta's part.

But Misty's silence at home and increasing quiet at school were taking their toll. Her compliance with Aunt Augusta's insistence that she not cry robbed her of natural healing of her wounds. The loneliness that tainted her memories with homesickness diminished the healing she had once received from her daydreaming. She continued drawing strength from her chats with God, for those turned her thoughts to others and away from her own sorrow.

Strength also came from three bright spots in her very dull world. Occasionally, instead of leaving the food Christina provided, Henry would find Misty and give it to her himself. Always, even the shortest talk with Henry delighted and cheered her. The feel of his huge but gentle hand on her shoulder or ruffling her hair seemed to lift pounds and pounds of weight from her small shoulders. He often brought messages or encouragement from Tommy, Bobby and even Daisy, or told her funny little stories of Tommy's latest 'bustin' out' that soon brought the sweet relief of laughter. Seeing Henry always forced her to fight hard with the tears, however, for his gentleness and concern showed love, and love releases pain. Had they been alone in his little room, she'd have given way to the tears without thinking, for there Aunt Augusta's rules were shattered by the prevailing great Truth. On the playground, however, Misty fought to do what was there considered right. Still, the refreshment Misty drew from Henry far outweighed any energy drained in the battle against the tears.

True to Henry's command, Misty had also been given several young students to introduce to the wonders of word problems. At times she thought the only thing worth living for in town was the hour she spent three times a week with half a dozen children. All the children she had were "difficult children," the only children Misty found lively or interesting at all. The children loved her easy way and happy games and soon found word problems as much fun as she did. When they first began to catch on, they didn't even realize they were doing arithmetic. Only after they had mastered everything she knew they needed, did Misty tell them what they were doing. Then easily she led them across the tiny bridge between playing the games she had played with them and solving the word problems on the tests the children must take in class.

All the teachers were astonished that their most difficult students could so quickly learn what they had been unable to teach for months and even years. One ventured to ask Misty how she did it but was no better able to do the job herself for having asked because Misty's answer made no sense to her at all. Misty's only comment was "I know they can do it, and it is fun." Some people can see neither simplicity nor truth. Misty knew and valued both and passed the benefits of them on to her young students. However, this pleasure was also mixed with pain in Misty, for seeing the struggle of the children and the destructiveness of the fear they had developed for something which, at worst was harmless and at best fun, hurt her terribly.

But the mix of pleasure and pain was perhaps greatest in the third bright spot in her very dull world: a letter from home. The Captain and Miss Lily had spent an evening together answering Misty's letter, and one day Mrs. Longacre found Misty on the playground at recess and gave her the reply they had sent in care of the school, since that was the return address that Mrs. Longacre had added to Misty's letter before mailing it for her. Misty could barely contain her excitement and simply clutched the letter for the rest of the day. Only when she was alone in her room did she open it and read it over and over again.

She read of the Captain and Miss Lily, of putting up the storm windows and tucking in for winter. As she had thought, they had taken care of the windows of all three houses. They had also added to all the woodpiles. They realized it seemed silly to top up a woodpile of an empty house, but it just didn't seem right to them not to do it. Besides, they would light the stoves from time to time through the winter so the house wouldn't get damp. The two old people very cleverly included all kinds of descriptions of Misty's favourite places and animals and included a few funny jokes they had shared. Misty read the letter until she had memorized it and even then she slept with it under her pillow and kept it tucked in a pocket or inside her sweater sleeve everywhere she went.

But even as her letter had said more to them by what it didn't say than by what it did, one line in theirs somehow spoke volumes and caused the great lump to rise up in Misty's throat. It said simply, 'Rusty misses you very much.' Misty would never have been able to swallow that lump had she known that what they didn't write was that every single day since he had watched Old Lundstrom's boat pull away from the dock with Misty in it, the faithful little brown dog had trotted the whole length of the island to gaze longingly and questioningly across the water from the end of the pier before slowly returning to the Captain's, stopping at Miss Lily's to check for Misty and get a drink along the way. She was, however, happy both to have the letter and to have sent them another and thus be able to hope for a reply from them. Hope is bright and life-sustaining.

The bright spots were enough for Misty, augmented as they were by her daydreams, her memories and her sleep. No matter how much tension there was in the air at night, Misty prayed until she could hear the gentle but strong sound of the old rocker lulling her to the sleep that she seemed to need more and more as the days and weeks wore on.

But her friends were worried. As bare branches replaced the leafy arms of the trees outside, Henry and Mrs. Longacre noticed Misty growing thinner and paler. Tommy sometimes asked Henry if he thought Misty was 'gonna be a'right cuz she looked so sad 'n' skinny somehow,' and though Henry reassured Tommy as best he could, he kept a close watch himself.

Though the child did grow pale, she also found strength, time after time, no matter how bad things seemed. Misty continued her game, lifting herself up and enabling herself to keep going with her thanks. Though Aunt Augusta was immovable and insisted on the ringlets, Misty was not only grateful that she gave up on the setting gel when she found it making stains on Misty's blouses and sweaters but also happy that the rain turned the ringlets back into free curls by the time she reached the school each day. Henry and Mrs. Longacre, however, did not know how long Misty's ability to see victory in defeat could keep her going and they grew more and more concerned. Mrs. Longacre had the nurse check her, but there was nothing physically wrong. She was much stronger than her tiny body looked.

But Henry could take no more the day he saw her walking to school in the rain with her head bent down. It was a blustery day, the kind of day he knew Misty liked. The rain swirled about with the wind, and Misty liked to tip her face rainward whenever she was outside on such a day. But this blustery day that Misty would once have called beautiful, she walked hunched over with her head down, looking even smaller and thinner than ever.

As soon as Henry was free, he took himself to the office to speak to Mrs. Longacre. Not even waiting for a chance to see her alone, he spoke, his shoulders drooping but his voice clear; "It is time, Jean. She's wasting away. Send her to me somehow." Mrs. Longacre knew exactly who he was speaking of and what he must do, though she didn't know how he would manage it. Still, she would do her part.

Misty was surprised to hear her name called over the loud speaker just after recess. She hadn't done anything wrong so she wasn't sure why she would have to go to the office, but, receiving a nod from Mr. Broadmore, she rose and walked down the corridor as summoned. She frowned to realize that more than anything else, more than nervous or curious or even confused about going to the office, she was just tired, too tired to be anything else. Only a sudden thought that Mrs. Longacre might have had a letter for her from home brightened her, so she had a slight smile on her lips as she went through the office door.

"Ah, there you are, Misty. I'm glad to see you smiling and not looking frightened. I didn't want to cause alarm but had to go by the rules, you know, and call you over the PA system. But don't worry; there's no trouble this time. It's just that Henry needs a helper for a while, and we don't have any naughty children to send him today, so I called you."

Together they laughed lightly both at Mrs. Longacre's little mimicking of "going by the rules" and at her exaggerated shock at having no naughty children. Misty thought for the two hundredth time how grateful she was that Henry had persuaded Mrs. Longacre not to resign from her position over the school's early treatment of Misty. Instead, Mrs. Longacre had apologized to Mr. Sullivan for her outburst and frustration, and he had been more than relieved to ignore the verbal threat that Misty had interrupted. Though Mr. Sullivan was relieved because Mrs. Longacre was experienced, very efficient and actually did much of his work for him, the others were relieved because she was a friend of the children. Misty was grateful simply because she was Mrs. Longacre. Now she said, "Thanks, Mrs. Longacre. You know I always like to help Henry, even though Henry never needs help, really."

"Now don't you let anyone know that, or I won't have much help with Tommy and the others who need Henry so much. I don't know what we'll do when he has retired. Actually, Henry came up and asked especially for you, Misty, and that is a first. Before you go, tell me, are you feeling well and getting enough sleep?"

"Sure, I'm fine, Mrs. Longacre. I get lots of sleep and I never feel sick or anything, just tired sometimes. But I'm okay. I should be getting a letter any day now, don't you think? This one is getting almost worn out, so I hope another comes soon."

Mrs. Longacre had her own battle with a lump in her throat as on the one hand she saw the light come into the child's tired face, triumphing once again through difficulty, and on the other hand she saw the worn and tattered letter that Misty pulled from her skirt pocket, evidence of the extent of the child's loneliness and suffering. No wonder she looked so gaunt. She hoped her voice was even and cheerful as she said, "Off you go, then. You can pick up a permission slip for going back to class after you've finished. I have no idea how long Henry plans to keep you out of class so I can't just make one for you now. See you later."

Through the partly opened door of Henry's little room, Misty could see him sitting in his big chair, his elbows on the table in front of him, forehead supported by his folded hands. Thinking he looked tired, she frowned slightly and knocked softly on the doorframe as she said gently, "Are you alright, Henry?"

The concern Henry heard in his little friend's voice smote him deeply but washed any tiny bit of doubt from his mind that he must do all he could for her. He turned, the kindest of smiles smoothing over his face and glowing from his eyes welcoming her as no words could have. Wanting to assure her, he added, "I'm fine now, Misty, just fine."

Relief rose up in Misty, erasing her frown and setting loose the tears that she had contained for so long. Henry gathered her in one great arm and quietly closed the door with the other, giving her the safety she needed. Sensing her pain and knowing the healing of tears, he let her cry for a long time, her face buried in his chest. He was glad Christina had made him change to his thick but soft winter shirt that morning, for the exhausted child had tears aplenty. From time to time a few of his own dropped softly onto the golden brown head as he quietly rocked her back and forth. When he sensed she'd washed herself about clean, he began gently to lift her thoughts, to turn her eyes, saying,

"I'd better find a cork for leaky eyes. There's enough rain about these days to keep your hair curly without an old fool dripping all over your head even when you're inside. This keeps up I'll have to get my 'Stina to pack a towel in my lunch bag so I can dry your hair before you go. But I'm sure glad you could come, Misty. I've made tea and I really couldn't think of having it alone today. Too many kids getting better and better all the time and losing that 'bustin' out disease' of Tommy's makes an old man lonely and his work seem harder. Besides, my 'Stina sent cookies in today and I can't eat them all myself. She's sure grateful that you told us about Tommy's family not having cookies. My 'Stina just loves to bake and she's so happy to have kids to give her cookies to. You've made her a happy woman, Misty."

As he talked, he felt more than saw Misty begin to respond, even felt a smile beginning to tug at the corner of her mouth, still pressed against his chest. Finally he heard the familiar tinkling chuckle as she lifted her head and looked into his face.

"Oh, Henry," she laughed, "you are the biggest kid of all. It's not my hair you're needing a towel for, it's your shirt. Look at the mess I've made. You'll catch a chill. Why, if you were lying down, there'd be a puddle there! Wouldn't Aunt Augusta carry on if she saw your wet shirt? I'm quite sure that shirts, like pillowcases, were not meant to be soaked. If your Christina fusses as much about laundry as Aunt Augusta does, I'd say we'll both be sent to our rooms today."

Even as they laughed together, Misty took the huge handkerchief Henry offered her and, after wiping her face, tried blotting up his shirt.

"Never mind that," he laughed; "my 'Stina doesn't fuss, and I'm not about to catch cold either. Besides, little Miss, take more than a hanky to mop up your puddles."

Again they laughed as Henry rumpled her pigtail and turned to get tea, blotting his shirt with some paper towels as he did so. "That make you feel better?" he grinned. "Can't have you worried about me." Again they laughed and Misty began to feel the refreshment of laughter adding to the washing of her tears.

"Thanks, Henry. How did you know I needed that? I didn't even know how full up I was or how long it was since I laughed. Funny thing about town. There's all kinds of noise, all kinds of activity, all kinds of chatter and hurry, but hardly any laughter. Even on the school grounds there's more yelling and hollering than there is laughter. Why is that, Henry?"

"I'm not sure, Miss. I think people don't spend enough time alone to get quiet inside, and we need quiet for laughter, at least for genuine laughter. I think some of the hollering you hear on the playground is a kind of laughter, at least for Tommy and his friends. Just like there are different kinds of laughter, there are different kinds of hollering. Tommy's hollering when he's playing football is laughter; his hollering when he's 'fightin' with the rich kids' isn't. You can hear the difference. You listen to the laughter of adults. Some of it is laughter and some of it is just hollering. People who have no quiet holler; people who have quiet laugh. You study it yourself."

"I'll listen, Henry, but already I think you are right just from what I remember hearing here. Boy, have I learned a lot about tones of voice and laughter since I came to town. There's so much I never knew before I came, Henry, and I am grateful to know so much more—at least I try to be, but lately it is getting harder and harder for me to feel grateful. The thought that the things I have learned were all things I was happy enough without keeps getting in my way, taking away some of the gratitude. And somehow there's just so much I miss. I think if I could have even a bit of what I had on the island while I am living here, then I would feel grateful for the new things I've learned because then I'd be adding them to what I already had instead of feeling like these new things are a replacement. Somehow I just don't seem able to fit in here, Henry. I have tried. But I feel like I don't belong anywhere. Even worse, I feel useless here, as if nothing I do makes anyone happy, and the happiness seems to be draining out of me. Do you suppose that in order to be happy, you have to make others happy, Henry?"

"Ah, little Miss, you are wise. But you are also mistaken in two things here. First, I know you feel that you haven't made Aunt Augusta and Uncle Hugh happy, and you may be right about that. But as Tommy once told you, 'they just are unhappy.' It isn't your fault. I admit, I had hoped that they'd feel happy having you around and I confess I'm saddened to see that they aren't, for only the deepest of unhappiness would fail to be alleviated by the joy that still bubbles out of you, even though you have become tired. But that is their struggle and their choice, Misty, not at all your fault. And you have brought a great deal of happiness to others, even to people you haven't met—my 'Stina, Tommy's pa, Mrs. Longacre's children at home. And what about me and Tommy? You do make people happy, Misty; you've just stopped seeing it.

"The second thing is that while making others happy increases your own happiness, you can be happy all on your own. You just don't realize how much people take out of you with all their rules and pettiness, Misty. You fit in this town about as well as Miss Lily did, and it just wears on you. That's not your fault. Besides, your heart is too big for the pain that is all around you, never mind the pain that they inflict on you most every day. I hear that it's still going hard for you at Sunday School. That means that every single part of your life has something chipping away at you. You mustn't blame yourself for getting worn down by it. Besides, I think that inside, beneath the wounds and scars and tiredness, you are still happy. Otherwise the fun wouldn't bubble up so quickly when you've had the little rest that comes from spilling over a bit on an old man's shirt."

After laughing freely again, Misty agreed that he must be right. "But Henry," she added, "if only I could tell what the good of this life is, or even just find a rhythm that I could rest in, I'm sure I would not feel so tired. But I can't find it. And sometimes I get afraid—afraid of what I feel like I'm losing. This morning when I walked to school, I was so tired and so little inside and so chilly, that I couldn't enjoy the wind or the rain. It took my whole walk to school just to get enough warmth and strength from God to straighten up inside. I don't think I managed to look up. Even when I first came and was so hurt to feel all trapped in tight shoes and silly clothes and stung every single time Aunt Augusta said anything, God was so close and quick to lift me up. Now I seem to have to fight just to get above the ugliness here to see the beauty of God that's so clear all around. I get afraid that the ugliness is coming right inside me."

Henry brushed away a tear before saying, "Tell me, little one, what made you so heavy this morning?"

"Oh, Henry," she said with a sob threatening her voice, "I just can't get things right. I couldn't eat all my porridge this morning and I was careless with my ringlets again, so Aunt Augusta just exploded. I know she was tired because she had gone on and on about how late they were last night and I know she is worried because she fusses on about Uncle Hugh's campaign, but when she exploded at me about my hair and spanked me for not eating all the porridge, I had to try so hard not to cry that my energy was all gone by the time I left for school. Somehow this morning I felt that it was my fault. Usually I can see that it is partly just Aunt Augusta's way, but this morning I couldn't see it. When that happens, I feel strangely cold inside. It's the funniest feeling, as if I'm hollow and cold at the same time. How can hollow also be cold, Henry?"

Henry couldn't reply right away as inwardly he fumed at a woman who would turn porridge and curls into a fight and hurt a child over them, so he said nothing for a moment, quietly patting Misty's hair as he calmed himself.

Warmed by Henry's caressing the offending hair, Misty added with a bit of a chuckle, "You know, Henry, I used to love porridge before I came here. Now it goes in the same category with lima beans, which I never liked much but never hated either until my first night here. But now I know the answer to a question I've always had. You see, my first night here, I asked God if He really made lima beans and mosquitoes because I've never been able to figure out how such a good God who made such a wonderful earth could have made lima beans and mosquitoes. But you see I know He made porridge because I used to know how good porridge is. That means I just haven't seen the good in lima beans or mosquitoes yet. It's good to have learned that, isn't it? And it will help me next time I have lima beans—and next time I have porridge, which will be tomorrow. I admit to you Henry that a couple of times now I've almost 'bust right out' over the porridge. I've felt like throwing the stuff, bowl and all, clean across the kitchen. Wouldn't Tommy laugh to hear that? But do you suppose the ugliness is getting into me, Henry?"

Though Henry suspected that Tommy wouldn't laugh, would instead get 'bustin' out mad' to think of Misty having such a fight on her hands every morning, he did chuckle at the image and joked a little to ease the strain of Misty's searching, saying, "Uh-uh, be ye angry but don't 'bust out', young lady. And what a mess you'd have to clean up! I can just see it."

Seeing Misty's grin, he dropped his voice again and continued more seriously, "but you mustn't worry so about the ugliness getting in. You are too full of love for ugliness to come in. And I surely admire you. Every time I see you win a battle or hear of the extent of the battle you are fighting, I see that you are even stronger than I first thought, and I knew right away you are a strong one. I saw your battle this morning, Misty. I saw you walking to school all huddled up, not looking up at the rain, not licking any raindrops from the sky, and I was worried. That's why I sent for you to share my tea and cookies. Don't you worry about the ugly getting in, for though you were so hurt and so tired that I could see it from the outside, what I heard in your voice when you came in here was concern for me. That's love, little one, not ugliness. So just you put that worry aside. It was another bad morning, but you just let a song rise up on your walk home and you'll be strong again. Remember, there's no room for ugliness where beauty resides, and there's beauty in your songs, Misty. Protect yourself with song.

"But Misty, I called you because when I saw you this morning I knew it was time for me to tell you a little more. This time I have no story for you, and what I tell you is going to seem incomplete and may not even make sense right now. But I know it is time to tell you something you wouldn't have thought of and may not have been told, and to suggest something else. I want you to look at me and listen carefully. First, your grandfather left his land to you; it is yours. An adult has signing authority, holds it in trust for you until you are 21, I believe, but the land is yours."

"Does Uncle Hugh hold it in trust, Henry? Or Aunt Augusta?"

"Neither one, Misty. And the land is yours. Do you understand? You can do with it what you want, for you need only the Captain's consent."

"The Captain? It's mine with the Captain holding it in trust? Oh, thank you, Henry! It is so nice to feel connected to the Captain again. Thank you."

Henry leaned back a moment, realizing that, as he had anticipated, she didn't yet understand what he was saying, but he knew she grasped the information and would use it properly when the time came. She was too pure to hear what he was suggesting to her, to see the possibilities that he hoped he was opening. He loved the purity and admired the strength that kept her pure despite her trials. It wasn't simply youth that kept her from seeing such a gift as anything but a connection to those she loved. She was like no other child he had know.

Drawing strength from her pure delight, he continued. "The other thing I must say is not the same kind of information, not just telling you a fact you didn't know. It is quite different and less clear but perhaps more important, so again; listen carefully. This town may be too dusty for you, Misty, so you must find a view of the water. Do you understand? Look at the water. That is all."

Misty looked puzzled, almost perplexed, but she stared evenly and trustingly at Henry as she said, "I'm not so sure.

And I don't know where to see the water. I can't see the ocean, for Aunt Augusta cancelled skating and won't take me out." Here she paused to chuckle a little and add, "She thinks it isn't safe to take me out at this time of year in case my hair suddenly 'looks a perfect fright' and turns me back into the waif she found on the wharf. How grateful I've been for this frizzy hair when I think of the things she would have me go to and the clothes she would make me wear if she didn't think my hair might spring out of its silly ringlets at any minute and turn me into a fright!"

The two laughed together before Misty continued seriously, "But that means I don't get to go to the ocean, and you know she won't allow me to go down to the bay. I haven't even seen the lake yet, Henry. I can't climb the apple tree in these skirts she makes me wear and I haven't anything else to wear. Besides, Tommy said he thought the apple tree wasn't high enough for me to see the lake from. So how am I to see the water?"

"You must, Misty. There is a way, and you must find it. Don't worry about it. One day in the quiet, you will simply know how to see the water. Promise me you won't worry about it? I had to tell you so that you will do the right thing on that quiet day when you do know. You understand that, don't you?"

"Oh yes, I understand. Gran used to call that having your bag packed a little before the boat came in. Okay, Henry, I'll keep my little bag packed. Thank you for giving me the things to put in it. I feel ever so much better now. Please thank your wife for the good cookies; they are as good as Gran's! And I do appreciate the food she sends, Henry. I can't eat very much at all any more but I can always eat what she sends to school. Today, though, it was you who made all the difference. I'm not hollow or cold inside anymore and I know I can sing a song again.

"I wish I could do something for you, Henry. I know! It's Friday and I'll have plenty of time alone over the weekend. Mrs. Longacre gave me some pencil crayons, and I'm getting quite good with them. I'll make a picture for your little room here, that's what I'll do. If I had a needle and some threads I'd make a towel for you to keep here, for you seem to have a mighty leaky little room, but a picture will have to do."

The laughter that filled the room was real and rich. When Misty stopped to get the permission slip from Mrs. Longacre, the secretary was relieved to see life and happiness sparkle once again from the eyes that had begun to look so large in the thin face.

20.

Grandy: Gift of the Lake

Misty did sing on the way home from school, and her eagerness to make a picture for Henry carried her through the difficult parts of her battle with dinner that night. It took her a little longer than usual to get to sleep, but it was her anticipation of drawing that kept her awake instead of the loneliness that so often threatened her sleep. Still, as she thought of what she might draw, what Henry might like, she began again to think she could hear the steady rocking of her grandfather's chair. Even as the rhythm she knew so well started to lull her to sleep, she wondered if she might draw the old rocker, maybe even draw the rocker and the mantle clock high above it. Hearing them, seeing them, imagining being able to draw them, Misty fell into a restful and refreshing sleep.

The morning brought a setback she had not anticipated, however. After being yelled at for not finishing her porridge, Misty was sent to wash her hair, a task the child looked forward to and enjoyed. She loved getting her hair clean and untangled after the many ups and downs it endured in a week. But in her eagerness to get to the picture, Misty forgot to wind her hair in the required ringlets, just combing it out to dry. Aunt Augusta could not tolerate two such flagrant displays of disobedience and obstinacy in a single morning and let Thomasina hear of her error in no uncertain terms. For the first time ever, Hugh stepped in, raising his voice. To Misty's dismay, however, he was yelling not at her but at Aunt Augusta for being unable to control the child and ensure a single meal without battle. Misty could take being yelled at but she could not stand thinking that she was the cause of someone else being yelled at, so she interrupted Uncle Hugh, apologizing and taking full responsibility for both errors. He was furious that she dared interrupt him and simply yelled louder at Aunt Augusta until she burst into tears and ran from the room.

Misty stood rooted to the spot, eyes wide, great thumping rising within her and pounding in her head. Silently she cried for help. Quietly she said, "I am sorry, Uncle Hugh; please forgive me. I honestly don't mean to be disobedient. I just can't eat all the food, and my hair just is curly and frizzy in winter. I can't help either one, but I will keep trying."

Not waiting for a reply, she walked steadily into her own room, closed the door behind her and knelt by the window. She could do nothing but look outside at the bare trees and the grey and dripping sky, waiting for the quiet to come, hoping for the quiet to come, praying for the quiet to come. Gradually the pounding slowed, faded and died altogether. She cried wordlessly for forgiveness and for Aunt Augusta's pain to disappear. She knew there was nothing she could do but she hoped somehow, someone could do something, for as little as she understood Aunt Augusta, the child could not stand to see her hurt so. Long she knelt at the window and long she heard nothing in the house, until finally she heard and smelled coffee perking. For a while she heard voices talking very softly before hearing bath water run. She rose from the window to reply to a knock on her door and was surprised to see Uncle Hugh standing outside.

"Augusta is getting ready to go out," he said; "I've made arrangements for what I hope will be a pleasant outing this afternoon, something that will give us both a chance to perk up. I've also made dinner reservations, so we won't be back before we attend the meeting tonight. We've both been overwrought lately, and you have not only done nothing to make life easier for us but have pushed us over the edge this morning. I expect you will apologize to Augusta sometime before the weekend is over, but leave her alone today. Under no circumstances are you to endanger our home in any way while we are gone. You will, therefore, stay out of the kitchen altogether. Perhaps missing lunch and dinner will make you hungry enough to eat all your breakfast tomorrow. I expect to see that you are indeed trying harder. Good night."

Misty fought with all her might to keep the tears from spilling. Never had she caused so much trouble or pain that she knew of. Surely she did more harm than good in this place. How could she stay where all she did was hurt people and cause them to hurt each other? How could she learn to bring happiness instead of sorrow? What was she doing so very wrong? What was happening to her?

She all but threw herself to her knees before the window again, dry, hollow, stunned inside, almost frozen yet encased in a searing, swirling, terrifying skull. She pressed her face against the window, hoping its solid coolness would keep her from spinning helplessly out of control, trying to keep the pounding head from hurtling off. She raised the window slightly to let in some of the coolness, taking great deep gulps of air even as she pressed her face once again against the cold glass. She hung on, breathing deeply and staring out the window, hoping, praying, asking for help. She saw the rain, great drops of wet, clean rain, and longed to be washed clean. Still she knelt, the pounding beginning to subside again, the swirling slowing, the heat burning out. For a time, only the hollowness remained as she watched the rain, great drop after great drop, imagining it was falling on her, cooling her, washing her, cleansing her, restoring life to her as it does to fields and forests. Exhausted, she fell asleep, face pressed against the window.

She woke to hear the sounds of the old chair and a cat crying softly. The sounds confused her, for one was a sound of sleep and the other a sound of the day. Puzzled she lifted the window higher and leaned out, looking around for the cat, wondering what a cat would be doing meowing about in the rain. She could neither see nor hear the little fellow anywhere in the garden or the trees. Turning her face up as much as she could, she enjoyed the feel of the rain against her skin before pulling back into her room and closing the window most of the way. Her fear was gone as were the intense confusion and the devastating hollowness. Left in their place was sadness.

Misty rose from the window, moved to the side of the bed where she knelt and asked forgiveness once again. She was surprised to hear herself move on to sing the Lord's Prayer as she had so often sung with Gran. Whether from the prayer, its singing or the reminder of Gran, she didn't know, but she felt calm as she concluded—calm and quiet, but not at rest. She missed Gran so very much.

Again in the quiet house she heard the old rocking chair, back and forth, back and forth, back and forth. And again, along with it she was sure she heard a cat meowing, not crying now but meowing softly, gently as if it could begin to purr. And suddenly in the quiet she knew.

She knew she had to see the water. She knew she had to get up from her knees and find the way upstairs, upstairs to where she had seen the cat on the windowsill, upstairs to where she could see the water from the window.

She didn't hesitate, just rose, opened her door and listened in the quiet for the cat. Yes; it came from above. Turning, she went down the hall, past the bedroom, around the corner, past the front door and into the doorway of the living room. Stopping, she listened again, stood still until she heard it. Yes; she was closer, but seemed to have passed below it. She waited, listening again, hoping for a sense of direction, a clue to the way up.

She hesitated only briefly when she realized she must open the door she had been told never, ever to open, hearing Henry's firm statement that she must view the water over Aunt Augusta's harsh list of rules. Yes; the door opened to reveal stairs going up! Her foot on the bottom stair, she paused, listening.

It was almost dark in the stairway and warm, pleasantly warm, and quiet, very quiet. She waited, tilting an ear upward, hoping, waiting, hoping. There; a soft meow. And something else. Back and forth, back and forth, back and forth, the same rhythm, the same slight click in the middle of each rock.

She began the ascent, certainly, steadily, eagerly, but cautiously in the darkened stairwell. Only at the top of the stairs did she pause again, listening. Yes; she could hear the steady rocking, back and forth, back and forth, and with it, the even, assuring tick-tock of a mantle clock. She glanced around.

It was less dark here at the top of the stairs, and she could see a room off to her right, but she knew that window would look out the same side of the house as hers did, so she turned to the left. From that side, she could see bright light coming in several directions, for she found herself in a tiny corridor, just a box really, with three doors opening off it, only one of which was closed. She waited, wondering, listening.

The meow came from the room around the sharpest turn from the stairs. Unhesitantly but a little timidly, she walked through the doorway.

"So you've come to see the water," said a sweet, musical voice that she saw at once came from a white head which rose over the back of a rocking chair almost identical to her grandfather's. "They've gone out, haven't they? I heard the car go. Come. Try not to be afraid."

Misty wasn't at all afraid but she was overwhelmed. Only when the woman held a soft, wrinkled hand out to the left of the chair did something suddenly set Misty free to move. She almost tumbled in her eagerness to take the soft hand in hers. Kneeling beside the rocker, the woman's hand grasped in both of hers, Misty saw the side of a beautiful, wrinkled, radiant face looking down on the cat curled in her lap, purring loudly.

"So you do have a lap to curl up in, Puss," said Misty. "No wonder you didn't have to bother with me. This is a fine lap, isn't it?"

"It was the cat let me know you were coming. I heard you talking to him one day when he was sitting on the sill, not the one in this room, but in the other: the little kitchen. You told him he should be looking out at the lake, not staring down at you, and then I knew you'd come. I've been waiting a long time, a very long time. But run on into the other room and look at the lake. When you've feasted your eyes, you can run back. If you want tea, you can put the kettle on while you are there. I'd like a cup with a friend besides the Dodger for a change."

"Oh, the Dodger? The Artful Dodger? Do you know Fagin, then? And Oliver? But why the Artful Dodger?"

"Like a beam of sunshine, a breath of fresh air. I knew it would be so. But slow down a minute, child. Go see your lake first. We've plenty of time to visit; you'll see."

Misty ran to the other room and looked out the window beneath which sat a small table with a chair. "Oh," she called, "it's beautiful! More beautiful than I imagined. How far does it stretch? How far can you see when the clouds aren't so low? May I open the window and breathe the lake air?"

"You can do better. Look to your left. Go ahead. Go out the door and onto my tiny patio."

Misty was amazed to see a door with small glass panes in it leading onto what was really nothing more than a small platform safely enclosed with closely picketed railings about three feet high. She stepped outside, flung her arms out at her sides and twirled around and around, breathing deeply as she did so. Smiling widely, she stopped, leaned on the railing and looked down over the road that Tommy followed home, saw houses and orchards all down the hillside and the log pond at the bottom where the bay met the land. The dark lake stretched out beyond, mountains rising on either side. Misty knew it must glimmer and glisten in the sunlight. Today it brooded slightly in the rain. It was wonderful! It was life!

She closed the door behind her against the rain as she stepped into the tidy little kitchen. Seeing the kettle on the back of the stove and a pot holder hanging on a hook above, she lifted the kettle to check that it had enough water, decided to add some before moving the kettle to the front of the stove top. "But where's your wood box?" she called.

With a chuckle, the woman answered, "It doesn't burn wood. It burns oil, not gas like downstairs, for I wouldn't have it, but oil. It works the same as a wood stove, but the firebox has a small oil burner in it instead of being stoked with wood. I'll show you some time how to adjust the oil to make the stove warmer, but you don't need to for boiling the kettle. I heard you move it to the front. It will boil in no time. The tea is in the cupboard beside the table, and I'm sure you've found the teapot by now."

Misty had and she was busily putting some hot water in to heat it. Carefully she moved her hand around the stove just above the surface, feeling for the coolest and hottest spots. It really was much more like the woodstove than the gas one downstairs. This one even had a warming shelf above, so Misty set the teapot there while they waited for the kettle to boil. She found cups and saucers on a different shelf in the same cupboard as she'd taken the tea from and put those down on the table all ready, before moving back into the other room.

"I think I've been rude," she said; "I came up here without being asked and didn't even introduce myself. I'm Misty."

"So that's what you like to be called, is it? I've heard Augusta down there fussing and fuming about Thomasina. At first I wondered why it took you so long to respond when she shrieks at you but I soon decided that you mustn't be used to the name for I knew you couldn't be a bad child, though to hear Augusta prattling on, you might think otherwise. I see you are trying to stifle some laughter. Don't bother. I like laughter and I know I sound funny when I start describing Augusta. It is naughty of me, but I just can't help myself. Besides, what else can one do but playfully mock a woman like that. Poor thing is positively, miserably wretched, and I haven't time to be wretched myself. Why what if life ended tomorrow, and I had spent this day wretched? It's just too risky, if you ask me."

"But who are you and why are you here and why didn't I know you were here and why did Aunt Augusta say I must never, ever open that door?"

The woman's laughter might have been as rich and tinkling as Misty's but it was slightly rusty and was fuller and a little deeper in its added age. "The kettle is boiling now," she said; "you go make the tea and run back. I'll allow one serious talk, but only as long as it takes for tea to steep, and we mustn't let it go bitter, so hurry back. To hear Augusta harping at you about the kitchen, you'd think you were an infant, but I know I needn't even warn you to be careful. The woman has forgotten what a brain is for, I'm afraid, poor thing. Must be that stiff hair preventing her from using her noggin."

Misty laughed delightedly as she poured the water into the teapot, put the kettle to the coolest part of the stove and put the teapot on the warming shelf. She did glance out the window at the lake again before returning to the other room.

"Turn the light on, pull up that footstool and sit at my feet a few moments, Misty. We'll get this terribly serious business over with. No, put it right in front of me. That's it. Now look up."

One deep and sparkling blue eye looked steadily at Misty as she lifted her bright and dancing hazel eyes to the old woman's face. A slight gasp escaped Misty's mouth but the only thing the woman saw in the eyes was a flash of pain and concern. Gently Misty reached out and laid her smooth hand on the scarred and disfigured right side of the once beautiful face. "Does it hurt?" she asked simply. When the woman shook her head, Misty asked, "Not even where your eye was? Are you sure?" Again the woman shook her head. Looking down, Misty asked, "What about your leg? Does it hurt?"

"The outside doesn't hurt anymore, the skin. But the ankle and knee were both damaged inside and they sometimes hurt, especially in the cold, damp weather—not much, but a little. It's really just arthritis that has set in as I've grown older. I use the stick, though, just in case my knee buckles, you know. I don't want to fall and damage anything else."

"Oh," said Misty, with a hint of excitement mingled with the compassion in her voice; "that's like Gramps. When his arthritis was bad, he used a stick, too. And he sat up at night rocking, just like you do sometimes. All this time I thought I was just remembering hearing him, but you were up here so close! You can't imagine how much you've helped me. I am sorry you suffer sometimes and don't sleep well, but your rocking has meant more to me than you'll ever know. So you see your suffering has not been for nothing, though I know it is far greater than a little comfort for me is worth. But you haven't answered any of my questions, and the tea will be getting strong."

"Come," said the woman, lifting the Artful Dodger gently from her lap and putting him in the seat of the rocker as she stood up. "I'll tell you while we have tea. Sometimes it may have been old puss you heard rocking up here. He loves the rocker himself."

"No," said Misty, slipping her hand into that of the woman as they moved into the kitchen, "it only sounds just like Gramps' rocker when you are rocking. Little puss cannot make the same sound. Have I been impertinent? I've asked ever so many questions, and you haven't answered many."

"No, you've been delightful. I've just gone slowly, not sure that you wouldn't be afraid of me once you saw how disfigured I am. Most children run away, and adults aren't much better. Augusta always looks at me as if I really should have known better or should fix it somehow.

"You'll forgive me if I chuckle at some of the shenanigans that go on downstairs. Don't think me uncaring, for I'm not and I know how much that woman's tongue can hurt. I've just learned to laugh. When I hear her going on at you about your hair, I near burst out laughing every time. She just has no sense, no sense at all. I'm sure if she took it in her mind to conjure up a sunny day and God turned the tap on that day, she'd manage to make the nearest person feel that the rain were all his fault and due to nothing short of a lack of trying on his part. When she wants something a particular way, she loses all respect for anything natural. I don't think it occurs to her that she is not God or even god-like. I have no more choice about this scarred face than you have about your beautiful hair. What makes me laugh is that you could solve the hair problem, but she won't let you yet goes on blaming you for what is her fault.

"I know it hurts you and I am sorry. But from way up here I can sometimes just see it as a cartoon, depicting only her antics and leaving out your pain. Then I laugh. Besides, with a face like mine, I had to learn to laugh. There are only so many tears a person can stand to shed in any given day. If I cried every time someone cringed at my scars, life would be nothing but a torture. God didn't leave enough land to grow the cotton it would take to make handkerchiefs for me if I hadn't learned to laugh.

"And we are going to have to laugh together, you and I, for we've both broken the rules. Just as you are never, ever to open that door, I am never, ever to go downstairs or allow anyone up here. But that's Augusta, just ordering about. How did she think I could prevent anyone from coming up if I chose to? Was I to tie you up? Was I to tie the Artful Dodger up?

"Don't tell her, but I actually coaxed him in. I get lonely sometimes up here and I saw the cat hanging around the lilac hedge down there. He was a scrawny wee thing, a stray, too young to fend well for himself, but he was a good climber. I often saw him up trees, quite high up. I guess he felt safe there. So one day I put a saucer of milk out on the railing of my patio and watched. He can climb that old oak tree whose bigger branches reach right through the lilac hedge. You probably haven't seen it. I never see you on that side of the house. It wasn't long before I saw him creep out on a big branch and hop down. He lapped up that milk like he was starved. I called him Artful Dodger because of the way he would dart down and drink or eat what I'd put there and then spring back into a tree to hide. He looked for all the world like one of Fagin's gang. He adopted me real soon after that.

"You should have heard the fights. I don't fight those two often, Misty; like you, I just keep quiet and try to keep the peace. Heaven knows it isn't difficult to keep quiet around Augusta; she doesn't give a person a chance to speak anyway. Hugh's not like that but he's easily upset and seldom comes up here. But when it came to being told I had to get rid of that cat and stop feeding him, I fought hard. It didn't take much, really. I think she was so shocked that I went stubborn on her that she gave in before she even knew what happened. Now, she even buys his food for him. She still hates him, though, and insists that he's filthy and brings dirt into the house, poor woman. He stays clear of her, so she never sees how wonderful cats are. Too bad when people can only look at one side of things. They miss so much."

While she talked, the woman had taken some biscuits from a tin and sliced some cheese and a pear she'd taken from the fridge and put these out with the teacups Misty had put on the table. She'd sent Misty into the far room for a chair that was in there, and they'd sat down at the small table for their tea. To Misty's great delight, the woman had automatically bowed and given thanks before passing things to Misty and helping herself. Misty ate easily and happily as the woman continued.

"You can call me Grandy, if you want. I always thought if I ever became a grandmother, I'd like to be called Grandy, just as my favourite grandmother was called. But let me quickly finish off this miserable stuff I said I wanted out of the way. I am

Hugh's mother. I grew up in this little town, but I left when I was sixteen to go to Normal School so I could be a teacher. After my training, I went North to teach and while I was there, I married. My husband died when Hugh was quite young. I decided to stay in the North and go back to teaching, for the people up there needed me. When into his teens, Hugh became so unhappy, I let him go to Vancouver, hoping that the influence of the men at a boys' school would help fill the gap losing his father had made. He never came back, choosing to work in Vancouver in summers and go straight to university.

"There was a terrible fire in the North and my leg was pinned beneath a beam when part of the burning building collapsed. When they finally found me, I was so badly burned and injured, they left me for dead. Even when a medic discovered I was still breathing and pulled me from the row tagged for the morgue, nobody thought I could live. They couldn't even tell who I was. But somehow, alone in the hospital in Edmonton, I just kept living. The coma I was in for months kept me from knowing how much pain I must have had and probably saved my life in more ways than one, for it kept me from thrashing about and tearing open the burns as they began to heal. There are almost eight months of my life of which I remember absolutely nothing.

"The few months after that are little more than a blur of pain and confusion for me, but somehow I came through those too. Eventually, I knew who I was and where I was but it was a long time still before I healed enough to leave the safety of the hospital or to try to rebuild my life. Then my real trials began. Nothing had prepared me for people's reactions. Every time I went out, people would shrink from me or even scream. If one of the hospital staff had not taken me to a boarding home she knew would make me welcome, I don't know what I'd have done. But going out was so difficult that it took me a long time to try to contact Hugh. Poor man had thought for years that I was dead, just one of the many lost in the fire. He had sold many of my things and spent my money on this house. Fortunately, he had put the furniture you see here upstairs. He never liked this old fashioned, homemade stuff, thinking it somehow didn't show that he is an educated man, but he had it in mind to let out this suite and thought this old junk would do for renters. I'm most grateful for that decision, for most of my favourite things are here.

"It must be a terrible shock to have believed someone dead and then hear from her, and he seemed worried about having sold my house and spent my money, though he had done nothing wrong. But when he was finally able to come to visit me, I think the shock of seeing how I look was even worse than the shock that I was alive. He has never been able to imagine that I could have a good life, looking as I do. And he was especially bothered to think of my returning to live in the town I'd grown up in but that he'd come to think of as his own. It was bad enough having a disfigured mother returned from the dead, but to have her already known in his community seemed too much for him. And he'd never told Augusta I'd grown up here so he was caught in some deception. It was a hard time for him.

"I don't know what happened to Hugh while he was at university, but what I found when he came to me after the accident was a hard man with a hard wife. He wasn't always ambitious and pompous, and it breaks my heart. Even worse for me is seeing his resentment, for though he brought me here to live, he seems to resent everything. Sometimes I think he wishes I had died in the accident. I know Augusta does. Somehow they are so taken with their small life, their notions of achievement and success, that they see everything and everyone only as a means or an obstacle to their goals in life. They respond to nothing else, nothing natural. It has been hard and sad, and I have tried to keep hope but I've about given up hoping either one of them will ever respond to good or desire it. I know it's wrong to think that way, but there does come a time when a person can keep praying out of obedience but stop putting herself through the torment of frustrated hope. There does come a time to brush the dust from the feet, you know. I've enough of a job on my hands keeping up with forgiveness, for my own son is ashamed of me.

"Since they moved me in here—it must be seven years ago now—I have not been down those stairs. They shop for me and they allow me on my little balcony, though I don't go out when it is cold, for I don't have a coat. That's it. Oh, I know it saves me the pain of being scorned by others and it saves me seeing the fear and discomfort my scars strike in other people, but nothing hurts as much as being scorned and shunned by my own son. I can pretend along with them that this is for my own good, but deep down I know it is just for their convenience. I can't help but get discouraged sometimes and I do have to forgive them regularly. I have nothing left of my own, so have no choice about staying here. I just make the best of my life as it is.

"So there you have it, Misty; that is the ugliness of my life. That is who I am and why I am here and why you didn't know about me. I refuse to dwell on the ugly parts, so if you have any questions, you'd better ask them quickly."

"But how can you stand it? Aunt Augusta may have hurt me with her sharp tongue but she hasn't wronged me really. They can't just lock you up here like this. It's all wrong! The only ugliness in your life is the way people treat you. Scars are just scars; they are not ugly. And nobody can judge you just on the basis of scars. It's all wrong, all wrong! How can they?"

Poor Misty burst into tears and flung herself into Grandy's lap, almost knocking the table over as she did so.

"There-there," said Grandy softly, as she stroked Misty's woolly hair. "It's not so bad, child. I have a wonderful view from up here and I have the Dodger for company. I have my books, too, and my knitting, and I have my rocker. And I've never lost God. Just look out that window. I can't watch the sky and the lake without feeling the strength and the love of God. And He gives me so very much. In summer, I grow flowers and tomatoes on my little patio. You can't imagine all the wonderful things I have and do up here. You're crying about the silly stuff and haven't even given yourself a chance to see the good parts of my life. I'm not often lonely up here, you know, and I am protected from much of the pain I suffered when I used to try to go out. And now I have you, Misty. Imagine that! For now that you have come, Augusta will not take you away from me any more than she took my cat. I might even take it in mind to settle that hair dispute once and for all. But I think we should go slowly at first, don't you? Come; let's move to the rocker. We can tidy this mess up later."

Misty could not stop her tears but she did get up and take the soft hand in her own as they moved back to the other room. The Dodger stretched and hopped down from the chair to let them sit down, Misty's tears turning to sobs as she settled on Grandy's lap and rubbed her smooth young cheek against the old, soft, wrinkled one. Back and forth they rocked, back and forth, back and forth, the only sounds in the room, the even rocking, the kind clock ticking and Misty's crying. Finally, her tears abated, her sobs turning to the smallest of shudders.

"It's all wrong in this town," she managed to get out between shaky breaths, "wrong for you and wrong for me. Yours is the first soft cheek I've felt. This is the first rocking chair I've seen. Everything here is hard, rough, loud, and chaotic. There's too much ugliness. It's all wrong. And nothing ever works out. Today I was excited to make a picture for Henry. Instead I made pain for everyone by not eating my porridge and by leaving my hair natural. And I'm crying again! Must I always cry here? But, oh your cheek is so soft, so wonderful, so warm, Grandy; I couldn't help but spill over, as Henry puts it. So I've gone and broken another rule, haven't I?"

"Crying is fine up here with me, child. It never hurt anything. Only not crying hurts. Poor Augusta doesn't know that, and Hugh just seems not to think about things as long as his life runs along as smoothly as he has planned it. I'm grateful I don't have to live with them. It is one thing to be banished to this little place, but would be quite another to have to live where their everyday lives and rules would have to be a part of my life. I couldn't do it, Misty. It's no wonder you are so thin, trying to find your way among them. Up here I am free. It only looks like I am caged in. Physical cages are nothing. It's the emotional and mental cages people force us into that hurt and stifle us. No; my little world is a free world. They can't take that from me."

"Oh, Grandy! That's why it is warm up here. I have all kinds of cold in this town, but it's the inside kind of cold, not the outside. Everywhere I go, but especially downstairs, I get cold inside. But Henry's little room and now your rooms are warm places. Funny how I know them right away. I didn't even try to fight against crying up here, same as with Henry, but I do my best everywhere else. Some things I just know. I am glad I came up, glad the Dodger called me. Do you get tired, all tired inside, Grandy? That is my biggest problem here, and I never felt it before."

"When I'm hurt again, I feel tired for a time, or when I get discouraged. But remember, I am free up here, so I'm usually not at all tired. I was tired when I faced people after the accident and I was tired most of the time I first came, but that was before I found the freedom in being alone and before I decided to laugh. But Misty, if I weren't alone so much, I would still be tired, for pain makes me tired, and people hurt me. It is enough for me to handle the pain of looking out my window and suddenly recalling that even right downstairs there are people, people who I care about, who cannot see that beauty. But then I weep; silly old fool, I sit in my chair and rock back and forth weeping. Soon I feel better. It is the other kind of pain, the jabs that people take at me, that I have learned to laugh at instead of cry over. So I get on fine."

"I feel much better right now, Grandy, but I know that I am very tired underneath. I don't seem to get enough rest, enough time to heal before the next blow comes along. I wish I were stronger. I wonder if I haven't let the Captain down and become polluted by this town. It seems like I have sometimes, but then, when I look outside and can see, really see, the rain or the clouds or some other beautiful thing, and the wonder bubbles up in me, I feel clean. It's hard to get rest here, that's all.

"But Grandy, shouldn't we tidy up the kitchen? I'll do it while you rock. The strangest thing of all here is that I have been allowed to do almost nothing but I am tired out. Back home I was busy all the time and never felt this tired. Isn't that something?"

"Tired is a little like rain, Misty. There are different kinds of tired. There are also different causes. Idleness is one of the things that makes me one kind of tired, not the emotional exhaustion that you are struggling with but not just sleepy tired either. I learned that soon after I moved here.

"And you are right. If you're better now, we'd best tidy up. But we'll do it together."

The two moved easily to the kitchen and began washing dishes and putting things away as they continued their discussion. "When I first came, Misty, I didn't do much. The shock of being banished to such a small place was greater than my relief at not being gawked at. I had lost any sense of purpose and I just sat. But one day as I sat feeling tired and dull, I saw the lake shining away in the distance, and it looked beautiful, bright and very alive. It looked more alive than I felt. I began to wonder why I had not just died, and suddenly it was as clear to me as the lake is on a sunny day that I hadn't died. It was that simple. There is no sense wondering why one is alive, why one didn't die; the simple fact was that I was alive. So I reasoned that if I was alive, then I must act alive no matter how small my world. I even thought that since I had been taken for dead but wasn't, there must be something important for me to do with my life.

"For a time, I couldn't think of what that might be, still don't know. But that very day I saw that I must just pick up and live a life as full as is possible in a small space. Right away I got up from my chair and went to my big basket in the closet, the basket where I keep wool and scraps and such. I started knitting. I didn't need anything myself, but I decided there were two things I could do. The coldness of the lake reminded me that far in the North, children need warm things in winter. I could make mittens, hats and sweaters for the Northern children. The coldness of my room reminded me that I could knit mats and hook rugs that would warm it up. So Misty, I began by knitting to warm people and my little place. Once started, I just kept seeing more and more things to do. From then on, I have stayed busy and been less tired."

"I can see, Grandy. Your towels are all like home, embroidered at the edges. Your tablecloth and napkins are handstitched. Did you braid your oval rug by the sink? We had one at home, too. Gran did it. Oh, Grandy, that must mean you have needle and thread! Could I borrow some? I need to move the buttons on my skirts. They're kind of loose, and Aunt Augusta doesn't notice. I'd feel more comfortable if they felt less like they'd fall off. Imagine what Aunt Augusta would say if my skirt fell off! Wouldn't she shriek and flap?"

The two laughed and laughed at the thought. "I'll tell you what, Misty. You run downstairs and get the things you want to fix. Bring up what you need to do your picture too, for there's no need to let a bad start keep you from doing what you had planned. We can sit and work together. I'll do some of the buttons so there will be plenty of time for drawing. We'll make some supper later too. And while we do these things, we'll decide what we're going to do now that you've made your way up here. Does that sound okay?"

"Oh, yes, but I'm not sure about supper. I'm supposed to have missed both lunch and supper for my disobedience. Was I wrong to take tea with you?"

"Of course not. But never mind that now. We'll sort it out later. And I'll take responsibility for supper. You will be my very first dinner guest. Isn't it about time I had such a house warming after all these years? It will be fun to make supper for two. Run and get your things. I'll get my sewing basket."

Misty fairly flew down the stairs and gathered the skirts she wore most often and her little box of paper and things Mrs. Longacre had given her. She was back as quickly as Grandy had retrieved her sewing basket from the closet.

"The light is best in the kitchen this time of day, Misty, so we'd best work in there. Let's see your waistband and mark how much we need to alter these. Good heavens, we need to take the zippers out, the skirts are so floppy. That's a lot of tricky work, though. How about we just put a little pleat each side of the front and take them in that way? That will be better."

The two chatted easily as they worked, laughing often and weeping occasionally. Once when Misty's delight at just living, just doing things alongside another bubbled up inside her, she leaned over and kissed Grandy's cheek. The simple uninhibited caress, the first of its kind the woman had received on her scarred face, sent warm tears coursing down the wrinkled cheek. Soon they were laughing again as the Artful Dodger, not wanting to be left out, began batting a spool of thread about the kitchen. Later, when Grandy reached out and stroked Misty's hair with nothing but love and admiration in the gesture, it was Misty's turn to spill over.

With just one skirt left to alter, Grandy persuaded Misty to begin her picture while she finished the sewing. As one stitched, the other became almost silent as she deftly sketched a rocking chair, the back of a shining white head showing above it and looking through a window and beyond to the lake. Grandy almost gasped to see what the child was accomplishing with only a cheap set of pencil crayons. A few more tears escaped as the picture neared completion. She hadn't seen anything like it for years, not since … not since … well, not since she cared to remember.

When Misty looked up with an almost comical frown wrinkling her small brow, Grandy chuckled. "Child, look at you all wrinkled at your age, and after such beautiful work. I believe you forgot I was here."

"Oh, I didn't, not for a minute. It was like drawing at home. Drawing just is quiet work, Grandy. But even drawing is frustrating in town. These pencils are much better than the wax crayons at school, but they are nothing like watercolours. You see, I don't have the lake quite right. Look. I can't get the misty blues of the lake meeting the shore, and the colour won't deepen gradually enough. That takes the life out of the picture, but if I keep trying to blend it, it will all go too dark. It's just so disappointing. I see it out the window and I see it in my mind. I can even see how I could get it with watercolours. But I can't get it on the paper with these. I think the rocker is okay, though, don't you? Maybe Henry will like the rocker."

"It's a wonderful picture, Misty. Though it's true you can't get the colour of the lake quite right with those pencils, you have managed life in the picture, for you've shown the warmth and the expanse of the lake. Yes, the rocker is good. Do you see the life that comes from the interplay of rocker and lake? Even without the right colours, the picture is alive, Misty. And you ought to be grateful to have crayons at all. Frankly, I'm surprised Augusta and Hugh have provided you with anything of your own."

"Oh, they didn't. Mrs. Longacre gave me these things. Thanks, Grandy, for not being silly about the picture, not lying. You know drawing and you know colour, but then lots of people do. But how do you also know truth about drawing? Only people who have painted or watched painting seem to know not to ruin a picture with ridiculous praise. You've painted?"

"No, Misty, I don't paint. But you are right; long ago I was often with one who did. I wonder, though, if we couldn't get you some watercolours. We're going to have to make a plan. Let's get supper. What would you most like to eat or to cook? Or," she added with a twinkle in her eye, "would you rather just have some porridge?"

"Grandy!" Misty said, "I didn't think you were a cruel person."

Their laughter was rich and full and warm, filling the small apartment and, had they known it, ringing through the empty house below. Happily the two cooked chicken with nice, rich gravy and enjoyed the best dinner Misty had since she arrived. As happily, they formulated a plan.

Grandy knew she must be the one to tell Augusta that she and Misty had met and would be friends, so they decided that Misty would go to her bed and to Sunday School as if nothing had changed. Grandy would speak to Augusta while Misty was out. She thought it best to give Augusta some time to get over everybody's "disobedience and flagrant disregard of rules" and then see what rules of their own they ought to insist on. To begin with, Grandy was going to demand that Misty be allowed to come up to visit her after school each day. She was quite sure the others would be able to view that as an advantage to themselves rather than a disadvantage. She thought she and Misty also might gain Saturdays. Both began to feel rich as they made their plans.

Suddenly Misty said, "He knew, didn't he? Henry knew! He told me to climb up to see the water. He knew about your window. And he must have known about you. You are the gift of the lake! Does everybody know you live up here, Grandy?"

"I don't know who knows what, Misty, and it doesn't much matter to me. It did once but it doesn't now. I'm ashamed to say that Hugh and Augusta can be less than honest. But, yes, your Henry knows."

"Then it's perfect; the picture is perfect, even though the colours aren't right! Oh, Grandy!"

Misty was so full of delight and awe that she danced, sang and wept all at once, striking such a comical picture that Grandy couldn't help but laugh the most rich and pure laugh Misty had heard from her. Together they danced around the kitchen, laughing.

"Ah, child," Grandy said, when they finally danced themselves out and sat down in the living room, "in one short afternoon and evening, you've filled my little place with life again—and set me to dancing, arthritis and all. And look at you. There's colour in your cheeks. You were pretty pale when you came up. We've just a little time before you'd best go down to bed. Will you read to me a while? I haven't heard anyone read for years."

"Oh, Grandy! You are perfect! Which book? What will I read? Where will I start?" Misty scurried around the room, moving from table, to bookshelf, to table, to china cabinet, everywhere she saw a book, touching first one, then another and another as the old woman shook with laughter at the child's delight and excitement.

Abruptly Misty stopped, books forgotten for a moment. In the sudden silence, Grandy heard her inhale deeply, then slowly, softly but clearly say, "Grandy! Look!" in a hushed voice filled with awe. Turning, Grandy saw her standing before the small glass-fronted curio cabinet, eyes wide and alight. "Look," she said again in a whisper.

"Go ahead, child, take it out."

"Oh may I?"

"Yes, take it out and bring it here."

Gently Misty opened the door and lifted the small, round, blue-hued metal box with its pearl-studded lid from its place on the shelf. She stepped over to Grandy's rocker and knelt in front of her, leaning her arms in the woman's lap, the box cradled gently, reverently in her hands as if she were carrying a newly hatched chick.

"Go ahead," said Grandy; "lift the lid."

As the tinkling sounds of the music box danced throughout the room, the tears ran freely down Misty's cheeks. Grandy's own tears spilled over to see the light in the child's face and the love with which she held the music box and listened, listened as if she'd never hear again. Neither moved. Neither spoke. Over and over, the tune rang out. As it wound down, Misty reached one hand up and ran it through the beautiful, soft, white hair of her new friend, saying simply, "Thank you," before rising and gently replacing the box in the cabinet.

Without a word, she took the Bible that lay open on the small table next to the cabinet, sat on the stool at Grandy's feet and began reading from the Psalms. Beside her, a smile lighting up the scarred and wrinkled face, the old woman rocked gently, back and forth, back and forth, back and forth, keeping even time with the rise and fall of the child's voice. Everything fit.

Finishing with Psalm 121, Misty closed the book and replaced it, kissed the old woman on the cheek, gathered her things and said very softly, very gently, "Good night, Grandy."

"Good night, Misty," replied the old woman, rocking steadily, "I'll see you very soon."

The even rocking that carried Misty safely to sleep and to rest that night fit perfectly with the hush that filled the house.

21.

The Rescue: A Place for Misty

Misty did not spend a lot of time the following day hurting because Sunday School contained none of the hush she and Grandy had enjoyed the evening before. She had long since seen that Sunday School, like the other school, had become self-serving and had little to do with knowing God. It still hurt her every Sunday to see such emptiness and misery where there should have been joy, and she was often hurt herself by the children there, especially after she was put in a grade above them at school, but she had learned to enjoy and give what she could and leave the rest. Her walk home provided her with time to recover from any pain and to celebrate life as it seemed it could be celebrated only out of doors here. But this Sunday, she knew it could also be celebrated indoors: in Henry's little room and at Grandy's. She went home singing.

She did not delay apologizing to Aunt Augusta as Uncle Hugh had demanded, but the apology seemed to go unheard. For the first time, Misty had to stifle a chuckle as she suddenly saw the ludicrousness of her walking in with her hair all frizzy from her damp walk home and apologizing for having left her hair frizzy the day before. She realized too late that Aunt Augusta would think she had disobeyed her again, for no one had been up when Misty, her hair carefully wound into ringlets, had left for Sunday school. Of course Aunt Augusta would rant on about disobedience, waifs, embarrassment, and unruliness with Misty standing before her looking as she did. But her laughter quickly vanished as she realized she had never seen nor heard Aunt Augusta as angry as she was now.

"You may have simply walked all over those buffoons at school and got your own way, young lady, but if you think you can do the same here, you are wrong. And if that crazy old woman thinks she can order me around, then she is wrong too. Even the two of you together are not a match for me. Hugh may be spineless about that woman, but I am not. She was supposed to be dead and she has no business not being dead. I'll not have her running my life. Hugh had no parents when I married him and he'll have no parents now. Upside down. Everything flips upside down. I won't have it. I told you never, ever to open that door and I meant it. First thing tomorrow, Hugh is putting a lock on it, since we obviously cannot trust you two. Who does she think she is to try to order me around? I've fed her and supported her all these years and what does she do for gratitude? Tries bossing me about. Next thing you know she'll want to go out. I won't have such embarrassment, I tell you, I won't. Hugh will get a lock for your door as well, for we have learned now that we've no choice but to lock you in when we go out. Those teachers were right; your disobedience knows no bounds and your attitude is atrocious. Now you will go to your room at once and stay there. Now!"

Misty did hurry to her room but stayed there only long enough to change. Inside her, something had snapped, just snapped. It didn't seem like 'bustin' out,' didn't even seem like anger, really. Something just snapped, gave way so completely that something else took over. It was as if she heard and saw nothing around her but what she needed.

Taking the Sunday clothes off, she put them neatly away before turning and brushing her hair. She brushed and brushed, divided the mass into two even sections and began braiding. One long braid, then another. Decisively, she tied the two braids together so they'd hang down her back before putting her plainest clothes on. Then she took the picture she had drawn for Henry, put her coat on and walked evenly down the hall and out the front door, closing it quietly behind her.

Down the path to the road she continued, turning at the corner to walk down the hill. On she marched, down, down, knowing where she had to go, but not really knowing how to get there. She simply marched on, sure at least that she would reach the lake and sensing that from the lake she could find an orchard that bordered it. Had she turned her head, she'd have seen a white-crowned wrinkled face watching her from the gable window. But she marched on, looking neither to the left nor to the right.

At the lake, she stopped long enough to put her hand in the water, to feel it and smell it, before following along the shore. She turned away from the logs and the sawmill and walked past houses, certain that if she carried on, she would find an orchard. On she walked. The houses got farther apart. She saw more grass, more trees. Finally she saw fruit trees, bare arms pointing in all directions. She left the beach and walked up among the trees, watching for an arbour. Yes; there it was, bare vines tangled, braided, woven all above it and through it.

Pausing only briefly below the arch, she continued walking evenly, certain she would find a house somewhere. Through an apple grove, through a plum grove she marched steadily until she came to a flower garden. Standing on tiptoe to see over the rose hedge that surrounded the garden, she peered ahead, finding both house and a break in the hedge. Turning, she followed the hedge to where she had seen the break, walked evenly through it and up the path that led to the door. She knocked loudly and firmly.

"Misty!" cried Henry, opening the door widely. "'Stina, it's the little Miss come in through your rose garden."

Misty stepped inside the door as a beautiful woman came from the kitchen, wiping her hands on her apron and reaching out for Misty. For just a moment, Misty slumped inside the circle of the arms before pulling herself up, standing back and saying evenly, "Thank you so much for all you've done for me. You are the best cook since Gran! And you have the best man since Gramps! Please excuse me for just marching in, but I need help."

Christina held the child at arm's length before giving her shoulders a squeeze and bidding her take her coat off and sit down.

"Thank you," said Misty, "but I'm not sure how much time I have." Crossing over to where Henry had sat in a large Morris chair, she quietly handed him the picture and said, "Henry, you packed my bag for me. How do I get the boat to come?"

Christina came and stood behind Henry's chair, looking over his shoulder at both the beautiful picture and the small child, eyes clear and wide looking steadily into Henry's face.

"So you found the water, little one," he said, wiping a tear from his cheek. "I didn't think it would be this soon. And you are sure you need the boat?"

"Yes, Henry. Today."

"Today, little Miss? Are you sure? You might be rushing into something."

Suddenly Misty began to cry. Henry gathered her onto his lap and listened as she sobbed out, "Oh, Henry. They are going to lock Grandy's door tomorrow and mine too. They said I can't ever go up there again and they are locking her in. They've kept her up there all those years, never letting her go out, keeping her in such a small place, and now they are going to lock her in. Lock! They can lock me in if they want, but not Grandy. She's beautiful, Henry, but hurt, all the time hurt. I have to take her to a place of our own, not just out of there, Henry, but home. She needs to laugh pure, Henry, not just to keep from crying. I have to take her."

"Okay-okay, child. We'll see what we can do. There-there." As Henry rubbed Misty's back, Christina went to the kitchen and put on the kettle before going to the phone. Henry smiled over Misty's head to see his 'Stina move so quickly into action. She never wasted any time wondering or talking. She'd have tea ready and things lined up before he had the child quiet. He rocked gently, stroking her head with his great hand.

"Ah, Misty; braids. Beautiful braids. I should have known when I saw the braids that the time had come. I'm going to miss you. We'll all miss you. But I'm glad you came. We've all gained something from your coming. You've suffered and suffered here, little one, but your suffering was not for nothing. And I'll have this picture on my wall. Tommy will like it, too, when he sees it. I'm glad you did it for me. That's our lake, alright. And that's one of your grandfather's rockers. 'Stina has one in the kitchen. Like him, you do good work, Misty. Now tell me, does Lila know you are taking her away?"

Misty snuffled a bit before asking, "Lila? Is that Grandy's name? That's a pretty name, isn't it? No, I came back from Sunday School, and Aunt Augusta flew at me, forbidding me to go up and telling me about the locks. I'm supposed to be shut in my room, Henry, but I just went in there, changed and came here. I couldn't get Grandy and her things by myself and I didn't know how to get a boat. What do we do, Henry?"

Even as Misty asked, Christina came in with a small tray of tea and biscuits, a fresh, new handmade handkerchief—a gift for Misty—and news. "I've called Old Lundstrom. He's in harbour today and will stay in until he hears from us. I've called Jean and she is getting a few people together to help pack what Lila needs or wants to take. It isn't likely Augusta will let her back in to get anything else once she's gone, so if there is anything she values, she'd best take it with her. The place is small and Lila doesn't have a lot, so I think with four or five of us working, we can pack and load all she wants this afternoon. Now drink up some tea, Misty, and eat a biscuit. You'll need strength. I'm going to pack food for you to take with you, enough to last until we can get an order sent up to you. It does seem crazy helping a little girl go off to reopen a house in winter. If it were anyone but you, I wouldn't think of it. But you'll be okay."

"Thank you, both of you. Had I better run now and get Grandy started? It will be a shock for her. Oh, think of what freedom she'll have soon! She told me she is free where she is, for nobody bothers her or stares or screams, but she is stuck in. Imagine living in the house of someone who thinks you should have died. Nobody can be free in such a place as that. Oh, think of it! She'll be able to walk outside, garden, anything she wants. Nobody will laugh. Oh, let's hurry!"

Henry and Christina exchanged a look that said volumes. It seemed no matter how long Henry knew Misty nor how much Christina heard of her, they continued to be amazed by her selflessness. She had said nothing at all of her own suffering in the past months and had criticized no one, not even the vain but abrasive Aunt Augusta. Instead, she was just excited at the happiness she could finally bring to someone hurt. Their quiet awe was interrupted by an outburst.

"The Artful Dodger! We'll have to take a basket or something for The Artful Dodger! Think of his freedom! He can come in and out the door, won't have to run up a tree and across the roof to get in. Oh, Henry, do you have something we can carry the cat in? Isn't it good that Rusty likes cats? Rusty! I'll see Rusty soon!"

Tears of joy spilled down Misty's face as she carried on, "I'll soon sleep in my own bed with my little brown dog beside. Maybe even tonight, Henry? Do you think tonight? Let's see, Grandy can have Gran's room, nice and close to the hall stove. The linen is clean. I did it myself. And it won't take me long to make her bed. Might be damp the first few days until we have had the fires on for a while. I hope it won't bother her arthritis. Oh, Henry, do you think she'll want to come with me? We'd better hurry." Misty could barely sit still, she was so excited.

Christina chuckled to see her and said, "I know you're eager, but you'd best slow down a little. You can't go to get Lila by yourself, so you'll have to wait. It won't be long now. Henry, you'll need the big pick-up truck, so you'd better get it ready. I think, too, you'd better get yourself a helper or two. We women won't do everything. Why don't you holler across to Bobby and Tommy, get them to help you put the sides on the truck? They can help you load too."

As Henry rose, Misty danced about again in delight, "Oh thank you! You think of everything. I'll be able to say goodbye to Tommy. It's perfect. It's perfect!"

Suddenly sobering, she said, "But wait. I should go alone for Grandy. I can ask for help but I cannot ask anyone else to do my own work, even if it is difficult. I'll go for Grandy."

"Yes, Misty, you can go," said Henry firmly, "but we'll be with you. You'll not walk in there alone. You wait with 'Stina while I go get the truck ready. And Misty, I do have a basket. I'll put it in the truck. We'll drive up the hill together when the others get here."

Christina thoroughly enjoyed the time she had with Misty helping her pack food. The child was delightful, everything that Henry had said she was, and very like her grandparents. As they put food into boxes, Misty chattered on about all the things she'd be able to do. Everything she mentioned was something she would do for others. She was excited to think she could paint a proper picture for Henry's little room. Then she decided she might even get Miss Lily to paint one for him. She would be able to write to Mrs. Longacre and she was sure she could help Tommy with his schoolwork by writing letters to him—as long as he took time to answer them.

She hoped she wasn't hurting anyone by leaving so suddenly and became quiet as she wondered how she could possibly have done something that might have made Aunt Augusta and Uncle Hugh happy. It troubled her that they remained crabby. Suddenly she wondered if taking Grandy away might make them even worse. But she decided she couldn't help it. Perhaps if she wrote to them sometimes she would know when a time might come that she could help them. Maybe they would use the top of the house, and the beauty of the lake would take the blinders from their eyes. She could hope that. And so she continued, eagerly carrying out her plan.

To say that Augusta and Hugh were shocked to see an old pickup truck and two cars pull up in front of their house and all sorts of bay riff-raff walk steadily to the front door behind Thomasina would be an understatement. Their faces were a study in shock, as they stood in the open doorway and heard Misty say, clearly and evenly,

"I am sorry to have caused you trouble and I thank you very much for having me these many months. It is time for me to go home now, and I am here to take Grandy with me. These people will help me pack her things and will drive us to the harbour, so we won't bother you at all. Old Lundstrom will take us back. I've left the things you bought me in the room. I'll send the ones I'm wearing to you by post. It was good of you to give me an opportunity to live in town for a while and to give Grandy a place to live all these years. You'll be free of us as responsibilities now, though, if you'll just stand aside so we can get to work."

The two seemed rooted to the ground, their mouths hanging open. Small as she was, Misty simply pushed between them and walked steadily up the stairs, brightly calling, "Grandy! I've come to take you home. We must hurry and pack. I've brought a basket for the Dodger. Is he in?"

Grandy met her at the top of the stairs, tears streaming down her cheeks. "Child, you can't do this."

"I can and I am, Grandy. Do you know about having your bag packed before the boat is in? Well, Henry helped pack my bag last week. The house is mine, Grandy, just mine. And when I came to find the water, I found you with it. Now I've come to take you home with me. I can't live there alone, they say, so I need you to come with me. You will come, won't you? I *need* you, Grandy. Please come."

Misty looked steadily and openly at Grandy as she spoke and soon saw the relief shine through the clear eye and spread across her face. "Yes, Misty, I'll come with you."

"Oh, good! I've brought people to help us pack so we can leave right away today. Let's get started. All you need is some clothes, for the house is complete, even has a rocker like yours. But you can bring whatever you want. You get The Dodger into the basket and then just tell these people what you want packed. Just think, Grandy, you'll be able to go outside whenever you want, and garden or walk or anything. You'll even be able to sit in Miss Lily's garden while we paint, for I have already seen that you are the quiet watcher, just as a painter needs. There's so much we can do together. Let's hurry! I'll go in the bedroom and pack up your clothes. You tell the women which of your other things that you want. Ask Henry what you need to know about packing. He has the truck. Hurry everyone! We're going home!"

Never had there been such a delightful time of packing, for Misty ran gleefully from person to person, continually singing out some exciting thing she would soon be doing again, some wonderful thing that Grandy would soon be free to do, some beautiful thing or person she would soon see. She exclaimed about fresh eggs, fresh milk and cheese, and fresh-baked bread, before laughing delightedly and announcing that there would be no porridge or lima beans in her house. No sooner had everyone laughed with Misty than she immediately and seriously apologized for her complaining before singing out yet another delightful thought about going home. No one could be anything but happy working in such an atmosphere. Misty's enthusiasm kept their own sadness at losing her from even entering their minds. They simply enjoyed the time with her.

Only one person struggled, but he struggled through to victory. Aunt Augusta and Uncle Hugh had stood to one side but otherwise remained motionless at the front door as Mrs. Longacre led the women she had brought to help past them and up the stairs. Only the sight of Tommy and Bobby coming down the walk and up the stairs with Henry liberated Aunt Augusta, sending her into a tirade.

"Leave? Yes, she can leave, the ungrateful wretch, and take that horrid old woman with her. But she will not drag this vermin-infested bay riff-raff into my house as she does so. Hugh, do something! Get them out of here. I never! There will be bugs everywhere. Stop them, Hugh, stop them! I won't have that waif of a child bring her filthy low friends into my house."

Only Henry's huge hand on one of Tommy's shoulders and Bobby's on the other kept the young boy from 'jist bustin' out.' He was so angry his face was even redder than his hair, and his eyes were wide, but he kept his lips tightly pursed, though his cheeks bulged out as if he'd pop at any moment. Silently he walked past Aunt Augusta and up the stairs to help carry things. He clenched his fists tightly at his sides as, behind him, he heard Aunt Augusta rant and rave on and on, insulting him, Bobby, his parents, Henry and, as always, Misty. Henry and Bobby could let him go only when Misty appeared at the top of the stairs and threw her arms around him, chattering wildly about how happy she was to see him, how proud she was that he had walked right past Aunt Augusta without "bustin' out" and how wonderful it would be to get letters from him after she got home. In just seconds, Tommy joined fully in both the activity and the happiness.

Hugh finally led the sputtering Augusta away from the door and into his study. Closing the door behind them, he began immediately to persuade her of their good fortune, listing all the advantages he could think of to this unexpected but wonderful solution to their two most bothersome problems. Though high on his list was the restoration of order to his life, most of the list showed financial and political advantages. They had done all they could for these people. Nobody could fault them for that. He was sure that they would soon show the whole community not only the great sacrifices they had made for both his mother and the waif but also the ill-treatment they had eventually suffered at the hands of that riff-raff who had so clearly persuaded the two to turn their backs on Hugh and Augusta without so much as saying goodbye.

That Hugh could even think either Misty or his mother capable of leaving without saying goodbye showed how little he knew either of them. When everything was packed and loaded into the truck, Misty took Grandy by the hand and led her down the stairs. As if by common consent, the two turned, walked down the hall and knocked on the door of Hugh's study before entering. Grandy simply thanked them for all they had done for her and assured them she would write when she was settled. Misty not only thanked both of them, the inextinguishable light of excitement shining from her eyes almost convincing even them of her sincerity, but also threw her arms around each of them and hugged them. At the door, she turned and invited them to come and visit any time, not in the least discouraged by either their failure to return her hugs or the sight of Aunt Augusta fiercely brushing imaginary bugs and filth from her arms and body where Misty had hugged her.

The Hughes did not go to the house door to see them off, but Augusta could not resist peeking through the window. At the sight of the old woman walking so steadily away beside the small child, Augusta turned to Hugh and said, "You are right. We are well rid of them. Did you ever see such a ridiculous sight? Those braids! So plain. And what on earth is your mother doing dressed like that, a great baggy sweater almost covering her body? Talk about a waif leading a waif. Good riddance, I say. Come Hugh, let's dress and go out for dinner."

The ride out to the harbour that had seemed very long to Misty on the way from the island seemed to fly by as she bounced along in the old truck with her friends. She had shed a few tears in spite of herself as Tommy and Bobby had turned to run down the hill, waving and winking as they went. But she soon laughed as she told Henry that he'd better be prepared for some lonely days in his little room.

When Tommy had said goodbye to Misty, he'd added, "Now don' you worry none 'bout me, Misty. Ya know, I walked right past thet blusterin' ol' bag, even when she said bad things about Henry 'n' you, 'n' I didn' even kick 'er 'r nuttin'. I maybe wouldna bin able ta do it 'thout Henry 'n' Bobby this time, but I swear, Misty, if I'm half as ugly when I jist bust out as thet ol' Augusta was when she got goin', then I'm done with bustin' out fer good!"

After Henry had finished laughing with Misty, she turned to him, serious for a moment, and said, "I hope you can bring Tommy for a visit some time, Henry. Maybe when his pa gets the boat done. You will remind them, won't you? And you'll bring your Christina?"

"Ah child, you'll have visitors in the summer, for sure. Why we have to come to see Lila, too! Augusta wouldn't have us visit in all those years, and we've missed her. And won't it be nice to see her tanned and healthy again? Mind you, to see the light just shining there now, you'd never know you've lived inside all those years, Lila. You look about as bright as Misty here! And it does my heart good to see you so alive again, little one. As much as I'll miss you, I'm happy to see you doing the right thing."

Misty couldn't keep herself from bouncing on the seat of the truck and exclaiming over everything they'd soon be doing, trying to describe for Grandy every part of their coming life all at once. Occasionally she'd interrupt herself to express some concern about someone she was leaving behind, but as soon as Henry gave her whatever assurance was needed, she'd move right on to some other gladness.

Grandy joined Henry's laughter both with and at the delighted child but said little. Being out of a house, down on the ground and moving along in a truck through the forest were enough for her. She could feel a profound peace descending on her and elevating her simultaneously, reacquainting her with things long since robbed from her. As they travelled along she realized for the first time what Misty had seen: as free as she felt herself left alone in the loft of a house, as positive as she had chosen to be, the inside scars had not healed as well as the outside ones had. She felt on the verge of life again.

As they neared the end of the road, Misty's bouncing and chattering both stopped. Concerned, Henry glanced over to see the child bent right over in the seat, reaching down toward the floor of the truck.

"Lose something?" he asked.

"No," came the reply, muffled by the wool of the skirt Misty's face leaned on, "just getting ready."

Henry and Grandy glanced at each other, a look of puzzlement on their faces. But Misty's face when she straightened up and looked around again was illuminated as Henry had never seen it before. As the truck crested the hill putting the forest behind them and the great sea before them, Misty stuck two wriggling bare feet up on the dash of the truck and burst out in a new song—a song of being ready, a song of being free, a song of going home.

As they began the short descent to the wharf, she interrupted her own song to exclaim, "Grandy, look! The ocean! We're almost home! Oh, the dock. The boats. There's Old Lundstrom's boat. Henry, look! Grandy, he's over there; he really is!"

Before Henry had the truck fully stopped and could say a word, Misty had opened the door and jumped out, running as rapidly and sure-footedly as a deer. Across the road, over the wharf, down the ramp and out on the float she ran, braids bouncing out behind her, skirt and coat flapping and swirling as she all but flew to Old Lundstrom. The crusty old fisherman turned just in time to catch her as she threw herself at him, laughing and crying at once.

"Are you ready? Can we go today?" she began. "Is the Captain fine? And Miss Lily? And Rusty? Have you seen them? Is the house fine? And Old Nobbin?"

The child's radiant face and battery of questions turned Lundstrom's tears to laughter. Holding Misty at arm's length, he threw back his head and laughed and laughed before he could say, "It is good to see you again, Miss T. The folks have missed you so much. We'll go today and give them the best surprise of their lives. I've put the running lights on, so we'll be fine. But what about your friends? I heard you are bringing home a friend. Come, we are rude standing here."

This time as Misty made her way up the dock with Old Lundstrom, she skipped easily and lightly at his side, beginning her chatter once again, telling him of Grandy and Henry and going home. The two men met with a steady handshake and a look above the child's head that conveyed all their concern for her as well as their hope. Lundstrom knew he would never hear from Miss T about the trials of life in town, just as he had never heard complaints from her grandparents or the other island folk. But he could see beyond her flush of excitement to the pallor, the sunken eyes and the thinness of her small body that showed she had suffered like the others before her. Henry heard the catch in the fisherman's voice as he thanked him for bringing her back.

"This is Grandy, Lundstrom. We're going home. Isn't it good I found someone who could stay with me so I don't have to leave the island? And Lundstrom, she was a teacher when she was younger, so Mrs. Longacre says they won't even make me come down to school! Isn't that wonderful? But we have to load the things. Grandy must tend to The Artful Dodger in his basket while we load the other things, don't you think?"

Old Lundstrom's firm, unflinching handshake and steady gentle gaze brought a tear to Grandy's eye, but she soon joined the laughter of the two men as Lundstrom said, "I'm not sure how you'll manage living with Miss T bubbling and bobbing about like she is. Looks like she might pop. Why her face is dancing just as fast as her feet are! How do we stop her?"

They all laughed louder as Misty answered, "By loading the boat! Come on!"

Grandy interrupted the child's scamper to reach the basket from the truck, saying, "Misty, you really should put your shoes back on. It is winter, for goodness sake. You'll catch your death."

Though Old Lundstrom was happy to hear the concern in the woman's voice and see for himself the love that was behind it, he put his rough hand gently on her arm and said, "She'll be fine, Ma'am. You just trust Miss T to know what she needs to wear and when. I have seen her put her boots on when the ground is frozen, but mostly she scampers around bare-footed, free and happy. Don't you worry none about her. She's full of good sense."

Henry nodded in agreement and Grandy relaxed, knowing they were both right. But Misty herself, wide, serious, gold-flecked eyes looking steadily at the three of them, fully ended the matter of shoes. Taking Henry's hand and looking up at the three of them, she said simply, seriously and sadly: "Sometimes you have to shake the dust from your shoes and let the peace return to you. And sometimes you have to take the dusty shoes themselves and leave them behind. Please Henry, throw them away so no other child has to walk in them. And don't worry, Grandy; I have clean rubber boots at home. I'll wear them when I need them. Come; let's load the boat."

The three old folks wiped tears from their faces as Misty walked from them to begin unloading the truck. But her cheerful chatter to The Artful Dodger about the new home she was taking him to soon brought smiles back to their faces. Her excited scampering about as they moved Grandy's things from truck to boat restored laughter, real laughter, to the whole group. Only when the truck was empty and the boat loaded did Misty grow serious again, for it was time for Henry to go back to town. Old Lundstrom shook Henry's hand and thanked him again before taking Grandy's arm to lead her to the boat, leaving the two friends their moment together.

Misty hugged Henry hard, tears dampening his great chest once again, his tears spilling over and dripping into her hair. But a quiet smile tugged at his mouth when she pulled back and looked steadily at him, saying, "Henry, when I think of town, I am going to think of you and your Christina, of Tommy and Mrs. Longacre and all nice things. You have your little room, and your Christina has her grape arbour. I have the whole island again, Henry. So we'll all be together, won't we? Thank you and come soon to visit. I have to go now. Grandy needs me."

Kissing his damp cheek, Misty turned and ran down to the boat, stopping twice to look back and wave and to wipe tears from her own cheeks.

But it was a child with a radiant face that untied the lines of the loaded boat and threw them aboard before hopping deftly and surely from the float to the boat deck. She hugged herself as the idling engine increased to the low throb that would take them slowly through the harbour. As the boat rounded the breakwater, the engine-throbbing increasing, she looked back through the gathering dusk and waved widely at the big man standing beside his truck at the end of the wharf. Seeing Henry's arm raised, the huge hand she had drawn so much strength from held as much in salute as in a wave, she called, "Goodbye!" before turning to move to Grandy's side.

The big man turned too, back to own place and his 'Stina and Tommy, Bobby, Daisy and all the people who needed him.

22.

Home

Misty was as a caged bird set free. She darted about the boat, always returning to Grandy to point out important things, urging her to breathe deeply the ocean air, to listen to the water folding back from the bow of the boat in rolling curls, to listen to the bubbles churned up by the great propeller, to look at the rich misty blues turning deep grey and on to black where the sea met the land and as the dusk met the night. She'd run to the bow of the boat and reach her face out into the wind of the moving boat as far as it would go before running back, first to report to Grandy and urge her to feel the life in the salt air and then to Old Lundstrom's side to watch again the perfect union of man, boat and sea. Back she'd run to Grandy, proclaiming the wonders of the peace and strength that come from rolling with the boat which rolls with the ocean. To Lundstrom she spoke of the rhythm of the rolling sea, the joy of floating, of being cradled in the water instead of bumping along the hard land in an unyielding car. Back at the bow of the boat, she spread her arms wide, imagining she was soaring with the gulls she could hear calling above the pulsing boat engine and see dotted white against the darkening sky. She was filled once again with the moment she was living, absorbed by the richness of the sights, sounds, smell and feel of her world. The simple joy of living rose so completely, it replaced even the anticipation of going home.

The life and joy in the child combined with the fresh sea air and comfortable motion of the boat filled the old woman as well, pushing any thoughts of change, any hesitation of beginning a new life in her twilight years, any questions of what was to come, out of her mind altogether. She looked neither behind nor ahead. Sitting in the middle of the boat, her things piled around her, The Artful Dodger in the basket on her knee, a heavy rain cape of Old Lundstrom's drawn over the huge warm sweater of Henry's keeping the chill from her, she looked up and breathed deeply: full, rich, content, alive.

But across the water there was a different feeling in the air. The day had begun as most days do there. The Captain had done his morning chores, tending to the animals and to his wood box; Miss Lily had done the same, and Rusty had set out on his daily pilgrimage to the pier. But this day, he didn't return as usual, and the Captain grew concerned, worried and finally restless. When the little fellow wasn't back even at dusk, the Captain could contain himself no longer. With Pilot, he set out to Miss Lily's, calling Rusty and whistling from time to time along the way but getting no response.

Miss Lily seemed even more anxious than the Captain, for she hadn't seen Rusty at all that day and she was sure something must have gone wrong. She pulled on her warmest sweater and set out with the Captain, determined to find the little dog. Neither was sure which was more overwhelming, their concern for the dog or their sense that they would have let Misty down if anything had happened to Rusty. Together they walked the island path, calling out as they went. Only Pilot seemed unconcerned, trotting evenly at the Captain's side as he always did.

It was almost dark when they reached the wharf, but, outlined against the darkness of both sea and sky, Miss Lily could see the light form of the faithful little fellow sitting at the end of the pier. He ignored their calling and remained sitting, head tipped to one side, eyes fixed out to sea. Even Pilot didn't interest him.

"Poor little fellow," said the Captain. "He has grown thin with running down here every day. Do you notice? I'd best carry him home tonight. We can't leave him here."

But as he stooped to pick Rusty up, the little dog growled and huddled down as if to fasten himself to the dock.

"He's baring his teeth, Captain. You'd better leave him be. I wonder what's going on. Do you suppose he's determined now to either wait it out or breathe his last right here where he last saw her?"

"Never seen anything like this, but you're right, we'd best leave him. I'll go along to Misty's house and get his old blanket and some food for him. At least we can make him comfortable and see if he'll eat. I'll bring water too. You can rest in the shed."

"No, I'll come with you, Captain. We may as well light a fire while we're there. It has been a week or so since we took the chill off the house. I still can't get used to seeing it empty. We won't have it growing cold and damp as well. It would break my heart, and I've enough of a job keeping cheered up without Misty around. Funny, isn't it? You were the one knew how hard it would be, and I told you to take a lesson from the child and not fuss about tomorrow. But I've been the one so lonely at times I could scarcely enjoy my painting. I don't know what I'd have done if you, Pilot and Rusty hadn't come by for supper often. I'd probably have grown as thin as Rusty himself."

"I'd have got thin myself, Miss Lily, that's what. Place has never seemed so empty. Everything I do seems to make me miss her. No matter how many times my conscience pricks me for letting sadness rob me of the gifts all around, I somehow can't help myself. I think it's losing Misty and her grandmother so close together. That's a lot of grief. Now we can't lose Rusty too. We'd best hurry."

The two made sure that the fires they built in both the kitchen stove and the barrel burner in the hall were well-banked and safe before they gathered things for Rusty and headed back to the pier. Night was full on them, the darkness broken only when the clouds moved and let the moon shine through. When they put the food and water down for the little dog, he didn't even acknowledge their return or look at the food or water, just stared out into the darkness, the two old folks standing behind him, shaking their heads, not wanting to leave him there alone but unable to interest him in moving.

As they stood there, the Captain suddenly tipped his head to one side, straining to hear. He took Miss Lily's arm and turned to face her, hoping she could see his lips in the darkness.

"Miss Lily, do you see anything? I hear throbbing, deep even throbbing, not rumbling like the freight boat just deep like a fish boat. I'm sure I hear it." Resting his hand down on the little dog's head and feeling it tipped eagerly to one side, he added, "I'm sure the little fellow can hear it too."

Miss Lily peered into the darkness. "Yes, Captain. There. Lights, just off the point. And you are right; they are not the freighter lights. Could it be Old Lundstrom? Does it sound like his boat?"

"Could be, though he knows better than to head out at night in winter. Storms can come up so quick, and he knows that. I thought he had more respect for the sea than to go out at dark. Still, it does sound like his boat. He's no fool, though. It must be someone else."

"No, Captain. Pay attention to Rusty. He's up, and his tail is wagging, though he's still staring out to sea. You don't suppose it is Lundstrom and he's bringing our girl home, do you? Whatever could have happened? Could it be?"

The rising excitement added both intensity and tone to the usually flat voice of Miss Lily and she found herself wanting to move around yet strangely glued to the spot at the same time, torn between wanting to hope yet afraid to think the child could come. It was too foolish.

But the Captain was growing more certain. "It is his boat. Old fool. But then what better reason to turn the fool than to bring our Misty home? You look at the dog, Miss Lily. He's barking now and wriggling. Is he turning circles and wagging his tail?"

Sure enough, the little dog looked almost ready to fly apart as he ran in a tight circle, tail wagging frantically over his back. Round and around he went, barking and barking and barking, a happy, excited, irrepressible bark the Captain had not heard in months.

Suddenly, the dog stopped in his tracks, face thrust toward the ocean, tail still wagging, muscles quivering, the barks replaced by excited whining and yipping. The little fellow shook all over.

"What happened? What's changed?" asked the Captain.

"Oh, Captain, the boat has its sweeping spotlight fastened on us now. It must be Old Lundstrom!"

"It's slowing, Miss Lily. I can hear it. Can you see anyone? Is it them?"

Tears fell freely down the Captain's cheeks even as he

asked. Seeing them washing down the shining, scarred face, Miss Lily gave way, collapsing against him as her own tears turned to gasps of joy. In front of them, the little dog quivered and yipped excitedly.

On board the boat, Misty's delight in the journey itself had changed to anticipation as they rounded the point, the island seeming to call out to every part of her being. "We're almost home, Grandy, almost home," she breathed, planting a kiss on the woman's cheek before scurrying to the bow of the boat and straining forward every bit as intensely as the little dog on the pier reached out to sea.

In the spotlight, she could see the Captain and Miss Lily standing together, waving and smiling, almost laughing, she thought, and the little dog straining at their feet, leaning over the edge of the wharf. Misty danced up and down, waving and laughing as she did so.

When the throb of the engine slowed and faded, and Old Lundstrom eased into the pier, Misty and Rusty were released as one. Before the boat had docked, Misty leapt across the water to the float as Rusty sprang up and into her arms, wriggling, yipping, and licking the salty tears of joy from her cheeks.

The bright spotlight danced on the two heads showing the rusty tones of the little brown dog blending with the golden glimmer of the rich brown braids. But Old Lundstrom smiled through his tear-dampened beard to see that it could not outshine the light that glowed from three scarred and wrinkled faces and burst forth afresh from the clear and pure, gold-flecked eyes of the other as Misty proclaimed, "We're home, Rusty! Home to stay."

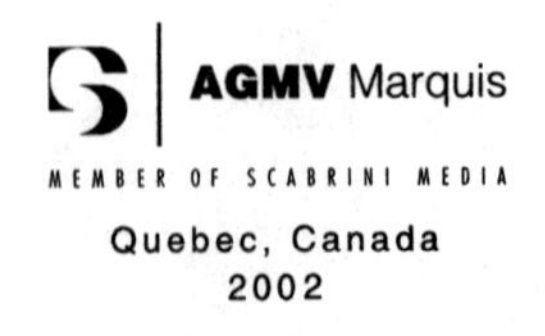

Quebec, Canada
2002